SOULSTAR

SOULSTAR

C. L. POLK

A TOM DOHERTY ASSOCIATES BOOK

New York

SOULSTAR

Edited by Carl Engle-Laird

A Tordotcom Book
Published by Tom Doherty Associates
120 Broadway
New York, NY 10271

www.tor.com

Tor® is a registered trademark of Macmillan Publishing Group, LLC.

The Library of Congress Cataloging-in-Publication Data is available upon request.

ISBN 978-1-250-20357-1 (trade paperback)
ISBN 978-1-250-20356-4 (ebook)

Our books may be purchased in bulk for promotional, educational, or business use. Please contact your local bookseller or the Macmillan Corporate and Premium Sales Department at 1-800-221-7945, extension 5442, or by email at MacmillanSpecialMarkets@macmillan.com.

First Edition: February 2021

Printed in the United States of America

0 9 8 7 6 5 4 3 2 1

To Robin and Maire, who stuck through it all

ONE

A Favor for a Favor

The knock came an hour after we had put up the stormboards and battened down to wait it out. Everyone in the second parlor looked in its direction, as if we could see who it was bracing themselves against the wind that scoured the street. Aunt Glory dropped her knitting on her lap to wave a burl-knuckled hand at me. "Robin. Go see who it is."

"I will!" Amos shouted, and he left the parlor quick as counting, pelting down the hall. I set down my notebook and *Bones of the Body* to follow little Amos, leaving my seat near the rear fire to step into the foyer. Joy followed, melting through the wall as spirits do, following her nephew down the hall.

Only trouble would come to Clan Thorpe on the teeth of a cyclonic blizzard. No other reason for it. The door lever was icy to the touch, and I pushed against the door to keep it from slamming into my face.

Trouble indeed. Grace Hensley had come to my door, holding a dome of still air while the Stormbowl's gift howled up the street. Trouble. Worse than trouble, and Grace had brought it to me without a moment's pause.

Amos wormed in front of me and craned his neck, pointing at Grace. "Ahoy. I remember you."

"Ahoy," Grace replied. "You should go inside; it's very cold out."

I put my hand on Amos's head and steered him back inside. "Why are you here, of all places? There's a storm on the way."

"That's exactly why," Grace Hensley said. "I have news."

I couldn't shut the door in her face, not with the snow swirling in the street. Even if I still mistrusted Grace Hensley, I couldn't deny her hospitality.

"Hurry inside," I said. "Put your skis anywhere they will fit on the rack."

Amos had already scampered back to the second parlor to tell the elders who had come to Clan Thorpe in such terrible weather. Grace shed her wet boots and found slippers in the seagrass-woven basket.

Grace stood up, and I fought a flash of irritation as she flexed her knees to half crouch to match my height. But then she spoke in my ear, her voice low: "Constantina abdicated. Severin's first act as king was to abolish the Witchcraft Protection Act. Is there somewhere we can talk?"

"Not just prorogued." A hundred responses trampled each other for the chance to be first. "Why would he do that?"

Grace's shoulders came up as she winced her way through a smile. "That's the reason why I'm here. But can we—"

"Ah. You want something."

"I do. But consider this: I ought to be with the Storm-Singers right now. I'm not. It's that important."

I could at least hear her out. She was here for the duration, as there was no turning her out in that wind. "Back parlor," I said. "But first we run the gauntlet."

The Witchcraft Protection Act was no more. What I had fought for these past twenty years, the fight I thought I would pass on to the next generation of my clan, was done. Too late to free those I loved, but our struggle was over.

"Why did Prince—excuse me. Why did King Severin strike down the law?"

"The Amaranthines wanted it."

"I thought the Amaranthines wouldn't get involved in our politics."

Grace sighed. "I bullied him into it. I don't know if I'll be able to pull it off again. What's the gauntlet?"

"Robin," Eldest called. "Who was at the door?"

I led the way to the second parlor, where four generations of Thorpes gathered next to hearth-fires and watched curiously. The children seated on chairs and stools knitted and sewed while the younger children sprawled on the floor to play Slap with four decks of playing cards. Eldest spotted Grace and grinned.

"You couldn't stay away," he said, wagging one finger playfully. "No one forgets our fish fry."

"I've had dreams about it," Grace said.

Eldest leaned forward in his seat, still smiling. "And what brings you here, Chancellor?"

"I wanted to speak with Miss Thorpe."

"In this weather?" Bernice turned her head to gaze at the snow flying on the other side of the window. "It must be important."

Grace nodded. "It is."

"We should go," I said. "Come with me."

"Not so fast," Aunt Glory said. "I want to know what brought you here, when the storm of a lifetime is at our doorstep and by rights you should be up on your hill with your Royal Knights trying to turn it back."

Grace's jaw dropped. "We didn't hide a thing from you, did we?"

"You did not," Glory said. "Strutting all over town with your auras blazing, imagining no one knew your secret. We knew. We had to know, if we were going to survive you."

"Aunt Glory," I said. "I don't think Grace has time to go over all this."

"Stay where you are." Aunt Bernice pointed at Grace. "There's only one reason why she's here at a time like this. She knows about our Circle. She's here to press them into service."

"We have to unite our power," Grace said. "It's our only chance."

"Mm-hmm," Glory said. "And then you'll round them all up—"

"She had the Witchcraft Act abolished," I said.

Gasps arose from everyone in the parlor. "Is that true?" Eldest asked. "Miss Grace, you said you couldn't—"

"Constantina abdicated," Grace said. "Severin is now king. His first act was to repeal the law—"

"Because you convinced him," I supplied, since she wouldn't tell the others. Modesty. I didn't expect it from her.

"It was the right thing to do," Grace said. "Every witch in Aeland is free and safe from persecution. And I did it just in time, because I need your people to help us fight this cyclone."

I knew it. She did want something, and she had changed history by abolishing the Witchcraft Act to get it. Abolished. Not just suspended in the legal oubliette of a prorogue, but erased from the books. I waited for the dream to switch, for someone to turn into a beast or a tree or a monster, so this would all make sense.

I wasn't dreaming. I knew I wasn't. But it still didn't feel real. "Did you bring a copy of the writ?"

Grace's shoulders slouched. "There wasn't time. But Jacob Clarke had to have heard by now—I half expected that the news had already spread."

"Everything's under storm alert," I said. "Parliament didn't meet today."

"I swear to you. It's true," Grace said. She slipped a white-handled witchknife from her pocket. "I will swear on my blood, before the entire clan—please. I need you to believe me."

"You should have brought Miles with you," I said. "Everyone would believe Miles."

"I couldn't bring Miles. He's still not well enough. Tristan was in no shape either."

Grace was no fool. Ignorant, where it benefited her to be ignorant. Accustomed to being treated as a figure of authority and respect. She knew that I could convince the others to believe her, if she convinced me herself. But I had seen the faces of neighbors who worked as navigators aboard our sailing vessels—pinched with worry and glancing to the west, bringing firewood and stove oil to clans who might need it.

"We know it's bad." I startled when the stormboards rumbled so loudly it was like being inside a drum. "But if you're here, it's worse than we thought."

"Worse than this?" Aunt Glory asked. A distant crack of thunder, nearly buried in the force of the wind, made us all look west.

"This is the edge of it."

Grace was prepared to swear on her blood. But still I kept my silence, standing in the midst of my clan. Could I trust her word?

Could I afford to doubt it?

"Please, Miss Thorpe," Grace said. "It's the best chance Aeland has to survive. And Aeland will demonstrate its gratitude for your witches. I will see to it."

She had the power—and a king who seemed sympathetic to the needs of his nation's citizens. She could pull a great many strings, and she would. I was just stalling. It was time to bargain.

"What do you plan to do once this storm is put down?"

"So many things I don't have time to list them all," Grace said. "With Severin's rise to the throne, we have an incredible opportunity to build something better. But to do that, I need you."

I took a half-step back. "Me."

"I don't truly understand the extent of the corruption in the system. I can't know. Up until recently, I didn't even know there was a real problem. I had dismissed you all as complainers."

I let an exasperated sigh escape my lips. "And why wouldn't you? From where you sat, everything was fine."

"I was wrong," Grace said.

How easily she admitted mistakes, ignorance, vulnerability—her candor disarmed me, her honesty meeting the walls of my suspicion and gently melting them away.

Glory sat up straight, her posture all icy dignity. "And now you need our Robin. For what?"

"Aunt Glory—"

"How do you know she isn't trouble?" Glory demanded. "How do you know what her promises are worth?"

"Ma'am," Grace said, "you have an excellent point. I'm not trustworthy, not yet. But I'm trying to be. You all know exactly what's wrong with Aeland. Robin knows what the people want. Which is why I want her—"

She turned back to me. "Which is why I want you to come work for me."

The parlor murmured. I put up my hand, forestalling comment. "You want me to work for you?"

"I need your vision. I want to give you access. Do you want to talk to the King? I can make that happen. Do you want to write new laws? We can do that. It's perfect. You can start right away. The salary is twelve thousand marks a year."

A thousand marks a month. That was what I could expect to make as a surgeon, and she was lowballing me. She did want me—but she couldn't know what she was offering.

"Chancellor Hensley," I said, setting my hands on my hips. "Do you know what my vision is? Do you know what the Solidarity Collective wants?"

She blinked, her face blank with thought. "Uzadalian democracy. You want Aeland to be like the countries in the League of Uzadal."

The word "uza" meant something that didn't quite translate to Aelander. It meant solidarity. It meant unity. But something more than that—it meant that the people banded together in a community had a moral duty to each other, to serve one another.

"We want more than just a resemblance to Uzadalian ideals." I gestured to include the clan in this room, but the circle went wider than that. "We want Aeland to join the league."

Grace stepped back, pushing herself away from my words. "Uzadalian countries don't have ruling monarchs."

"They do not."

"They support the common vote."

"They do. Is that job offer still on the table?"

Grace's face lined itself as she thought. A gust of wind bashed itself against the window, and Grace turned her face westward, intent on whatever she sensed out there.

She went pale. "There's no more time. And I need you on my team, even if you do want to upend all order and tradition. So yes. The offer stands, only please, we need to go now."

"How do you think we're going to make it to the hall?" I asked. "That wind is—"

"I can shelter us with my power," Grace said. "It'll deplete me, but we must."

Aunt Glory sighed. "You can't. They're pretty words, Robin. Maybe even true ones. But they're not enough to risk exposing the Circle—"

But she couldn't be lying. Not about the law, and not about the danger. If I didn't take her, would we survive?

"We need her," I said. "We can't risk letting this storm howl across Aeland. I have to take her."

"Robin," Glory said. "Are you certain?"

I'd get in deep trouble with the Circle for this. They'd censure me, distrust me, maybe even shun me, but this was the only choice.

"Yes," I said. "I will face the cost of doing this. We have a storm to put down."

We arrived at the Maritime Hall gnashed by the teeth of the wind. The front door slammed shut when I pulled it open, but Grace wrestled it far enough for us to slip into the vestibule. Boots, skis, and winter gear filled the space with only a few pairs of felted slippers left in the basket.

Grace eased yellow and green half-socks over her feet. "Thank you for doing this."

"I don't see how I have much choice—Carlotta."

I smiled as the biggest gossip in the Circle caught sight of me and hurried over.

"Robin, what are you doing here? Circle's about to—" Carlotta Brown stopped in the doorway, staring straight at Grace. "You."

I checked my urge to stand in front of Grace like a shield. "She's here to help."

Carlotta turned a look of betrayed surprise on me. "You told an outsider about the Circle? No, it's worse. You brought a Royal Knight to us?"

"She convinced the King to strike down the Witchcraft Act," I said. "The law is no more."

Carlotta lifted her chin. "I know that. Jacob Clarke is here. But we're still a secret."

Grace coughed. "I knew there was a group of witches out here. I kept it a secret. But Aeland cries out for your aid. We must strike the storm together. I will join our groups in magic—"

"You can't just walk in here and expect to order us to—"

"Peace, Sister." Marlon stepped out of the knot of witches. "Miss Robin. I trust you have an explanation. I'm sure you have a very good reason for exposing us to anyone, let alone this woman in particular. So tell me—do you trust her?"

I couldn't stop a sharp breath. "I trust that Grace isn't lying about the Witchcraft Protection Act."

Carlotta dismissed my words with a wave. "We already said that Jacob Clarke told us—"

"She's saying that she didn't have the news from Clarke, Sister,"

16

Marlon interrupted. "You're saying you had only her word, and you believed her."

"Yes." The band around my chest loosened. "I brought her here because I believe Grace would unite us with her Royal Knights if it meant stopping the storm, and she would use her power to protect us."

"I don't know if our groups together are enough," Grace said. "But we have to try."

"Truly spoken," Marlon said. "Storm-Singer, you are welcome here. What is your plan?"

Grace stared at him astonished as Eldest welcomed her. "I can join our power, but I won't be able to do that and fight the storm too."

"You will gather; I will weave," Eldest said, the smile stretching the lines on his face. "The storm calls. Come, Dame Grace. You will stand in my Circle."

Marlon took Grace away. I joined volunteers at the buffet to stir salt and vinegar into fresh-pressed apple juice. The wind roared past the walls of the hall, flinging snow smack into the many-paned windows. It battered against the rooftop, screeching as it tried to pry the roof loose. It nearly drowned out the song rising from the witches. But the hall had been built by shipwrights, and not a breath of a draft snuck into the room.

A loud crack made everyone jump. Trees would crack and fall in winds like this. Anyone who had been caught outside was dead already. The witches sang, united against the fury of the Stormbowl, and Grace's voice blended into the choir. My fingers went cold as we glanced at each other, the same question in our eyes: What if it isn't enough?

All around us, the wind screamed like a death-herald. Too strong. If the witches weren't enough—if they couldn't protect us from this—the storm would rip across Aeland. It wouldn't be possible to count the dead. The Circle had to hold.

Marlon's younger brother Maurice took off his apron and shuffled between the singing witches, his hand on his ring-husband's shoulder. Octavius smiled as he took up the thread of Maurice's power and added it to the Circle. Tressie Lawrence followed Maurice's lead, dropping her apron on top of his. All of the medical recovery crew's witches followed suit, joining their power to the Circle that had one chance to stop the blizzard that would bury us.

It was heroic. Was it enough? There were only twenty witches on the recovery crew. The storm had crashed into us. It was too late to get more people. Every witch but me was in the weaving, adding power to the work, but were we enough?

It wasn't. I knew in my bones that it wasn't.

The wind didn't let up for a moment. It hadn't slowed; the sky cracked with thunder, louder still. They didn't have enough power, not even combined. It was too late to bring in more witches. All we had was the magic in this room, and it wasn't enough.

I could walk into the Circle and add my power to theirs. But I was only one witch. They needed a hundred.

And then the answer lit up my mind, bright and sudden as lightning.

I leaned against the chilly, hand-paneled wall and closed my eyes. I slowed my breath and stretched out my senses, cutting through the wind with a song of my own. I reached out through the wind and howling snow and found them—huddled in doorways, standing in the shelter of a stranger's home, drifting and unfocused until my power touched them.

I pressed my back against the wall. I braced my feet. I pushed until blackness crept to the edge of my vision, singing, calling. My net spun a little wider. It touched two more souls. I had done all that I could.

The dead slid through solid walls and gathered around me, curious at my summoning. Dozens came to my call, and I held out my hands in appeal as they crowded around me.

"We have used you so terribly. But we need you."

A ghost in a pin-striped college jacket scowled at me. "You never want us. Now you need us?"

"Most of us can't hear you or talk to you. I can. And if you need me, I will try to help you."

"All of us?" the ghost demanded.

"If I can help you, I will," I said.

"Done," he said. "What do you need from us?"

"This storm is too strong to fight alone. Will you join with the witches here? Will you help save our lives?"

"Because you asked," a woman said. "Because you see us, and you hear us, and you asked. We will help."

The ghosts took up stations next to this Storm-Singer or that, dressed in the fashions they had died in: narrowly cinched waistlines, short jackets with too much padding in the shoulder—and one little ghost gathered the drooping velvet hem of her mother's bag-sleeved tea gown as she walked.

Outside, the wind faltered, as if it were capable of surprise.

Every ghost laid a spectral hand on a witch's shoulder. The dead lent their strength to the Circle of weather-witches who sang their power into something greater than themselves, a force powerful enough to calm the whirling fury aimed directly for our shore.

Living witches and the unquiet dead poured their souls into the work until the wind stopped screaming past the rooftops. The Windweavers of Riverside unwound the weaving of their voices, dropped the threads of their magic, and slumped into chairs, thirsty and dizzy.

The medical crew tottered back to the restorative station and poured juice with shaky hands. The ghosts drifted around, pausing to stare at the living as often as they gazed at the huge murals of Samindan ships at sea, their white sails paunched with wind. The chandeliers swinging above us made everyone's shadows slide dizzily. And just there, not quite in the center of the web of Storm-Singers, Grace Hensley collapsed to hands and knees, breathing hard.

I wove my path through the witches to crouch beside her, offering a cup of salted apple juice. "Drink this before you faint."

"Thank you. We couldn't have done it without you." Grace lifted her head and gave me a pale smile. I laid my hand on her forehead, and she was clammy. My fingers slid to the pulse on her wrist. Thready.

I clucked my tongue before I could stop it. "You overdid it."

A fine thing to say, when for me the room still tilted and I felt too hot, but Grace quaffed juice and wiped her mouth with the back of her hand.

"We needed every scrap of power to avert that storm," Grace said. "Bringing in the ghosts was genius. And your people, these witches, they're . . . startling."

"You didn't expect them to be powerful."

Grace shrugged. "I'm used to being the best. In this room, I'm not even in the top ten. And won't the Royal Knights scream when they find out they're middling to ordinary?"

"That kind of resentment could be dangerous," I said. "You came to me to unite the witches with the Royal Knights. We've done that. Now it's time to hear what it's going to cost you."

Grace nodded and plucked a lumpy, russeted apple from a passing attendant's basket. "I'm ready."

"You took the prorogue and convinced the King to abolish the Witchcraft Protection Act, and now we're all free. Except there are hundreds of witches flung to the corners of Aeland and locked in asylums. I want you to get them out. Now."

Grace stopped chewing. She watched one of my medics tending Loretta Green, who would faint in a stiff breeze if it meant being fussed over.

When she spoke, it was in careful, rehearsed tones. "It's not that I want to say no. And I'm not saying no." Grace swallowed the last mouthfuls of fortified apple juice and blotted her clammy forehead with the cuff of her sweater. "But saying yes is empty. I could say 'Certainly! The witches are free to go as of this moment,' and that would mean exactly nothing, because there's nowhere for them to go."

"They have somewhere to go," I said. "There's always room for one more in the clan house."

Grace's eyebrows rose. "For near on a thousand witches?"

"We'll take them," I said. "Next objection."

"Aether's still out. There's no way to even get word to the asylums to tell them they're free. How am I supposed to get them home?"

"On the trains," I said.

Grace cocked her head. "How's that, now?"

"We have a new king. The law dictates that a new monarch must call an election and name a new Cabinet within ninety days of his coronation. That means getting the word out. And with no telephones, no telegraphs, and no wireless, that means the proclamation must be spread in person."

"The rail lines are snowed under," Grace said.

"So King Severin calls for anyone in National Service to report in to clear snow. Send passenger trains. Staff them with Service workers and get to work. What choice do you have?"

"You're right. That's the only choice we have. But that will still leave the witches locked up for weeks."

I huffed and shrugged at her criticism. "If you can think of a way to fetch them out faster than that, I want to know about it."

Grace bit into her apple. She weighed the question in her mind, as if there were a way. "Actually, I might."

Grace surveyed the room, her gaze settling on the witches quietly replenishing themselves with salted apple juice. Grace pushed herself out of her chair, swaying only a little.

Of course. It was perfect. "Come with me," I said. "I might as well ask them while they're irritated."

TWO

The Greystars

When Grace gave her word, she didn't dally. I hovered in the drafty front parlor the next morning, clad in my best daytime suit. I hadn't brought the smart gray jacket and pleated skirt out of my closet since the day I signed the nurses of Beauregard into a fair labor agreement with Dr. Matheson. My shiny black heeled shoes pinched at my toes.

We had done well. Only a foot of snow had fallen, and that was soon cleared off the sidewalks and tamped on the street. Marlon had called it an astonishing success. He had praised me as Aeland's savior.

It wasn't actually me. It had been the dead acting to save the people they loved. All I'd done was ask their help. Grace had gone home talking of reorganizing the Royal Knights to coordinate the efforts of both Circles, promising to bring me to the King the next morning.

Grace's flashy orange sleigh and gait-matched horses pulled up to the clan house, and I threw my cloak over my shoulders and dashed outside, the cold seeping up through the frozen sidewalk.

Grace sat cozy and snug under a blanket woven from the downy undercoat of northern longhair goats on one side, and lined with the skins of sheared beavers on the other. She shared the blanket and the foot warmer as the horses trotted back up the hill and up Main Street to the King's Way and Mountrose Palace. We smoked. Joy set herself on the bench beside us. Grace nodded to her as if she was there in the flesh.

I rode with one of the wealthiest Royal Knights of Aeland, the one who held the most power as Chancellor to the new king. That didn't stop me from raising my fist in the air for the knot of people gathered in the square in protest. Some of them returned the gesture. Some turned their backs.

"I'm sorry," Grace said. "This blasted sled."

"Some people don't think we should consort with the likes of you. You're a corrupting influence."

Grace smiled. "Is that so?"

"They're right to worry," I said. "I could wind up in your pocket financially, and then the next thing you know I'm preaching meaningless displays of incrementalism I'm calling compromise."

"But compromise is how politics works."

"Politics works on compromise. We want transformation."

"Severin has a plan," Grace said, leaning into me as the sled turned a corner. "He's going to announce it at the coronation. I want you to come and hear it for yourself."

"Do you have an opinion of this plan?"

Grace gave one curt nod. "I think it's too cautious. I want bolder action. That's why I need you—I need to be able to present what you truly want, couched in the art of my persuasion."

A flock of birds took wing, the sound of their flight agitated. "When I come work for you as your consultant. For eighteen thousand a year."

Grace sat up in surprise. "I said twelve, but I can see you to fourteen."

I was worth more, I told my leaping stomach. She knew it. "Sixteen, plus paid vacation."

"You'll have weeks of downtime between sessions."

"Which I will use to gather wisdom from my community. Sixteen, plus paid vacation. And I quit on Frostmonth one. I'm going back to medical school."

"Do you honestly think you can get enough done that you can stop after less than one year?"

"If I'm not satisfied after Frostmonth one, we will have wasted our time," I said. "I don't mean to chat over tea while I work for you. I'm going to leverage my position into as much change as I can move."

"With my office as the fulcrum," Grace said. "All right. Sixteen. Paid vacation. I'll even throw in a travel allowance, so you can go in-country if it suits your needs."

"When do I formally accept the offer?"

"After you've convinced your people that it's smart," Grace said. "The day after the celebration for the freed witches? That will give our advocates weeks to fight over the contract."

An advocate. Oh, dear. Was this something Cousin Orlena could negotiate? I'd have to ask her at dinner, and if she couldn't, I'd need a referral. I papered a smile over my face. "Three days after. We'll be busy getting ready for the celebration, and I will want a rest."

"Very well. Three days," Grace agreed. "I have a feeling we're going to do excellent work together."

"Done." I slipped my hand out from under the luxurious sled blanket and shook on it.

I had been to Government House before. But Grace's driver George took us around to the empty square and wide stone steps where Queensguards—well, they were the King's now—stood in the cold with scarlet cloaks over their dress uniforms. The guards at the door took down the particulars of my identity card, compared the photo of my face to my living countenance, and finally allowed me inside.

I had been inside the Royal Gallery when I was a schoolgirl, but this entranceway outstripped it. Marble tile, from wall to wall. Gold on the aether-powered chandelier hanging dimly from the soaring ceiling, while portable gas lamps did the actual work of lighting the vast, chilly foyer. A collection of marble statues stood in a circle in the center of the room—seventeen of them, all veiled, identifiable by what they carried.

Menas the Just carried his scroll and quill. Halian the Maker, with a sculptor's chisel in one hand and a hammer in the other. Grace sailed past them with the carelessness of one who had seen the devotional statues so many times they were just people to her.

I had always been fond of Lilia the Compassionate, as her teachings governed the ways of healers. I touched her toes, smooth from the fingertips of visitors with enough faith or superstition to make such a gesture, and gripped the knotty stave of Amael the Traveler, the Lady at the Gates of the Solace, the Shepherd of the Dead.

She was my clan's patron. And mine, since I carried her sight. I had to hurry to catch up to Grace, who was halfway to the exit she meant to take.

Mountrose Palace would have been more beautiful if I could stop thinking about those who tried to outrun starvation and homelessness, but I wasn't about to forget. I laid my eyes on every alabaster figurine, every deftly cut crystal vase filled with fragrant herbs and evergreen boughs, every painting ignored by the guards stationed in the hall. They watched me go past as we took ourselves to a wing of the palace that stepped backward in time, decorated and furnished in the ornately carved wood of a hundred years ago.

The guards here were Amaranthines, garbed in short-hemmed voluminous trousers, their tunics belted by tooled leather. They wore swords at their hips and carried curving, powerful bows, their hair braided away from their faces and silver-decorated ears. Only a few of them were white. Grace nodded greetings to these guards, and they all smiled, not at all the stoic, half-scowling expressions of the Kingsguard.

"What are we doing here?" I asked.

"You guested Grand Duchess Aife for lunch," Grace said. "We're here for refreshments."

"With the Daughter of the Gates?" I swiped at the front of my cloak, trying to bat away lint that wasn't there.

"And Severin Mountrose," Grace said, and I swallowed just as she stopped before a set of double doors carved in concentric rings.

They opened on a light-filled jewel box of a room, an ornate latticed cage of crystal and iron. I gawked as butterflies, bright and impossible, danced to the luminous music of the tawny brown-skinned woman perched on a guitar stool. No one sang an accompaniment.

She lifted her gaze from her fingers on the fretboard and stopped playing. The butterflies winked out of existence, diminishing to a single firework spark and then gone. The Grand Duchess rested the beautiful guitar on a stand and—splendid in a layered gown of the most delicate shades of blue—set her slippered feet on the floor to approach us.

I hadn't been especially religious. I knew the stories; I had attended temple for the important services. I had seen the stories of the makers and the tales of the Amaranthines as allegory.

But Grand Duchess Aife was no story. She was so tall I had to look up at her the way I craned my neck to look Grace in the eye. She had the sort of lovingly sculpted face and deep night eyes that could have been beautiful and terrible, but instead were kind and inquisitive. Her golden hair curled loosely, each coiling lock stretched under the weight of hanging down to her hips. My scalp hurt imagining what it took to comb all that hair free of tangles, how long it would take to put up and wrap in silk before she slept. A Samindan's hair was their glory—and from the impressive styles I had seen on all the Amaranthines, they agreed.

"I thank you again for the excellent meal," Grand Duchess Aife said. "I hear you are the one who saved Aeland from terrible destruction."

"I didn't," I said. "The dead did that."

"You were the one who thought to ask them," Grand Duchess Aife said. "Their additional protection will see you through the winter, and it took your ingenuity to make it happen."

"Thank you, Your Highness," I said, because while you can deflect praise once, twice is throwing someone's respect back in their face.

"I'm happy to assist you in your endeavors today," Aife said. "Between the three of us, I have every confidence Aeland's new king will see reason—ah. Here he comes."

The doors opened and King Severin Mountrose walked in. I bowed my head, but he came straight to me, stopping at a distance. Joy swooped closer, and Severin's lips curled in revulsion before he turned a stern look at me.

"So you are the person responsible for the protesters outside the palace," he said.

"I am," I said. "I and the rest of the Solidarity Collective."

"That's not an apology for disrupting the flow of visitors to the palace," the King said.

"Your Majesty, it is not," I agreed. "You are currently suffering an inconvenience. We're doing it to ask you to build a better Aeland."

"Robin's quick thinking saved us from the storm," Grace said. "As I told you when I asked you to meet her."

"You did." The King looked me straight in the face. He would have been handsome enough for the stage if he hadn't been a king, dressed in the height of fashion, though the deep, nearly black violet wool suit couldn't have been donned by anyone but a king. Not even the barely suppressed scowl smirched his handsomeness. "Aeland thanks you. And my friend Chancellor Hensley tells me you have a plan you'd like my help with."

Oh, blast! I had prepared myself to answer questions, not pitch the idea, and so I scrambled for words. "I did what I did because Chancellor Hensley promised that she would do everything in her power to help me with what I want."

"And you wished to ask me to help you."

"Yes, Your Majesty. You have abolished the law that my comrades have fought for decades. For that you have our sincerest gratitude."

"But you won't call off your protestors."

"The work is not yet done, Your Majesty," I said. "The witches are free on paper, but they fester in asylums waiting for the snow to thaw. I want them truly freed, as quickly as possible."

"That is also my wish," Grand Duchess Aife said. "I know you understand my position on the imprisonment of these innocents, and how I condemn the motives of those responsible for this outrage. Miss Thorpe has proven to be a woman of great ideas."

"How can I withstand you both?" Severin asked, his smile more charming for the Grand Duchess. "But the rail lines are buried so deeply that we probably wouldn't finish digging them out before the Firstgreen thaw."

"But you have to call the election," I said, "and that means the trains must run. And I think I know how to accomplish the task faster than the labor of strong backs and shovels."

"Very well. I'm curious to hear it."

I had to trust this man. I had to believe that he would protect us when the dangerous winter was past. "You call your Royal Knights Storm-Singers, which refers to their actions of calming weather patterns. But in Riverside, we call witches with the power Windweavers, because the most common occupation for a Samindan Windweaver is ship's navigator."

"That's why Samindan sailors are so fast," King Severin said. "So you propose that we use Windweavers to clear the rail lines."

"Yes. They will need staff support on the trains, of course, with plenty of food and ample rest, with medical staff and other amenities. They will be working very hard to clear the rail lines. You can't just dole out Service pay for that level of skill."

"Aha. Very well. How much?"

"Twenty marks a week."

Severin blinked. "That's four times Service pay. We generally double for emergencies."

I shrugged and risked it. "Well, this time it's more."

King Severin finally looked at me with a little surprised respect. "This is a service to the kingdom. But I could probably see two and a half times Service pay, for extraordinary—"

"Four times Service pay, Severin," Aife interrupted. "You have to free them, and I like the idea of it being done as swiftly as possible. Miss Thorpe understands the worth of the people with the skills to do the job quickly and well. They ought to be paid what they usually get."

"Actually, ma'am, as navigators they stand to make considerably more than that on a voyage," I said. "They get a share of the sale of their cargo, but since this is an emergency the reduced rate is fair."

"There you have it," Aife said. "Will you pay them?"

Severin stole a glance at Grace. "You had this in mind when you suggested we all meet."

Grace didn't try to simper or look innocent. "They deserve it, and you know very well that they do. And you won't get the rail lines cleared this quickly without them."

"But the Cabinet—"

"The Cabinet's about to be dissolved. You don't need to consult them."

Severin sighed. "Fine. Send messages to the engineers and the staff. How long do you need to get the operation in motion?"

"The day after tomorrow," I said. "I have some wrangling to do."

"When will you stop all this?" the King asked, gesturing to the yellow ribbon pinned to my jacket sleeve. "The activism."

"When the work is done, Your Majesty. When the sun rises on a better Aeland. And may it be soon."

He blinked at me, then collected all his surprise and tucked it behind a grave expression. "It may be sooner than you think. You may leave us."

Tea hadn't yet been served. Aife gave him a sharp look, but Severin watched as Joy and I took three backward steps before turning for the door. My stomach growled, but I would eat at home. The plan was on, and I had work to do.

We couldn't bring the witches home to nothing to wear, but I could organize a clothing drive in my sleep. I had crews ready to visit our neighbors the next morning. Five Corners wasn't the wealthiest part of Riverside, but even their residents could find an extra sweater or hat to donate. I traveled alongside a cargo sled already half-full of clothes that didn't need too much mending to make whole. Residents of every tenement on the block lined up to donate what they could and then speak to me of the ones they had lost, and what they remembered of their whereabouts.

I stood at the back of the cargo sled with my clipboard and pen, standing in a shaft of morning sunlight. The woman in front of me tied her layered shawls together and shoved her hands into the pockets of a food-stained apron.

"Lonnie Fisher," she said, her straight hair escaping the knotted bun at the back of her neck. "Lonnie's my cousin. They took him to Norton. You're going out to Norton, aren't you? You're going to them all?"

"We won't stop until every asylum is empty." I noted Norton as Lonnie's possible location in the ledger. "And can you take him in?"

"I've only the one room, Auntie, but I won't leave him to the cold either. If his family uphill won't have him, then I will."

"And you're Ginny Fisher?"

"Smith. I married. Lost him to the Laneeri War. The widow's pension is half of nothing."

"I'm sorry," I said. "What did you do?"

"I was a factory baker."

I fished a stiff little card from the stack in my pocket. "Would you stop at the Service offices and tell them you're a baker? We need staff on the trains, and they could use someone like you."

"Thank you for the tip, Auntie. I'll do that." She took my card for the Service office and turned away.

The next to talk was a red-nosed man smoking acrid tobacco in his pipe. The sour smell made my nose wrinkle. He offered old suits and a story about his missing niece. I wrote it all down and caught up to the sled, ready to speak to the next person who had lost family and friends to the asylums.

Some of the people I talked to hadn't given up hope. They were alive with it, brimming with the possibility that their loved one would come home, free at last, and they would get their lives back. Their sons, their siblings, their spouses would come back and fill the empty space they had been torn from.

I tried very hard not to disturb their hope. It was a powerful feeling, so easily shattered by reality, and a fall from its heights could break one's heart in a breath. I rubbed at my chest and fought the urge to envy them. They didn't know what had happened to their people, so hope still nudged their hearts. They still believed. They still had a chance.

"I've been alone for so long now," one man said to me. "Wouldn't it be something to be two of us once more?"

I smiled and wrote down the name of his wife. "It would be something, indeed."

"She was everything, my Marcia," he said. "Sang sweet as a bell, nursed every animal she could find that was sick or hurt or starving. She was so kind—she is so kind," he corrected. "And the birds will sing when she comes—"

He wasn't looking at me anymore, gazing at a sight that turned him waxy-pale.

"Excuse me," he said. "Good luck."

He shuffled around and made his slow, careful way back into the tenement. People who hadn't had a chance to talk to those of us with clipboards and pens about their own connections scurried back inside.

Standing in the intersection of East Second and Cockle were eight Greystars, so called for their smoky attire and the shine of sunlight on the dark-tinted snow goggles they wore year-round. They watched people melt back inside and hastened their flight by moving toward us.

I moved too, past the volunteers who watched the Greystars, staying still and quiet, until I was in the lead of the group. I planted my feet. I held my head up. My breath came too fast, and anyone looking at the cloud I exhaled in the cold would know it.

The Greystars walked in step. The crush and crunch of their boots on hard-packed snow played a rhythm that made my heart kick in my chest. They marched toward me, a wedge that filled the street, the point of their charge the woman in the center of them all.

I suppressed a tiny flutter in my middle. Jamille Wolf came strolling over, clad head to toe in shades of gray from mist to charcoal, glare goggles over her eyes. A yellow ribbon fluttered from her left arm, matching the band on my coat.

"Good morning, Auntie." Jamille grinned, showing off the gap of a missing front tooth. She shook back her braided hair, and bone beads clicked together as the ends swung free.

She called me Auntie out of respect, like everyone else, but Jamille was a cousin—distant, and out-clan, but still one of my relations, though the respectable Thorpes didn't make a point of displaying their connection to the wild, disreputable Wolfs. I nodded to her and her followers, standing my ground.

"Good morning, Miss Jamille."

"I see you've come out to collect donations in Five Corners," she said, and cocked her head to one side. "I don't remember you coming to ask me if that was all right."

If you asked Jamille Wolf, she owned Five Corners. Every business that wanted to keep its doors open, every tenant who wanted to keep their belongings—they all paid Jamille the cost of keeping their roof safe. They paid her again when they filled runners' pockets with coins, playing the game where they predicted the closing numbers of the Kingston Stock Exchange for a share of half the day's take. They paid her even more when they bought their poppy resin and smoked their way into forgetful dreams.

Jamille had taken her family's gang of drug peddlers and extortionists and organized them into an efficient, money-generating enterprise. She was as good at making money as any prince of industry. She was at least as heartless. When Jamille said Five Corners belonged to her, few would dare to disagree. Only a fool would deny her to her face.

"We didn't ask," I agreed. "We were coming your way next, however, to see if you had any extra clothes to spare. We're still in need of everything, but we're on the lookout for shoes."

"Shoes," she said. "I've always admired your dedication to the community, Auntie. But really, I admire your sheer nerve. What are you doing here?"

"We're collecting clothing and taking down the names of family and loved ones who were sentenced to life in the witch asylums," I said. "We're bringing them home."

Jamille went still, and the pressure of her gaze kept me transfixed. Her mouth opened. She covered it with one gray-gloved hand.

"You're going to save Jack," she breathed. "He's coming home."

Hope had Jamille Wolf. In just one instant, hope had her by the scruff. "Will you tell me where they took him?"

"Clarity House, in Bywell. Basil." Jamille raised her hand and beckoned.

A blocky, pink-faced man with colorless blond hair and a thin white scar curved over one cheek stepped forward. "What is it, Jams?"

"These people need shoes and winter boots," Jamille said. "Fetch them."

The Greystars moved as one body, slipping into a nearby shop.

"You don't need to do that," I said.

"I won't give my brother used shoes. Or secondhand clothes. You shall have the best, Auntie. I'll see to it. Whatever you need, just ask."

"You could take your brother shopping instead," I said. "I can't accept looted goods. I appreciate the gesture—stop them. Please."

Greystars marched out of the shop, arms piled with shoeboxes. "Auntie. They're donations."

I sighed. "Miss Jamille. Don't. They won't be able to pay insurance if you take all their stock."

Jamille sighed. "Fine. Take them back, lads. Save one pair. Proper brogues, size ten. Give the rest back."

They turned around to return the newly looted goods. Jamille turned back to me. "Anything you need, Auntie. Just ask. But please make sure Jack gets his new shoes, will you? And tell him I'm waiting for him to come home."

She rounded up the Greystars and took them away, hope gently stroking her hair.

THREE

Clarity House

The morning of the liberation dawned bright and clear, and I climbed up King Philip Hill with a company of thirty Windweavers in stout layers. We were greeted with coffee brewed to a strength I hadn't tasted in weeks, and pastries fresh and warm.

Marlon handled the Windweaver shifts and sent two of them to board the train's engine car. It looked strange to see its stack smoking with the leavings of burning coal, but all trains could run on coal if there was an emergency. People gathered on the platform, some gathered in clumps organizing their roles on the trains, others getting in the way with their gawking.

"They're going to start clearing. You all are going to want to stand back," Marlon yelled. "Go inside. Inside!"

No one moved. Marlon shrugged and let himself in. Grace stepped outside, joining me in the crowd of spectators.

"What's going on?" she asked, and then gripped my arm. "We should go inside."

"But I want to see it."

"Not from out here. Come on." She pulled on me, and the breeze changed direction, blowing harder. Faster, and snow flew, smacking me in the face. I had to lean into the wind to join the others who staggered toward the door and took refuge inside the train station.

Outside, the wind howled. The train was little more than an

outline as snow filled the air, slicing sideways as if a tiny blizzard had overtaken the train station.

People inside exclaimed in amazement, but they shuffled away from the Windweavers, whose rows of pierced earrings, long hair-locks gathered into buns and high headwraps, and ornately knitted woolen sweaters marked them out from the spectators and officials.

It was one thing to sit in their parlors and declare that witches didn't frighten them. But when confronted by the uncanny, impossible gift of witchcraft, those stout-hearted opinions flinched.

The wind died. Tiny, sparkling snowflakes fell glittering to the ground, dusting the carefully cleared platform. The tracks were clear, scoured by the efforts of the Windweavers. Marlon clapped his hands together, and the echoing slap made the crowd jump.

"That turned out well enough," Marlon said. "Let's board."

The Windweavers headed for the doors. Grace and I followed behind them. And the spectators muttered to each other as we greeted the sun on our heads with squinting and snow goggles.

The trip took longer than usual, but we beat the estimate of sundown. We pulled into Bywell Station with the long afternoon sun shining off the heaps of snow piled on the town. We ate in the dining car while people toiled to lead horses from the livestock cars and hitch them to sleighs for the rest of the journey to Clarity House. Grace and I shared a sleigh, bundled against the glittering cold.

"We'll be back in Kingston late tonight," Grace guessed, and then pointed at a mound in the snow. "I think that's my car."

"This is where you broke the network?"

"The very same. I wonder how Dr. Fredman's doing?"

"Who's Dr. Fredman?"

"The head physician," Grace said, and took a deep breath of cold air. "It's so much better than it was. When we were here before, the air was agonizing. Just horrible."

We passed through the gates and stopped. The building sprawled in snowdrifts, long arms angling away from the center. The roofline was peaked with tall gables and a drift of snow fell from the steep pitch to pile just under ground-floor windows. Grace didn't wait to be helped from the sleigh. I scrambled out after her, and we studied the building while waiting for the guards and medics to sort themselves out.

I caught a glimpse of a small face in an upper window. I blinked and stared at the empty space, willing the face to appear again.

"What is it?"

I shook my head. "I think I saw a ghost up there. Just for an instant."

Grace nodded. "Maybe a lot of them stayed here."

She led the way to the front door and marched inside, halting as we encountered an empty, silent foyer.

"What's going on here?" she asked. "Where is everyone?"

"Ahoy!" I shouted, pitching my voice to the ceiling. "Ahoy! Who's here?"

Heavy boots thudded on the stairwell, becoming a white-uniformed porter—did they have porters, in witch asylums? He stared at us in offended, slack-jawed surprise, his eyes lighting with fear as he beheld the Chancellor of Aeland and uniformed King's guards.

The porter caught his heel on the stair and toppled—backward, thank luck, so he landed on his backside. He scrambled a few steps away from us. "What do you want?"

His name was embroidered just above the pocket, just like my uniforms at work had been. I pushed forward, a far less intimidating figure than Grace. I was small, kindly, my expression unpainted with the fakery of a smile, and he looked at me with a little relief.

"Are you Jordan Sellers?" I asked, and he clapped a hand over his embroidered name.

"I am."

"We're here to release the witches, Mr. Sellers," Grace said, presenting a ribbon-tied scroll of paper. "Here is a copy of the writ signed and sealed by the Crown. Take it to your director, and then have the staff report to me for further instructions."

"Director's not here," the porter said. He got back on his feet, adjusting his too-big uniform.

Grace waved his excuse away. "The proctor, then."

Sellers shook his head. "They left after their shifts. They didn't come back. Most of them didn't. And then the storms hit and now we're snowed in."

There was something wrong. This man looked tired, his eyes sunken into violet-tinged shadows. His uniform should have been white, but it was dingy, and his belt was looped past holes that showed the wear of a waistline that had lost an inch or two around the middle.

Grace made an astonished noise. "They abandoned you?"

"No one has walked through that door in weeks," Sellers said. "Since you came and broke everything. Director no-showed first. They say he packed up and left town. There's only three of us left, and we can't go home—we couldn't leave them alone."

"They left," Grace said. "Ran away. The cowards."

"We can still get to the barns. There's goat milk, as long as we have hay," Sellers said. "But we're running low on everything. They would have died without us. We couldn't leave them."

"Thank you for your humanity," Grace said. "You could have left them, trying to escape whatever your superiors fled."

"Is anyone ill, or injured?" I asked. "Will anyone need assistance to get to the train?"

"The train's running? How? The line's buried. What are you going to do with the witches?" Memory made him shake his head. "You're going to release them? Why—you can't do that. It's not safe."

"The Witchcraft Protection Act has been abolished," Grace repeated. "We have come to bring them to Kingston, where they will be reunited with their families, or sheltered until they can return to their homes elsewhere."

"You can't—you can't do that." He shook his head, reaching for the baton hooked into his belt. "You can't set them loose—in Kingston? It'll be a bloodbath."

"Please stand aside," I said. "We've come to free them. If you won't assist us, then get out of the way."

"You can't. They know how to behave here. They'll go wild without us." He backed up another step, still fumbling for his baton.

Guards stepped forward. I stayed them with a gesture. "I know what you've been led to believe, but it isn't true. You work with witches every day. Have you ever seen any of them fall into believing something that wasn't real? Did you ever see them use violence?"

"That's the therapy," Sellers said. "The therapy keeps them from using their power. The power makes them violent. But if we're not here to correct them—"

I shuddered at what these doctors, isolated and empowered, could

have done to the people imprisoned here, and how the witches were
"corrected." I didn't have time to convince Porter Sellers. "I'd like the
keys, please. You kept the witches safe. We'll make sure you're not
held responsible for their abandonment."

"We're here by direction of the King," Grace said. "The keys."

"You'll frighten them," he said. "There's no telling what they'll
do. They've had no therapy for weeks."

"I am tired of arguing with you." Grace put out her hand, palm
up. "You are obstructing the wishes of the King. Hand over the keys
or be arrested."

Very few people defied the Chancellor, but he put the keys in my
hand instead of hers.

"This will end in tears," he said. "They don't know what the outside world is like. They're not prepared for it."

That was ridiculous. They had all had lives outside the asylum.
But there was no more time to waste if we were going to get everyone out of here.

I led the way up the stairs and sorted through dozens of keys,
reading their labels. Grace nearly danced with impatience. "What did
he mean, they don't know what the outside world is like?" she asked.

"I wondered that too," I said. "It doesn't make sense. Ah!"

The key turned. I pulled the door open, and held up my hand for
quiet. "Do you hear that?"

Grace and the guards went silent. Floating down the narrow corridor lined with barred cells came the sound of an infant crying.

"Children," Grace said. "They have children."

How had that happened? The usual way, of course, but how had
hospital policy allowed a child to be born in captivity?

Sellers's words came back to me in a nauseous rush. "They," he'd
said. The baby we heard crying wasn't the only one.

"We have to find out what happened here," I said, "after we get
them all out."

I led our party past empty cells. They were narrow and bare, with
a few pegs holding gray pajamas. They smelled like unwashed laun-
dry, stale and musty. There were no pictures, or keepsakes, or anything to distinguish one narrow little cell from another until we
found ones with cribs crammed inside. One, two . . . no. A dozen.
More.

"This is too many babies," I said.

"Far too many," Grace agreed.

"This isn't right," I said. "This shouldn't be happening. There are rules against this."

One of the guards cleared her throat. "Ma'am. Down the hall."

"Hm?"

The end of the corridor was blocked. Three gray-clad, barefoot witches crowded the end of the hall with their fists up, every one of their wrists encircled with copper bands. They were too thin, their cheeks hollow, and—

Their heads were shorn nearly to the scalp, fuzz growing on their heads, black witches and white ones alike. No braids. No locks. No curls to the shoulders—their pride had been stripped from them.

They guarded a larger room, where the others—the children—must have huddled, not knowing who invaded their unit.

"Ahoy," I said. "I'm Robin Thorpe. I've come from Riverside. This is a rescue."

They glanced at each other. "How did you get here?"

"We're from Kingston," Grace said. "The laws that locked you in here have been abolished. We're here to release you."

The witches glanced at each other. "We're free?"

I shut my eyes and blinked my vision clear. "You're free."

They looked at each other again. One of them looked back at us, his lip quivering. "But where will we go?"

My heart cracked open. "Home. We're taking you all in to find your families. And if you weren't from Kingston, we will shelter you until you can travel back to your hometown."

"But what if they don't know us?" that same witch asked, and then I looked at his face. Hunger had thinned him, and that had aged him, but he couldn't be much older than fourteen.

Children. Children born here, raised inside prison walls. I smiled at him, fighting nausea. How had this happened?

"You have a place to go," Grace said. "We're not going to punt you into the snow."

"We'll find your families," I promised. "Who is your father?"

The boy's shoulders went up. "The doctors don't tell us that. They don't tell us who they picked to make us."

Who they picked to . . . Oh, Solace. Solace, no.

An older witch covered the boy's bony shoulder with one hand. "He has forty fathers," he said. "We don't talk about it."

"What is going on here? Were the doctors forcing you to—" Grace stopped talking and covered her mouth.

"Breed more witches," I said.

"Only the channelers," the older witch said. "They needed them to power the aether engines, and no one they bring in from outside has the power."

I was going to vomit. The floor didn't even feel solid. "I'm Robin Thorpe," I said to the young witch. "What's your name?"

"Murray."

"I'm Grace," Grace said. "Murray, did they make you go downstairs to the basement?"

He nodded. "Only a few times. I didn't like it."

"What did you do down there?"

"I linked with the other witches," Murray said. "And then I let the visions come through me. I had visions and feelings, like I'm very old or a woman or in strange places. I feel sad, but I'm not sad. It's the vision. And then there was another one, and another one, all day long."

"And now that you don't go downstairs anymore," I said, keeping my voice gentle, "do you see people only other channelers can see?"

Murray nodded. "They're all dead. That's what the visions were. Dead people, and their memories."

I really was going to be sick.

"He's a Deathsinger," Grace said.

"Like me," I said.

Only I lived outside, believing myself powerless. I grew up outside, wishing I could do something more than just make a witchlight, while Murray and the children like him were bred and raised to use the magic of a soul to light our homes and play music on the wireless and lighten the burden of our lives.

Grace covered her mouth again. "Excuse me."

She dashed into a cell, and I held onto my dignity with all my might as the sounds echoed through the hall.

I strode forward, pulling my own keys from my pocket. I pinched between my fingers the manacle key I carried with me from my days monitoring patients in restraints, and held it up so they could see.

"I can unlock your bracelets," I said. "We're getting out of here."

Behind the three witches, others gathered, curious now.

"The Witchcraft Act has been abolished," I announced for all of them to hear. "You are all free. We're getting you out of here. You're going to be free."

"Robin?"

I knew that voice. The witches stood aside as one of their number shoved through the line of defense, halted at the front of the crowd, and stared in disbelief.

I knew that long, narrow nose, even if the planes of kher cheeks were sharp and underfed. I knew kher eyes: heavy-lidded, long lashed, resting under eyebrows arched like ram's horns.

Years had changed kher hair to silver streaks, cut cruelly short. Khe hunched bony shoulders covered by a sweater mended with whatever wool came to hand, its loops and twists and bobbles the clan pattern I knew by heart. I had knitted this sweater. I had given it to kher, twenty years ago.

"Zelind," I said. "You're still alive."

I had forgotten how to dream of this moment. I had fought to set kher free. As the years wore on I fought in kher name, and then in kher memory.

But khe was here, and I had forgotten how to dream of seeing kher again, to imagine what it would be like. What I would do, what I would say—and the moment to seize kher in an embrace sped past. The moment to take kher hand wandered off, leaving me to stand here, staring, unspeaking.

Zelind watched me as if I would vanish if khe looked away. Khe said nothing. Khe shifted kher weight from one bare foot to the other, long fingers tracing over the bends and curves of kher spirit-knitted sweater.

"I tried to visit you," I said. "I filled out the paperwork over and over. They always refused. And then they told me that you were permanently unavailable to visitors, and I—"

"So you broke in, trussed up the guards, and came to see for yourself." Zelind smiled, and it wrenched at my heart. "Thank you."

Now. Now. Go to kher now. I didn't move. "We have to get you out of here. Are you all in the common room?"

Zelind stretched kher arms out and shuffled backward, making way for our entry. "How are you here? The road's been impassable for weeks."

"The Windweavers cleared the snow off the tracks to get here," I said. "They're exhausted, but it worked."

Zelind licked kher lips. "Is he here?"

I turned my head to the left before I could control it. "He never joined the Circle."

Zelind's eyes went narrow and hard. "I shouldn't be surprised."

But before I could say anything, more people crept into the room filled with ratty, mended furniture and not much else. Behind them, children cried, probably picking up on their mothers' fear. More thin faces. More shorn heads, and every eye was too wide to be anything but afraid. All were barefoot—and then I wished I hadn't refused the boxes of new shoes Jamille had extorted.

Murray ran to one of the older patients, and they let Murray wrap them up in long, skinny arms as he said, "They're here to set us free."

"But—"

"They said they'll take us to Kingston," he said. "Zelind knows one of them."

"It's true?"

Zelind nodded. "It's true. Get your things, everyone. Come back here when you're ready."

People moved cautiously to their rooms. Others waited, watching us with carefully blank expressions.

Zelind turned to me. "There's someone here you should meet."

"Who?" I asked, but khe was already moving across the room, headed for a young woman who made me stop in my tracks. The shape of her eyes and the short rounded nose, the gap between her two front teeth—I had seen her face before, in photographs made back when the subject had to sit very still to get a good image.

Zelind offered kher hand, and the girl took it. She stared at me, studying my face as intently as I had hers, and I knew before Zelind cleared kher throat.

"This is Jean-Marie. Her mother was Ophrah, and her grand-mother was—"

"Mahalia Thorpe," I said. "Jean-Marie, you're my cousin."

Jean-Marie slouched. She bit on a chewed corner of her nails, then set her hands in her lap, clenching one hand around the other. A movement caught her attention, and a ghost drew near, hovering beside her in the shapeless gray dress of the asylum.

"She looks like your grandmother," the ghost said. "No bigger than a robin."

Jean-Marie turned to me. "Mother says it's true."

"I heard her. Funny thing. My name is Robin," I said. "Robin Mahalia Thorpe."

"You're a channeler too?"

"We call ourselves Deathsingers," I said. "We only just learned what our power does."

"Why didn't you know?" she asked.

"Because there were no ghosts to talk to," I said. "Because . . ."

She looked away.

Because the channelers had been forced to pour them into the soul-engines. No more. I'd live in the dark for the rest of my life if it meant getting them free.

"You're getting out of here. You're never coming back."

She shrank into herself. "But I have nowhere to go."

"You do," I said. "The Thorpes live in Kingston. Our part of Kingston. We live in clan houses, surrounded by family. You can live there too."

"You'll let me live with you?"

"Let you?" I smiled wide. "You are a Thorpe. The clan is your family. The clan house belongs to you by right. You'll be coming home where you belong. Why don't we go get your things?"

She stared at me for long, anxious seconds before she nodded and pushed herself to her feet.

Zelind offered Jean-Marie kher hand. "I'll help you."

I should have moved to follow them, but I didn't.

FOUR

Kingston

We had made it all the way to the train before we found out just how deprived the asylum-born had been. They stood before their seats, each one supplied with a warm blanket, a box lunch from the train kitchens, and a small selection of books—none of them suitable for children. Jean-Marie picked one up and gazed at it upside down, ignoring the writing board with its paper and pens.

She offered the books to me. "I don't need these."

"You don't like reading?"

"I don't know how. None of us do."

Zelind put a comforting hand on Jean-Marie's shoulder. "That's not quite true. You know some words."

"Flour, eggs, sugar, tea." Jean-Marie shrugged. "Hay. But the others got in trouble if they tried to teach us more."

"They don't speak Samindan either," Zelind said. "It wasn't permitted. People got in trouble if they spoke it."

Inside I boiled, but I kept anger or pity from my face. "You can learn," I said. "You all can learn. It's your right."

"What does that mean?" Jean-Marie said.

I thought for a moment. "A right is something you don't have to ask permission to have. It's a freedom no one can morally take from you. You are supposed to have hundreds of them—and the right to speak the language of your people is just one. The right to a minimum standard of education is another. You have the right to know how to read and write."

"They didn't tell us that," Jean-Marie said.

"You will all learn your rights," I said. "Every one of you. But for now, I can read to you."

They stared at me, quiet and unsure.

"She means stories," Zelind said. "She's going to tell you stories."

All the asylum-born turned to me at that. They gathered close, curious. "You can read stories?"

The question hurt my chest. "Any time you want."

They listened to me read for a moonlit hour, the train speeding past miles of fields and farms. When my voice gave out, Zelind took over. So long as one person was awake, another was reading to them, and they were careful with the books on their seats, which were treated like precious things.

It was deep night when the first train pulled into Main Street Station, and the platform was full of people holding candles and cheering. The windows filled with witches staring at the assembly, glancing at each other, groping for a hand to hold.

"It will be all right," I said. "The people here are waiting for you."

"Not for us," a young Deathsinger said, her white face tight with worry. She bounced the baby in her arms, backing away from the windows.

"For you," I said. "Look how many people came. They're here to see you come home."

"I just want to sit here for a minute." She took a cushioned seat away from the windows. "Just for a minute."

"All right," I said.

It took a while for the asylum-born to move. The others couldn't wait to get off the train, and were soon enveloped in the arms of their families. But many didn't move off to go home. Instead, they waited.

And since the witches weren't going anywhere, the crowd stayed.

Then some of the witches came back to the train. One woman pushed back the brim of her knitted green hat and came to the Deathsinger who wouldn't look out the window.

"Come with me, you and your littles," she said. "I talked to my family. There's always room in a clan house. We'll get you sorted."

The Deathsinger rose, looking fearful, and followed the woman off the train. Joyful cheering faltered when she stepped through with her daughter tucked in the crook of one arm and her son clinging to her free hand.

All the mothers and children went through, greeted by horrified murmurs, but one by one, a witch took them along to their family or their clan and gave them someone to belong to. Others were taken to the clans of their grandmothers and great-grandmothers, until there were only a few left.

Those mothers clumped together, huddled against the stares and muttering. They watched as Jacob Clarke and his wife drew near. They shivered as the breeze stole away their body warmth.

Jacob stopped a few feet away and bowed. "I'm Jacob Clarke," he said. "Welcome home. We're so glad you've been returned to us. We have extra sweaters and blankets. Will you come and pick out what you like?"

Winnie Clarke offered her hand to one of the women with a baby. "What are your names?"

She curled protectively around her child, studying Mrs. Clarke. She was thin—all the witches were, some painfully so—and her mouse-colored hair made her look like she'd recovered from a long illness. "I'm Emma. My baby is Cora."

Mrs. Clarke blinked, and her eyes filled with tears. "You were born in the asylum. What was your mother's name?"

The baby woke up with a thin cry. Emma stroked her back and answered. "Jane Parker."

"We'll find your people," Mrs. Clarke said. "But for now we have room for you."

"Plenty of room," Jacob agreed. "Ah, Miss Agnes. Ahoy."

"Ahoy, Member Clarke. What are you going to do about these poor girls?" Miss Agnes Gable, tall and dressed head to toe in deep navy blue, leaned on a cane and stared at Jacob through delicate silver-rimmed spectacles. "We can take a mother. Not enough babies in our house."

Shouts of joy went up as witches were recognized and claimed by the clans. Clanless inmates shook hands with families from Riverside and uphill, welcomed into strangers' homes.

But near the back, I kept an eye on a cluster of people clad entirely in gray, their faces obscured by dark-lensed snow goggles covering their eyes. They lurked near the hot urns of apple tipsy, effectively keeping one of them for their own enjoyment.

A shout cut across the crowd. "Zelind! Zelind Bay!"

I clamped my lips shut as Bellita Bay's voice scraped against my ears. People parted for the matriarch of the sailing, trading, building Bays, who moved with slow dignity. She wore a gleaming ankle-length coat made from blue fox skins, a matching hat perched on her head. Her kid-gloved hand rested in the crook of Jarom Bay's elbow.

Jarom Bay wore a stylish black coat, his long, beaded locks hanging in a neat queue down his back. Zelind's younger cousin was tall, and fashionable, and moved through the world as if every inch of it owed him rent. He made straight for Zelind, who stood unmoving as cousin and mother came near.

"You're home. All our prayers, answered."

The Bays were here. I should have realized that they would be. I had prepared myself for whatever painful, horrible thing they would say when I returned from the asylum and told them Zelind was dead. But Zelind was alive, and here they were to take kher away to the mansion on top of the hill that held a handful of the numbers a clan house would. They would set Zelind at the head of the business, and the next time I saw kher, it would be at a distance.

I watched, my tongue struck silent. Mrs. Bay beamed, tears in her dark eyes. "Oh, my child—what is that rag you have on?"

She reached to stroke Zelind's cheek, but Zelind backed up a step, putting kherself out of reach.

"Don't touch me."

Everyone in hearing range gasped. I gasped. Mrs. Bay glared at me so fiercely spots of heat bloomed on my face, and I wasn't so sure it wasn't her feelings burning me.

Mrs. Bellita Bay had never liked me. Not when I was Zelind's school friend. Not when I was Zelind's study partner. And especially not when khe had taken me to formally meet the woman who had always looked past me with little more than a tepid smile.

I had worn my best daytime outfit then, borrowing from cousins for this bit of jewelry or that pair of shoes, and had held Zelind's hand as khe brought me into the parlor where Bellita drank tea with a thin slice of lemon floating on top.

"Mother," Zelind had said. "I know you've met Robin before, but that was different. This time, I want you to meet Robin Thorpe as the girl I love."

The teacup went still. Her eyebrows rose. She inspected me, from the toes of my borrowed shoes to the drop pearls hanging from my ears, looked me in the eye . . . and then turned her face away, uninterested.

"She's a null," Birdie Bay had said, and that should have been that. But it hadn't been.

Now, Jarom moved, blocking me from Mrs. Bay's sight, a frown on his face. "Zelind. That's no way to treat your mother."

"Neither is locking up your heir in an asylum," Zelind said. "I am no child of that woman."

Murmurs rose from the crowd as Zelind wove around them. Jarom turned, an impatient scowl on his face.

"Zelind. Be reasonable. Aunt Birdie did no such thing—"

"Spare me." Zelind turned kher back on kher mother and younger cousin and walked away. Curious faces swiveled to follow as Zelind stopped in front of me. "Robin. Did you—did you get an annulment?"

Birdie pressed one hand to her chest, her fingers splayed across her clavicles. "Zelind!"

Now the voices exclaimed in scandalized delight. Everyone watched us, everyone. The ground trembled under my feet.

Zelind hadn't accepted kher mother's rejection of the powerless girl khe loved. We had found a ship captain who would wind a line around our wrists and bind our fortunes anyway. So what if khe was disinherited? Khe had laughed at the very idea. "Is that the worst they can do? I don't want the business anyway. I don't even want their name."

Twenty years later, khe still didn't want it.

I swallowed and shook my head.

"No."

"So we're still married?"

"These last twenty years."

"I am a Thorpe," Zelind said. "I have no other family. May I come home with you?"

Birdie Bay warned me with the set of her mouth, the flint in her eyes—if I answered wrong, she would become war in a blue fox coat. She'd do her best to destroy me if I dared to cross her. I had dared to cross her before, and I was grown now, a woman of my community. But I wasn't a head of my clan. I didn't have the right to speak for them.

But I knew what they would say.

"Yes." It came out as a whisper. I cleared my throat. "Yes. Come home, Zelind Thorpe. We've been waiting all this time."

Zelind ignored Birdie and Jarom while khe caught up with witches who were going home with their clans. Khe touched their shoulders, speaking earnestly while they looked each other in the eye, folding adults and children into hugs. Khe settled their nerves, straightened their backbones, and sent them on their way.

None of my clan were here. We had been lucky, I suppose—we had lost the witches of my grandmother's generation to Clarity House and had received the death notice for her and my father years ago. The rest of us survived, hidden.

Jean-Marie had found a corner to huddle in, where she could watch the swirling crowd collect themselves into groups and take their newfound clan and their billets home. I hadn't really spoken with her yet. Every time I turned around, someone had a question, a request, a complaint.

I started toward her, but Jacob called out, "Robin, come and tell her she's wrong?"

I tried not to grumble and walked over to where Jacob Clarke and Grace Hensley stood, having a perfectly calm and civil argument. Grace opened a cardboard box and offered me one of her ready-made cigarettes; I put up my hand and shook my head regretfully. She nodded, and put the box back in her pocket without lighting one.

"It's a goodwill gesture; it's easy to implement; we have a system in place right now," Grace said. "Why are you saying no?"

"The witches need justice," Jacob said. "They can't even be completely compensated for what has happened to them. But we must. If we're to get past this, we must hold those responsible accountable. And the Crown must do what they can to repair the wrong done."

Grace rubbed her gloved fingers together, washing over the knuckles with her thumb. "I understand your reasoning, and something must be done, but we just don't have that kind of capital."

"You're saying Aeland can't afford them?"

Grace shook her head. "We can't deny what happened here. Veterans get pensions. Adding witches to the pension rolls is literally the least we could do for them. Let me start with that."

"A pension?" I stared at Grace. "That's all?"

The pension rolls were simple. If you were disabled, a retired employee of the government, or an injured veteran, you received an income that was equal to the national minimum wage in Aeland—but the cost to paying people on pension was the excuse Aeland had used to not raise wages in twenty-two years.

"To start," Grace said. "Just to start."

"We have to come in with complete demands," Jacob said. "If I let you lowball us with a token payment—"

"I don't feel comfortable turning uneducated people into the streets without a dime," Grace said. "It feels cold and unfeeling. This is the absolute least they deserve. I know they deserve more."

"But will they get it?" I asked. "You know people like Jessup will fight kicking and screaming. They'll say the witches are greedy and entitled. They'll ask why the pension's not good enough."

"It could be decades before any witch sees a cent if you hold out for a lump sum," Grace said. "Why don't you give me some time to gather some reports and work on Severin? He wants to do what's right. If you give me some time to show him the extent of this cruel and unjust treatment, we might rely on his conscience."

"You have your way and I have mine," Jacob said. "Do your best, Chancellor. Will you come back here to see the rest of the witches return?"

"I'm going to try," Grace said. "But this action is guaranteed to cause a stir up at the palace. I might better serve your cause by managing reactions."

"I think you may be right," Jacob said. "I should go and find Winnie and Miss Emma. We should get her and the children settled in."

"Children," Grace said, her tone weary with horror. "When Severin hears of this—I should go too. I have an appointment."

"Anyone I know?" I asked.

Grace's smile told me enough. "I never thanked you. For taking Avia in."

We had an entire network designed to hide witches for years. One lone reporter was hardly a task. "Why did you do it? King Severin doesn't seem like the sort who'd convict her."

"It wasn't Severin I was worried about," Grace said.

"What do you mean?"

Grace waved her hand dismissively. "There are a couple of difficulties at the palace. Nothing I can't handle. I had better get going. I don't want to be late."

"Farewell," I said, and turned back to searching for Jean-Marie. She watched me approach with wary eyes.

"You're one of the people in charge here." She said it almost like an accusation.

I smiled while my nervous stomach fidgeted. "Not me. Jacob is our leader."

"You're important. People come to you more often than they go to him."

"That's because they're looking for the answers to simpler questions. I'm on the committee, but I'm not in charge."

She shook her head. "It's the same thing. The head doctor, Dr. Fredman, he made the big decisions. The proctor was the one who did the work. You do the work. He gets the authority, but the people trust you more."

I was easier to talk to. And anything they would have told Jacob, he would have delegated it to me anyway. "I suppose that's a fair assessment."

She turned her face away. "Dr. Jane should have been in charge," she said. "Maybe you should too."

"No, I shouldn't. Some people are meant to stand in front. It takes something special to lead more than a handful of people. Others find their place in the operations. That's where they do best."

Jean-Marie shook her head. "I think you'd be a good leader anyway."

"I'm good at what I do, and part of that is knowing where I can do the most good."

I was good at organizing. I was good at managing projects and people. I could lead, but not the way Jacob could.

Jean-Marie pointed. "What are those people doing to Zel?"

I turned my head, searching for whatever dismayed her. Zelind stood in a knot of reporters avid for details of the asylum. They took pictures of kher shorn scalp, of kher hunger-pinched face, of the darned and mended sweater, peppering kher with questions.

"If it's not one thing, it's another," I grumbled, and headed in that direction. I pushed my way through with elbows and leverage, not caring to be gentle.

"Where did the children come from?" a reporter asked, and Zelind hardly had time to blink before someone else asked another.

"Are you returning to your family's development firm?"

"What does it feel like to be free of the asylum?"

"That's enough," I declared. "No more questions. Zelind."

Zelind gave me a grateful look and wiggled out of the scrum. "Thank you. That was—are they always like that?"

"Not always. You're big news, though. There they go, off to bother Grace and Jacob. Let's go."

We headed back to Jean-Marie's perch. "Do you mind walking?"

"From here? It's not far."

"Two miles," I said, and slowed.

A knot of people in gray approached. Front and center strolled Jamille Wolf, flanked by Basil Brown and a fistful of toughs trailing after, and that's when I remembered that Jonathan "Jack" Wolf hadn't been listed on the rolls of witches at Clarity House.

Jamille bobbed at the knees, ever so polite. "I came over to personally thank you for the deed you've begun here today."

"I am happy to hear it," I said. "But—"

She smiled that missing-tooth grin at me. "I've come with a proposal. I will loan out some of my best to help you with the liberation of the other asylums."

"The Crown's security team is sufficient, but it's a very kind offer," I said. "Did you hear we needed children's shoes and clothes?"

"We'll take a walk through the neighborhood tonight," she said. "For the sake of Five Corner's uza."

I kept the skeptical look off my face. "Thank you."

"Robin?"

Zelind came closer and eyed Jamille with wary suspicion—khe knew the Graystars, of course, but they had been little more than a street gang twenty years ago.

"Welcome back, Zelind Bay," Jamille said, flashing her grin again.

"Zelind Thorpe," khe said. "Is everything all right?"

"Miss Wolf was hoping to lend a hand with the liberation," I said. "They took her brother, and she's eager to have him back. He wasn't at Clarity House."

Zelind cocked kher head. "Wolf, you said? Was your brother Jonathan Wolf? Answered to Jack?"

Jamille's face lit up. "Yes. You know him."

"I did."

"You did?" Jamille's sand-golden face went chalky. "Why isn't he here? Why isn't he with you?"

"Miss Wolf," Zelind said. "I am sorry."

She backed up. Her locks swirled around her shoulders as she shook her head. "No. No. You go back and fetch him, you hear me? You fetch him here right now."

"Miss Wolf." Zelind shook kher head, slowly and so, so sad. "He died this past Leafshed, about a week before the network shut down."

"No," Jamille said. "No. You're lying."

"The asylum killed him. He couldn't bear what they made us do there. He—"

I had never seen Jamille anywhere close to tears. She held them back through the naked tension on her face, in the stiffness of her spine and her sharp, gasping breaths. "What? What are you saying?"

Zelind looked so sad. Khe stroked her shoulder, daring to comfort the Gray Wolf. "You don't need to know how he did it, Miss Wolf. But he's gone. I am sorry."

Jamille batted kher arm away. "No. He wouldn't. He wouldn't! You're lying! Bring him back!"

Jamille's shouts caught the attention of the other Greystars, who gathered around their leader. Basil Brown slipped his arm over Jamille's shoulders. "What is it? Jams, what—"

This was the shelter she needed to crumple. "Jonathan's dead," Jamille said. "He—the asylum killed him."

Her people exchanged worried glances behind her back.

"Oh, shit," one of them breathed.

"Those bastards," another grumbled. "Blast them all to the void, every one of them. Rich, evil bastards."

"They'll pay." Jamille swiped at her face. "They will pay for what they've done."

"Come on now, Jams," Basil coaxed. "Time enough to talk about all that. First, we've got to remember him."

"We do," Jamille said.

She slid open the front of her coat, and I tensed when I caught sight of the butt of a pistol holstered under her arm. She dug into her inside pocket and pulled out a battered silver flask, thumbing the lid open. The other Greystars followed suit, and the air smelled like gin as they poured out a draft for the dead from their flasks.

"Here's to you, Jack," Jamille said, and drank. She swallowed twice and poured out the rest. "I swear to you. I promise you. I will get revenge."

"Revenge," the Greystars echoed, and gin puddled over the snow. They emptied their flasks and turned their backs, marching out of the park with purpose stiffening their shoulders.

FIVE

Everyone at Once

We managed to get a taxi sleigh. The three of us took the long way home, crisscrossing the hillside that housed a lovely public garden and smaller homes than the clan houses of the river flats. Zelind turned kher face away from Bayview, looking down King Philip Hill at the snow-covered rooftops; the steepled, jagged edges of Riverside's downtown; and the dark ribbon of the Blue River sparkling just beyond.

Jean-Marie stared around at every sight. She swiveled her head to take in the shops of central Riverside, the bare-branched apple trees lining the road, and the huge, colorful clan houses that stood on each block, which grew grander and larger the farther we went west.

Zelind stayed quiet, studying streets khe already knew from twenty years ago. But khe held kher jaw tight as the shops and cafes weren't quite the streets khe knew—the details had changed Water Street into something that wasn't quite home.

We hardly spoke for the whole trip, and I was fighting the urge to fidget by the time we climbed out of the sleigh. The horses trotted away, leaving us to stare at the green-and-white-painted house fronted by a porch with its furniture packed up for the winter.

"This is the home of Clan Thorpe," I said. "The door never locks and you are always welcome."

Zelind watched the front windows filling with curious faces.

"How many people live here?" Jean-Marie asked.

"Permanently? About sixty." I led the way up the walk and looked back to see if Jean-Marie followed.

She stood on the sidewalk, her arms hugged around her middle.

"What's wrong?"

Jean-Marie stared up at the house. She had to be freezing, even with two more sweaters on. "What if they don't like me?"

"They're your family," I said. "You're bound to squabble with one or two. Tell one of the elders if it gets out of hand. Tell me, if you don't think you should bother the elders."

She didn't look satisfied by this comment, but she joined us on the porch.

The door burst open, wafting out the scent of roasted goose. Amos bounced up and down, grinning like he'd light the stars on fire.

"You brought witches home!" He let go of the doorknob, and a pack of children tumbled out of the chilly front parlor to stare.

"That's our clan pattern," Halima said, pointing at Zelind.

"It is," Zelind replied. "Your aunt Robin made it for me a long time ago."

"Second cousin." She tilted her head and gazed at Zelind skeptically. "But it's our clan pattern," she persisted.

"Well," Zelind said, smiling, "there's a reason for that. But we can't tell until everyone is in the second parlor to hear it."

Halima's eyes lit up and she herded everyone out of the way, shouting at them to move.

Jean-Marie watched it all with big eyes, staring at the wide central hallway and the clutter of shoes, jackets, skis, and mittens, past it to the front staircase that led to the bedrooms and suites that slept everyone in the clan. She backed up until she stood flush with the front door.

"Is meeting everyone at once too much?"

She looked at me with panic widening her eyes. "What if they don't like me?"

"Then we'll figure out something else," I said. "We'll go up and find you a room, Jean-Marie. Then we'll come down for supper."

I only got as far as the first stair before Aunt Bernice's voice rang out.

"What do you think you're doing?"

Jean-Marie spun around, gasping for breath. Zelind flinched. I turned to face our questioner. "Jean-Marie needs a room."

"Time for that later. Come here. Now." Aunt Bernice beckoned us inside. We stopped just inside the door, and I gave the elders a shallow bow.

"This is Zelind. Some of you know kher," I said, and before anyone could ask, I pushed Jean-Marie forward. "And this is Jean-Marie Thorpe, daughter of Ophrah Thorpe, who was named by her mother—"

"Mahalia," Aunt Glory said. "You're the spit of her, girl. I thought I was seeing a ghost, you look so much like her."

Jean-Marie patted her hair. She dug one slippered toe into the parlor rug, and her voice came out like she was a long way off. "I never knew her," she said. "I'm sorry. Zelind told me khe knew who I was related to, but I don't—I'm sorry."

"You're a Thorpe. You are Mahalia's granddaughter. Come and meet your family." Aunt Glory took her feet off the small tufted stool and gestured for her to sit.

"Don't distract us, Glory," Bernice said. "Did you know about this foolishness twenty years ago?"

I stepped back. "How did you—"

"Did you think you could just announce to half of Riverside that you got married—married!—and someone wouldn't run straight to our doorstep to ask if it was true?"

I licked my lips. "Carlotta Brown?"

"She was the one who got here first," Aunt Glory said.

Zelind and I exchanged a glance. I hadn't thought—I never thought, when it came to Zelind. I never took the time to reason it out. I just went ahead and—

"Married? What in the world were you thinking? That the Bays would just give over?"

"Plainly we were wrong, Aunt Bern," Zelind said. "But I don't take it back. I won't."

"Who married you?"

"Captain Errol Brown of the *Sandpiper*."

"A ferryman?" Aunt Bern exclaimed.

"A ship's captain is a captain no matter the vessel," I said. "Did you think anyone else would dare?"

"What's done is done," Hiram said. "Tell me you would have objected."

"That's not the point," Bernice snipped. "The point is that if we had known, we could have supported them."

"We were going to tell you," I said. "We were going to tell you the next morning."

"Why didn't you?"

The lump rose in my throat so quickly it hurt.

"Because Zelind was gone by then," Aunt Glory said.

"I walked into an ambush," Zelind said. "They were waiting right outside Bayview. They took me that very night."

One of the older children looked on in horror.

"Examiners, lurking in front of the Bays'? They were looking for you," Eldest said. "And your family didn't buy your way out?"

"Is that possible?" Zelind asked.

Uncle Hiram nodded, his bald head shining like he polished it. "They did it for Charles William, oh, thirty-five years ago. He walked right out of that jail and got on a ship and his feet never touched land again, but they bribed his way out."

Zelind's deep brown complexion went gray.

"They didn't buy my freedom," Zelind said. "They didn't even try."

"Maybe they did," Aunt Glory said. "Maybe it wasn't possible."

"It doesn't matter," Zelind said. "I was inside the sentry points. They arrested me in front of that clan house. Someone in that family allowed them to come through. Someone in that family wanted me gone. I am not a Bay. They are not my clan."

"You didn't ask your elders permission for the marriage," Eldest said. "And if you left for home after the rite, then you didn't get the chance to seal your marriage. It's not complete."

No. They could forbid it. They could apply for an annulment, and—

Zelind swallowed and nodded. "That is true. But I spent every minute inside that asylum a Thorpe. I have come home to my clan and my wife. Do you deny it?"

The eldest Thorpes exchanged glances. Bernice set her jaw. Glory gave her a withering look. "Now you know why Robin never brought home a sweetheart."

Bernice sniffed. "I thought the doctor was a fine-looking man—"

"You're not so sharp if you didn't see how he stammered the first few times he met Handsome Michael," Uncle Hiram cackled. "Give over, Bern. They kept faith with each other for twenty years."

"Twenty years together is different from twenty years apart," Bernice objected. "They were married to ideas. Now they're flesh and blood together, and—you grew differently. Both of you did."

"Bernice, can't you see the beauty of it? The romance?" Hiram asked.

"Of course I do," Bernice said. "That's the problem. It's romantic. It's not practical. They don't have what they had when they defied everyone and married. They—"

I wasn't listening to another second of this.

"Aunt Bernice," I said, and unclenched my fists. I smiled. "I thank you for your caution. But if you forbid the welcome of my spouse to the clan, we will find our own roof."

"Now see what you've done, Bernie," Glory grumbled. "This is what looking for rain in a clear blue sky will get you. Can't you be happy? Zelind has returned to us!"

"I don't forbid it. Zelind Thorpe is welcome here. I'm just point-ing out—"

"You're just poking holes," Hiram grumbled. "Zelind Thorpe is welcome here."

"Zelind Thorpe is welcome here," Aunt Glory said, beaming bright enough to light the room. "Rosabelle."

Rosie stood up. She crossed the room, her first child bundled in her arms. Rosie had barely been old enough to walk the last time Zelind was in this house. She put the sleeping, serene Zola in kher arms. Zelind handled the baby like khe did it all the time, swaying as khe gazed down at the youngest infant in the clan house.

"You are now this child's clan-parent," Hiram said. "You are charged with her protection. You are to teach her, guide her, be her confessor. She will be a sister to your own children, when they come."

That was just part of the charge, but it slid between my ribs.

Zelind nodded. "I will. This child has the strength of my arm and all the wisdom I bear. I promise. What's her name?"

Hiram answered. "She is Zola."

Zelind smiled at the baby. "Ahoy, Zola."

Aunt Bernice nodded. "Welcome to Clan Thorpe, Zelind. This day was long in coming."

Zelind lifted kher tear-streaked face to smile at the Thorpes gathered around the newest of the clan.

Hiram levered himself out of his chair, took up his cane, and made a slow plod to the door. "What are you waiting for? Come to the kitchen. We need to feast."

The children raced to line up and be chosen to sit at the big table. A line of Thorpes covered the table with dishes that had been baked in the enormous ovens or simmered over the gas burners in the kitchens. Cousins exclaimed over the new arrivals, and Cousin Delia laid her hand on Zelind's shoulder when she saw kher.

"Here you are at last," she said. "I see you've been charmed by my grandbaby."

"I'm completely under her spell." Zelind twisted around to smile at Delia, who had a tear in her eye.

"There's another one coming," Delia said in a conspiratorial tone. "Lorne's wife is expecting for Summerstide. Can't keep a bite of food down before noon, poor thing, and after that she eats everything in sight."

"Congratulations," Zelind said. "I look forward to meeting the new little one."

"Robin," my cousin Jedrus said, sounding a bit irritated. "Will you please pass the salt?"

I used it as an excuse to look away.

The children shouted and poked at each other at a low table of their own. I passed dishes to the right, holding them for Zelind, so khe could serve kherself one-handed. Khe passed the dish to Delia in time to catch the next plate and dish out some duck breast.

Baby Zola watched every move Zelind made. Zelind talked nonsense at her the way one does to babies and smiled at me as I passed kher a dish of pan gravy.

"You're supposed to put food on your plate," Jedrus said. "Do I have to dish you up while you moon over your spouse?"

"That's fine," I said. "I'm not really hungry."

"You should have something anyway."

"I couldn't eat if I wanted to," I said, and passed a bowl of black-berry sauce to Zelind.

Zelind didn't take kher eyes off Zola for the entire meal, eating one-handed. Khe laughed when Cousin Delia took a knife and cut kher meat into bites. I chewed bread spread with sweet butter and set the crust down when my throat spasmed in protest.

"What is wrong with you?" Jedrus asked. "You have to eat more than that."

I stood up. Jedrus huffed and offered kher shoulder for support as I climbed over the bench. "I'm going to get started on tidying."

I left the dining hall to a chorus of questions.

Fifty-nine people make a lot of dirty dishes, and with no aether, we couldn't just load the washing machines. I turned on the wa-ter, and steam billowed up around my face. I added vinegar to the bubbles carrying the lemon-fresh trademark scent of Mrs. Sparkle's Squeaky Soap.

No children. I scrubbed pots. Soft steam from the water damp-ened my face. No grandchildren. I concentrated on the texture of the pot smoothing out under the efforts of my scrubbing off the burnt bits, handling the pot with careful fingertips when I dunked it in the scalding water and dropped it on the rack. I tested the pot soaking in the soap, putting some muscle behind the scrubbing steel.

It hadn't bothered me. I would never let it. But all those years were gone. Gone—

"Robin."

"What?"

I kept scrubbing, even though khe came closer. Zelind didn't have Zola any more. Khe stood five feet off. "Everyone is worried about you."

"I'm fine."

"Because after a long day of hard work, you always eat half a slice of bread and volunteer to do the dishes." Zelind leaned on the pantry door. "You hate dishes."

"Everyone hates dishes."

"Just tell me what's wrong," Zelind said. "Or I'll have to guess."

"Everything's fine." I slid pots into the sink, plunging my hands into the too-hot water. "And your supper's getting cold."

"I ate it."

"Already?"

"I learned to eat fast." Zelind picked up an oiled linen towel and wiped the first iron pot to come out of the wash. "These still go under the stove?"

"Yes. The catch sticks."

"Is the toolbox still where it was?"

"Yes."

Zelind took the green wooden box down and had the drawer catch dismantled in a trice. Khe could rebuild a simple thing like a spring catch without even thinking. Khe had built the wireless that still sat in the second parlor when we were still in school at the academy. Khe put the device back together, and the pot drawer worked like new.

"I'm not going to badger you," khe said, standing up and shoving the pot drawer closed with kher toes. "We'll just wash dishes."

"All right."

I scrubbed four more pots. Zelind strolled across the kitchen to put them where they belonged. We worked in quiet, the same way we had when Zelind first came to Clan Thorpe for dinner and we volunteered to get an early start on the dishes, and therefore a chance to be alone. I scrubbed down a roasting pan, bathed it in clear rinsewater, and Zelind tugged it free of my grasp with kher power. The pot floated across the air to kher hands.

I used to be used to that. I went back to washing the dish in front of me.

Zelind cleared kher throat. "It was Zola."

I nearly dropped the roasting rack into the water. "What?"

"You were thinking our grandchild should have been at that table," Zelind replied.

Zelind had once had a knack for seeing into me, seeing the thoughts that hurt to voice—the selfish, angry, unfair things that I felt ashamed for feeling. But khe never made me feel like I should be ashamed. Zelind accepted my petty feelings, holding them gently. Today, though, I couldn't feel anything but hurt.

"We should have had the chance to discuss our child's future with their would-be spouse."

"We should have." I wrapped the dishcloth around a kitchen knife and carefully cleaned the edge. "We should have had our own babies. We should have a line of descent—"

"There's still time."

I shook my head and rubbed at the twinge of pain in my chest. "Women my age rarely get pregnant."

"But—"

"Because when they do, they risk their lives and their baby's lives. High blood pressure. Early delivery. Complications in pregnancy. It's too late."

"Then we'll have Zola," Zelind said. "And little Unknown, when Lorne's nameless wife finally has her child."

As I scrubbed cooking tongs, something awful lurked in the back of my thoughts. "Zelind. Did you—are you a parent already?"

Zelind shook kher head. "They only bred the channelers. They'd never want my child. I was too dangerous."

"It's so atrocious. Solace hold them all." I pulled water-wrinkled hands out of the sink and let the water drain. "Did they get Jean-Marie?"

A shadow passed over Zelind's face. "It's still too early to know."

I dug my teeth into my lip. "Blast them. She's a baby. Fifteen?"

"Sixteen."

"Still. She shouldn't have gone through that."

"She shouldn't. And she won't. She's safe now. You made her safe."

"I just brought her home where she belonged."

"Yes," Zelind said. "You did."

Zelind gazed at me, and it was like all the times I would notice, and when I noticed, I would say—

"What?"

And Zelind would say—

"I'm just—"

The door from the dining room swung open, and Jedrus led the way with a stack of dirty plates.

"You're excused," khe said, "since you made a head start already. There's enough left over for sandwiches at midnight. Go."

Zelind had spent many an evening perched on the roof of the clan house, but khe had never climbed the wide walnut stairs that led from the clan house's public floor to the private rooms above. We moved quietly, as if someone was going to catch and scold us.

Zelind stayed behind me, past the second floor that kept families grouped together, to the third floor, where my rooms were tucked into a corner at the back of the clan house.

"This is it." I moved all the way into the room and opened the curtains, catching what little light was left.

My view gazed out to the Ardelia Densmore Canal, now frozen, leveled, and scuffed by hundreds of ice skate blades. Three panes of glass separated the frigid outdoor air from my modest little sitting room, a chamber insulated by books climbing to the ceiling and an oval rug braided from torn-up bedding and outworn clothes.

Zelind took a deep breath before crossing the room to sit in the rocking chair with the best light. Khe gripped the chair arms, looking all about the room.

" You still have Saria's adventure stories."

"The whole collection."

Khe turned to the side table, where a stack of my surgery texts rested, a basket of yarn just below. "I stole your seat. Sorry."

"You always had an eye for the best seat in the room." I moved to the door on the right and pushed it open. "I'll have to make space for you in the dressers."

Zelind set the chair to rocking. "Do you get much time to sit up here?"

"Not usually. Sometimes, a half hour here and there. I've kept busy."

Khe turned an ear to the open door, where Ramona played the aria from *A Strand of Stars for Your Hair*. The performance began with a single melody played in darkness representing the singer moving through the darkness of the Solace, searching for the Amaranthine she loved, and lost, and sought.

She could have picked something else.

"It's lovely," Zelind said. "It sounds tragic."

Khe had never heard it. Had never seen Hyacinthe Chalk on the stage—did they have the wireless, in the asylum? No. They would have heard the news of the outside world if they had, and that could have made them difficult.

"Is it tragic?"

"Yes."

"What's it about?"

"Lost love."

Zelind turned kher face away.

"I have my own bathchamber," I said, desperate to talk about something else, anything else. "The tub's tiny, but it's better than waiting for six teenagers to finish primping in the mirror . . . and I finished a quilt a few weeks ago."

"You have time to quilt, when you have to read all these books?" Khe ran a knuckle up the spines of *Richardson's Abdominal Surgery Encyclopedia*. "You have to learn all that?"

"I already know a lot of it. I've watched hundreds of surgeries. Maybe even thousands." I closed the door to the hall and Zelind tensed. "Are you all right?"

Khe glanced at me, then turned to my knitting. "I know how to knit now."

Kher hands landed in her lap, grasping, tangling over each other and then twisting free.

"Do you want your own kit? There's a bushel of yarn in storage. You could make something. You could—"

"What's in there?" Zelind asked, nodding toward the door on the other side.

"That's a closet. I'll have to make space—"

"You have to make a lot of space for me," khe said. The rocking grew sharper. "I don't know if I can—"

Khe settled long, reedy fingers in the grooves carved in the tip of the rocking chair's arms and squeezed. Khe rose to kher feet and stood in front of me. "I want a bath."

"In here."

I led kher into the bedroom and gestured to the narrow door. "You'll want some clean clothes," I said. "We have a closet of hand-downs. I'll find you something."

That room was too small. Too warm. Overstuffed with Zelind's unease. I fled down the stairs to a storage closet, where I sorted through canvas trousers and singlets and button-front shirts. I found a collar that barely showed any wear; machine-knitted woolen stockings, and a knee-length pleated bottle green kilt. It was enough to change into.

When I came back to my suite, the bathroom door was firmly closed. I left the clothing on a nearby chair and shut the bedroom door behind me. What would I want, if I had gained my freedom? I'd want to wash the asylum off me. I'd want to put it all behind me. I'd want to hold the person I loved.

I wrapped my arms around myself and shut my eyes tight.

Zelind hadn't even held my hand, and now khe was in my room. My domain, laid out and designed for my comfort and preferences, furnished with only one bed—a bed khe wouldn't even look at.

I didn't want to have that conversation. I already knew what we would say. I took another trip down the hall, and I had a bundle of canvas, lashing cord, and a folding wooden camp bed. I was still fighting with it when Zelind emerged from the bedroom smelling like my soap, dressed in the kilt and stockings, the much-mended clan sweater worn over a fresh shirt.

"What's that?"

"A cot. I thought perhaps you'd like to use it."

Zelind studied the mess I was making trying to fit the pieces together, and then knelt on the rug to help me build it.

I tried fitting one wooden pole into its brass corner join, but I lost my grip at the last moment. A snap, and a hot, painful line bloomed across my middle finger. I popped it in my mouth, broken nail and all. "Why is this so difficult?"

"Because you can't do it alone." Zelind took the corner join and held it steady. "Try now."

We assembled the cot easily once Zelind was there to help, and a narrow wooden frame stretched the laced canvas surface taut.

I stood up, groaning at the creaky resistance of my knees. "I'll get some blankets."

"It can wait a minute," Zelind said. "You hurt yourself."

"I'll tend it after," I said. "It's nothing."

"None of that," Zelind scolded. "Let me see."

I held out my hand, and Zelind bent over it, examining the break. "It's in the quick. That's going to sting."

And then, gently, khe took my hand in khers.

Kher hands were dry, the skin tight over the joints, the ridges of kher fingertips textured against my fingers, the back of my hand. Kher touch was so gentle khe could have been holding a butterfly instead of a hand. Like khe touched something that would break with a careless touch.

"This needs cleaning." Khe didn't let go as khe rose and led me into the still-steamy bathroom and guided me to sit at the edge of the tub.

"Washing first, hm? Warm water and salt."

"In the cupboard without a mirror. There's a little basin wrapped in paper."

It crackled in kher grip. "Carbolic soap in the box?"

Khe didn't check for my answer. Soon khe knelt beside me, offering the basin, and I hissed as my finger met salty water.

"Hold that." Water ran in the sink, and the medicine-herbal smell of carbolic soap rose in the air as Zelind washed kher hands. "Still soaking that finger?"

I would leave it in the water until it was pruny, if I had to. "Yes."

Khe used a fresh towel to dry kher hands, and knelt to tend my wound: washing, dressing in ointment, and carefully wrapping gauze around the tip. Khe focused on my finger, not me, but I sat fuzzed, warm, and aetheric under kher attentions. I had taught kher how to do this, and khe hadn't forgot a thing. Khe would undress the wound and tend it tomorrow, and the day after that—

In this way, Zelind could touch me.

Zelind held my bandaged hand balanced on kher palm.

"I'll need to look at it again in the morning."

SIX

Coronation

Zelind accompanied us on rescues for the rest of the week. Khe slept in the cot we set up each night and broke down each morning, and never got close enough to touch. My broken fingernail healed under kher attention. We sat one on either side of Jean-Marie while she balanced a book on her knees and turned the pages, reading the books we gave to four-year-olds. We brushed elbows at the table. I avoided Aunt Glory's inquisitive looks. Zelind didn't seem to notice them.

But Zelind took the two-day trip to Red Hawk while I stayed behind, riding in the discreet black sled Grace had sent to bring me up the hill to Mountrose Palace. I wore Aunt Glory's cape and one of Ramona's concert suits over a pair of sweaters and woolen leggings, prepared to withstand a long outdoor ceremony to crown the King.

Joy floated beside the sleigh until it stopped at the back of the palace, where portable rising seats were assembled and then draped with violet scrims. She moved by my side until I set foot on the carpeted path, and she disappeared with a gasp. I paused, staring at the carpet. The pile had been dusted with a light layer of salt. Clearly the dead weren't invited to the ceremony.

I took my seat before a tall slab of black stone, its weathered face scoured by wind for so long that the markings historians believed to be an ancient language were hardly more than scratches.

No one knew what was written on the stone, but everyone knew what the place was—one of dozens scattered across Aeland where the distance between our world and the Solace was thin enough to pass through. But this one was more special than all the rest, for it was the place where Queen Agnes had accepted the crown of Aeland.

Grace showed me to a seat in the front row of the rising benches. She moved on to join the colorful display that was the court dress of Amaranthines, clasping hands with Grand Duchess Aife. I glanced at the person sitting next to me in a hand-tailored coat and a green silk muffler.

Albert Jessup scowled at me. "She invited you."

"She invited me," I replied. "How have you been, Member Jessup? Legislated any good profits lately?"

"The House session's been cut short by this." Jessup flung out an irritated hand at the ring of red roses bordering the stone. "And then we'll be disrupted again once the crown is on King Severin's head and we have to hold another election in Firstgreen."

"It is the law," I said. "But I suppose you'll have to spend a lot of money getting reelected so soon."

Jessup went red as a lobster. "What are you implying?"

I widened my eyes. "Aren't election campaigns expensive? Don't you have a great deal of expenses to pay your canvassers, and print handbills, and then woo the eligible voters in your district? There's about fifty of them, isn't there?"

If he could have slapped me, he would. Jessup presided over a riding where about sixty thousand people lived, but most of them couldn't afford to pay for a permit. The leader of East Kingston–Birdland came from the votes cast by representatives of this business association or that, pooling their money to pay the 250 marks for a permit.

"Ninety-one."

"As many voters as that?" I murmured. "That's a lot of roast quail dinners and handshake promises, Mr. Jessup."

"It's hard work," Jessup said. "You and your entitled protesters should try it."

I hated this man. I hated his greed, his callousness, and the power he held over us. His family was one of the worst employers in Kingston, and I was going to make a point of advising Grace to do everything she could to knock this man down.

"What are you doing here, anyway? There's no rabble here to rouse."

I smiled so sweetly at him that anyone watching would imagine that I just pretended not to understand something he'd said. "I was invited. Twice."

"Mrs. Thorpe!" exclaimed Jacob Clarke. "My apologies for being late. Mrs. Thorpe. We're all so delighted that your spouse is returned to you."

He took the seat next to mine. "Member Jessup."

"Member Clarke," came Jessup's curt reply.

"Chancellor Hensley told me the King is making an announcement at the coronation—"

I hushed as children dashed into the circle, scattering rose petals. Music swelled from the other side of the stone, where guards and support staff waited to do their parts. We all quieted as Grand Duchess Aife rose from her place on the bench and glided to where a mother and child stood, clad head to toe in colorful wool cut in the fashions of a thousand years past. Aife took the child's hand and guided her to her place within the circle of rose petals.

Every monarch of Aeland had been crowned at the foot of this waystone since the founding. None of the coronations had ever been witnessed by an Amaranthine. The little girl held the simple, ungemmed golden circlet made for Queen Agnes nearly sixteen hundred years ago, and we watched a pavilion's door flap open as King Severin walked out, flanked by his elite women guards.

Murmurs rose from the crowd. Severin wasn't dressed in the tunic and robes of Queen Agnes's day. Instead he wore a splendid morning suit, the peak of formality for daytime affairs, caped by a trailing cloak of white fur lined in violet silk. He had broken with tradition. Was it a signal of things to come?

Severin didn't have a daughter to crown him as Queen Agnes had. This had to be one of his cousins, once or twice removed. Severin knelt, and the gaily dressed child carefully set the circlet on Severin's head. Severin scooped her up, holding her on one hip as if he'd carted around toddlers all his life.

"I am honored to be your king," Severin said. "I come to you this day excited for our future, and optimistic for the people of this fine country. My vision is filled with the brightness of new possibilities, with the chance to shape our kingdom for the better. I see a better Aeland on the road ahead. A fair and just Aeland. A prosperous, comfortable Aeland. But the vision needs more than just bright-eyed optimism. We need to work. We need to change.

"My rule will accomplish that," King Severin said. "I've already begun by righting a terrible injustice done to our own people. I have torn down the lies and manipulation that led to the unspeakable treatment of our own citizens—citizens who were vilified as unstable, dangerous monsters so a few could profit from the many. That liberation was the right thing to do, even if we all have paid the price.

"But we need aether back. Burning oil has saved many lives in this crisis, but we can't continue its use in the long term. And so I am pleased to announce that I'm calling for the brightest minds and the cleverest hands to develop a method that generates aether power for the country."

Murmurs rose on the frozen air. Severin paid them no mind.

"This is not a popularity contest. This is a race. The first person who comes to me with an effective method of producing aether without burning wood, oil, coal, or gas will be honored with a Medal of National Service, inducted into the Order of Aeland, and given a cash prize of two hundred and fifty thousand marks."

That was a fortune to some, a nice profit for others. But it was enough to get the attention of the attendees, including the curiosity of reporters who scribbled down every word the new king said.

"But to do that, Aelanders need time. They need time to rest. Time to spend with their families. Time to dream. So I'm announcing the beginning of the Labor Fairness Act—an act that will define the full-time work week as forty hours per week."

Was he, now. Severin was getting ahead of Grace and me with this declaration—Solidarity had protested and written to our Elected Members for years, but Grace and I hadn't yet begun work. Was this a sign that Severin was going to cooperate with us?

Around me, the murmurs turned to dismay. Plenty of people in the audience owned businesses, and they were the ones who had to figure out how to make their factories, offices, and shops run smoothly when they couldn't work their employees as hard. The people around me weren't happy with Severin's proposals, and I felt no sympathy for them.

"Employers may decide to structure five days of eight hours of work or four days of ten hours of work. And because the work week has been decreased, naturally, the base wage of the ordinary Aelander has to increase, but with the new work week, the rate of pay will remain the same, so a citizen will take home the minimum of five marks a week."

I folded my arms. Five marks a week was chicken scratch. Five marks a week was three people crammed into a one-bedroom apartment just to make rent. I glanced at Jacob. We still had work to do.

"Finally, I know people have been asking about what compensation the witches will receive for the years stolen from them to endure hardship and horror. Certain citizens have come up with a formula to compensate the imprisoned witches—and in many sad cases, their survivors. But the figures they've calculated add up, and Aeland can't afford that up-front cost."

People around me muttered, but they nodded their heads.

"We need to put this sad time behind us. It's over. Those of us who actually put the old system into place are dead or dying. We didn't make the laws that imprisoned our citizens. We are sorry it happened to them. But we are not responsible for that hardship."

Beside me, Jacob sucked his teeth. A chorus of hisses sounded from the Amaranthines in attendance, and we all looked at them, our faces turned to regard the Guardians of the Dead and their displeasure.

Severin cleared his throat. "I have an alternative," he said, his voice pitched over the sound of vexed Amaranthines. "I wish to grant every surviving witch a guaranteed income on the Service pension rolls, the same as we give physically wounded soldiers who went to war. They will receive this pension, the equivalent of Aeland's minimum wage, for the rest of their lives. Survivors of the citizens institutionalized will receive the usual lump sum paid to survivors of soldiers killed in wartime."

That was nothing compared to what they had gone through. It was a token payment. But the Royal Knights and Elected Members around me grumbled at even that pittance. Jacob and I exchanged another determined glance.

Severin smiled at everyone as if they had cheered his every word.

"That is my vision, and I require a sober, orderly government to make it happen. As of this moment, I declare that an election will be held to begin the work of government as swiftly as possible. We must elect a new ministry even sooner than the ninety mandated days. Therefore, Election Day will be Snowglaze thirty-five."

That wasn't enough time for anyone to seriously mount a campaign against incumbent members. It actually made the people around me relax—Severin might have introduced unpopular changes, but the election wouldn't change anything in government. There hadn't been much doubt before, but this sealed it. Grace, Jacob, and I needed all the fight we could get.

"My new government will work hard to realize my vision of a better Aeland, and I look forward to meeting with them. Thank you. I'm sure you're all freezing. Let's go inside and enjoy the refreshments and warmth of the palace."

Severin walked away, bouncing the little girl on his hip, his opulent cape trailing in the snow behind him.

Jacob rose to his feet, took my arm, and walked me away from the hearing of others. "It's as I feared. Too little change. Too comfortable. It's not good enough."

"It's not," I agreed. "Let's get together and draw up our own vision. We can meet with Grace as soon as we have it in hand, and then talk to the media, and—"

"We need to call a meeting. Fast," Jacob said. "But first. Winnie's been after me to have you for dinner. Will you bring your spouse?"

"We'd be happy to. When?"

"Tomorrow night," Jacob said. "I'll let Winnie know you're coming."

We shook hands. I smiled. But I didn't want to stroll inside the palace and try to be courteous to people who despised me as much as I did them.

Zelind would be home late tonight. Maybe I could purloin a loaf of bread for us to sneak off and enjoy, the way we did when we were young.

I avoided the palace and took my hired sleigh home.

Zelind and I put on our boots and walked to a modest apartment building perched on the side of King Philip Hill. Soft golden candlelight glowed in the windows, and the pianochord's music spilled through the glass.

"Duke is here," I said.

"His name is Duke, or there's a duke upstairs?"

Khe watched me with the half smile and raised eyebrows of someone who just tried to make a joke.

"Duke isn't actually his name, but his name is Gersham, so he prefers Duke."

"Hold on. Duke Corbett?"

"The same."

The music led us up the stairs to an open door, so we let ourselves inside, shedding our outside shoes for knitted slippers. Althea bustled out of the kitchen to take our coats and ask, "Will you take a brandy?"

I glanced at Zelind, who nodded.

"Yes, please," I said to the woman who cooked and cleaned for the Clarkes.

"Robin!" Jacob called, and he waved us inside the large chamber that served as a retiring room and a library. We took a place on a sofa surrounded by tall bookshelves, and Zelind took the corner closest to Emma, the young woman Jacob had taken in from the asylum. Perched on her knees was her baby, Cora, who was fascinated by a corner of the room. Nothing particularly bright resided there; what could she be looking at?

Emma was watchful too, and where her baby was just fixated, Emma was tense. She turned her gaze to me and, after a moment, tried to smile.

Zelind went to her instantly. "What did you see?"

"They're haunting us," Emma whispered. "We can't run far enough. They're everywhere."

"The ghosts?" I asked. "They are everywhere. They're all over Aeland."

Her already pale face was pinched. "They look at me," she whispered. "They know what I did."

She was haunted by more than just ghosts. I tried a question Miles would have asked a patient at the hospital: "Have they said so?"

She stared at me, and for a moment I feared what she would say.

"Do you think your friend Miles could talk to her?" Jacob asked me. "She's terrified of the dead. We don't know how to help."

"I can ask Miles," I said. "Where's the ghost?"

"Gone. They come and go," Jacob said. "Once I got used to it, I hardly notice. But Emma . . ."

I turned to Emma. "They come to you because you have the power to speak to them. Have you ever tried?"

Emma shook her head. "Never."

"Well, let's try that."

"After dinner," Winnie said, and trailed a gentle hand over Duke's shoulder to get his attention.

Duke was one of those white Aelander men who had been unfairly good-looking in youth, and beauty, being so used to his presence, lingered on in the fine bones of his face even after years. The lines at the corners of his eyes matched his charming smile. A sweep of snowy white streaked the center of his carefully styled hair. And he had a way of focusing so completely that he made everyone's hearts flutter when confronted by the full force of his fascination.

He gathered me in a gentle hug. "How happy I am to hear of your reunion, my dear. And this is khe?"

I stepped back and lifted my hand in introduction. "My spouse, Zelind Thorpe."

"I am delighted," he said, shaking Zelind's hand. "Both by your freedom and your devotion. I am Duke Corbett."

"I know who you are," Zelind said. "I saw you at the Riverside Music Festival of '61."

Duke turned that devastating smile on my spouse. "Oh Solace, you've heard of me. I'm soaring."

"Duke's being modest," I said. "But we should eat before it gets cold."

Althea had simmered her clear-brothed crab-and-vegetable soup, roasted a pork shoulder, and used an herb blend on skirrets that made tasting one after the other an experience. I ate the green things on my plate, as it was my duty and they were nutritious, but Althea had managed to add something that made winter greens and broiled hazelnuts tastier. She dashed between kitchen and dining room, bringing dishes, serving, and then waiting to see how she would be needed. Jacob and Winnie hardly noticed her.

Winnie led the conversation, and it pleased her to speak of the theater, as she had once been on stage until she and Jacob had married and she became a politician's wife—a particular sort of unsung hero, to my mind. And if Winnie wanted to talk about stage plays, then we would talk of plays until the dessert came—a rich, elegant custard, the sugared top crackled and brown from broiling in the oven. Coupled with hot whiskey toddies, it was a perfect ending.

"I don't know if Robin told you of the King's promises at his coronation, Zelind." Jacob mentioned it casually, as if the event hadn't burned him.

"She did," Zelind said. "I'm of mixed mind about it. What do you think?"

"It's not enough," Jacob said. "The national pension. It's an insult."

"They didn't pay us at all in the asylum," Zelind said. "So that's an improvement, at least."

"Back pay," Jacob said. "It's a slap in the face."

"It is," Zelind said. "But how can I expect more than that?"

"And this contest to replace aether. As if he could just sweep the atrocity of it under the rug—"

Zelind glanced away. I watched kher, but Zelind wouldn't look at me.

"There isn't a sum in this world that would make up for what happened to us," Zelind said. "But that's going to be the reason why we won't see a cent beyond the pension."

"The fight for reparations is going to be a hard one, even with the threat of the Amaranthines' displeasure hanging overhead. Severin's trying to buy time."

Duke toyed with his spoon, trying to scrape the last morsels out of his custard pot. "And he'll use the resistance of his government to justify doing as little as possible. Snowglaze thirty-five is election day! You could watch the time go by on a wristwatch. He doesn't want to change a thing."

"It might be a good idea to raise awareness and make it clear that the fight's not over yet." I still had a bite of custard, and I savored it.

"More actions. Make people understand the fundamental violation of witches' rights."

"I have a different idea in mind." Jacob accepted a second toddy from Althea, barely noticing that she'd had one ready the moment he'd finished his first. "We'll do all that, of course. But I realized during the King's speech that we had an incredible opportunity in front of us, and I mean to seize it."

"What do you mean to do?" I asked.

Jacob grinned. "We're going to have an election. A true democratic election, Uzadalian style."

I sat there with my mouth open. That was huge. That was organizing on a national scale. That was completely mad.

"In a month?"

"I'm sure you can handle it," Jacob said. "You hustled the witches out of imprisonment so fast the doors are still swinging shut. This may be the greatest challenge I've set you so far, but—"

He wanted *me* to organize it? I shouldn't be surprised. I led the organizing of everything, and when the lights had gone out and I couldn't attend school, I had turned my attention to the movement and all its many projects. I had done hard work, and the witches were probably free because of it. But this burned my ears. He wanted a national project organized and managed by me. He wanted a near impossible task, and he assumed I would do it. How did he think I could manage that and work for Grace?

I thought back. Had I even told him about it? Had Grace? Maybe he didn't know. But my next words spoke themselves, rather too close to the truth to be gentle:

"What makes you think I'm going to organize your election without you even asking me first, Jacob?"

Everyone went still as deer who'd just heard a human voice in the wood. Emma hardly even breathed. Even the baby on her lap stopped trying to grab everything in sight and stared, as babies do, unsure of whether she should cry or not.

Zelind touched my hand, a gentling gesture.

Jacob just gave me a quizzical look. "I'm asking you now."

Really! Jacob was my friend, but this was too much. "Oh, forgive my confusion."

He left the hint on the floor and kept talking. "We have to find a candidate for each electoral riding. Hopefully a person of sound reputation. I don't know how you're going to determine that, but you'll come up with a way—"

He wasn't listening. I set down my fork and placed my folded hands on the table. "No."

Now Jacob caught the danger that had everyone quivering. He picked up his toddy and cocked his head, as if I were doing something peculiar. "Is there something wrong?"

"Plenty," I said. "You didn't ask me to do this, first of all—"

"I said I'm asking you now."

"You have a funny way of asking," I said. "Secondly, I didn't hear you offering me a salary to organize this for you."

"It's volunteer work," Jacob said. "I'm not getting paid either."

I ignored that. "Grace Hensley, however, is paying me."

"Grace Hensley! What for?"

"She wants to know what we want, so she can try to twist the King into doing it for us," I said. "She's paying me, and my contract will be up in time to go back to school. So thank you for asking me, but I regret to inform you that I don't have time to run your election project."

"But this is important," Jacob said.

"Jacob, dear," Winnie said. "Robin's already dealing with a full plate, as she said."

"But this is vital," Jacob insisted. "If we don't take this opportunity now there won't be another one for five years. Imagine it! Everyone in Aeland casting their vote. Everyone in Aeland given a voice. It would show everyone what the people of Aeland really wanted—and how big money and power kept the decisions hoarded to themselves. How could you—"

"I think it's a lovely symbol, Jacob. I really do," I said. "But even if I didn't already have a job I'm excited about—"

"We'll find a way to pay you," he said.

"Not fifteen hundred marks a month, you won't."

"So I've lost you to the Chancellor's pockets," Jacob complained.

"Only my labor, which you assumed you could have for free. I still think it's a good idea. I simply am not available to organize it."

"Then what can you do?"

"I can help you convince the others," I said. "At the meeting tomorrow. I'll come up with a list of people you can ask to organize the action."

"They won't be as good as you."

"I know. But they'll still be good."

"Will you at least come to the next meeting? Will you help me convince the others to do this before you leave me for Government House?"

I shook my head. "You don't have to put it that way, Jacob. I'll come to the next meeting. It's at the studio?"

"Yes." Jacob glanced away from me and frowned at something behind me.

Cora squealed and pointed. Emma made a noise high in her throat.

"He's back," she said. "He's come back."

Now I saw who had been disturbing Emma, and this was a ghost I recognized—he had helped us turn the storm back, the one in the old college jacket.

"Excuse me," I said. "We'll speak of this later."

I stood up, and Emma screamed as the ghost came closer, making me shudder as he tried to grab my arm. His fingers passed through my flesh, leaving a sensation like cold water creeping over my skin.

"I remember," he said. "I remembered you. Help me find her."

SEVEN

The Princess Mary Hotel

We finally made it home—Zelind, me, and Cortland Brown, the ghost who had frightened Emma at dinner. We barely made it inside the front door when Joy zipped toward us, shaking her finger at the apparition. She even hovered a few inches off the ground to loom over the other spirit.

"You just turn around and go back. There's nobody for you here."

"It's all right, Joy."

Jean-Marie looked up from wiping polishing paste off a portrait of Great-great-grandfather Walter. "Who's that?"

"Cortland Brown. He was one of the first ghosts to help with the storms. What took you so long to find me, Cortland?"

"I forgot. I forgot until I saw her. You have to tell her. You have to tell her it's going to be all right."

I sighed. "And you want to do this now. But I need at least a full night's sleep before setting off on a folly. Zelind, do you—"

"I'll be fine here," khe said. "But take Jean-Marie. She could use the fresh air."

"It's likely to be a bit of a goose chase," I said. "It depends on how solid the ghost's memories are, so I could be gone all day."

"Jean-Marie's frustrated by all-day lessons. Take her. She should see what Deathsingers are supposed to do."

"All right." I turned to the ghost. "I'm Robin. What's your clan name? Clan Brown of the Sure Winds?"

He shrugged. "Clan Brown of the Sheltered Harbor."

"Sheltered Harbor," I said. "I didn't know there were—" I closed my mouth. That was rude.

He slumped. "The clan dwindles."

"Robin," Zelind said. Khe held kher scarf in one hand, kher expression rumpled with intrigue. "The Bays had dealings with the Browns of the Sheltered Harbor. I know where you can start your goose chase."

The next morning, Jean-Marie and I pulled winter bicycles out of the shed and pedaled along the long, straight streets. My cousin was still scared of taking a spill, balanced on two tires, but she had picked up the trick of riding after a few lessons from Amos. I kept a sedate pace with my heart pounding at the thought of our destination—or rather, the neighborhood that housed our first place to look.

We came to a street where the windows were more likely to be covered with boards than expose their shining, expensive glass to breakage. We locked our bicycles to a track, then locked them to each other, and turned to regard the gray stone building across the way.

"This is it," Cortland said. He stopped in front of the tall, ornate iron fence that blocked us from passing under the arched breezeway. Just beyond its shadows, snow piled so high it made the space indistinguishable. Was it a driveway? A courtyard?

"This isn't the way in," I said.

"Yes it is," Cortland protested. He tried to grab the gate latch, and his hand passed right through.

"It used to be. It's not the way in now." I looked left, then right, and pointed. "That way."

Cortland bristled. "That's the service entrance."

"You're welcome to glide through the front doors, but my flesh and blood needs to use the service entrance." I set off along the only sidewalk cleared of snow, turned into the alley, and pulled the half-rotted bell cord in front of a paneled set of double doors.

Cortland followed me, but he looked sulky. "What's happened to this place?"

"It shut down . . . must have been eight years ago, now. I'm sorry, Cortland. It was still going when you were alive?"

"I died here," he said. "All of this happened in eight years?"

Jean-Marie hadn't stopped staring at the building. "It's beautiful."

"It's a wreck," the ghost complained. "The Princess Mary was the finest hotel in Riverside, and the service the best you could get in the city. What happened to it?"

"I don't know everything," I said. "But I have heard that the hotel was too hard to keep up."

"But Nolene was supposed to take care of that," Cortland said. "What happened to her? What happened?"

"I don't know," I said, and tried the door handle. My insides shivered when it opened.

"Ahoy," I called into the darkness. There was a light ahead, a dim lamp flame, and I cast a globe of light on my fingertips to shine as we stepped inside.

The light touched crates filled with trash next to twenty-gallon jugs of water and shelves and shelves of stable staples. We moved closer to that other light, but Jean-Marie sped impatiently forward, headed for the threshold.

We caught up with her quickly. She studied the floor, covered in colored tiles that built the image of water lapping on a sandy shore speckled with seashells and tiny crabs. She touched the walls, feeling the grain of hand-carved panels, the wood so pale it made me think of bones.

"It's so beautiful," Jean-Marie said.

"It's a shadow of itself," Cortland muttered. "What happened to this place?"

He sped ahead, stopping as he stared. "Aunt Minnie? She's still alive?"

He had found someone? "Ahoy," I called. "Ahoy, it's Robin Thorpe of the Peaceful Waters."

"Ahoy yourself," came the thin, reedy voice of a woman who had accumulated many years of life. "Come in here where I don't have to shout the walls down."

"Come on." I tugged Jean-Marie's arm, and she followed me past the seashore-tiled floor and into what must have been a custodian's apartment.

Jean-Marie had plenty to gaze at in here, even if it was shadowed with the light of a single lamp and the flickering glow of a hearth-fire. A woman with a cloud of snow-white hair and papery, dark brown skin sat straight and poised in a lightly padded chair, a froth of lace knitting puddled in her lap.

"Come in, sit down, who's that hovering—? Cortland," she said with a gasp. "Oh Cortland Jubilation Brown . . ."

"You know him," I said.

"I do," she said. "He's my own grandnephew, even if he is dressed a complete fool. You graduated from Queens forty years ago, Cortland. Clinging to your schooldays like that. I don't think he ever grew up."

"I'm Robin Thorpe," I said. "And this is Jean-Marie Thorpe, my cousin."

"Come closer and let me look at you, young lady." Minerva stretched out one hand, her grip strong on Jean-Marie's fingers. She tilted her head, studying Jean-Marie's face. "Are you Ephla Thorpe's line?"

"You knew Great-grandmother Ephla?" I asked.

Minerva nodded, her eyes bright. "We were school chums. And you have her gift, if Cortland sulking about is any evidence."

Cortland grumbled. I smiled. "He says he doesn't sulk."

"Oh, they all think that," she said. "I'm Minerva Brown, but before I was married, I was Minerva Seaman of the Distant Sky."

"It's a pleasure to meet you, ma'am."

She laughed. "What brings you here?"

"Cortland had a wish to speak to his daughter."

Minerva's mouth turned sour, but she masked it quickly, showing off even, perfect teeth that had to be mounted into a denture. "She should be here soon, if you'd like to wait. And you, young lady—"

Jean-Marie yanked her attention away from the glass globe chandelier. "Yes?"

Minerva waved her hand. "The building's closed, but it's still sound. Go and explore."

Jean-Marie's face lit up. "Really?"

"Go before I change my mind," Minerva said.

Jean-Marie was gone before I could tell her to be careful. Minerva picked up her knitting and worked a complicated pattern from memory, scarcely glancing at it while her fingers guided knit stitches from the left needle to the right.

"So the dead have come to Aeland," she said. "I see them drifting through the halls sometimes, on my walks. Sometimes, I think I know their faces. Cortland's the first one to remember that we existed, though he only cared about Nolene."

I took a guess. "Your great-granddaughter?"

"Great-grandniece. And there are no great-great-grandnieces, which Cortland undoubtedly hoped for."

Cortland staggered. "She never married?"

Minerva addressed the answer to Cortland once I relayed the question. "She did. No luck carrying a child. The Browns of the Sheltered Harbor are no more. I am one hundred years old, and I have seen the end of my clan."

It put a lump in my throat. "I'm sorry."

"I am too," Minerva said.

"Granny Min?" a voice called, the tone rising to panic. "Granny Min, was someone here? Granny Min?"

"Here," I called, and footsteps pounded along at a run.

A woman with a worry-furrowed brow halted in the entrance, her hair worn loose and curly in the fashion that was overtaking the traditional locks of Samindans. "Who are you? Who is—Daddy?"

She set down a hamper and crossed the floor, staring at Cortland. They shared the same broad jaw and high cheekbones, her face a little more finely drawn around the eyes and nose, the legacy of handsome parents. As she came closer, I could smell tobacco smoke on her clothes.

"We came to find you," I said. "I'm Robin Thorpe of the Peaceful Waters. Cortland wished to tell you that he loves you."

She regarded me with wide eyes. "You're a Deathsinger."

"I am," I said. "Cortland wished to speak to you, and he did me a big favor when he helped us soothe the storm."

"Cortland. Tell Granny Min she should live in Greenfields," Nolene said.

"Nolene, we've discussed this," Minerva said. "If you want to stop bringing me meals, I'll hire someone to do it for me, but I am not leaving my home."

"But you could fall," she said. "You could fall, and break a hip, you could bleed internally, and then you could—"

"Die," Minerva said. "Child. I am a hundred years old. I know I could die. But this is my home, and I will leave it feetfirst."

"Stop talking about death," Nolene said. "It's morbid. It's horrible. If you'd only just let me take you to Greenfields—"

"No," Minerva said. "I'm perfectly fine here, as I told you. I'm not going to Greenfields. I'm staying."

"But Granny Min—"

"No."

Nolene sighed. "I made you chicken soup. But I'm afraid I only made enough for the two of us."

"I can collect Jean-Marie," I said. "I came for Cortland's sake. Is there anything else you want to say, Cortland?"

"Tell her she should see a midwife. It's not too late to—"

"I'm not telling her that," I said.

"Telling me what?" Nolene asked.

"Your father wants me to badger you to have a child."

Nolene's face melted into sadness. "Tell him I'm sorry."

"He can hear you," I said. "When I'm nearby, he can hear you, understand you, is alert and aware. But he'll fade again when I'm gone."

"Daddy, I can't," Nolene said. "I'm so sorry. I tried."

Cortland watched his daughter, his expression folded up with sadness.

Their clan was ending, and Nolene blamed herself. It wasn't fair. Minerva reached for Nolene's hand, and I couldn't break the silence that hung over us. Cortland hung his head, his hand passing through Nolene's shoulder.

Jean-Marie appeared in the doorway. "It's the most beautiful thing I've ever seen. There's a statue in the lobby. She's so lovely. And the stairway—it's so elegant, I could explore for hours, but I thought I should come back before I made Robin worry."

Minerva caught a little of Jean-Marie's delight. "You like it?"

"I love it," Jean-Marie. "Thank you for letting me explore."

"You haven't seen it all yet," Minerva said. "Why don't you come back and explore it properly?"

"Yes! Thank you! Can I come tomorrow?"

I had never seen Jean-Marie elated. I had never seen her brimming with excitement and curiosity. I nodded permission. "You can bring cakes for tea."

"I would be honored to have such a lovely guest," Minerva said. "I look forward to your visit."

"Thank you! I'll come tomorrow morning. I want to know everything. It's the most wonderful place I've ever seen."

"It is wonderful, isn't it?" Minerva had stars twinkling in her dark eyes. "And I have a hundred stories. More. I'll tell you the first one tomorrow."

"And then you can meet us at the park for the homecoming," I said. "We'll pass by the park so you know what streets to take."

Nolene kept her mouth closed so firmly she had to be holding back an objection, but she didn't voice it while we said our farewells.

Zelind was in charge of the kitchen for the evening meal, and so we had a huge pot of crab chowder served with crusty hot bread covered in sautéed mushrooms and cheese sauce. I was in charge of cleanup, and Zelind was already stretched out on the cot when I finally made it to our rooms. I watched kher breathing, a little moonlight shining through the window, until I slept, and dreamed, and woke to thumping coming from the sitting room.

Zelind was the source of those noises. Dressed in a singlet and athletic shorts, a light glow of sweat across kher broad shoulders, Zelind jumped, flexed, and balanced on one hand or one foot or kher seat as khe ran through strength-enhancing exercises.

Even a few days of feeding up had filled the hollows in Zelind's ribs, dulled the sharp peaks of kher spinal column, and wiry strength gained some sleekness across kher arms and legs. Khe worked every muscle and then moved into a fluid series of poses meant to enhance balance and flexibility before khe spoke to me.

"Did I wake you?"

"I get up early anyway."

"Sorry."

"Don't be."

"I am. Do you have a busy day today?"

"I wanted to visit the library downtown."

"I'll come with you," Zelind said. "Do you want to skate?"

And so we hurried through breakfast. We laced skate blades to our boots and glided along the Densmore Canal, the ice shushing under our strides. Zelind offered kher arm, and we skated together in pairs hold, skating in time with each other.

We had to skate two miles like this, and two miles back, matching pace and rhythm to move as one. We glided past a class of children skating in pairs, and Zelind nudged me into skating before kher, so I sped backward and faced kher.

"Do you remember our trick?"

"Yes—" And then I squawked as Zelind hoisted me in the air, much to the delight of the class, who watched me spread my arms and cross my skates at the ankle.

Zelind twirled around twice, skating backward as khe set me down. My knee gave a loud pop as I landed on one foot, my other leg stretched out in an arabesque.

Zelind went wide-eyed. "That was an alarming noise."

"My joints make a lot of alarming noises. It's fine."

But khe stuck to skating side by side after that, taking no more risks. I settled under kher arm across my shoulder blades, in a pairs skating hold and smiled at the sunny day and the other skaters playing on the canal.

"This was a good idea."

"We could do it again tomorrow," Zelind said. "Is Mama's still there?"

"Mama's is still there, and Mama still makes hot smoked hog."

"Now I want to go there today."

"After the library?" I paused at a bench and unlaced the blades from my boots. "It's not far."

"I've been thinking about what you told me about the King's speech," Zelind said. "About the contest."

"Do you have an idea for it?"

Zelind shrugged. "Maybe. I need to catch up on research. What do you want from the library?"

"Lesson books on figuring for Jean-Marie."

Other people with asylum-born witches had the same idea, and the lesson books were picked over. Illustrated books with more story than pictures were gone as well, and I should have thought. No Samindan would sit still while someone near them couldn't read and write.

"We're going to add surplus lesson books from the schools as soon as we can get them," a librarian told me, and I put our name down for the waiting list. Zelind found some books khe wanted, all of them bound editions of kher favorite mechanical magazines.

"What are you going to make?" I asked, and Zelind crammed the last book in the canvas sack I had brought.

"Not sure yet. I have an idea I need to research," khe said.

"You can use the work shed."

"I'd like someplace more secret."

I raised my brows at that. "Be mysterious, then. I guess we're getting that smoked hog sooner rather than later," I said to Zelind as we returned to the street.

"I'm sorry you weren't able to get more books for Jean-Marie."

"They will come," I said.

Mama's wasn't quite full for lunch, and it smelled like hours of careful, slow cooking. We sat at a table for four, and Zelind took off kher gloves and scarf. "If they come, I want a sandwich, extra hot sauce."

"It'll be here soon," I promised, and khe left for the comfort room.

Today was a good day. Zelind was merry, smiling and at ease, as if the fresh air and exercise had buoyed kher mood. It had felt a bit like when we were young, though we had known more daring skating tricks than the flying swan lift. Khe had pulled me into that move with sure confidence. Would khe do the same if we were at a dance? Would khe promenade with me at the homecoming? I rubbed my healed finger. Khe had insisted on tending it. I had let kher, because if khe had a reason to touch me, khe would. Maybe we would whirl about in each other's arms. Maybe—

Someone slid into the seat next to me, wafting sweet amber perfume and damp wool. "Miss Thorpe."

My stomach sank as the fragile happiness of the day shattered. Jarom Bay was at our table, fine deerskin gloves in one hand, clothed in luxury, smiling that sure, smug smile.

"Mrs. Thorpe," I corrected.

"I need your help."

"No."

"Khe won't talk to me, Robin—"

"Mrs. Thorpe."

He blustered on, leaning down to put his face close to mine. "Khe won't talk to me." His voice rose with that last statement. "Sorry. It wasn't supposed to be like this. Khe was supposed to—"

"Come home to you," I said. "But that wasn't kher choice."

"I just need to know if khe's all right. I need to see kher. I need kher to know that I love kher. We all do, but I'm the only one who didn't mind that khe took up with a—"

I tilted my head. "Were you about to say 'null'?"

"I know you're not," Jarom said. "I've read all the papers. Kingston is beside itself, and I don't think it's really sunk in yet. They really took the dead and—"

Jarom shook his head, his lips tight with horror. "But we thought you were a null. You did too, in case you don't remember. And Zelind had a responsibility to continue a legacy. The two of you simply couldn't expect to be together, even if it was romantic. I thought it was romantic, back then."

"You certainly made that clear when you took Zelind's side against Birdie."

"I was fifteen," Jarom said. "No one was going to listen to me."

"You were Zelind's favorite. You two were the perfect team. You could have stuck together. But instead, you became the one whose hand will guide the firm—"

"I would step down in a heartbeat if khe would just come home and—"

"Jarom."

Zelind stood at the table, lips pinched and nostrils flared. Khe stood every inch of kher five and a half feet, and though Jarom was a head taller, khe loomed. "It's time for you to go now."

"Zel," Jarom said. "Zel, I need to explain."

"Oh, excellent. Start with why there were examiners waiting for me when I came home that night."

Jarom shook his head. "I don't know."

Zelind folded kher arms. "Then find out. I want the truth."

"It was just—"

Zelind rolled right over Jarom's protest. "I want to know who sent them to our street, when Ma doubled the captain's salary out of her pocket to keep her people out of their hands."

"She didn't have anything to do with it."

"You're a fool if you believe that," Zelind said. "And I want to know why, if it really was misfortune, they didn't buy me out of the examiners' hands."

"You can't do that."

"They did it for Charles William."

Jarom gave Zelind a skeptical look. "Who told you that?"

"Eldest Thorpe."

Jarom opened his mouth to protest—and shut it. He licked his lips and glanced down at his hands. "That's all you want? The truth?"

"That's all."

"Then ask Birdie. Ask your mother."

"You really think she's innocent."

"You didn't see her," Jarom said. "When she found out what had happened to you, she screamed and wept and broke every mirror in the house. She had to get stitches. And then she shut off. It was like someone flipped a switch. We had to dress her. We had to feed her. It went on for months. Would she grieve like that, if she had done what you suggest?"

"What happened after?"

"She was never the same," Jarom said. "Father took on the firm. I gave up my dreams of sailing past the archipelago, because I had to learn everything they had crammed into your head for when the firm was going to be yours—"

Zelind gripped the top of the seat-back and leaned closer. "She grieved?"

"For years."

Zelind looked at me. I nodded. "I never knew all the details, but I heard some of it."

"I'm still a Thorpe," Zelind said. "And I still want the truth. Suddenly I'm not hungry, missus. Maybe when we get home."

Zelind donned kher hat and gloves. I put my own back on, and Jarom got to his feet.

"I'll leave you to eat."

"I said I wasn't hungry," Zelind said. "It's time to go home."

Khe didn't utter a word on the two-mile trip back.

Zelind spent hours shut up inside our rooms, poring over the library books khe had borrowed about steam engines. Khe pushed kherself into the endless housekeeping tasks of the clan house, even venturing into the attic to clean and organize.

If khe wasn't busy in the kitchen, minding children, or knitting in the parlor, khe was in the attic, using spare bits of old-model aetheric gadgets forced into obsolescence to make whatever had captured kher imagination.

But khe didn't disappear entirely. Khe drew models and wrote notes from the journals khe'd borrowed from the library, sitting with me at the dining table while I firmed up the details of the celebration we planned for the return of all the witches, checking the expenses against our donations in preparation for our committee meeting. Zelind made a child's windflower, making it spin with kher talent for moving things without having to touch them.

I sat back from my notes and watched the toy spin. "What are you doing?"

"Thinking." Khe let the toy wind down. "This is the key. What are you doing?"

"Finalizing my estimates for how many volunteers we'll need for Jacob's project." I blew on the windflower, and it spun obediently.

Khe handed it to me. "You can put it on your bike."

We used to do that as children. I tilted my head. "Does it have a wish on it?"

"Can't tell," Zelind said. "They're secret."

I reached out and took the windflower from kher, and it spun with a fluttering rattle as I pedaled to the eastern end of Riverside, then climbed the stairs to the top floor of the building where Gabrielle Meadows kept her light-filled painter's studio. I opened the door carefully, avoiding disturbing noise.

They were already gathered, and Preston Grimes, our group's pessimist, spoke as I shut the door. "We can't do it."

What, already?

Preston leaned against the back of his wooden chair, his arms crossed over his chest and his knees splayed apart, his bony ankles showing below the hem of his trousers. "There's not even a month to Election Day. It's impossible."

Jacob rolled his eyes and set down his teacup. "Honestly, Preston. Can't you wait until I'm finished presenting the idea before you pour cold water on it?"

Preston planted his feet on a paint-splattered drop cloth and gave Jacob a reproachful look. "And while you were floating around on the high of a beautiful idea, did you even think about the resources this action would need?"

Slowly, discreetly, I took a deep, grounding breath, and the scents of linseed oil and gassy-smelling paint thinner slid up my nose, rising to press against my forehead. I studied a still life painting drying on an easel—student work, and not the graceful, talented hand of Gabrielle Meadows, whose atelier we used for our meeting.

Jacob lifted his chin. "It's going to take everything we have. This is the biggest, most significant action we've ever considered. This even outdoes the work we did on fighting the Witchcraft Protection Act. That makes it worth every drop of sweat and tears it will take to make this happen."

"Jacob's right," I said. "The scope is wider than anything we've done."

"And you're doing the organizing, of course," Preston said.

My shoulders came up. "Actually, I'm pursuing work with the Chancellor—"

"You are?" Preston looked even more dubious. "Jacob, how do you expect this to work?"

"This action will reach millions of people," Jacob said. "They'll join us."

"If we have the coin," Preston said. "And if we spend every dime on this action, which at worst is a shallow publicity stunt."

Around his section of the circle, his companions nodded, eyes trained on the landscape gardener who used his magic to make Riverside's public spaces lush and healthy.

I had expected caution from Preston. He always wanted to know the scope. He always questioned enthusiasm, testing a wild idea until the inspired either came up with a plan to address the weaknesses Preston poked at or abandoned it as foolishness.

Jacob had the vision, but Preston's hand was on the tiller, and he wouldn't set course in a new direction until he knew the way was clear. If we convinced Preston, his coterie and Jacob's would unite and get to work moving whatever mountain the two of them pointed at.

If he didn't agree, Jacob's idea would founder. Would that be my fault, if it did?

"It's more than that." I set my hands on my knees and caught the eye of everyone in the circle. "Once we have all those ballots counted, once we have physical proof of what the people of Aeland want— that's more than just a symbol. That's evidence in a legal appeal to the Chamber of Justice."

"That's thousands of marks in advocate fees." Preston planted the point of one finger into his palm.

"We have advocates in the movement who could—"

Preston sent his gaze to the ceiling. "It's thousands of marks in legal fees that will get us—what? What do you imagine? That the justices will dissolve the power of the Crown because we asked nicely?"

I swallowed down the words that would make me look like a foolish girl and not the steady-tempered, rational woman I was. "I imagine that the people will see how hard we're fighting for their freedom and power."

"We'll talk about money in a moment," Jacob said. "I want you all to appreciate this idea and what it could do for us."

Someone in the neighborhood had started a hearth-fire. The faint smell of smoke filtered through the scents of linseed oil and solvent. A draft swirled around my ankles, and I sipped weak tea while I listened to them debate.

Preston inclined his head. "I agree that it's a beautiful symbol, Jacob. It's an inspired idea, and it will capture the imagination of millions. But I have to consider the practicalities."

He lifted the cup resting on the small table next to his seat, then grimaced at it. "I need more tea. Tell me how you mean to get the message across the country in time."

He stood and moved to a potbellied silver urn full of tea made from second steepings and took it black, leaving the scant supply of sugar lumps and dribbles of milk to someone else. There were still molasses cookies, and he took one to dunk in his cup. He made a sour mouth at the first sip of tea, and then turned his attention to Jacob.

But I spoke up. "King Severin has cleared the railways to announce the official election, but they didn't clear the secondary stations. They will need people to dig those stations out. We'll just ride on his back."

Preston mulled this over. "Send our volunteers with the Service workers."

"It's the fastest way to contact movement members across Aeland. It's not fast. But it's the quickest means we have."

"That's clever," Preston said. "They'll be paid, fed, given a bed—"

"And then they can bring the news to the networks in-country. We can tell them to name a candidate for each riding, spread the news about the shadow election, and every riding organizes their vote."

"It's tidy," Preston admitted. "But after that, we're long on ideas and short on money. This is going to take funds . . . and I can tell you, it's going to be more than we have."

"We'll have to raise money," Jacob said. "But—"

"Our people are stretching dimes to keep fed and warm," Preston objected. "And the kind of money we need, we can't collect it in coin jars. We need a patron. We need an investor."

Our people didn't have that kind of money. There weren't many people who profited off Aeland's system who wanted to see it fall— but that didn't mean there was no one.

But you couldn't make a plan if you didn't know the goals. I cleared my throat. "How much do you need?"

Preston shifted in his seat. "I have no idea."

"Guess."

He shrugged his shoulders and dunked his cookie in the tea, buying a minute by chewing. "At least thirty thousand marks. If you can find thirty thousand marks, we can raise the rest."

Thirty thousand marks. I factored it. Two investors at fifteen thousand. Three at ten. Five at six thousand. But that may as well be a million—I didn't know many people with that kind of coin, and all of them would want something in return for that money. Power, or favors, and how do you reckon the value of a favor against the cash that bought it?

Who could we afford to climb into bed with? Who could we recruit who wouldn't cost us that much?

"We'll get the money," Jacob said.

I stared at him. "We will?"

"We will," Jacob said. "I have ten thousand I can liquidate quickly. That's a third done already."

Then Preston spoke up. "I'm good for five. That's half. Find the rest."

"We should still take personal donations," I said. "We could make up the rest that way. People will want to help. But I can lay my hands on a thousand?"

"From your savings?" Jacob said. "We can't accept."

"You'll have to," I said. "And I know someone else I can ask—"

"Anyone I know?" Jacob asked.

"Miles."

He shook his head. "Your Royal Knight friend? He might, but—"

"Miles believes in the cause."

"But his sister can't find out about this until it's in motion."

"Then I shouldn't be here at all."

Jacob grimaced. "You'd keep our confidence."

"I'll be our woman on the inside, but I won't spy for you or mislead her while she pays for my counsel. If you don't want her to know about the shadow election, I shouldn't be here."

"Maybe you shouldn't," Preston said, and moved toward a window. "But you won't tell her what we're planning; I know you."

Preston raised the sash. The smell of smoke filled the room, hustled in by the chilly air from the window.

"Fire!" Preston hollered. He pulled the paint-splattered draperies wide, and through its panes leaping orange flames danced on the roof of a building in the distance, its pointed spires burning, black smoke unfurling across the sky.

"Solace," Jacob said. "That building's done for."

"Isn't that . . . it is," I said. "That's Kingston Asylum."

"Good riddance to it," Preston grumbled.

"They kept patients who weren't witches too," I said. "They were overflow for Beauregard Veterans'. There are innocents in that building. We have to go."

It was over before we even got there. Fire had Kingston Asylum in its grasp, and only a handful of people—all young men, shivering in pajamas and wet woolen blankets—had survived the fingers of flame that belched out the window to lick the stone walls.

Preston stopped on the street and shook his head. "Lost cause."

"Some patients got out," I said, hefting the metal case holding a pathetic measure of first aid supplies I'd taken from Gabrielle's building. "Ahoy. I'm Robin Thorpe. I'm a nurse. Does it hurt to breathe right now?"

The soot-streaked young man nodded. "Had to run through smoke to get out."

It was too dark to see down his throat, but he turned away coughing and spit a black gob onto the snow. I gave him a gentle smile and held up a stethoscope.

"Let's have a listen," I said, and he went obediently still. I placed the cold disk on the left side, and the right. I took his hand and pressed on a fingernail, watching the pale spot take its time to fill up.

He'd be dead by morning. "Come this way," I said, and gave him a cup of water. "Is that better?"

"No," he admitted.

"Stay quiet. Don't exert yourself. Tell this man your name; he's going to write it down." I nodded at Tupper Bell, who clutched a writing board and pale pink paper, the only kind Gaby would write on. "I'll be back to check on you."

"Sure thing, Doc."

I left him to tend to the next one.

"I wet a handkerchief in the sink and tied it over my face."

"Good thinking," I praised. "Come over here. Stay with this man." I pointed to the man whose airway would close up, who'd struggle to breathe and suffocate anyway. "The fire wagons will be here soon."

And on to the next, a man in a black-streaked white porter's uniform. He coughed. He wheezed. He grabbed my wrist.

"I unlocked all the doors I could," he said. "Second I smelled smoke. The fourth floor was gone. Nobody could have made it up there—"

He coughed again, and tears streaked his face. "I should have tried."

"You did," I said. "You saved your patients. You got them out."

But I sent him to sit with the first two men and moved on to the next.

"It must have been a chimney," a patient said. "It's cold as a murderer's heart in there. We stripped the extra beds for blankets and sit near fireplaces all day—"

Talking to fill the air. Breathing just fine. This one would make it. I moved on.

There were so many ghosts milling around the grounds, all

of them wearing the means of their death—blackened by soot, or horrible burns. I left them alone until I had sorted all the survivors, moved them to their groups—Urgent and Fatal, but I didn't call them that—and kept examining, kept listening for clear breath sounds, or the fluttering hiss of a lung overcome by smoke.

The fire wagons came too late to save the building, but they fought the blaze regardless. When the medical rescue people came, they came to ask me questions and sorted patients out. "There's no-where to put them," one of the medics said to me, wiping soot off her cheeks. "We'll take them, but they'll be on cots."

"Cots will be fine," I promised.

She stared at the translucent, burnt, and smoke-blacked ghosts. "What a way to die. Horrible. How did it start?"

"Not aether, obviously," I said. "One of the patients thought it could have been a chimney."

"Awful," the medic said, and she turned away to help a patient into a sleigh.

I didn't know how to determine what started a fire. The ghosts drifted to me, attracted to someone who could hear them, and they told me what had happened to them.

"The door was locked. I couldn't get out. I couldn't breathe any-more. And then I was here."

"Hurts," said a ghost, blackened by burning. "The floor collapsed. I fell. There were flames everywhere. It was so loud."

"What's your name?" I kept asking. "Who are your people?"

They told me. I wrote their names. "How did it start?"

None of them knew. Grease fire in the kitchen? Chimney fire on one of the floors? I talked to the dead and learned what they had all been doing. Sleeping. Reading penny novels. Singing to themselves, just to hear a voice.

I made my way through all of them, but one ghost made me drop my pen in the snow. He wore the white uniform of a porter with a wool coat over it, as if he had to go outdoors, or worked somewhere particularly drafty. But he wasn't covered in soot. He wasn't charred with burns.

His coat collar was soaked in blood, all of it having trickled from a bullet hole in the back of his head.

I swallowed down nausea. Not a chimney fire.

Arson.

I insisted on staying with my patients until the medics came, and then I marched across the trampled sooty snow to speak to the senior constable. I told him what I knew from talking to the living victims and the dead.

I had thought it would go better than this.

"I know you can't talk to them," I told Constable Weaver for the fourth time. "I'm telling you what they told me, so you can use the information to—"

Weaver sighed and capped his pen. "Look, we don't have time to chase after your fancies. We have no proof that the fire was deliberately set that isn't coming from your imagination."

Rolling my eyes didn't endear me to the constable, but they rolled anyway. "Fine. Do whatever you like. I tried to tell you—"

"Weaver!" The shout came from the burnt-out asylum's open front door. "This one was shot."

"There!" I pointed at the ghost of Caleb Grimes, still staring up at the asylum with his coat collar soaked in blood. "Just as I said—"

"Even I can see that ghost's been shot." Constable Weaver closed his notebook. "Excuse me."

I stared after the brown-coated policeman's back, and if I'd had iron to chew I would have spit nails. It was arson! What else could it be? That stubborn, shortsighted, unimaginative—

"Robin," Jacob said, and I turned to his gentle expression. "You tried. But it's going to be a while before people accept magic, let alone what Deathsingers can do."

"What do you think he'll do when he finds out I'm correct?"

"I'll tell you what he won't do." Jacob offered his arm, and I took it. "He won't come to you with an apology. Did you leave anything at Gaby's?"

"My scarf."

"Let's see if she's still up," Jacob said, and we skirted the fire wagons and the medical sleds and the ice-spiked tires of the police's winter tricycles, headed up the street to the six-story building that had been snapped up by artists years before when the business operating inside it went under to the competition of the Bays' sailing empire.

Tokens of the Solidarity movement hung out the windows and the fire escape grates; strips of yellow ribbon even decorated the mailbox. Gaby was outside, sweeping a soft drift of snow off the stairs, hiding the comings and goings of our secret committee meeting.

"Good evening, Gabs."

Gaby startled so hard she jumped in the air. "I didn't hear you coming."

"I'm terribly sorry. Robin left her scarf upstairs—"

"Stay here. You don't want to trudge up six flights just for that." Gaby unwound a fluffy yellow scarf from her neck. "Borrow mine, and we'll trade at the next meeting."

"Six flights isn't so bad. Beauregard didn't have a lift, so I'm used to it." I craned my neck to look up at the windows and caught a blur of movement.

I smiled at Gaby's nervous expression. Honestly, she was going to have to tell us who her mysterious paramour was eventually, but I couldn't fault anyone for keeping their romances private.

"Come to think of it, your scarf will do nicely. Thank you," I said. "Sleep well when you get there."

EIGHT

Louder than Thunder

I woke up glad I had washed the smell of smoke out of my hair. I had laid out my outfit for the celebration the night before—a full, swirling skirt, proper underlayers, my soft gray clan sweater. I'd loaned the dark gray one to Jean-Marie, as Zelind hadn't finished knitting one for her yet. My boots were freshly polished, even though they would be trampled and dull by the time the party was over.

Zelind hadn't followed my lead, and morning saw kher dressed only in a singlet and woolen hose while khe fussed about tidying the tiny rooms we shared. Khe stripped the linens off my bed and remade it. Khe sorted books back onto the shelves. Khe had been arranging brightly dyed balls of yarn by color in the basket when I put my foot down and declared, "We're going to be late."

"You can't be late to a festival," Zelind said. "How long do we have to stay? Twenty minutes?"

"We have to be there for the acknowledgments," I said.

"You have to be there. How about I just slip off and—"

"This is supposed to be celebrating you," I said. "You and all the other witches. You're free. You've come home. No one will ever trap you again—"

Zelind's expression shuttered closed.

"What?"

Zelind sighed. "Nothing."

No, something. Something about being trapped again. Did Zelind feel trapped by the clan? Trapped by me?

"Are you worried Jarom will be back?"

"I know Jarom will be back. Look at this." Khe stretched to grab a letterbox and presented me with envelopes. "He writes one every day. Every day! What could he possibly have to say every single day?"

"You haven't read them?"

Khe flipped the envelopes over. Every seal was intact.

Khe hadn't opened them, but khe hadn't thrown them away, either. "If we see Jarom, we'll give him the cut. Fiddle with your boots."

"I don't even think that would stop him," Zelind said. "And I don't want to have a big scene in the middle of everything. Can't I stay here?"

"We'll dawdle," I said. "We'll be fashionably late. Just in time to hear the speeches. We'll eat fry dough in sugar and drink apple tipsy until we get drunk."

"In the middle of the day?"

"So what? We'll be too busy giggling to notice. Maybe Mama will have her cart out—I'm sure she will. Smoked hog buns?"

Zelind gave a gusty sigh. "Fine. But only because there will be smoked hog buns."

Jean-Marie was in the middle of a book that had to be too advanced for her to read, but it was the illustrations she gazed on: diagrams and sketches of the architectural details of the Beautiful Age, the heavily carved and ornamented fashions of the last century.

"The tiles making pictures on the floors are called mosaics," she said. "The black-and-white geometrics of modern architecture design are abstract. Mosaic tile is representative."

"You read that?"

"Yes," she said. "Tiles are made from stone, clay, and glass. They're set in mortar. Mosaic artists would be paid a half-year's income for laying an eight-foot-by-eight-foot mural—"

"You learned all this because of the hotel?" Zelind asked.

"It's the most wonderful place," Jean-Marie said. "And Granny Min was the face of her day. Did you know that?"

Jean-Marie chattered like a whitewing once she got started. She told us all about the architecture and design of the Princess Mary. She repeated Minerva Brown's stories. She had even talked to the apparitions who drifted through the hotel, haranguing them for their memories of the place. Zelind and I glanced at each other, sharing smiles for Jean-Marie's enthusiasm, and she didn't quit talking even when we found somewhere to park our bicycles by Clarence Jones Memorial Park.

But the crowd soon sobered her. The park was teeming with people, all gathered to play in the snow, eat deep-fried food, and dance to the merry-sounding brass band on the amphitheater's stage.

I joined the line for Mama's lunch cart and nearly perished from the peppery, savory scent of smoked hog wafting from the smoker. I sent Zelind and Jean-Marie off to look at snow sculptures while I waited in line. If I kept Zelind a moving target, perhaps khe could avoid—

"Mrs. Thorpe."

Oh, blast it.

"Mr. Bay," I said. "I am unsurprised to see you here."

Jarom wore his clan sweater under a stylish pin-striped jacket and a smoke-gray overcoat. His left sleeve was bare of the yellow ribbon that signaled favor for radical change, and his hair clicked with purple beads, subtly declaring loyalty to the Crown and the status quo. "Where is Zelind?"

"At home," I lied. "I came alone."

He tilted his head, and his lips stretched out flat and skeptical. "Alone? With an order chit in your hand for three smoked hog buns? You have a healthy appetite, even for a witch."

Not that long ago, he wouldn't have called me a witch so easily. Not that long ago, he'd have had nothing to say to one of the talentless children who quietly distressed witch families all over Aeland. "I'm starving. I haven't eaten in nearly an hour."

At that, a line worker took the chit and handed me three buns wrapped in foil and paper, hot and steaming. I stepped out of the line and unwrapped one, biting into it right in front of Jarom.

"Delicious. I should have gotten four."

Jarom sighed. "Please let me talk to kher. Has khe read my letters?"

"Burned in the fire," I lied. "Unopened."

I saw the exact moment my words slid between his ribs; the second a little of the light died in his eyes. I took another bite of my bun and looked him in the eye. I couldn't search for Zelind's bright yellow knit cap. I was alone. I had come by myself. And I was going to burst if I had to eat all three of these buns, but eat them I would, if it would make Jarom go away.

"Robin!"

I held out a bun for Grace, who kept her patient pace next to Miles, who had recovered enough to walk without depending on his cane too much. The astonishing web of magic that took him from the brink of death to nearly hale made witches on the path stop and stare, but what made them back away in openmouthed awe was the crown of thirteen soulstars wreathed around his head, a glittering halo of souls bound to an already vibrant healer's aura.

"There you are," I lied again. "Hurry and eat them before they get cold."

"I've heard so much about Mama's smoked hog—oh!" Grace covered her mouth as she chewed. "I could eat seven of these."

Miles took the other foil-wrapped bun and eyed Jarom, who was dumbstruck by the sight Miles presented to witchsight.

"I'm Miles Singer," he said to Jarom. "And this is my sister, Grace Hensley. Have you ever met the Chancellor of Aeland?"

"No," Jarom said. "It's a pleasure. But I mustn't disturb you any further. Please enjoy your food."

He didn't quite scurry, but he left. I sighed in relief. I picked out a chit for two buns and got back in line. "You're eating Zelind and Jean-Marie's share right now. That was Zelind's cousin—"

"I remember," Grace said. "Zelind caused quite a stir when khe rejected him and kher mother at the station."

"Jarom's been trying to see Zelind ever since," I said, exchanging more coin for a pair of buns. "Zelind's been cooped up in the clan house, trying to avoid him—it's a mess."

"He should respect Zelind's wishes," Miles said, and at the same time, Grace declared, "It's impossible to just give up on family, no matter how hurt they've been because of it."

They looked at each other ruefully.

"It worked out for us," Grace said.

"Only because you accepted how very wrong you were."

"I was wrong. You were right. But I can't help feeling sorry for Jarom."

"I know," Miles said. "And if Jarom deserves to be taken back, he'll do something to prove it."

Miles had the right idea. Jarom had to prove to Zelind that he was worth taking back. Zelind shouldn't have to forgive kher cousin just because he was family. "I should find Zelind and Jean-Marie; the buns are getting cold."

I moved toward the collection of snow sculptures artists were carving out of pristine blocks of dense-pack, looking for the brightly colored caps protecting Zelind's and Jean-Marie's shorn heads from the cold.

"There." Miles pointed, and there was Zelind, helping to build a tower of snow blocks by lifting them through force of will, stacking them precisely before amazed onlookers.

One day, it would be commonplace to see an act of magic on the street. One day it wouldn't be remarkable. But now the people around Zelind fought the urge to either press closer or back away. I moved to kher side and offered kher a bun.

"Jarom's here," I said. "He ambushed me at Mama's cart."

"How'd you get rid of him?"

"The Solace's own luck," Miles said. "We showed up just in time to play along with Robin's story. I'm Miles."

Zelind stuck out kher hand. "Zelind. You—I've never seen any-one with that many soulstars in my life."

"It's new to me too," Miles said. "Do you mind if we tag along? He seemed nervous around me."

Zelind smirked. "A thirteen-starred witch? I wonder why."

"I have to go to the stage," Grace said. "The speechifying part is about to start, and I'm supposed to be there."

"We'll come with you," Zelind said. "I appreciate the backup, Miles."

"My pleasure," Miles said, and we wove through the crowds to gather in front of the stage, where Duke was finishing a foot-tapping number that had young people shimmying and lifting each other in stunts straight out of figure skating. When the music ended, the crowd closed in on the stage, ready to cheer as Jacob bounded onto the stage, clapping his hands over his head and smiling his brightest.

He led a call-and-response patter of clapping hands and stomping feet, punctuated by cries of "Uza!" at intervals between more and more complicated rhythms. When we were one voice, a crowd rather than a collection, he waited for the cheering to die as he raised a bellower.

"Friends—"

A smattering of cheers interrupted him, and he smiled as he tried to shush them with a finger to his lips.

"If you all keep that up we won't have any time to hear more music. Duke Corbett and his Wandering Brass, everybody!"

Another chorus of cheers while Jacob cleared his throat and began.

"I stand here today a grateful man. Today, all the Aelanders locked away by the Witchcraft Protection Act stand with us, and I want us all to take a moment to reflect on our victory. Our triumph. Our gratitude."

"Uza!" the crowd shouted, and they were right. We had worked together for the community. We had given; we had fought for those of our people torn from us. It was uza, without a doubt.

"When the last witch set foot in this very city, free to come and go wherever they pleased, the sun shone on a better Aeland. And Aeland is a better place because of you.

"You have shown me what Aeland is capable of. You have shown me that together, we can move the course of justice to the correct direction. You have shown me that together, we can dream of a better Aeland—and then we get out of bed, roll up our shirtsleeves, and make it so.

"All we need is a dream to chase, and the will to make it happen."

Satisfied murmurs all around. Someone shouted, "Make dreams real, Uncle!"

Zelind's fingers brushed against mine, but instead of moving away, khe slipped kher hand around mine. I squeezed. Khe squeezed back. I felt my rib cage loosen as we stood hand in hand.

Jacob lifted the bellower to his lips. "I stand here before you to say I have a new dream."

Someone cheered, but mostly, everyone was quiet, listening to the man who'd led Solidarity to this incredible victory.

My victory, an annoyed little voice whispered. But that wasn't fair. Jacob had worked hard for this. While I made priority lists and managed action teams, Jacob had put the prorogue of the Witchcraft Act on the table. It was teamwork.

"The dream dazzled my eyes when the morning sun reflected off King Severin's crown when he stood before the King's Stone and promised the Royal Knights, the landed, and the princes of capital that he would change Aeland—but not too much." Jacob lifted a finger and waggled it, quelling an idea.

Ugly grumbles, and the click of women sucking their teeth in disapproval. "Typical," someone muttered behind me.

"That's what Prince Severin promised. Change—but not too much. Because we mustn't upset the landowners. We mustn't upset the businessmen. We mustn't upset the Royal Knights. Those people on the street, those people in your factories, those people in your tenements?" Jacob shrugged, playing the gesture to the back of the crowd. "They'll just have to be patient."

"Same lies, different day!" someone shouted, and a soft chuckle followed the cry.

"We're expected to be patient, because the government is not for us. King Severin called an election. But it's not ours. It won't elect our government. It doesn't belong to us."

Here we go. The crowd around me muttered. They folded their arms and nodded. It was true, what Jacob was saying, even if he said "we" while living in a ten-room flat with a full-time housekeeper and a day maid. Jacob said "we," and everyone around me nodded along with him. Jacob scanned the crowd, and at the perfect moment, let the bellower send his question over the crowd:

"But friends, what if it did?"

He held my eye. He held Zelind's. He held the audience in that moment, letting them think, letting them wonder, *What if?*

"What if you were the one with a ballot in your hand? What if you had the power to vote them out? What if your candidate were one of your neighbors, instead of one of your landlords?"

Dead silence from the crowd. Even the breeze stilled, as if the air were listening. Everyone was quiet, leaning toward Jacob Clarke as he asked them to dream with him.

And in that quiet, in that spellbinding moment, my hands went cold. The hair on the back of my neck stood up. Something wasn't right—

"This is my dream. While the King runs his sham of an election, we'll have one too."

The crowd whistled. "Yeah!"

"A fair election."

"Yeah!"

"A free election."

"Yeah!"

"And at the end of it, we will have six million ballots to speak for us. We'll have to work hard to make it happen, but every one of you past your sixteenth birthday on Election Day will hold a ballot in your hand, and you will have a voice—"

I heard it first—a pop, like the afterthought of a nightflower blooming in the sky. Beside me, Miles ducked, pulling me down with him.

On the stage, Jacob stumbled backward, one hand flying to his chest. He kept his feet, pulling his hand away. Red, red blood smeared his palm and seeped into the twisted cords of his knitted clan sweater.

He looked at us with wide, startled eyes. And then he fell, crumpling to the stage.

"Jacob!"

Everyone around me scattered. Screams rang across the cold afternoon air. I dodged a pair of schoolgirls clinging to each other, crouched on the ground and crying.

"Run!" someone shouted at me. They grabbed my arm, trying to drag me along with them. I yanked my arm loose and sprinted over the dirty snow, not running away from the stage, but headed straight for it.

I had jumped fences one-handed as a girl. Today I sprang, my hands on the lip of the stage, and barely made it, scuttling half on hands and knees. I tore a tin case off the shelf and skidded to a stop in front of Jacob.

It wasn't good. He panted, as if it was too difficult to get air. Collapsed lung? I popped the clasps on the first aid kit and nearly screamed. Rubber gloves. Bandages and tape. Iodine. A cute little pair of scissors. Silk thread and suture needles, as if anyone would be doing stitches in the field. Tweezers, in case anyone complained of a splinter.

But there they were, wrapped in paper—drinking straws, to go with the tiny bottle of replenishing apple juice in case someone fainted.

Scissors turned Jacob's clan sweater into scrap yarn. I felt under his back, but the bullet hadn't exited his body.

"Miles!" I shouted. I didn't even know if he was there, but if anyone could help a man with a bullet in his lung, it would be the miracle man of the Laneeri War.

I needed something to seal the hole. I plucked up a thick ochre-brown rubber glove. First, cut off the fingers. Then pierce it with a suture needle, wiggle a straw through, and then I stuck the straw directly into the bullet wound.

This wasn't the right way to do it. I should have a long needle, a sterile field—I shouldn't be crouched out here. Behind me, people still screamed trying to find cover. And here I was, out in the open trying to save the man an assassin had wanted dead.

I ignored the crawling sensation between my shoulder blades and pressed on the rubber bandage. I didn't have anything but the contents of a tin box and prayer. But air seeped through the straw, and Jacob's distress eased.

Tape. I needed tape. Who in the blasted void packed a first aid kit with a syncope kit and no tape?

"Robin." Jacob's voice was full of air. He lifted one hand, its palm red, and gripped my wrist.

"Don't do that. I'm keeping you breathing, but I need both hands."

"Robin."

"Shut up." I looked into his eyes. You did that with patients who were scared. You looked into their eyes and told them they were going to be all right. That you had it under control.

"Lie still and just breathe," I said, and then I shouted, "I need some help over here!"

There was an emergency station three streets away. Someone could run and get the medics. I could hold pressure all the way to the hospital, if I had to. It was going to be all right.

"Take my hand." Jacob tugged on my wrist, and the dressing came loose.

"I need both my hands," I said. "My hands are keeping you breathing. How bad does it hurt?"

"It doesn't hurt," he said. "That's bad, isn't it?"

Could be adrenaline. Could be the shock—no, it was definitely shock. "Put your hand on my cheek."

Cold. So cold. That could be the air, but I looked into Jacob's eyes and I knew.

He knew, too. "Promise me."

"What?"

"Take care of the movement. Take care of—" He lost the words to a cough, and red painted his lips.

"Don't talk!" I cried, but I knew, and so did he.

"Robin."

I looked into his eyes.

His fingers touched my face. Warmth radiated from them—warmth that spread across my scalp and down my neck. It wrapped around my shoulders. It glowed, the stormy violet-white afterlight of a lightning strike, wrapping me up like a shroud.

"No." I pressed harder on the dressing. "Don't you dare, Jacob Alexander Clarke. Not today. You hear me? You don't get to die today. You have work to do."

"Yours," he said, and the last sound was a sigh.

Jacob died. I knew it, the same way I knew in the operating theater—the weight of his soul, lighter than a feather, had left. I could pump his heart, fill his lungs, but he had fled the shell of his body, his light squeezing around me, seeping into me, filling me with might—

I was young. I danced with Winnie, and she spun from my arms into Duke's, who took a kiss before Winnie was back in my hold, and I kissed her too. I sat in the stern of a tiny boat, my senses woven into the air around me as I directed a wind to fill the little skiff's single sail. I stood on a stage and thanked every volunteer who worked so hard to elect me. I stood behind the stage and rehearsed the last speech I ever gave . . . the speech I hadn't finished.

The Deathsinger visions faded. But the words trampled over my tongue to get out.

Jacob was dead. He had bound his soul to me. And it wasn't quite my hands that lifted from the wound. It wasn't quite my limbs putting me on my feet and walking back to the edge of the stage, carrying the bellower.

The crowd had come creeping back. They had watched as I tried to save Jacob. They had seen the power winding around me, and they watched as I lifted the bellower to my lips and pitched my voice to the back of the crowd:

"You will have a voice. You will be the power."

I saw a woman lift one hand to her mouth, her eyes wide.

"This dream is scary. It scares me. It maybe scares you too. But I

know it scares the factory owners and the landlords and the noble order of the Royal Knights. I promise you, they will try to stop it."

A nudge inside me, not mine, prompted me to talk over the crowd
who stared at me in disbelief and awe.

"I can't do it alone. I need your hands. I need your help. We need
to do this together—because when you stand as one lonely voice, you
will be silenced."

I swung the bellower away from my face and let them see the
blood staining my hands. Jacob's blood soaked into the protective
charm of my clan sweater and smeared against my cheek.

Everyone was listening now. All those eyes were on me. I trembled, but the words came, the right words, and I let them ring over
the crowd.

"But dreams of a better Aeland, of an Aeland for everybody—that
dream will never falter."

"Uza!" Zelind cried.

The crowd took it up. "Uza!"

Now I shouted into the bellower, roaring over their voices.
"Together we are louder than thunder. Together we are stronger than
steel."

Did Jacob feel this, when he spoke to the people? Did he feel this
pull between him and those who listened to him, this glowing feeling when the words touch them? Did he feel this, when they shouted
and raised their fists in the air? I felt six feet tall. Jacob's spirit in me
made me brave, made me welcome the focus of the crowd. This was
how it felt to be the face, to be the one who the people saw, the one
who carried all the results of the people behind them.

I had always been too afraid to stand here. It made me tremble.
Ecstatic with terror, flush with elation, I lifted the bellower again.

"And when we win, when the sun shines on a better Aeland,
when we gather once more in victory, in triumph, in gratitude—then
we will join hands and dream again, and lift our voices to the sky."

They screamed. They raised their hands. I had them. I had them all.

"Louder than thunder! Stronger than steel!" I shouted, and they
shouted it back as I stood before them with my fist in the air. The
crowd shouted, one thought from a thousand mouths.

"Louder than thunder! Stronger than steel!"

NINE

The Interview Room

Full of Jacob, I stood and chanted with the crowd. His power filled me to overflowing. I felt the breezes playing over the park, knew the pressures of warm air and cold, and gazed at the three tall, narrow tenements across the park. I touched the spot on my chest that had hurt, breathed freely and without pain.

Then someone darted across the stage. Winnie knelt on the boards, her arms around Jacob's body. She rocked his corpse as if she were sending him to sleep one last time.

Oh, Winnie. An ache unfurled in my chest. Duke knelt by her side, and Winnie buried her face in his shoulder while Duke clung tight, murmuring comfort into her hair.

I wanted him to take care of her. She shouldn't be alone, and neither should he. They would need each other more than ever now.

The feeling of containing Jacob Clarke eased and left only me, caught between the chanting crowd and the distraught widow. I moved closer to Winnie and Duke.

"He loves you," I said to her. "He's glad you have each other. He's sorry."

Winnie nodded. "He has nothing to be sorry for. But whoever did this has to pay."

Another mourner, vowing revenge. But I understood. "We'll find them."

Winnie took my hand and stood up, then backed away as medics swarmed around the body.

"Dead," one of them said. "Ballistic trauma. Someone tried to treat it."

"That was me," I said. "Robin Thorpe. I was a nurse at Beauregard Veterans'. His lung collapsed. I couldn't save him."

I couldn't. Not alone. But I had been standing right next to someone who could—where was Miles? I had shouted for him. Had he heard?

"Miss?"

Brown-coated police constables surrounded me. I looked at the only man with insignia on his shoulder and nodded. "I'm Robin Thorpe. I tried to save him."

"Would you come with us, please? We'd like to ask you a few questions."

I nodded consent and they marched around me, ignoring several out-of-the-way corners where we could have talked to stand beside a sidecar trike. I stopped, planting my feet so hard they grew roots.

"What's this about?" I asked.

"You're an important witness," the corporal said. I looked for his name badge. Moore. "We need to know exactly what you saw, and what happened on that stage."

"And you'll be safer at the station."

"Safer? Why do I need to be—"

I shut up. Jacob hadn't just been murdered. Jacob had been gunned down in front of a thousand people. Jacob had been assassinated. And I had rushed to the stage, tried to save him, and then, after our soulbinding, stood up and finished the speech that had been interrupted by his death.

You didn't go through the trouble of a public assassination just to eliminate people. You did it to destroy symbols. And if Jacob had been one, then I had just become one too.

"Someone needs to find Zelind Thorpe," I said. "Khe's my spouse. We came together. Khe'll be looking for me."

"We'll find kher," a constable said. "We need to get you to the station."

I climbed into the sidecar and helped the corporal pedal us across the snow and onto the street.

I stopped at the threshold when I spotted the mirror-coated window. "This is an interrogation room."

"We use interview rooms for witnesses," Corporal Moore said. "There's little chance of interruption. The calm helps witnesses recall more accurately than trying to recount the event in a busy staff room."

"We still have some tea, if you'd like," the constable who had stayed with us said. "There might be wheat cookies too."

"Thank you, I'd love some tea," I said, and the constable left.

Corporal Moore pulled out the chair for me. "I don't have any of the forms I need for your interview. Will you excuse me?"

"Of course."

They left me alone, and I wished they had let me stop in the restroom. Blood had dried on my hands, on my face, had soaked the cuffs and front of my clan sweater. I was restless with the power brimming inside me, the full heft of Jacob's soul bound to me.

I looked at my reflection and, to witchsight, a softly glowing distortion floated just in front of my head. It made me a stronger witch, but did a Deathsinger have need of a deeper reservoir of power?

Jacob hadn't bound to me for no reason. He wanted something.

Nothing. The sense of his presence had faded back at the park. Now that I was at Central . . . Why was I at Central? There was a neighborhood station a few streets away from the park. Why come all this way just for an interview?

The door opened, and the constable carried a tray with three mismatched clay cups. The sugar bowl held three half-size lumps, barely enough to go around. I dropped one in my cup and let it dissolve in the too-hot tea, which was a little lighter than it really should have been. There was no milk, not even canned.

"Thank you. I appreciate the tea."

"It was the least I could do." The constable—Brewster, his name tag said—slid a writing board out from under the tray. "I need your information for the forms."

"The tyranny of paper," I said. "I used to work in a hospital; I know how many forms go into a day's work."

"Where do you work now?"

"I don't," I said. "I was supposed to attend medical school, but—"

"The term was cancelled," he said. "Bad luck. How have you been keeping busy?"

"I'm the operations manager for Solidarity," I said. "It's volunteer work, and that's why there's always so much to do."

"Operations manager," he said. "So you organize civic disruptions?"

Careful. "That's one way to put it," I said. "We usually call it direct citizen action."

"But you fill up the streets with people and stop traffic," he said. "You organize gatherings in front of the palace, where people stand around all day with signs. Don't you think you should turn all that energy into helping people find jobs?"

"These people were all dismissed from their positions for taking actions against unsafe working conditions, grueling hours, and unfair wages."

"But they had jobs before you filled their heads with the idea that they're entitled to more," Constable Brewster said. "Did you organize the celebration in Clarence Jones Memorial Park today?"

"I didn't," I said. "But I supervise the committee that did. I had to take time away for family reasons."

"Your spouse," Constable Brewster said, and unease twinged in my stomach.

"How did you know that?"

The door swung open.

"I hope I haven't kept you waiting too long," Corporal Moore said, bearing another writing board full of forms and a file folder already thick enough to hold a criminal case. "How's the tea?"

I took a quick sip. Weak. Bitter with tannins the sugar couldn't touch. "It's lovely, thank you."

"Good! Now that we're all here, I want you to tell me everything you remember about this afternoon's events. Even the trivial details. You never know what's going to be important."

"Certainly," I said. "I was close to the stage, but not right next to it. I had a partial view of Jacob as he spoke to us."

"And what was he speaking about?"

"He was telling the people what he wanted Solidarity to do now that the Witchcraft Act has been abolished, and all the witches are free from asylums."

"And what is that?"

"Jacob wanted to hold a shadow election. One where anyone over sixteen had a vote, with no need to buy an expensive poll ticket."

"All this for a symbol?" Constable Brewster asked.

"Symbols are powerful," I said. "Jacob Clarke was a symbol. He represented change. And fairness. He was the face of gaining greater rights and protections for the people. And someone wanted that symbol extinguished."

They both watched me very carefully. They didn't touch their pens.

"They say you stood up and finished the speech he was giving," Constable Brewster said. "You stood in the very spot where he had been shot and picked up what had fallen from his hands."

Did they want me to explain that? "It wasn't me," I said. "It was Jacob."

They glanced at each other. "How is that possible?"

"Since it's no longer illegal to tell you, I am a witch," I said. "I have the power to speak to the dead. Jacob was a Windweaver. Like those Royal Knights you read about in the paper a couple of weeks ago. He could control the effects of the weather. When he died, his spirit bound itself to me. He was the one who knew the rest of the words. I just spoke them."

"I'm not sure how I'm supposed to believe that," Constable Brewster said. "He possessed you?"

"Yes."

"Because he bound his spirit to yours," Corporal Moore said. "I don't really understand anything about magic, but that's important, isn't it?"

"It can be," I said.

"And you weren't important before today," Constable Brewster said. "You weren't anyone important."

I shrugged. "Not really. Not in the sense of being prominent."

"But you were vital to the operations of your protest group," Constable Brewster said. "Operations manager. That's how you described your unpaid position."

"Yes," I said. "I was the lead organizer of our group. Jacob worked his side in Parliament; I oversaw our citizen efforts."

"So you were partners," Corporal Moore said. "You worked together to make your protest group work."

"Yes."

"But he was the leader. You worked your fingers to the bone, and he shook hands and thanked people and got all the credit," Constable Brewster said.

"Did anyone know how much of his greatness came from the person standing right behind him?" Corporal Moore asked. "Did anyone even realize how much of his success was actually yours?"

What was this?

How many times had I heard about these kinds of tactics? How many times had I imagined that I would never fall for them, that I wouldn't be gulled? I wasn't any cannier than the next person.

"Why don't you tell me what you're implying?" I asked.

"Just an observation," Constable Brewster said. "You weren't important before."

"But you're certainly important now."

"And you think I conspired with a rooftop sniper to kill my friend so I could catch a little fame?"

They leaned back as if they were one body and traded a glance. Blast, and blast again.

"We never said anything about a sniper," Corporal Moore said.

I shut up. I was being clever. I was being so clever I was telling them how it was done, and they were taking my conjecture as involvement.

"Do I need an advocate?" I asked, and the police in front of me went sour around the mouth.

"We're just talking about what happened."

No. No, we weren't. "Am I under arrest? If I am, would you be so kind as to tell me the charge?"

"This is an interview. It will be easier if you cooperate," Constable Moore said.

"I don't think so," I said. "I would like an advocate. Please send for one. I'm not answering any questions until they are present."

"That will take time, and we're nearly finished," Moore said. "Just a few more questions."

"Advocate," I said, and said no more.

They didn't look friendly anymore. They got up and left the room, leaving me with only a cup of lukewarm, bitter tea for company.

I knew, from fetching out dozens of Solidarity members, that those men weren't making any effort to find an advocate. They were probably grumbling to each other. They'd leave me to stew in here for hours, and the pressure on my bladder didn't have hours.

I closed my eyes and reached out.

"Joy," I said. "Mahalia. I need you."

I stretched my senses west and south, and the clan house was in easy reach. I would have had to strain to spread my senses that far before Jacob bound his soul to mine. I touched them both, and they came, swifter than birds could fly.

"What happened to you?" Joy asked. "Are you in trouble?"

"I'm in deep trouble," I said. "Please find Jean-Marie. Tell her where I am. Tell her I need an advocate. Hurry. I don't have a lot of time."

I was pacing around in little circles by the time the door opened again.

"What's your advocate's name?" Constable Brewster said.

"Why does that matter? I asked you to get an advocate, not my advocate. Now let me—"

"There's someone here claiming to be your advocate," Brewster said. "We need to know if that's true."

"It's irrelevant." I said. It hadn't been that long. If they'd had to go to get Orlena, they would have had taken hours. That meant someone on the spot had volunteered to do it. Someone who had reason to stick around with Jean-Marie and Zelind.

Jarom? No. He was a doctor of laws, but he was no advocate, and he wouldn't help me anyway. Who?

Only one choice left.

"Do you mean to tell me you're making the Chancellor of Aeland cool her heels in the station?"

"You guessed."

"I reasoned it out," I said. "I had been with her before the shooting happened. I'm not surprised she took an interest. I think you had better let her see me."

He didn't quite slam the door when he left. I went back to pacing around. Grace was here. She was going to get me out of here.

But I didn't know why I was in here in the first place. Did they think I hired a sharpshooter to stand on a rooftop and kill my friend because I was jealous of his spotlight? It was ridiculous. It was something out of a cinema matinee!

The door opened again, and Corporal Moore blocked the way out. "You're free to go."

"Thank you," I said. "I would like to visit the restroom and wash—"

"Water's out," he said. "Sorry."

Of all the petty, childish—"Then get out of my way, please."

He stood aside with a flourish, and I hurried down the hall.

"You have a habit of collecting powerful friends, Mrs. Thorpe."

I ignored him and joined Grace. "Thank you for coming."

"We had gone to the closest station to find you," Grace said. "Are you all right? Do you want to wash—"

"Apparently the water is out. I'm eager to leave."

"Good."

Grace led me outside and into her sled. "Don't talk to the police," she said. "Don't say a word to them besides 'I want my advocate.' Don't even give them the correct time."

That was the advice we gave our people. I hadn't followed it. I hadn't thought I had to. The sled rumbled underneath our seats, gliding across hard-packed snow. "They told me I was a witness."

"A popular lie," Grace said. "They wanted to stitch you up after the end of that speech—what happened up there? When you stood up there and finished Jacob's speech, my hair stood on end."

"I don't really understand it. I didn't know the speech, but I did. I knew every word. It was a triumph, and I felt like a fool. I looked at Winnie and I felt so much love for her. And then it faded off and I'm alone in my head."

"So he's with you."

"I don't know if he is, still." I tried not to touch the sled blanket. Dried blood cracked and flaked off my neck. "I'm a suspect in Jacob's murder. How does that make sense?"

"Listen to me," Grace said. "I'm not in criminal law, of course. But

I know that in big public cases like this, the police don't like to look like fools. They want an arrest, and they want it fast."

The sled jostled over some ruts. We turned right, and the moon, not quite full, glowed soft silver in the night-black sky. "But how could I have arranged this?"

"It doesn't matter if you're only using the facts that fit," Grace said. "No more talking to police without an advocate."

"Will they try to find another suspect?"

Grace glanced at me. "You have to prepare for the possibility that they won't."

They could. They could just bother me and never look for the real killer. Jacob would never get justice, then.

"So I need an advocate," I said. "Orlena might not be cut out for this."

"I know a good one," Grace said. "I'll get her for you. And I should have said this before: I am so very sorry for your loss."

I had been talking about it for hours, but Grace's sympathy made me feel it. Jacob was gone. Our leader was gone. My friend—how could I walk through the rest of my days without Jacob to argue with? "Thank you. But it's your loss too."

"Jacob was a good colleague. He was your friend, and he died in your arms."

"I couldn't save him," I said. "I should have. Miles could have."

"Miles—" Grace sighed. "He reacted badly to the moment, and now he feels awful."

"The war?"

"The war," Grace said. "That blasted war. I hate everything about it."

"I don't know if we could have saved him," I said. "He was drowning in his own blood. It would have been a miracle."

"Miles wouldn't forgive himself for not providing that miracle," Grace said. "We're here."

The sled stopped in front of the clan house. Every window glowed with light, and the front door swung open. But instead of one of the children, Aunt Glory came out to stand in the chilly air and wait for me.

"Do you want to come in?"

"I should go home," Grace said. "When will the funeral be?"

"Two days," I said. "Someone's probably doing the death examination now. They'll release him to the funeral home in the morning."

"All right. I'll be there."

I climbed out of the sled and set myself for the porch, but I stopped, turned around, and let my breath out in a great heaving sigh.

"It was the wind."

Grace looked at me. "What do you mean?"

"There was a breeze during the speech. Jacob stilled it, made the sun come out from behind the clouds to shine on him. Pure drama. But it meant the killer had ideal conditions for the shot."

"He couldn't have known," Grace said. "And a breeze wouldn't have stopped this from happening. If he blames himself, tell him to stop."

Did you hear that? I wondered. But nothing stirred in response.

TEN

Free Democracy

They had to drug Winnie just so she could make it through the receiving line. Duke stuck by her, speaking the words Winnie would have said if she hadn't been so overcome. She could only nod at whoever paused in front of her bearing a widow's casserole and a promise to come by to get the dish another day.

Hundreds of people had come to walk down the central aisle, carrying single flowers, evergreen fronds, sprigs of herbs—every one of them a tribute to Jacob, who rested in a lightweight canoe just large enough to hold a paddle, a fishing net, and gold for his travels through the Solace. Jacob had already been buried, there were so many offerings piled on him.

Aelander mourners wore white and enameled butterfly jewelry. Samindans wore blue, with motifs of white-capped waves—born to the sea and returned to it. But the Amaranthines—

For not just Tristan attended the funeral of Jacob Clarke. Grand Duchess Aife wore pewter gray silk, all the layers of it floating from her shoulders. At her side was her taller, dark-skinned secretary, clad head to toe in unrelieved black. He reached into one of his sleeves and produced a bundle neatly wrapped in waxed hemp fabric.

"For you," Ysonde said, and the black dove on his shoulder cooed.

"It's apple bread," Aife said. "I made it."

She was the Daughter of the Gates. The living embodiment of our myths and legends. One day, she would be the Queen of the Solace.

She had rolled up her sleeves and kneaded sympathy and cinnamon into bread dough, baking it to bring to the widow.

Winnie wrapped gentle hands around the package. "Thank you. That's very kind."

"I like your husband very much. He's a fighter. I admire people with vision like his."

"He had so many plans. He wasn't finished," Winnie said. "He wasn't done."

The Grand Duchess touched Winnie's cheek. "He's not lost to you forever."

Winnie handed the apple bread to Duke, who set it on the table with the rest. "But I miss him now."

"Yes," Aife said. "I miss him too. If I remember right, I'm supposed to call on you to retrieve the bread wrap later. We can talk more then."

They clasped hands, and then Aife took her secretary's arm. They joined the line of visitors come to pay their last respects, leaving the reception room astonished.

"She came to the funeral," someone said.

"She bakes apple bread," came Carlotta's reply.

"Don't you dare ask her for the recipe."

"But don't you want to know?"

"Carlotta."

"They walk the streets of Kingston, you know," Carlotta's voice went on. "They wear ordinary clothes, but they're all so tall, and if you're kind to them, they're kind back. One of them gave a gold coin to a housemaid who helped them chase a loose hat."

"You can't expect me to believe that."

Knowing a few Amaranthines, the stories could be true. I glanced at Zelind, and Zelind shared kher smile with me. But that smile melted as khe spotted someone over my shoulder.

I didn't really have to guess. "Jarom?"

"Yes."

"Escape plan?"

"Yes."

We turned to duck into the sanctuary, where talking was not permitted, when someone in deep indigo blue waved, just at the corner of my eye.

"Robin." Gaby caught my arm. "There you are. Come on, we need you."

"We were just about to go in the sanctuary."

"No time for that. Emergency meeting. Preston's getting impatient."

"But—"

"Go," Zelind said. "I'll be there."

I huffed out a sigh and let Gaby drag me along to a room mounted with paintings of floral still lifes. I stopped just inside the doorway, staring at those assembled.

The committee of Solidarity sat in a horseshoe of uncomfortable wooden chairs. There was one left, the seat facing the assembly. Preston gestured for me to sit in it.

I remained standing. "What's this about?"

"We have questions concerning the events around Jacob's assassination," Preston said. "Particularly around your actions."

"I couldn't save him," I said. "There was too much bleeding. He would have died on the way to the hospital even if the medics had been on site."

"Never mind that." Judita Linton stretched her crossed ankles out in front of her, leaning back in her seat in the casual way that probably made her congregation feel comfortable. "Did you know Jacob's speech before he gave it?"

"No."

She looked around at the others. "You see."

"I don't know what happened," I said. "I had to finish the speech. I couldn't help myself. But if you're thinking I have contact with Jacob because of the soulstar, I don't. It was only for a few minutes, and then he was gone."

Tupper Bell, the headmaster of Riverside Public, nodded as if this was exactly what he expected. "It's probably within your skill to speak with him, Miss Robin. If you applied yourself to the task of making that contact—"

"Jacob didn't bind with Robin to make her his mouthpiece." Gaby shook her head, and the beaded tips of her locks shifted along her shoulders. "She's the only clear choice, and you know it."

"Choice for what?"

"I don't know if you understand what people believe about what

C. L. POLK

they saw at the rally." Preston tilted the head of his cane toward me. "The sight of Jacob's magic wrapping you up and then condensing into a soulstar, then when you stood up and told the people they were stronger than steel—it's had a profound effect."

"People want me to, to channel him? Like some mountebank with a spirit guide? Like some sideshow fortune-teller? I can't," I said, and a long needle of hot pain poked at my throat. I'd never speak to Jacob again. "It was only long enough to tell Winnie he loves her. Then it was over. He hasn't made a peep. And even if I could, even if Jacob were sitting in my head judging your mourning outfits and commenting on the covered dishes, I wouldn't do it."

"That's not what he meant," Gaby said.

Preston shrugged. "Though it would make the choice easier if you did have contact."

"The choice for what?"

"Solidarity needs a new leader," Preston said. "We need someone who can stand at the head of the Free Democracy Party, to run for Jacob's seat in South Kingston–Riverside Central."

"And you wanted Jacob's blessing," I said. "I'm sorry I can't give it to you, but you are our best choice—"

But Preston lifted his hand, and I fell silent.

"We want you to do it."

What.

Words careened against each other in their frenzy to escape. I grabbed the back of the chair I had never managed to sit in, and I stared at every single member of the committee, studying their expressions for suppressed smiles or laughter in the eyes, because this wasn't funny.

But that was just my disbelief grasping at straws. This was serious. They wanted me to lead Solidarity. They wanted me to run for Parliament. But they would have felt better about it if Jacob had still been chattering in my ear, and I could just be a relay for his wishes and opinions.

I was the poetic choice, not the rational one. If they'd had the chance to discuss it, my name wouldn't have come up. But we had left them with no choice—struck by the drama of it all, the people wanted me, not the committee, to lead them.

And they were right. I couldn't refuse. And part of me, the part that pouted every time someone else got the praise for the results of my efforts, seized the silence and spoke into it.

"No," I said. "You don't want me to do it. You want Jacob back, and you were hoping he was sharing flat space in my head."

"You are who the people want. You were anointed the moment you picked up that bellower and finished Jacob's speech." Preston stared me down, but the set of his shoulders, the walking stick planted between me and him—he wasn't the picture of joy at this situation. "They will clamor and demand you if we offer up anyone else."

"But you would have chosen someone different."

"There really isn't another candidate," Gaby said. "It isn't just your contact with Jacob. You're the one who carries water around here. You know how to organize and manage people. You operate from a whole-picture view, but you never forget the details. Your plans are sound and solid—"

"But I'm not a visionary," I said. "I'm not a figure of fire and dreams. I'm not the spellbinder who can make people believe that anything is possible. I'm a planner."

"We'll help you with that," Preston said. "Headmaster Bell will write your speeches—"

"No."

The committee leaned back, their faces sour and affronted at my interruption. But I had to take control. If I couldn't convince them here, every one of them would waste time trying to make me their mouthpiece. If I was going to do this, then we were doing things my way.

I stood up straighter. I looked at Preston, because he was the one most likely to manipulate me with his help. "I'm telling you who I am. I'm telling you what kind of a leader you're getting," I said. "Now listen."

They went silent. I nodded once and continued.

"I'm the one who sees the whole project. I see the whole beautiful, interlocking mess underneath all that shiny dream-stuff. I see the pieces and how they fit. I'm the person who writes the list of goals and breaks them down into jobs for people to do so the work gets done. That's what you're going to get."

The committee stayed quiet. They listened. Preston's sour doubt wavered in the corners of his mouth. Gaby folded her hands in her lap

and nodded along. Headmaster Bell, Miss Agnes Gable, Reverend Judita, Dr. Theresa Smith—they all listened.

"Jacob had the dreams. You're not going to get vision from me.
You're going to know your part in building the vision. You're going
to know that you're part of a bigger whole, and every one of you is
needed if we're going to build Jacob's dream. I don't get dreams. I see
the work. That's what you're going to get."

"Practicality," Miss Gable said. "You're the one, Robin. Please accept my approval."

"I've seen you organize at the clinic for years," Dr. Smith said.
"Please accept my approval."

"You're the reason we got anything done in the first place," Gaby
said. "Please accept my approval."

"I have no objection," Judita said. "I will trust the committee on
this one."

"I believe that if Jacob were here, he'd tell us that you were a nat-
ural successor to his legacy," Preston said. "You have a level head.
That's going to matter. Please accept my approval."

"I do," I said. "I'll be your leader. I'll run for Parliament. I will put
Jacob's dream to work."

They all smiled now, every one of them pleased. I stilled deep inside, listening for a nod from Jacob, a shrug, a whisper of any feeling
at all.

The inside of my mind was quiet and alone.

Flowers and offerings spilled off Jacob's funeral boat as they carried
it out of the memorial hall to doleful music and Winnie's heartbreak.
She walked behind it, following the bearers to the enameled hearse
sled that would bring Jacob to the unfrozen shore of the Ayers Inlet.
Once there, they would take Jacob out to sea and set him on his voyage to the Solace. We spilled out to the sidewalk, all the smokers gathering downwind before sharing matches and sighing in relief when
the first draw hit their lungs. Miles and I gathered in the opposite direction, staring a little too longingly at those still indulging.

"You quit too. That means I have to really quit," Miles said. "You
were my supply."

"Zelind doesn't like the habit, and there are better ways to get
outdoors."

Khe hadn't mentioned the smell on my coats and gloves, but I'd emptied my tobacco pouch and put it away. I still reached for it, before I remembered that I had quit the habit and counted the cost a bargain.

But I wanted one now. I wanted the calming ceremony of rolling tobacco into paper, of cupping the match to protect it from the wind, of that first inhale that rushed straight to my head. But I didn't smoke anymore, and so I breathed in the river breeze carrying the sap from cut spruce boughs, the mingling of warm wool and perfume from the mourners. "Now we revel in fresh air."

"It'll be better for us both," Miles promised. "We should make Grace follow suit. Look at her over there, with that dapper gentleman."

We smiled, for that dapper gentleman was Avia Jessup in a breast binder and a net mustache. Grace couldn't stop smiling as they chatted with each other.

"We should stop staring," Miles said, and we turned around, as subtle as a stampede of cattle.

"Is this better?" I asked.

Miles's lips twitched. "It's really not."

"There you are," Tristan said. "I was waylaid by a little girl who had a hundred and nine questions, and I could only answer three. Why aren't you smoking?"

"Robin quit. I can't borrow from her anymore."

"Poor dear—wait."

Tristan turned his sharp gaze to a mailbox, of all things, that someone had gently tagged with a bright yellow bow. But Tristan walked right up to the mailbox, examining all sides of it before returning to us.

"Take me somewhere private," Tristan said. "I have to tell you something."

"About the mailbox?"

"Shh."

Well, all right then. I led them back inside the funeral home and into the main chamber, now empty save a few floral arrangements. I put us in the center of the room, and we each faced an entry, so no one would catch us talking.

"Is this sufficient?" I asked.

"Perfectly," Tristan said. "I think you have a spy."

"Because of a mailbox?"

"Yes," Tristan said. "I've lived here for a year now. I have some experience in finding information someone might not want divulged. I've recruited informants. And someone operating in Kingston has a fondness for leaving drop signals on mailboxes."

"The ribbon," Miles said.

"More the clockface marked in chalk," Tristan said. "The informant tied the ribbon. The handler marked the clockface. That's a meeting, scheduled."

"Where?"

Tristan shrugged. "No idea. But it's at five o'clock."

"What information could anyone possibly have because they went to a funeral?" I asked.

"All kinds of things. People gathered here. They talked. They gossiped."

They called secret meetings and chose a new leader for the movement. What if it was someone in the committee? "What do I do?"

"You keep an eye out," Tristan said. "And you assume that whoever it is spying, they're accessing the most important information in the room."

I pressed my lips together. "You mean to say that someone's spying on us," I said. "On the Solidarity Collective."

"Exactly," Tristan said. "Assume it's one of your people."

"How do I catch them?" I asked.

"Be sharp. See if you can find the result of leaked information. Follow it to the person who benefits the most. Solidarity has plenty of opponents, so it might be hard to narrow down."

A thought made me go cold. "What if Jacob's death is a result?"

"What do you mean?" Miles asked.

"What makes you think that?"

"No one save the committee knew that Jacob was going to announce the shadow election in his speech. It was a secret. But then Jacob was shot."

"And you took over his speech," Tristan said. "That implies two things. One, that whomever is organizing intelligence gathering does not like the idea of the shadow election—"

"And two," Miles said. "They're going to be watching you now, to see if you're a new threat to their goals."

Blast. Blast it to pieces! Was I a new threat? Oh, to be certain. I had stepped in it up to my neck.

"Can you lie low for a while?" Tristan said. "While we Amaranthines have a slightly different view of death, I'd rather you were corporeal."

"I can't," I said. "I have a responsibility."

"She's going to be working for Grace," Miles said. "Policy advisor to the Chancellor."

I wasn't. I would have to tell Grace, and as soon as possible. "Actually, the plans have changed."

Miles tipped his head back. "They made you leader of Solidarity."

"I'm afraid so."

"Then you need security training," Tristan said. "And you need to find out who's leaking your secrets to an interested party, because once they find out what you're up to, you're next."

My stomach gave a terrified little thrill when I approached the funeral home's front door. There was a spy in Solidarity. It wasn't too hard to imagine that the person responsible for planting that spy and the person responsible for assassinating Jacob were the same person. Or a group. And Jacob had enemies. Plenty of people didn't want him stirring up their workers, instigating their tenants, fighting against the laws and traditions of Aeland.

But who had it all? Plenty of people disliked Jacob. Who hated him? Who—

I pushed open the door and stopped, my heart sinking.

Zelind stood on the sidewalk, bundled against the river breeze, gloved hands in the pockets of a knee-length cloak. Khe stood with kher back to the street, watching me finally emerge from the funeral home.

Beside kher stood Jarom, who gave me an irritated glance before turning his attention back to Zelind. "What I'm saying is that your arrest shouldn't have happened. Birdie was funding the Riverside Division's mounted unit. She was paying for the whole thing."

Zelind said nothing.

I remembered the mounted police. I remembered how they used horses to corner and intimidate people on foot. "Riverside Division doesn't really have much of a mounted unit anymore."

"Birdie wouldn't give them another cent after they snatched

Zelind. They had to dissolve. She didn't have you arrested. She would never. Zelind. Please see reason."

"I've been waiting for you for a long time," Zelind said to me. Jarom sighed in frustration, and Zelind ignored him like he was wind. "You never met me in the sanctuary."

"I'm sorry. I got caught up in a discussion." I looked at Jarom. "Could you excuse us?"

"You can't just dismiss me."

"Go," Zelind said. "Leave me alone. I don't want you here."

Jarom's expression crumpled into shocked hurt.

"But I told you what you wanted."

"Go away, Jarom," Zelind said. "I'm about to have a fight with my wife. Go buy something expensive. Just go."

Jarom glanced at me, sneered, and looked at Zelind.

"You can't make me give up," he said. "We need you. You can have anything you want. Just come home to us."

Zelind turned kher back and walked away, leaving me to hurry after kher. "I'm sorry I didn't go to the sanctuary to get you. Everything just kind of happened, and I never realized—"

Zelind focused kher unsmiling gaze on me. "You didn't sit with me during the service."

"I had to talk to Winnie." And I had to break her heart again when I told her Jacob wasn't chattering away in my head. But that didn't stop her from dragging me to sit with her and Duke in the front row, where she went through four handkerchiefs and I feared that maybe she couldn't stop, now that the sedative had let go of her emotions.

"Then you ignored me after the service to talk to your Amaranthine friend," Zelind said.

"Tristan needed to tell me something important."

"What was so important, then?"

I sucked in a breath. "I can't talk about it here on the street."

"You forgot I was even here. Because of all your secrets."

I had. But it wasn't on purpose.

"That isn't fair," I said. "Winnie needed me. Tristan had something important to tell me, and I have obligations to the movement. My work wasn't done after getting you all free. There's more to be done, and—"

"It's more important than me."

"No," I said. "I was just where everyone who needed to talk to me was all in the same place, and it went too far. Please, can we talk at home?"

"I had a surprise for you," Zelind said. "I've been waiting to tell you for hours, but you forgot me."

"I was just busy," I said. "But now we can go home, and then you can tell me. Please."

"You don't even know what it is," Zelind kept kher gaze straight ahead.

"You said it was a surprise."

"That isn't the point. You didn't notice me sneaking off. You didn't notice that I wasn't in our room or in the parlor or on kitchen crew or even whether I was in the clan house or not. You had no idea I was up to something."

"My friend died," I said. "He was shot. By an assassin. And then the police wanted to pin it on me. And then the funeral, and the meeting, and then Tristan—I have been busy. I have a busy life. Dozens of people depend on me."

Zelind hunched kher shoulders and watched kher feet. "All I wanted was for you to notice I was gone."

We stepped into an intersection, and the wind shoved our shoulders. "I'm sorry," I said. "I'm sorry I wasn't home enough to realize that you were making something. That's it, isn't it? You made me something, and you wanted to give it to me, and you worried I'd catch you sneaking around. And then I didn't. And it made you feel like I don't care about you. But you never once wondered about how I feel."

"You're too busy to feel things," Zelind snapped.

I flinched. "You won't touch me!"

Curtains twitched open. Bernard Blackstone opened the front door of the Clan of Full Sails and called across the street. "All right there, Auntie?"

"We're fine! We're almost home," I called.

"Just so," Bernard said. "Have a peaceful journey."

Stop screaming at each other in the street, he meant. But I wasn't done, so I lowered my voice to a growl. "I know you've been through something terrible, something I can't even imagine, but you won't talk about it. You act like nothing's wrong, but it's all wrong, Zelind.

You won't touch me, and I'm not even supposed to be sad. Or angry. Or hurt."

"But you have to deal with it," Zelind muttered. "Your damaged, traumatized spouse, the witch made out of glass, and if you touch kher, khe'll shatter to pieces."

"You're not ready for—"

"No," Zelind said. "We are not making this about my failings. I have tried to share happiness with you. I wanted to share it with you today. But you're different too."

"I am not."

"You are. You just don't see it. You don't see how little you need people, while they need you for everything. You work and work and work and you don't resent it for a minute. It's your life, and I don't seem to have anywhere in it that fits."

"You fit."

"Do me the courtesy of being honest with me. The government lied and told you I was dead. You grieved. You mourned. And then you built a life that only has room for you in it."

Had I? My blood rushed, cold and anxious.

"Then let's rebuild it," I said. "Look. I know I have a lot of secrets where the movement is concerned. I don't tell you things. But I have to tell you. You need to know, and I should have told you sooner. And if we worked together, then maybe we'd have a life for us."

"No. Tell me your secrets. But I don't just want to be your tagalong. I have something important too. I have something to work on too. That's what I wanted to show you."

"Then please show me," I said. "I really do want to know."

"All right."

"And I'm sorry I made you feel excluded. And I had something to tell you. I should tell you it all."

"All right. But me first. Straight to the attic."

We didn't make it three steps inside on slippered feet.

"What took you so long?" Eldest said. "Even I made it home before you did."

"I had a few things I needed to take care of," I said. "And Zelind wants to show me something—"

"That contraption khe's making in the attic?"

I had missed it. Zelind had hinted at what khe planned, and I missed it. I should have noticed. I should have asked. I nodded, not trusting my voice.

"Bring it down, Zelind," Eldest said. "Show everyone what you made."

"It's just a prototype," Zelind said. "It's crude."

"Go fetch it," Eldest said.

Zelind knew better than to wrangle with Eldest. Khe jogged up the stairs to obey.

Aunt Glory looked up from her heirloom lace knitting. "And then Robin can tell us what was so important the committee hauled her off for a meeting in the middle of their leader's funeral."

Aunt Bernice clucked her tongue. "I'll bet you a button I already know."

The elders didn't miss a thing. "That should wait until we have made a formal announcement."

"Ha! Just as I thought," Aunt Bernice crowed. "They chose you to lead Solidarity. Didn't they?"

Footsteps faltered on the stairs behind me. The skin just between my shoulder blades crawled with aversion. "You can't tell anyone. We're doing a press conference after I talk to the Chancellor, and then—"

"And then you'll be busier than ever," Zelind said.

"Yes," I said. "But there's more, and I wanted to talk to you about why I wanted you to get involved, and—"

I pointed at the wooden plinth in Zelind's hands, shuddering. Copper wire wound from a child's windflower to a cylinder coated in the stuff to an old, chipped mounting base for a lightbulb. "What is that?"

"It's aether," Zelind said.

Khe concentrated, and the windflower spun, slowly at first, and then fast enough that the bright paper was a blur as it whirled.

After a few heartbeats, the lightbulb glowed.

"The wind blows; the fan turns the rotor; energy builds in the coil; the light turns on." Khe smiled. "I just earned the clan a quarter of a million marks."

ELEVEN

Clan Cage

Zelind and I went to bed in the sulky silence of an unfinished argument. I tried to leave kher asleep, but Zelind's eyes popped open the moment I stood in the narrow channel between my bed and kher cot.

"Just me," I said. "I'm on breakfast."

Zelind eyed the outfit I had laid out the night before. "And then you're leaving again."

"I am. I won't be gone all day. Can we talk when I get back?"

Zelind rubbed kher hand over the springy, dense coils of kher hair, then pressed kher hands over kher eyes. "Sure. We'll discuss it."

I fled the flat animosity in kher voice to cook a hundred pieces of goose sausage, flinching every time a tiny bubble of grease pricked my hand. I concentrated on my task, ignoring the talk, which was nothing but Zelind's invention.

"Why doesn't it sting, though?" Halima asked. "It used to hurt my ears."

"I don't know, treasure," Halima's father, Boyd, said. "Robin! Did Zelind tell you why it doesn't sting?"

"I don't know." But I had a guess. The invention used wind, not souls. What we used to hear was their pain.

"What's with you?" Jedrus asked, spreading butter across fresh toast. "Did you stay up all night?"

"No."

Jedrus picked up another piece of bread from the toasting grill. "Is everything all right?"

"It's fine."

"Mm-hmm. You had a fight."

"Jedrus, not now."

"It's all right. Fighting with a spouse is a knock upside the head. So long as you don't try to win, it'll turn out just fine."

I didn't need advice. We were going to talk later. For now, I made a plate in the kitchen and ate at the counter. I snuck to the front, found an old coat with a beaver fur collar, and pedaled up to Mountrose Palace.

I knew my way through Government House, and the golden oak door to the Chancellor's office swung open at my touch. A strange man perched on the edge of the office secretary's seat, facing a desk that was far more cluttered than I was used to seeing it.

"What happened to Janet?"

"Early retirement," the new secretary said, and pushed his glasses up his nose. He stared at Joy, then turned an uncertain look on me. "I don't—" He pawed through papers, searching for an engagement calendar. "Do you have an appointment?"

I could say yes. How would he know if he forgot to write it down? "I'm Robin Thorpe," I said. "Joy is my companion. The Chancellor would like to see me, I think."

"You're Robin Thorpe," the secretary repeated. "I'm James. James Hammett. Is this your first day? I thought that was tomorrow—"

Oh, James. It wasn't comfortable, watching someone new on the job drowning in all the tasks their predecessor handled flawlessly. I desperately wanted to stack up every piece of paper on that desk and show him how to three-box his work. Did he even have a process notebook? I needed to stop. I wasn't here to rescue secretaries today.

"It was," I said. "But I'm here today. Could you find out if she has a minute for me?"

What if she didn't? I could manage tomorrow if I had to. The press conference wasn't until noon. If I hurried, I could handle all of it.

James piled up all the paper he'd had balanced on his lap in the mound with all the rest, and I craned my neck to see his face all the way up there. He was easily as tall as Grace, but lanky as a lamppost.

"I'll just—please have a seat, I'll—"

Poor James. He knocked on Grace's door, went in, and said, "Your consultant's here today. Robin Thorpe? I know she was supposed to be here tomorrow, but—"

"Send her in," Grace said. "And then play something suitable for morning."

"You can go right in," James said, and I stepped inside Grace's fortress of books. All the bird feeders mounted directly on the windows had been removed. Her second room had a parlor's worth of furniture, balanced on a soft silk rug.

Grace slipped the papers she was working on in the center basket of three and capped her pen, though she twirled it around in her fingers. "You're here a day early."

"I am," I said, and then stopped as music, sparkling and gentle, played to mask our conversation. "Oh. He's very good."

Joy swayed and let one hand glide through the air, describing the tempo and melody. "He's marvelous."

"Joy likes his music very much," I reported.

"James Hammett studied music with Joanna Wensleydale. He's excellent," Grace said. "But he's so nervous when he has to take the main desk in the morning."

"He's not your new secretary?"

Grace smiled and gripped the pen as if she were writing. "Oh, no. He's an under-typist. But my new secretary's children aren't in school until nine, and so I need someone warming the seat until she comes."

"Well, I'm relieved," I said. "He's quite overrun at your main desk."

"You didn't come here to chat about my staff," Grace said. "You're here a day early. Why?"

Best to just get it all out immediately. "I can't work for you," I said. "I'm the new leader of Solidarity."

"You're concerned about conflicting interests?" Grace asked. "I think you can do both, but we can consult someone—"

"I'm taking Jacob's place," I said. "I'm the candidate for South Kingston–Riverside Central, and the leader of the Free Democracy Party."

The pen in Grace's hand went still. "So you're going through with the shadow election," Grace said. "You're maintaining all of Jacob's plans."

"Yes," I said. "And I have to get started right away if we're going to run everything on time."

Grace nodded slowly, but she sat back with her arms crossed. "I think you'd make an effective Elected Member, but this shadow election . . . there's poetry in it. I see the symbolism. But that's a lot of effort and a lot of money to spend on a symbol."

"I know," I said. "But it could be more than that. It could be a real step in gaining free democracy—"

The music stopped. We listened for voices, but the music started again.

"Who—was it the mail?" Grace wondered, but then the door opened, and King Severin let himself in. He stopped, staring at Joy tight-mouthed and scowling.

"Good morning, Your Majesty," we said, and Severin eyed me, head cocked in puzzlement.

"I'm sorry to interrupt your appointment," Severin said. "I'm surprised to see you here, Mrs. Thorpe. I thought formal mourning wasn't over until tomorrow."

"It's not, but I had to speak to the Chancellor today."

"I see. What business brought you here, then?"

"I had wished to engage Robin as an expert in civic matters," Grace said. "But with Jacob Clarke's death, she's taking on his responsibilities, including his candidacy for Parliament."

Severin's head came up as he looked at me, a tiny frown knit between his brows. "Well! That's very ambitious, Mrs. Thorpe. Have you held office before?"

He had to know that I had not. "The closest I've come is secretary to the president of the student union at Queens University. It was around the time you graduated."

"A time I still remember fondly," Severin said. "Didn't the students at the time stage some kind of protest? Over books?"

"Over unfair pricing of textbooks, yes." I smiled at the King. "We won. Queens University no longer produces 'academic editions' for six times the price of books available on the public market."

"And you remember all this because you typed up the reports."

I had to admit, I'd been snubbed with faint praise hundreds of times in my life, but never by a king. What a morning! "Something like that."

"Well, I wish you luck," Severin said. "But I'm afraid I came with an invitation for the Chancellor. I hate to cut your appointment short—"

"I understand," I said. I had said what I needed to say, regardless.

Grace circled her desk. "Perhaps we should meet again sometime next week," she said, and helped me into my coat. "Whenever's convenient for you should be fine."

"I should think Mrs. Thorpe would have buried herself in the work of an election campaign by then," Severin said. "It's a grueling project, by all reports."

He stepped into the room, as far from Joy as he could get.

So Severin assumed that I would go on with the election, where Grace thought I would cancel it. I had to remember that Severin, for all his frivolous romances with theater actresses, was a clever, insightful man.

"I'll see when I have a spare moment," I said. "Good morning, Your Majesty, Chancellor—"

The door shut on my last words. Well. He was the King. Everyone had to jump to his bidding. I gave James an encouraging smile and headed out, feeling my pockets for gloves.

The smooth, crisp edge of a folded piece of paper met my fingertips. That hadn't been there before. I pulled out a hastily folded note, the letters blotted on the blank lower half of the message:

I will help where I can.
Never lie when the truth will do.
Everyone has a hidden reason for their actions.
When you find someone you can trust, don't let them go.

I folded the paper along its crease lines and put it back in my pocket.

I pulled my bicycle off the rack outside Government House, and took my time pedaling, but I was home soon enough, tucking my gloves into a box and replacing my coat on a hanger. I walked past the second parlor, but the people inside only waved. There was no delaying it. I climbed the stairs and nudged open my door.

Zelind sat in the good chair, knitting a row of ribbing in soft gray yarn, kher needles still sliding against each other as khe looked up from kher work.

"You're good at that."

"We all knit," Zelind said. "Sweaters, socks, mittens, hats, blanket squares. All of it plain, but we learned to cable in secret. Small charm patterns, mostly."

I shut the door and came closer. Zelind lifted one hip and reached into kher trouser pocket, producing an angular sailor's star knitted on a square of yarn. Khe handed it to me, and I traced my fingers over the knotted arms of the star. Perfect. Not a single mistake.

"They used to take my sweater away when they wanted to control me. I always did what they wanted so I could get it back. People used to touch it. For luck. For safety. When it was you who came to free us all—they're too shy to tell you what that meant."

"Because they touched our clan pattern for luck."

"You mean a lot to them," Zelind said. "Even though they don't know you."

There had to be a reason why khe was starting here. "I'm glad our clan helped you all survive."

"I felt abandoned yesterday," Zelind said.

"You were disappointed," I said. "You wanted to share your invention with me, and I wasn't there."

"Because of Solidarity," Zelind said. "And because of the election. And that's going to take you away from me."

"It will," I said. "It's going to take a lot of my time."

"But I understand. The others need you too," Zelind said. "I mustn't be selfish."

So we weren't going to fight. I leaned against the door and nodded. "You can be selfish," I said. "You get to tell me that you need my time. I am supposed to give you my time."

Zelind returned kher focus to kher knitting. "Thank you."

"But it's not going to be easy. If I win the seat, it will be just as bad as campaigning. But Jacob and Winnie did it together. You could help me—"

"No."

I blinked at the interruption. "No?"

"I'm going to be busy enough on my own. I invented a device

that generates aether," Zelind said, knitting needles sliding as khe worked. "Did you forget?"

I hadn't, but . . . "No. I just didn't think about how much of your time it would take."

The needles never stopped moving. Zelind held the yarn in kher left hand, like an Aelander, and both needles rocked in kher hands. "Orlena's looking over the contest rules and conditions today. She's going to advise me. And I am surprised you didn't realize that providing aether for an entire nation just might be important too."

"I know it's important." I had a sudden, fierce craving for a smoke. "I had just . . . hoped that you would team up with me."

"And now it is I who has no time for you," Zelind said. "Doesn't feel good, does it?"

Heat flushed my cheeks. "That's not fair," I said. "I didn't know you were brainstorming the invention of the century. Forgive me if I'm a little behind."

"Well, now you do," Zelind said. "I have something that's just as important as yours."

Did khe think I didn't know how important aether was? "All right." I gritted my teeth. "So you'll do your invention, and I will lead the nation to democracy, and everything will be just fine."

The knitting landed in kher lap. "Why aren't you proud of me?"

"I am proud of you! What you've done is enormous! It's going to help everyone in the nation and you will be a hero!"

"Maybe an even bigger hero than you," Zelind said. "And that's what you can't stand!"

I went still as the words wrapped around my throat. "Is that what you think of me? That I need to be better than you?"

"You need to be the leader of Solidarity more than you need me," Zelind said. "You're happy to have me as a follower, but I want something of my own."

"Then have it!" I cried. "Didn't I already say you should?"

"But that isn't what you want. That's just what you think you should say—and then when I do it, you'll resent me. Because I'm not around to admire you."

"I don't need you to admire me! I need your help!"

"My help," Zelind scoffed. "Why would you possibly need my help?"

"Because no one really thinks I can do this!"

Zelind shut kher mouth, understanding flooding kher eyes. "Oh, Robin."

"Jacob was the leader. He had the vision, and now he's gone, and I can't—I just held on to him long enough to finish his speech, but now everyone thinks I'm—" My throat closed tight. My sinuses burned, clogging with tears. "Nobody can do it but me," I choked out. "Everyone assumes that Jacob is there, in my head, but he's not and I'm alone and I don't want to be alone and I—"

"All right," Zelind said. "All right. And you want someone to— come here. Let me . . . there."

Kher arms closed around me. Khe cradled my head, and rocked kher weight from one foot to the other, as if we swayed in a gentle spring breeze.

"I don't want to be alone," I said, my voice still watery. "I can't tell anyone but you. But you can't—"

"Yes, I can."

"But the turbine—"

"I'll need some time to fill out the contest form. I'll probably need to meet with people who work for the King. We can help each other. I'll help you, and you'll help me, and we'll work it out."

Which is how we should have done it in the first place. If I hadn't been so secretive, so stubborn, we could have figured this out last night.

I didn't pull out of kher arms, and even though I'd stopped crying, khe didn't let me go. I sniffed. My breath hitched. Zelind held me and swayed. Khe stroked my back, and I sniffed and finally leaned back, tilting my head to look at kher.

"Thank you. I'm sorry."

"I know you are," Zelind said. "I was cruel to you. I'm sorry too."

"I was hurting you," I said. "I've been all caught up in my own nonsense—"

The knock was timid, but it shut my mouth. "Who is it?"

"Jean-Marie," the voice came through the door. "Are you—"

I opened the barrier and she held my sweater in her hands, the fabric neat and even from a proper washing and blocking. She flinched and backed up a step.

"Are you fighting?" she whispered.

"We were," I said. "But we're done now. Thank you for taking good care of my sweater."

"I can come back," she said.

"No. You're fine. What's on your mind?"

She shook her head. "It can wait."

"No it can't," I said. "What is your wish?"

"I need to show you something," Jean-Marie said. "And please don't get mad."

"Show me what?"

"It's at the hotel," Jean-Marie said. "Please come."

We followed, of course, and soon we were looking for a place to lock our bicycles among twenty more that had taken up space just outside the hotel.

"Who's here?"

"You'll see," Jean-Marie promised.

Muffled voices made it out to a much cleaner entry. All the trash was gone, and someone had organized all the food on the shelves. Some of it was gone.

"You're cleaning up for Miss Brown?"

"Yes. But come on."

She dashed past the custodian's apartment and led us to the main lobby, where twenty asylum witches, their shorn hair growing into tight coils or loose curls or straight tresses, sanded and swept and mended the grand entryway. They'd even lowered the chandelier, and two young people wiped each crystal pendant free of dust.

Seated on a heavy green brocade sofa was Minerva Brown, pouring out powdered tea mix and serving jam crackers to anyone who needed a break. Jean-Marie dragged me to meet the grand dame, who smiled to see her.

"It hasn't looked this good in years," she said. "I'm glad you came."

"I'm so happy that you have volunteers to help you," I said. "I imagine you've wanted to see the beauty of this place for a long while."

Jean-Marie knotted her fingers together. "We need to ask you something—"

"We have a proposition for you, Mrs. Thorpe, and I hope the Solidarity movement has room for another project."

"You want to restore the hotel? Open it to guests again?" Zelind asked.

"Not quite," Miss Brown said. "Not to guests. Residents."

"We want to live here," Jean-Marie said. "The witches, I mean. I told them about this place at the celebration in the park. We could have a home."

"But you have homes," I said. "No one is putting anyone out of the clan house."

"We want a home together," Jean-Marie said. "We're used to being together. Even the witches from the other asylums are better with us than they are feeling like outcasts in the clan house. It's lonely."

"Because you're not with your people," Zelind said. "I understand. I feel lonely too sometimes."

Zelind felt lonely too. A sick, heavy feeling rolled over in my stomach. "You don't want to live with your family?"

I kept my gaze squarely on Jean-Marie when I spoke. Whatever shadow passed over Zelind's face, I couldn't bear to see it.

"I don't know them the way I know my friends. We understand what we went through. We know what it was like. We don't have to hide it for fear of upsetting people."

Upsetting people. Miles told me once that many of the soldiers didn't open up to him until they knew that he had been in the war, that he had known its horrors. That they couldn't talk to their experience with anybody but each other, because it was too much for their spouses and children to bear.

But it was Zelind who spoke first. "You want to be your own clan."

Jean-Marie sighed through a relieved smile. "Yes. I don't know if we can be, but that's what we want."

They needed each other. I glanced at Zelind, but khe stared at the lowered chandelier.

Jean-Marie didn't want to live in the clan house. She was lonely in a house full of family. And she was afraid that the reaction would be less than supportive. That I would . . . do exactly what I was doing.

Miles would understand why they wanted this. Miles would trust that they knew what would make them feel safe.

"You need a name," I said. "For your clan."

"Cage," Jean-Marie said.

"Clan Cage. It isn't subtle," Zelind said.

"It's so we don't forget," Jean-Marie said. "This is what we want. Granny Min is our Eldest. We'll live here, together, eat together, work together—"

How would they do that? "But you need money," I said. "Most clans have a healthy amount in savings. They own their property outright. But you don't have anything in the way of income—you will have your pensions, but they're meager."

"We know," Jean-Marie said. "But we can make do. They weren't exactly serving up the butcher's finest at the asylum. We know a lot about making what we have stretch farther—"

"I have a hundred thousand marks," Miss Minerva Brown said.

We all stared.

She nodded, twinkling at our shock. "Well. A little less than that. My clan will want for nothing, Mrs. Thorpe. I hate the idea of dying and leaving the Princess Mary alone and abandoned. And it isn't every day you get to found a clan. We are Clan Cage of the Sheltered Harbor, and this is our home."

"If you're sure," I said, "we can get a doctor of laws to advise you."

Jean-Marie whooped. "She said yes!"

All the witches cheered. Some of them jumped up and down. Others hugged each other. Murray kicked over a wash bucket, which led to laughing and scrambling for a mop.

And into the midst of this celebration walked Nolene Brown, carrying her basket of hot food and a bewildered expression.

"Granny Min? Who are all these people? What's going on here?"

The witches went still. Jean-Marie gasped, but Miss Minerva covered her hand, patting it.

"It's a happy day," Miss Minerva said. "The Princess Mary will rise again."

Nolene stared at the witches, then cultivated a patient smile. "Don't you think that would be expensive? It would be. The hotel needs more than just cleaning off the dirt, and the renovations needed to attract a certain caliber of guest—"

"I'm not reopening the Mary to guests," Miss Minerva said. "We are founding a new clan, and this hotel will be their clan house. They're going to live here, with me."

Nolene went gray. She stared at her grandmother with her jaw hanging open, until a thought blazed across her face. "Con artists. Grifters. Taking advantage of an old woman!"

"She was the one who suggested it," Jean-Marie said. "It was Granny Min's idea—"

"Don't you dare call her that," Nolene seethed. "You won't get away with this, you hear me? I'll have you in jail, all of you. Trying to steal my inheritance—you won't get away with it!"

She dropped the basket on the floor and marched straight out of the lobby. Miss Minerva watched her go, and then tugged at my sleeve.

"If you'd just pick up that basket, dear, that would be a great favor. And you were mentioning a doctor of laws before. Do you happen to know a good advocate?" Minerva watched the doorway Nolene had disappeared through. "I think we're going to need one."

TWELVE

Rules and Regulations

Zelind coasted beside me on our bicycles, kher arm held out to signal a turn. "Doesn't Nolene have to prove criminal intent on the part of the clan?"

"Yes. And that's what's going to save them," I said, coasting down the slight hill from the Princess Mary.

We were taking the zigzagging, scenic ride along Hillside, the part of Riverside that marched up King Philip Hill to the rest of Kingston. Zelind sat upright, taking kher hands from the handlebars, and stretched. "So the logical thing is to march all those witches onto the stand and let them testify. If they have the nerve to trust the court."

"Some of them will. The rest can submit written statements," I said. "My worry is if Nolene gets an advocate who isn't below the occasional dirty trick."

"Like what?"

"Endless motions, for one," I said. "They take time and money, and if they ask for the activities at the hotel to be suspended . . . they could drag this out until Miss Minerva dies."

"And then it'll be a mess."

Zelind leaned over the handlebars again. "What will we do if Clan Cage loses?"

I sighed. "I think we'd have a hard time finding them somewhere as suited to their needs as the Princess Mary Hotel. But if they need to be together—"

"They do," Zelind said. "It's how they grew up. Together. Doesn't it make sense to you?"

"Yes. It does now," I said. "And I think I need to get Solidarity behind this. Public opinion could drive this story in the direction we want."

"We can win this," Zelind said.

"We can win this," I repeated. "With the right advocate, it'll be over before we know it."

We arrived at the clan house in good spirits, and Zelind held my hand to steady me as I slid out of my shoes.

"Robin, is that you?" Aunt Glory called from the second parlor. "Come in here, please."

"We're coming," I called. "Is Orlena here?"

"I'm here," she called. "Is Zelind with you?"

"Why are we shouting across the house?" Zelind muttered, and then raised kher voice. "I'm here!"

Orlena sat with a printed contract in her lap sitting on top of a folded copy of the *Star of Kingston*.

Orlena was a first cousin. Whip smart, more interested in the law than in her power to speak with birds, she was a slender, elegant figure in the custom-fitted suit she didn't even notice anymore. Gray streaked her tidy, tight-braided hair, and she had chosen polished agate beads for the ends. She watched us, and I doubt she missed a detail of our attire or our demeanor.

"I'm sorry we're late," Zelind said.

"You're not. I came early," she said, her soft, girlish voice startling out of such a handsome, mature-looking woman. "I've read the contest rules, and there's a problem," she said. "I've underlined the relevant portions."

Zelind took the long document and paged through it, squinting at the tiny print. Khe traced one finger over a passage and scowled. "'Applicant agrees to a transfer of rights to their entry upon application,'" khe read, and looked up from the document. "Hold on. I get a quarter of a million marks, but they hold the rights to my invention?"

"It's worse than that," Orlena said. "They claim the rights of all entrants, not just the one who wins."

"Thievery," Aunt Glory said. "All these Mountroses, they're all the same."

"No," Zelind said. "No, that's not going to happen."

It was dirty. How many people had an advocate to read the jargon of the rules to find out what they were giving away?

"That clause is completely unfair," I said. "You can't enter the contest, Zelind."

"I won't," Zelind said. "Word of my ancestors, I'll never fall for thievery like that."

"But what do we do?" I asked.

"I start my own business."

Glory glanced up from her knitting. "With your pension? That you haven't been paid yet?"

"All I have to do is build one turbine," Zelind said. "When the neighbors see the lights shining through the window, that will do the rest."

I sighed. "It won't be that simple. You need an investor. You need manufacturing space. You need employees—"

"Ownership share workers," Zelind said. "And maybe we can do it on orders—there would be a lot of backlog at first, but—no. We need an investor. But who?"

"Let me think about that," I said. "But we have to do it fast. You need to register your invention—"

"Here," Orlena said. She held out a sheaf of papers. "I thought you might want them. If we fill it out today, I can start the registration process tomorrow."

"Orlena, you are the best," Zelind said. "We can work in the dining room—"

"There's one more thing," Orlena said. "The offices are close to Main Street. We get the afternoon paper an hour before delivery makes it to Riverside, and today's headline is—Robin, I am so sorry."

"What? What is it?"

Orlena unfolded the paper. The *Star's* headlines were bold, often one word and a picture to drag two cents out of a reader's pocket. This one read UNFAITHFUL, and beneath it read JACOB CLARKE'S SECRET MAN COMFORTS WIDOW.

The subtitle floated above two photographs. The photograph on the left was of a younger Jacob Clarke standing with his arm around Duke Corbett, who laughed as Jacob tried to blow a note in the bandman's trumpet. I'd seen this picture before—it hung in the hallway at the Clarkes'. But I had never noticed the soft admiration in Duke's eyes. How had I missed it?

The photograph on the right was taken outside the funeral home. Winnie Clarke stood beside Duke, whose head reached up to nudge the widow's chin higher, saying something, by the set of his lips.

But Duke wore that same tender look when he looked at Winnie. The caption under the photo read THE WIDOW AND THE OTHER MAN.

"Oh no," I said. "This is all over Kingston? Right now?"

"It's spreading as we speak," Orlena said. "They'll talk of nothing else at the press conference tomorrow. What are you going to do?"

I smoothed my hand over my skirt pocket. "Handle it. I'm sorry, Zelind. I have to go see Winnie."

And if I was right, Duke wouldn't be hard to find either.

Every reporter in the city crowded the entrance of the co-op where the Widow Clarke lived, and I spotted the chrome fenders and white enamel of Duke's favorite bicycle.

"Excuse me," I said while I shoved a reporter off-balance and snuck into the gap. "I beg your pardon. I'm going inside."

"It's Robin Thorpe," someone said, and the scrum spun around, notepads and cameras thrust in my face. "Miss Thorpe. Is it true that you have trapped Jacob Clarke's soul to do your bidding?"

"Is it true that the spirit of Jacob Clarke leads Solidarity through you?"

"Miss Thorpe. Does Jacob have any comment about his long-standing unfaithfulness to his wife?"

"These questions are all nonsense and I have no comment," I said. "Excuse me."

I pushed, trod on toes, and bullied my way through the scrum, only to be confronted by the double row of brass buttons shining on the coat of the doorman, who scowled.

"You know who I am," I said. "She'll want to see me."

"Mrs. Clarke said she didn't want to be disturbed. I can't take you up."

I slipped one hand inside my pocket and pulled out my card holder. "Send my card," I said. "I'll leave if she says no."

"Miss Thorpe!"

"Miss Thorpe! Did you know about the affair? Were they still having liaisons?"

I kept my back to them and watched the doorman disappear up the stairs. It took twenty minutes for the doorman to return, gesturing me inside with a sharp nod. I jogged all the way up to the fourth floor, where Emma hovered in the doorway, looking peaked.

"She's in terrible shape," Emma whispered. "She's groggy."

More sedatives. I nodded and stepped inside, crossing the foyer to the plush, carpeted parlor, where Winnie leaned on Duke's shoulder, still weeping. She lifted her face and stared at me through a starry veil of tears.

"Did he say anything?"

I went still. I listened. Would the sight of his wife and his lover stir him to any kind of response?

Winnie's face fell as I waited for something, anything to happen.

"There's nothing. I'm sorry, Winnie. How long?"

Winnie blinked. "What?"

"How long have the three of you been married? Does your clan know that Duke here should actually be Duke Clarke and not Corbett?"

"They know," Duke said. "My family doesn't. They would never have accepted it. And now people think that we betrayed Winnie? We'd never do that. It's been thirty-two years."

"Longer," Winnie said. "Since college. Aelanders don't understand triangle marriage. It confused Duke for years. Do you remember that song, the delight of three?"

It was before my time, but I knew it, and I followed Winnie's sedated chain of thought. "Yes."

"It was banned." Winnie reached for Duke's hand. "That only made us want to play it more. We were inseparable friends."

"You and Jacob and Duke the third wheel."

"It never felt like that," Winnie said. "We'd sit up and wait for Duke to come home from a performance or a tour and—you couldn't take us apart. So we did it. We were three. But now—" Winnie shut her eyes. "He wasn't done. There was so much left to do. There was so much we were going to do. . . ."

Triangle marriages were illegal. But you couldn't stop a trio from saying vows. You couldn't stop them from ordering rings with two names engraved inside them instead of one. You couldn't forbid anyone to name whomever they pleased as a beneficiary of their estate. And that was good enough for any Samindan to bind themselves to the person—or people—to whom they belonged.

No one would go to jail for the crime of bigamy. Winnie and Duke weren't legally or illegally married to each other. But white Aeland would be aghast at the truth of their relationship. There would be talk for weeks, and so they kept it quiet.

"Who knew?" I asked. "Who witnessed your vows?"

"Our clans," Winnie said. "The Clarkes. Some of my mother's clan came, too. We held it at the Princess Mary Hotel, on Duke's birthday."

"And you kept it quiet all these years," I said. "The Clarkes, the Windhams . . . people from your mother's clan—"

"The Brewers of the Fragrant Meadows. And Preston, he was at the ceremony."

I went cold. "Anyone else from the steering committee?"

"Tupper Bell showed up early one morning—seven years ago? And found us all at breakfast," Duke said. "You're trying to figure out who told the papers."

"It could have been any one of dozens of people. Did anyone disapprove?"

Duke shrugged. "A few people were concerned for Jacob's respectability during his first political campaign, but the worry was unfounded."

"Until now," I said. Tupper had the charge of hundreds of children. He'd worry about appearances. Preston was our most reliable plan-breaker, who never let us take a step until he was satisfied. And he wasn't happy I was succeeding Jacob.

And dozens of family members. But I felt it in my bones: It was one of those two. But which one?

"We have to figure out how to handle the press," I said. "They're not going to go away until they get their answers."

"I can't face them," Winnie said. "I can't."

"I think you have to," I said. "You and Duke both. At the press conference. Tomorrow."

"At your press conference?" Duke asked.

"Yes. And I think I already know our strategy."

"What is it?"

"Never tell a lie when the truth will do," I said. "You're going to give the press a love story—the love story of you, and Jacob, and Duke, and how triangle marriages are a part of Samindan culture denied by the law."

"I can't— Oh, Robin, please, I can't say all that." Winnie clutched Duke's arm. "Not like this, not right now."

"You will. You will both go. Winnie, you will wear your veils. Duke, you will wear butterflies, as you should, since your spouse has died. You're bereaved spouses. You tell the truth, because the truth is beautiful, and anyone who doesn't like it can kick rocks."

"We will," Duke said. "Do you want to fight your way out of that mess tonight? We have plenty of room."

"I didn't bring my clothes for tomorrow," I said. "If I'd been thinking, I would have. But I'll come early. At breakfast?"

"Please," Winnie said. "And if you— I know he doesn't talk to you. You said so. But if you could just stand by my side, in case he can hear me. . . ."

"I will," I promised. "I'll be with you through the whole thing."

Breakfast at Winnie's was delicious, and I hardly ate any of it. I had to go downstairs and speak to an entire curiosity of reporters, and that was nerve-wracking enough when all I had to do was announce my candidacy. Now I had to head off a scandal, and so I ate half of my custard and blueberry sauce and paced when it was time to go and Winnie wasn't quite ready.

I nearly lost hold of my normally dignified stomach when I saw them all spilling out onto the street, pressed against the small wooden podium where I was going to stand and speak.

I couldn't do it. My hands went cold; my throat dried up. This wasn't where I belonged—not up there, trying to catch the attention of a crowd. But I had to do it. If I was going to lead Aeland, I had to do it.

I climbed the wooden steps and stood, now head and shoulders above even the tallest of them.

"Thank you for coming. I have a statement," I said to the assembled gathering of reporters. "I've provided copies. Please take one. After that, I will take questions for five minutes."

Because if I had to stay up here any longer than that I was going to be sick. I looked out at the faces of the reporters with green spots in my vision from all the flashes, and the smell of a hundred extinguished matches in the air. Beside me, Winnie squeezed my hand and leaned on Duke for support.

That had the reporters in a mumble. "The first thing I want to talk about is the accusations of infidelity smeared across Jacob Clarke's good name. The truth is, he and Winifred Clarke and Duke Corbett entered into a private commitment ceremony known as a triangle marriage over thirty years ago."

Shouts from the reporters. More flashbulbs, and someone off to the side hand-cranked a strip-film camera, optimistically hoping there would be a way to replay it soon.

"Ring marriages are not uncommon among Samindans, who have historically recognized that marriage should encompass more than two people. Aeland has known and looked the other way for centuries."

"But that's . . . that's bigamy," a reporter stammered. "How could an Elected Member indulge in such an immoral practice?"

Aelanders! There was nothing immoral about it, but they controlled the lawmaking process that kept traditional romantic bindings between two people, and they had to be between people whose bodies configured exactly the way Aelanders expected. We Samindans let them have their law, working around it with legal designations other than registered marriage.

It was silly. But the people assembled in front of me were rocked by the idea. The truth scandalized them, however they thrilled to romances between men or women at the cinema.

I had to get this under control. I couldn't backpedal from my earlier statement, though, and so I spoke over the babble. "Winnie, Jacob, and Duke engaged in a Samindan cultural practice with thousands of years of history behind it. There is no controversy here. Duke was Jacob's husband. Winnie is Duke's wife. Both have lost their beloved. They ask for privacy while they mourn the loss of their husband. Please treat them with respect."

Skeptical faces looked back at me. Some of the reporters were tight-lipped. Some paper would follow up with a piece about Samindan triangle marriage and smirking stories about historical triples who loved each other as spouses. I had made it worse, telling the truth. But Duke stood up beside me, facing the curiosity as they dropped flashbulbs in their pockets and loaded fresh ones.

One of them spoke up as Duke wrapped his arm around Winnie's shoulders. "Duke, are you worried that the revelation of your peculiar love life will reflect badly on your musical career?"

"I'm only worried about one thing, and that's Winnie's happiness," Duke replied. "For thirty-two years, I wore a ring very like the ones some of you wear, and cherished my family, just as you do. These questions are ugly. I won't dignify them with a response."

He took Winnie down from the tiny stage and guided her inside the co-op, leaving me to face the reporters alone.

"Thank you. Duke and Winnie are not taking questions."

"Miss Thorpe, is your own marriage to Mx. Zelind Bay legally sanctioned?"

I fought to keep the outrage from my face. "That's none of your business. The period for questions about Jacob's marriage to Winifred and Duke is closed. I'm moving on to the next matter."

Half the reporters rushed off, eager to get their copy typeset for next morning's edition. The man with the strip-film camera covered the lens with a cap, as my announcement wasn't worthy of motion film. But enough reporters stayed to listen, and so I cleared my throat.

"Jacob Clarke was murdered in broad daylight. His murderer is still at large, while the police expend minimal effort to bring justice for a man who fought tirelessly for the rights of Aeland's citizens. Jacob's assassination was meant to silence him and shatter the Solidarity Collective. It has left a hole in our hearts, but we persist, even with guns pointed at us. We stand firm against their hope that if they cut the head off our movement, the body will die.

"Instead, we have selected a new leader."

I held up my hands, and the force of their questions pressed against my palms. "I humbly accept leadership of the Solidarity Collective. I am also taking Jacob's place as the candidate for South Kingston–Riverside Central in King Severin's election. My platform retains the same values and promises as Jacob's had, and I have a lot of work to do, so I'll only be taking questions for five minutes."

"You wouldn't answer the question regarding the legal status of your marriage to Zelind Bay," that same reporter spoke up. "If your marriage is not genuine by Aelander standards, how can we trust that your decisions will have the moral weight that Aelanders demand of their leaders?"

"Aelanders understand that the work of government is to manage the smooth and orderly operation of its resources to serve its people, including the distressed and endangered. Aeland did the right thing in freeing witches from the horrors of their labors in the asylums. They rejected the atrocity legislated by those Aelanders in government who destroyed the very souls of their loved ones. Aeland understands moral action better than you think, sir."

Reporters spoke up to try to have their questions heard, shouting over each other for their chance. I pointed at a woman in a pinch-fronted hat and a press card from the *Kingston Daily Herald*. "Yes."

"You were a labor organizer in your days working for Beauregard Veterans'," she said. "Is it true that the weight of the demands from your united nurses are the root cause of Kingston's only veterans' hospital's financial woes?"

"I don't think that's true, no," I said. "If you research the actions of the last Cabinet of Queen Constantina the First, who now await their sentences for treason in palace prison, I believe you will find a series of deep funding cuts to secondary service hospitals, including Beauregard Veterans'."

More uproar. I disregarded them, finding a friendly face in the crowd. "I see you, John Runson of the *Star of Kingston*. What is your question?"

John raised his voice to drown out anyone rude enough to keep talking. "Did anyone else announce their intention to run for the seat?"

"Not before Jacob's death," I said.

"Today is the last day to sign up for candidacy." John tossed his hair, and shell beads clicked against each other as his locks shivered back into place. "You could be running unopposed."

"The day's not over yet," I said, and some of the reporters laughed. "Someone might come and make this a race."

"And indeed, someone has."

The voice came from behind the crowd of reporters and pulled them around to stare at Jarom Bay, graying locks hanging neatly around the hand-eased shoulders of his gleaming, midnight blue coat. Beside him stood a smugly smiling Albert Jessup.

"I'm Jarom Bay," the man said. "You all know Albert, of course. We've come to announce my intention to become Riverside's Elected Member of Parliament. The loss of Jacob Clarke saddens me, and I mean to carry on his legacy, with sound and sober decisions to help guide and protect the people who employ and house thousands of citizens."

None of those reporters were looking at me anymore. But Albert was, and I wanted to punch him right in his supercilious face. This was Jessup's doing. He had hated Jacob, the leader of a small but effective coalition bent on bringing fairness to government. They had squashed Albert's efforts to line his own pockets more than once.

Jarom was cut from the same cloth. When aether-powered vessels had outrun even the fastest sailing ships, the Bays had turned to real estate, buying and tearing down the homes of poor people and rebuilding neighborhoods for a profit. Together they'd empty the pockets of ordinary Aelanders and put them in the street.

Reporters asked them questions. Jarom answered with keywords like "tradition," and "stability," and "preservation"—nothing like the ideals that had moved hundreds of voters to chip in for a permit to elect Jacob. Would they do the same for me? Did I have what it took to beat the barrels of money Jarom could spend on voters who could see how a Bay in Government House would fatten their bottom line?

I had to. I had to get every clan and shopkeeper I could, because Jarom Bay in Government House was a disaster.

I stepped off the platform and pushed through the reporters, headed straight for Jarom. He watched me approach, the stern lines between his eyes furrowed and deep.

"I come to wish you good luck, Mr. Bay," I said, and stuck out my hand. "It will be a pleasure to have such an influential competitor."

He stared at my offered hand, stripped of its glove, and then gazed at me. "I'm sure I won't need it."

I cocked my head. Reporters shot photographs of Jarom refusing to shake my hand, at the cold sneer on his face as he denied me courtesy.

"I wish luck on you regardless," I said. "Good morning."

"Mrs. Thorpe!" a reporter cried. "Is this rivalry personal?"

"Oh, I don't think so," I said. "That would be awfully petty, don't you think?"

I smiled at Jarom and Albert, waggled my bare fingers at them, and strode off.

I had expected a fight. But this was going to be a nasty battle, one that I would have to fight with all my strength if I was going to stop Jarom from buying his way into Parliament.

THIRTEEN

At the King's Pleasure

The next week, I knocked on doors all over Riverside, traveling from the comfortable clan houses of Water Street to the tenements of Five Corners. Today Zelind had taken the time to accompany me. Our last visit before our lunch break saw us perched on fifty-year-old chairs adorned with frothy crochet doilies as we drank Mr. Alfred West's best tea—properly strong, if a bit stale from hoarding.

"You want to know what the government can do for me?" Mr. West asked in a soft and reedy voice, his bent figure pitched forward with his years. A white Aelander living in a building across the street from Clarence Jones Memorial Park with creaky floors and decades of water stains on the walls, the halls filled with the scent of simmering shellfish stock. Mr. West was small of build, with a dapper air and a chin that had never needed a razor. He slurped his tea loudly, and the cup rattled as he set it back on the saucer. "I want them to turn the lights back on. How can your government do that?"

Zelind glanced at me before setting kher teacup back in its saucer. "We want to bring light into your home that costs less than your old bills for aether."

"Don't see how you can promise that," Mr. West said. "How are you going to get the lights back, with all those witches on the loose? They were making the machines work."

We had run into a surprising number of people who didn't believe the story Grace had published in the *Star*, each with their own
explanation for the power outage—that the Amaranthines had done
it, usually. And that they had brought thousands of ghosts with them
to haunt us into doing what they wanted, which was anything from
letting them take over the government to turning them into walking gods.

Some of them took one look at Zelind and kher short halo of unlocked hair and shut the door in our faces, convinced that witches
had come to hurt them. Some of them stared uncomfortably at Joy
until I regretfully left her behind on canvassing days. But Mr. West
hadn't so much as batted an eye. Then he invited us in for tea so he
could tell us all about how the witches needed to be enslaved again.

"There's another way to make aether," Zelind said.

"Not without witches. You need witchcraft to make it, don't you?
It's the only way this makes sense. And good luck trying to round
them up now that they're scattered all over the country, doing Solace
knows what. We need the Royal Knights to save us from the weather,
so they can't do it. It's got to be the witches. You've got to bring aether
back."

"Believe me," Zelind said. "We're working on bringing aether
back, and we won't need witches to do it."

"Hmph. You'd say so, wouldn't you? Tell me this, though—" Mr.
West sat up a little straighter, a probing glint in his eyes. "How is going out to vote in your mock election going to change anything?"

"There are six million people in Aeland," I said. "Two million of
them live right here in Kingston. A fraction of that population actually has the power to vote individually. The Free Democracy Party
wants to demonstrate the will of the millions by taking all of those
ballots and bringing them to the justices of the highest court and asking them to make our election legitimate."

Mr. West planted a dainty hand on his knee and led with his chin.
"And you think they will agree."

"I think that we're not going to stop until we make free democracy
a reality," I said.

"You should organize more voting collectives," Alfred said. "Even
if a thousand people chipped in to make one vote—"

"Work within the system," Zelind said. "We could do that. And if we did, the elite would just find a way to shut us out of their system. We can't rely on that."

"That's how we elected Jacob Clarke," Mr. West said. "That's how we're going to elect you, Auntie. We'll pay for the permit, and we'll vote you in, and show the country how it's done."

"I'm grateful to you for that," I said. "And I want to ask you to come out and cast your own vote as well. Our polling station will be in the dancing hall at the far end of the park—"

"Where Jacob died," Mr. West said. "I don't get out much. I watched from the windows. You can hear the music in the summer-time, you know, and I could hear him. And then the shot—oh, it made me jump!"

I leaned forward. "You heard the shot?"

"Like a firework going off just over my head," Mr. West said.

Zelind and I looked at each other.

"When the police came," Zelind said, "did you tell them that?"

"The police never came here," Mr. West said. "I watched every-thing from my window. It takes too much out of me to take all those stairs unless I need to, and no one came to my door."

No one had come to see Mr. West. There were others in the build-ing, though, and perhaps the police had only talked to the building custodian. "Mr. West, I'm so happy I came to see you today. I need to meet your neighbors. Who would you say could give me some good ideas about what Aeland's government needs to do for them?"

"You should see Marjorie Potts," Mr. West said. "Beware, though—she'll keep you all day."

"I'll save her for last, then," I said. "Thank you so much."

Zelind and I shook hands, and when we left, we hurried to the stairs. Zelind went up, not down. "The police never came here. We have to look. Has it snowed since—"

"No," I said. "Do you think it was here?"

But we climbed the stairs. We pushed open the door, and we stepped wide of footprints molded into pristine snow.

Five snowmen stood sentry on the rooftop, their heads peaked with fresh fall, the impressions of small boots nothing more than dents.

"Look," Zelind said, pointing past the snowmen.

The edge of the roof was a waist-high wall crowned with snow, except in the place where it had been cleared off. Footprints paced around the spot, dusted with snow. Zelind went to hands and knees before one, and alternated blowing on the powder filling it, and dusting snow away with kher gloves.

Zelind's efforts revealed an impression of a Service boot's heavy-lugged soles, but the size was smaller than most men's boots, the heel impression a little narrower.

"Small feet," Zelind said. "They were up here."

"How'd they get up here with a sniper rifle? Did they carry it in a loom bag? A broom case, for skiprock?"

"A guitar case," Zelind said. "It could have been anything."

We skirted around the footprints and peered over the mound of snow on the walls. There was the stage, visible in the winter with no leaves on the trees. The assassin had been here. Had watched and waited through the music. Had waited here with a long-barreled rifle and infinite patience, waiting for a clear shot, for Jacob to stand in one place, for the wind to still.

Had the assassin stared down their scope at me? Had they waited with all the patience of an egret as I fought to save Jacob's life, and then stood in his place to save his dream? Cold trickled down my back.

"This is it," I said. "But the police never came."

"You can't go to them," Zelind said. "They'll think you're interfering with their investigation."

"They stared right at this building," I said. "They couldn't have missed it. But—"

But they had already taken me away. Why bother with evidence when a good story would do? I scanned the park again. You really could see everything on the outdoor stage. This had to be the place.

But how were we going to convince anyone to look into it?

"Look at this," Zelind said. "They dug around in the snow for something. Cigarette butts?"

"Shell casing," I said. "They pocketed it before they left."

"Taking the evidence," Zelind said. "That's clever."

"That's thoughtful," I said. "If we can assume this shoe print can determine gender, we're looking for a woman sharpshooter."

"I think it's fair to assume the shooter is an adult," Zelind said. "The boot size is small, suggesting the shooter is also small."

"Right. I don't even know how one goes about finding the kind of expert gunsmithing you need for a rifle to fire accurately at this distance—"

"The army," Zelind said. "She or khe probably joined the army."

"The army would have her in the records as a woman, most likely."

Zelind made a rueful face. "True."

"And was so adept at shooting they put her in combat. I like that story. But can we prove it?"

"We can request a dive into the records," Zelind said. "How many women sharpshooters can there be?"

"Let's look into it," I said. "Thank you for thinking of it."

I started for the door and had swung it open before I realized Zelind still stood next to the assassin's perch. Kher brow was knit with worry, and khe crouched next to the shoe mark one more time.

"Zel. Are you coming?"

"Robin." Zelind licked kher lips, looking at the shoe marks in the snow. "You can't look into it."

"What do you mean?"

"She saw your face through a scope," Zelind said. "We have to assume that she watched you try to save Jacob's life, and that she decided not to take it. If you suddenly show up asking questions about her, do you think she'll show you mercy again?"

"You have a point," I said. "First spies in the steering committee, and now this."

"What?"

Weariness stole over me. "When we were at Jacob's funeral, Tristan showed me a mark on a mailbox he believes is a signal between a spy and their handler. He believes that someone informed on Jacob's plans, and that's the reason why he was murdered."

"To stop the shadow election?"

"Or to shatter the collective," I said. "But yes. Jacob made enemies while he was in Parliament. He was frighteningly effective. There are people who wanted him gone."

"Who?"

"Albert Jessup is on the top of that list," I said. "He hated Jacob. It wasn't just opposing his goals in Parliament. It was personal. Jacob used to delight in thwarting him. Any of the Royal Knights would have the money to pay an assassin, but many of the men and women who hated him most are imprisoned in the Tower for treason."

"So Albert Jessup."

"Yes," I said. "And—and Jarom Bay."

"Why him?"

"Kingston has a housing crisis," I said. "Jacob used his leverage against the city council to stop the Bays from buying up cheap land, squeezing out the tenants with intimidation tactics, and rebuilding commercially profitable properties—apartments, mostly."

"How much money could that mean these days?"

"Hundreds of thousands of marks," I said. "Jacob used to push the council into forcing rent controls and maintenance orders onto Bay-side Properties, sucking money out of Jarom's and Birdie's pockets."

"And Jarom thinks that I would come home, join the business, and kick the poor out of their homes?" Zelind asked, disgusted. "But now the two of them are working to take your seat."

"Correct. Because I will continue Jacob's work. I will tweak their noses at every turn."

"You're not safe," Zelind said. "You realize that, don't you?"

"Yes."

"But you're doing it anyway."

"Yes."

"But you can't chase down this assassin. You have to assume she'll kill you if you try."

"You're right," I said. "But I'm not going to just let her hunt me, either. Let's figure out what to do over lunch. I'm starving."

It wasn't as simple as that, however. I spotted Grace's sled the moment we turned the corner onto Water Street.

"Now what is that about?" I wondered.

Zelind sped kher pace. "We'll know when we get there, I suppose."

Grace was sitting at the table next to Eldest, who grinned and shoved another filet of pan-fried salmon at her. Next to her perched Tristan and Miles, who cut globe sprouts into quarters before eating them. Orlena had a tiny portion on her plate and was picking away at her salmon.

Zelind and I sat on the bench across from them. "What are you doing here?"

"We're here just to get out of the palace," Miles said. "Grace said she had news for Zelind."

"For me?" Zelind asked. "I'm sorry, Chancellor Hensley, but I don't see how we could—"

"It's your invention," Grace said. "You applied to protect the rights to your technological innovation, specifically an animated generator of aether."

"I did," Zelind said. "But how did you know that?"

"The person processing your application request forwarded it to the King by way of the Chancellor. My under-typist, turning over an efficient new leaf, had it taken to the King this very morning. And now the King is—well, he's wondering why you didn't present it to his contest."

"I think the word you used on the way was 'perturbed,'" Miles said.

"He wants you to come and submit your invention to the contest," Grace said. "But I don't understand why you didn't do that to begin with."

Zelind's fork hovered over kher plate. "Are you familiar with the contest's rules?"

Grace, having just stuffed the last bite of salmon into her mouth, shook her head. "I didn't write them. What do the rules grab at?"

"Just entering forfeits your rights of invention to the Crown."

Grace coughed. "That's—oh! That greedy, conniving—I should have monitored that more closely. I need duplicates of me to stay on top of palace intrigue."

"Wait. Go back to the part that's about me," Zelind said. "The King wants to see me?"

"Yes."

"Because I didn't give away my invention to him."

Grace nodded. "I don't know what Severin was thinking with those rules."

"I do," I said. It made my shoulders tight. "He wanted a method that would keep Aeland Power and Lights in operation. That monopoly is worth millions."

Grace nodded. "Now that you point it out, yes. That's exactly what he was thinking."

"Is he expecting to see me today?"

"This very afternoon."

Zelind glanced my way. "Will you come with me?"

"Of course I will. Orlena?"

Orlena touched a napkin to her lips before speaking. "The sled's going to be crammed."

"We'll sit in front with George," Miles said. "Or we'll hire a sled to get back."

"I need to talk to you and Tristan first," I said.

"Oh? What about?"

"I want you to discreetly try and find someone for me."

"Oh, a mystery!" Tristan said, half rising from his seat to grab the platter of fish. "I'll do it. I'm deadly bored. Want to come, love?"

"I still think you could open your own investigation firm," Miles said. "But I'm not going to let you have all the fun."

"Who do you want me to find?"

I glanced up and down the table. "I can't say at the moment."

"Very well. Later, then."

We finished our lunches, and while Zelind and Grace helped with the task of washing dishes, I led Tristan and Miles to the tiny back parlor, setting Joy at the door to tattle on anyone who tried to eavesdrop. Tristan leaned against the door, securing it.

"Who do you want us to find?"

"We had the chance to do a little investigating," I said. "We found the place where the assassin probably took her shot—"

"Her," Miles said.

"A guess based on the shoe marks we found in the snow. There aren't a lot of places to learn long-distance shooting—"

"You're thinking army records?" Miles asked. "But you could—"

"I could," I said. "But if she's vigilant, and she notices I'm on her trail—"

"You're right. You can't get anywhere near this," Miles said. "We'll have a look. There are more women snipers than you might expect—I met one in Laneer. It wasn't common, but we'll have a number of women to check out."

I nodded. "Thank you. Did Grace tell you the police tried to pin it on me?"

"Yes," Miles said. "I suppose they don't want you poking around their investigation."

"That's the other thing. The police never went to the building in question. They never saw the site."

"Hmm." Tristan scratched at his chin. "That's interesting."

"Isn't it?" Miles asked. "I will stop in at Records and have a poke around for lady sharpshooters. I'll know something in a few days, I'm sure."

Tristan gasped as Joy slid through the door, hovering half in his body.

"Sorry," Joy said, even though he couldn't hear her, and she passed all the way through. Tristan shivered. Joy gave him an apologetic look before turning back to me. "They chased Grace out of the kitchen. That girl never got hot water on her hands for anything, but at least she tried."

"We'd better get going, then," I said. "We can't keep the King waiting."

Grace couldn't stay with the three of us, but she did walk us up to the tall double doors leading into a room that could have been called a parlor if it wasn't so large. We three perched on the edge of a plush green velvet sofa nested in the middle of the room, its curving, asymmetrical shape the height of modernity.

A maid in black and white wheeled in a tea cart and poured out three cups of floral-scented tea, perfectly brewed to a deep burgundy brown, over delicately molded sugar snowflakes. Fresh unskimmed milk clouded and lightened every cup, and we balanced cup and saucer on our knees, every cup joined by a lacy, crisp, ginger-spiced tea cookie, the efforts of a dedicated pastry chef.

Red-uniformed guards stood at stations around the room, guarding every door and window in the place. All were armed. All were women. I tried smiling at one near the window, but she stared right through me.

I took a nibble of the cookie, rich with butter and sugared ginger. Nothing but the best for the palace—and it would be a shame to leave a drop of this tea behind when the King called us into his office. I stole another glance at the two women dressed in the scarlet, ivory, and gold of the Kingsguard who stood on either side of that door. They stared straight ahead, expressionless.

This long room was simultaneously spare and opulent. Cool winter light poured in from tall windows that offered a view of a snowed-over garden. Snow sculptures of the mourning wives of the first Aelish rebels clustered in the center of the oval lawn. They huddled together, weeping, keening, screaming as the Edaran Empire executed their husbands, their sunlit faces awash with grief. Only one woman stood upright, gazing at the horror of the example the Edarans made of their men and warriors—Agnes, whose clenched fist depicted her resolve to pick up her husband's sword and fight on.

What did King Severin see when he looked out the window? Did he dwell on the anguish of the women, or the stony determination of Aeland's founder? I sipped my tea, dwelled in the round fullness of the brew, bit a petal off my cookie, and wondered.

Beside me, Zelind's knee jogged with nervousness. Khe tugged at kher shirt collar and tugged the hem of kher kilt over kher knees, stilling for a moment—but the bounce came back as khe leaned toward Orlena.

"Can he order me to give over the turbine?"

"Technically, yes," Orlena said. "But it's more likely that he will ask."

"Can I say no? I can't, can I?"

"You can." Orlena looked up at the ceiling thoughtfully. "You can negotiate. That's what we're doing here. We're negotiating."

Zelind blew out a long breath. "All right. So he can take it from me, but you don't think he will?"

Orlena glanced at the pair of guards before leaning over to answer in low tones. "Technically the monarch is absolute ruler of Aeland, but no monarch has stepped past the structure of constitutional law since King Philip signed it into being. He will ask. We will negotiate. Eat your cookie."

"I can't."

"Give it to Robin, then. She's already eaten hers."

I had. Zelind handed khers over and I took a bite, sipping my half-full cup of tea. I hadn't expected to drink so much of it.

I took another sip. Another bite. And another, until all the tea was gone and the cookie was little more than a few crumbs on the lip of the saucer. I set the dishes on the knee-high table in front of me and waited.

Three empty cups sat on the table. The sun tracked three hand-sized panes across the windows, twisting the soft blue shadows on the snow. Orlena had caught Zelind's fidgeting. She tapped each of her fingers against her thumbs in complicated guitar exercises. I reached out for any ghosts wandering around the palace, and one came, flowing through the wall to look at me.

"What is the King doing in that room?"

I barely let my lips move, my voice nearly inaudible. The ghost, a clerk with the stiff, broad lace collar of his station, drifted toward the office door.

The guards stiffened. They tracked the ghost's progress, and when the apparition was in reach, one dipped into a pocket and flung a pinch of salt at the ghost.

The spirit flinched and discorporated, banished to the location he had been most attached to in life. I blinked. None of the guards had repelled spirits with salt when I had been coming here to visit Miles as he recovered. Something had changed in that time.

Neither of the guards looked our way, but disapproval hung in the air. I refused to avert my gaze or look anything but innocently surprised. Orlena gave it away, though, by the way she gaped at me, and I would have kicked her ankle if Zelind hadn't been in the way.

At last, the office door opened. The King had a previous appointment, and that person was finally leaving—

I gaped at the man leaving the King's office. A tall man with white hair carefully styled in rich waves. His once perfectly tailored suit hung off bony shoulders, and the collar of his white shirt gaped around his wattled neck, but that tie—

Orange silk, exactly the color of Grace Hensley's sled. The long elegant nose, the curving lower lip—I knew those features. They were a harsher, colder version of Miles's own perpetually thoughtful expression. Miles's hair curled in exactly that way. I knew this man, though I had only seen him in newspaper photographs.

The traitor Christopher Hensley didn't even acknowledge our presence. He could barely put one foot in front of the other, but he walked unassisted by the guard who flanked him. Was she his jailer or his bodyguard? She could have been either. Both.

The man responsible for the asylum system that leeched the dead for aether took another step, then bent over his cane as his ribs rattled with a deep, terrible cough. I recognized it as the body's desperate urge to rid itself of blockage in the lungs. Sir Christopher Hensley was in the last stages of cancer. He would die of it, and probably soon.

But he should be coughing his lungs out in the Tower of Sighs. He should be behind bars, living his final days in a cell. He should be paying for the things he had done, not walking freely about the palace after a nice chat with the King.

How could Severin condone this? How could he choose this man, of all people, to advise him—how could he unlock the traitor's cell and let him out?

This was the man who had devised the contest to bring aether back—and had greedily tried to seize someone else's innovation for the Crown's profits.

I wanted to get to my feet and walk out. I wanted to refuse to speak to the King. But I followed Orlena and Zelind as they rose and moved to the office door, now summoned to attend King Severin.

I followed into a room full of books—and I cocked my head, because these weren't the identical spines of law books, dictionaries, encyclopedias, or authorized histories. I squinted at yellow linen spines of an underground press I knew in passing—a press whose books were banned the moment they were published. This was a library of forbidden publications, and probably one of the biggest collections of books on witchcraft I had ever seen.

"Thank you for waiting," King Severin said, as if we could have left. "I am surprised to see so many of you attending me."

"Thank you for the invitation, Your Majesty," Zelind said, remembering the etiquette lessons of our school days. "Orlena Thorpe is my advocate. She's a contract law specialist. Robin Thorpe is—"

"Here out of concern for her community," Severin guessed.

"My spouse," Zelind said. "And one of my business partners."

Zelind had never mentioned that before. "I suppose we should explain why we decided that submitting to the contest wasn't the wisest choice," I said.

"My client has no wish to surrender kher intellectual property rights to this invention, Your Majesty," Orlena said. "But according to the full contest rules as outlined on the application, Zelind would be forfeiting those rights in order to enter."

"The prize is a fortune," Severin said. "It's enough to live on for the rest of your life."

"And the income from the national aether network reaped millions of marks for its shareholders," I said. "We have no interest in reviving that system, and so we're pursuing other means of manufacture and distribution."

"You have no funding and no infrastructure," the King said. "The Crown already has a system in place. It would be wasteful to duplicate the same system for private profit."

"I'm sorry, Sire," Zelind said. "While my invention certainly could be used in a national network, there's no reason to restrict distribution in such a way."

"I offer you five hundred thousand marks," King Severin said. "Induction into the Order of Aeland, and the Medal of National Service."

Zelind pressed kher lips together and glanced at me. Not at Orlena, who could offer sound legal advice. Me.

Five hundred thousand marks? It was more than a fortune. It was riches. But the ease with which the King doubled the figure—it was too much, on the one hand, and not enough on the other. The King wanted it badly.

I met Zelind's eyes, and slowly shook my head. Khe nodded and turned back to King Severin.

"It's a generous offer," Zelind said.

"You don't have the means to spread your invention across the country. For the sake of Aeland, you must say yes."

"I'd like to take the time to think about it," Zelind said. "I understand that your offer is very generous, but there are other matters to consider. As an inventor, it's not enough to simply make things. I have to consider how the device will change the daily life of every citizen, and I want to be sure the people of Aeland don't suffer because of my machine. I will consider your offer, but I want to understand it."

"There could be another applicant, and then you could lose the prize money," Severin said. "I mean it. This is a race, not a popularity contest. We need to bring aether back to Aeland, and we must do it as quickly as possible."

"I understand," Zelind said. "Thank you for the meeting. I'm grateful for your offer. But I must take some time to think about it."

"You will retain the rights of invention," Severin said. "The Crown will pay you an annual license fee for the use of your device."

He was desperate. We had to get out of here. Severin had a reason why he didn't want to let us go without an agreement, and we had to know what it was.

"Perhaps if your people drew up an agreement," I said, "and then sent it to Orlena, so we know exactly what we're being offered? It's never a good idea to bind a promise on a handshake. But if we had the offer on paper, that would help make the terms clear."

Severin stared at me, his expression troubled. "Very well," he said. "I'll have an offer drawn up. Expect it soon."

"Thank you, Your Majesty," Orlena said, and bowed. We followed her lead, echoing her thanks.

Severin picked up an amethyst pen with silver overlay and turned his attention to a document on his desk. "You may go."

Three steps backward, nod, and turn. We filed out of the office, and the remaining door guard led us out of the parlor and through the palace, dumping us out near the palace square, where the protestors that irritated Severin so much still stood.

There was no sleigh waiting to take us home.

"I have to get back to the firm," Orlena said. "Are you certain refusing the King is the best idea?"

"No," I said. "But now we have more time to figure out what to do, at least. We can talk about it at dinner?"

"I might have to stay late," Orlena said. "I never told anyone I was going to be gone all afternoon. But as soon as we can, yes."

Orlena waved and set off toward downtown, leaving Zelind and me on the edge of the square.

"I just turned down half a million marks," Zelind said. "Am I doing the right thing?"

"You can always change your mind," I said.

"I know," Zelind said. "Who was that man, anyway? You went stiff and angry when you saw him."

"That was Sir Christopher Hensley, the man who had you locked up, and who made millions because of it."

"And he's a confidant of the King," Zelind said. Khe looked back at the palace, at its hundreds of windows, and a decision set in kher eyes. "No. I'm not giving my invention to the King. Not for half a million marks. Not for a million. Let's go canvas Hillside. You have an election to win."

FOURTEEN

The End of a Judge

We covered all of Riverside in the following days. Volunteers reported to the Solidarity Center by the hundreds. In the evenings, Zelind built a larger model of kher turbine, refining the design and looking for improvements, readying kherself to present the idea to the public after the election.

Four days before voting day, Zelind and I received a carefully printed invitation from Jean-Marie, inviting us to the housewarming feast of Clan Cage. Zelind wore kher worn and patched sweater for the evening, and we cycled on a thin dusting of snow to Riverside's newest clan house.

The Princess Mary Hotel gleamed. We exclaimed over the hard work Clan Cage had done to rehabilitate the hotel, now flaunting its grand decorations and elegant design. Jean-Marie took us on a tour that walked us through a kitchen capable of producing a banquet for hundreds, steamy and delicious-smelling with braised goat stew and baked apple tarts.

"I'm so hungry already," Zelind said, lifting a pot lid.

"You put that down!" Murray scolded. "You're our guests. Go be guests where you belong."

Banished, we found a seat at one of three long tables, nodding to neighbors from the clans invited to mark the first night members of Clan Cage would sleep in the Princess Mary. We dug our thumbs into crusty bread and dipped buttered chunks into the rich sauce the goat had simmered in.

Jean-Marie sat with us, full of talk about how well the sturdy old building had held up, their plans to restore additional floors of the hotel, and the volunteers who were coming to start teaching the Cages what they ought to have learned in school.

"Everything's coming together wonderfully," I said, but I couldn't hide my glance at Miss Minerva and the empty place set beside her. Nolene hadn't accepted the invitation to celebrate the new clan house. She hadn't been back since vowing to put the law on Clan Cage. Minerva had gained a clan, but had lost her last relative, and that was a loss that ached.

"Thank you for the yarn," Jean-Marie said. "And the spinning wheel. Emma and Darrell are already scheduling who gets to use it and when."

Emma had moved out of Winnie and Duke's apartment, but they were her guests at the table. Duke held Cora in his lap to give Emma a chance to eat, telling his part of the table stories that had everyone spellbound. Everywhere I looked were animated, happy people, excited for their new clan and their new home.

"It's a good night," I said. "And you remember, if you're short on anything—"

"We'll say so. But we have enough for now," Jean-Marie said. "Everyone has been so generous."

"Everyone looks so happy."

"We are. This is exactly what we needed," Jean-Marie said. "We're together, and we're in charge. We can come and go as we want, we have a home, we have the clan—thank you so much for helping us."

"It's uza," I said. "We're all happy to do it."

"Headmaster Bell brought schoolbooks. They're worn out, but still good. And he went to the school board to bully them into hiring our volunteer teachers, so they'll be paid, and Dr. Singer will be coming so anyone who wants to talk to him can—"

A draft billowed through the room, chilly on the skin. Jean-Marie stopped talking as the room fumbled its way to silence. I leaned back to look at the people who had walked inside, my heart dropping as I recognized Nolene Brown. With her was a man with a sealed document tube that made my stomach churn. I recognized the blue ribbon tied around the tube, signaling that it was a notice of a civil lawsuit and not criminal charges. Nolene was suing.

The third person with Nolene made Zelind duck kher head, for Birdie Bay strode in beside her, cold and glittering in a blue fox coat. She patted Nolene's hand and stood by, solicitous as an aunt as the court clerk presented the tube to Minerva.

"Thank you. You may leave now," Miss Minerva said.

The court officer stood firm. "I need to determine whether you understand the nature of the suit laid on your behalf."

"On my behalf?" Miss Minerva asked. "I haven't any reason to sue anyone. I never asked for you. You may leave now."

I knew then what was inside that tube, and I shot a fierce look at Nolene before leaning closer to Minerva. "Nolene is suing for guardianship," I said. "She's arguing that you are incapable of making sound decisions, or that you're infirm, and no longer mentally competent."

Minerva gazed at me, and I saw it when the light in her eyes cracked in half. Then she rose to her feet and took the tube from the court officer's hands.

"I disagree, naturally. I reject this document. It is scurrilous, it is grasping, and it comes from no family of mine."

Nolene gasped. "Granny Min—"

"You may call me that no longer," Minerva said. "To you, I am Miss Minerva Cage, and no relation of yours. Your suit holds no water. You are on my property. Get out."

"Miss Brown," Birdie said, "I can see you're distraught."

"And you," Minerva said. "You've been sniffing around this hotel's skirts for fifteen years. I told you then and I'm telling you now: The Princess Mary is not for sale. Now it belongs to Clan Cage, held in cooperative trust by the whole of the clan—"

"Enclosed is the motion to block the founding of your cooperative trust, pending the findings of your mental state in court," the court officer said. "You have taken the notice from my hands. The suit is now in motion. Though frankly, Miss Cage, I wish you luck."

Nolene gasped again, but the clerk ignored her as he walked out of the dining hall.

"Granny Min—"

"Get out," Minerva said. "Get out right now, and never come back. No flesh and blood would do this to me. You're trespassing. Now leave."

"I've seen enough." Birdie took Nolene's arm. "Come along. We have to report this to your advocate."

Birdie's advocate, if you wanted to be honest about it. I could see the lines of this particular web—Birdie had wanted the hotel, or maybe the land the hotel occupied, and now she'd found a way to get it. She could see the case go to trial, but Miss Minerva was as sharp as a needle. They'd never win it that way.

"You need an advocate," I said into the astonished murmurs in the room. "You need one now."

"I'm an advocate." A man stood up. "Charles Brown of the Sure Winds. If you'll allow me to consult for you, I can look at these motions immediately."

"You'd better come with me," Minerva said, and she unhooked her cane from the back of her chair. "Serve dessert. This is not going to stop us. We're going to fight back."

But the mood had broken. Zelind and I made our excuses with everyone else and left the hotel, standing on a smoke-scented street.

"That's too strong to be a chimney," Zelind said, and the small crowd around us ventured to the intersection to get a better view of the evening sky.

"There," someone said, and we swiveled our heads to a billowing cloud of black smoke. "Up the hill."

"That's a house fire," Zelind said. "If the wind shifts wrong, the whole block could go up."

"Let's go," I said. "They might need a nurse. Make sure the firehouse down on Eighth Street has sent a wagon. Anyone who wants to help, come on. We've got to keep that from spreading."

The whole family huddled on the lawn, and I wanted to cry. An older man in judicial robes; his younger wife in a long, shimmering gown; a coltish, lanky girl in a lace frock that must have been her Merrymonth festival dress; and identical boys in short pants and long hair all watched the fire that belched through the roof.

Every single one of them was dead. Reddened, blistered skin and black patches smeared their arms and faces. The young wife clung to her daughter's shoulders, holding her back from trying to run inside, though the flames couldn't hurt her any longer.

I moved to speak to them, but Zelind slipped kher arms around me, pulling me back from the lawn and into the street, away from the thick smoke and intense heat. Volunteers sweated over the water pumps, and firefighters sprayed the neighboring houses, trying to keep the blaze from jumping from one roof to another.

The fire blazed on, ferocious and starving. Zelind found the sergeant in charge, dragging me along to his side. "What can we do to help?"

"Pump," the sergeant said. "If you can pump water, all of us can fight the blaze."

"Whose house was this?" I asked. I had to shout to be heard.

"Belonged to Judge Battle," the sergeant said. "All of them are dead in there. Every room's lit up. It's going to come down any moment."

The roof shifted at his words, half of it falling into the house below.

"And there it goes," he said. "Water on!"

Firefighters directed their hoses to the burning house, soaking everything they could. Two more fire wagons showed up, and the emptied ones moved aside to trade places.

The family watched until their home was a smoking, blackened heap. The house leaned backward, pulling away from what had once been a pretty covered porch. I turned to the sergeant and pointed at the family.

"Do you want me to ask them what happened?"

"You can do that?" He pushed his helmet back on his head. "I want to know. It can't be evidence, but they had fire ladders outside the upper windows. They could have escaped."

I nodded and came closer to the family. "Ahoy. Do you know what happened to you?"

The judge turned his head. "They were banging. All the windows and doors, banging all at once. Hammering."

That made no sense. "The windows were banging?" I asked. "Why were they banging?"

"They were hammering," the judge said. "Hammering them shut. We couldn't get out. We shouted at them. They looked in the windows at us. And then the fire in the grate rose to the ceiling. The house burned. We couldn't get out."

People with hammers and nails and the will to do murder, to make the last moments of these poor people horrible and terrifying. "I'm so sorry."

"They were monsters," the judge said. "Who would murder my wife? Who would murder my children? They never did anything to anyone."

He didn't include himself in that protestation of innocence. Judges made enemies every time they handed down a conviction. But who would do such a terrible thing as nail shut the escapes and then burn the house down around his family?

"Mrs. Thorpe," a stranger said.

I beheld a constable in brown tunic and brass buttons. "Constable?"

"Come with me, please."

"If you need to ask the family questions," I said, turning to face Constable . . . Miller, her shiny name tag read. "I know they're not evidence, but if it will help—"

"Come with me, please," Constable Miller repeated. "We want you to answer some questions."

Another figure turned away from a crowd of neighbors, and I recognized Corporal Moore.

"Please come along quietly," Moore said.

I stepped back. "I will not. What are you charging me with?"

"We have the authority to question you, as a person of interest in an investigation."

"Nothing, then. Am I free to go?"

"I could hold you on suspicion. Instead, I ask you to submit to questioning in an investigation."

He took my arm, then, and led me away from Zelind and the crowd. He stopped at a sidecar bicycle. "Please get in."

Fuming, I pedaled back to Central Police. I refused an offer of water, and sat in the interview room's uncomfortable, odd-legged chair.

"Thank you for coming along quietly."

"I won't answer any questions without an advocate present to protect my interests."

"Now, that just makes you look more suspicious," Corporal Moore said. "This is the second arson case we've found you at. It's reasonable to wonder at your connection."

"There is no connection," I said. "Arrest me, if you have the evidence."

Now the corporal's patient expression vanished. "First we find you at the burning of the asylum where witches were held before trial and transportation to the asylums. Now we find you at the burning home of a judge who presided over dozens of trials that convicted witches. I think you have a connection to these fires, and I mean to find out what it is."

I scoffed and crossed my arms over my chest. "What do you think, Corporal? Do you think that I set fire to these places and I murdered Jacob Clarke for—what could I possibly want from these actions?"

"Revenge," Corporal Moore said.

The scent of gin tickled my memory. "I assure you, Corporal. I didn't set these fires. I didn't kill Jacob Clarke. And you can't charge me with these crimes based on what a good story it would make. But if you keep trying to pin me, you're going to let the real criminals escape."

"Oh? And who are the real criminals?"

"I don't know," I said. It wasn't a lie; I only had a guess. "Now either get me an advocate—who will tell you to let me go—or just let me go yourself. I didn't have anything to do with these crimes, but you keep harassing me instead of looking for the real culprit."

He licked his lips and shifted his weight. "I can keep you for a full day."

"Then take me to a holding cell," I said. "It'll be one more item in my civil complaint, is all."

Moore blew a frustrated breath out of his nose. "You're good. But I'm better."

"I hope you are," I said. "Because then you'll stop harassing me and set to finding out who did this."

He had to let me go, but not before he blacked my fingers making impressions of the ridges on the tips. I stood out in the street, three miles from home, and set off down Eighth Street.

When I got to the corner of Eighth and Quimby, I turned my back on the way home and ventured east, headed for Five Corners.

The Rook Saloon's triangular building was the only open establishment in the intersection of five streets in the heart of East Riverside, and tonight it smelled like a bonfire extinguished by cider. I sidestepped gobs of filth nestled in sawdust, taking a careful path between tables where drinkers sprayed laughter and talk.

Conversation faltered when someone caught notice. He scrambled off the tall stool and took off his hat, looking like he'd just been caught lazing about at work. "Auntie."

I searched about for his name and nodded. "Henry. You've recovered well, it seems."

"Yes, Auntie." He lifted one hand and waggled his fingers, twisting his wrist to show how well the break had healed. "It aches when the weather turns, but it's sound."

"Good," I said. "I've come to see Miss Wolf. Is she in?"

Now more people from more tables watched me. I knew most of the people here, as patients from the clinic or from medical examinations in the local jails or strictly by their reputation, but I didn't frequent the Rook. I didn't drink in saloons at all, much less the one that was the roost of criminals and ne'er-do-wells.

Perhaps I should have hesitated before walking straight into Jamille's domain. But I waited politely while they buzzed and whispered and shrugged. Finally, Henry escorted me to a door within the saloon flanked by a pair of gentlemen who hadn't had a drop.

"Wait," one of them said, and disappeared inside. I stood in place, heels together, hands clasped before me, and fought the urge to look behind me for whoever's gaze bored into my back.

Presently, the man came back. "She'll see you. Don't touch anything. Don't talk to anyone."

I nodded, and he led me inside. Gas lamps flickered in the draft, steadying as the door clicked shut behind me.

I entered a room filled with tables of women wrapping coins in paper and tallying the results. The bonfire smell was replaced by cigarettes and perfume, with a thread of unclean water sliding beneath.

You don't talk to counters. You don't touch a counter, or their tally, or anything in that room if you like your face the way it is. I slipped past their curious gazes and headed for the chamber beyond the counting room.

Basil leaned against the wall, smoking a gasper. He winked, and I could smell smoke hanging on him like an accusation. "It's quite a surprise to see you here, Auntie."

Jamille Wolf sat behind a desk that shouldn't have surprised me—she had turned petty crime into a business, and so she had ledgers, and reports, and all the other trappings of a manager. Her pen was silver filigree, matching the ornament on a box of pipe tobacco, open to release the sweet, creamy scent of Miller's Black Cherry. She picked up a fat-bowled pipe and gestured at a chair on the other side of her wide oak desk, where a glass of water perched next to an ashtray. "Basil. Get Auntie a drink."

"I'm fine, Cousin, thank you for the kindness," I said, and Basil leaned against the wall once more.

I ventured across the office, taking the chair before Jamille. Above her head hung a portrait of elder brother Jonathan dressed in the round-cornered collar and striped jacket of a Queens University scholar. It was garlanded with a white ribbon, tied in a bow that resembled a butterfly in flight.

"Cousin? Family business, then. What brings you here, at an hour when you must usually be snug in your bed?"

"I was in the area when Kingston Asylum burned," I said. "And now tonight, I've come back from the fire that killed a judge and his family."

"It did?" Jamille asked, glancing at me over the bowl of her pipe. "What a thing."

"I spoke to him," I continued. "They reported something awful— that people nailed the doors and windows shut, and then set the house ablaze."

Jamille cocked her head. "Really."

"People died at Kingston Asylum too, all to smoke inhalation and the flames. Save one."

"And that one was special?" Jamille asked.

I ignored the mean little smirk on her face. "That last person I mention was the first to die. Shot in the head—probably by the people who came to set the fire."

"What a thing," Jamille repeated. "And why have you come to me with this news?"

"Because I can add two and two," I said. "Because I can draw the line between the asylum that held witches to be examined, and a judge who convicted witches. I am certain that Jonathan was held at Kingston Asylum, but here's what I'm wondering, Miss Jamille. . . ."

Jamille sat perfectly still, the unlit pipe cradled in her hand. She listened to every word without moving so much as a muscle. She stared into my eyes, her mouth just slightly open, the gap from her missing tooth showing. When she finally spoke, it was so quiet I nearly missed it.

"What do you wonder?"

"If I were to visit the archives, would I find that the judge who died tonight was the judge who convicted your brother?"

Basil shifted his weight and took a step toward me. Jamille lifted her hand, and Basil stopped.

"You're telling me this instead of the police," Jamille said.

"I am," I said. "I have no proof. Just an interesting story. But if that story is true, Miss Jamille—these fires are not going to solve anything. They're making things worse. If someone makes the same connection I did, that's a story in the papers accusing us of violence, of being dangerous, that every lie told about witches that put them in asylums for their lives is actually true."

"It's an interesting story, Cousin," Jamille said. "And it is as you said. Just a story. Not proof. Do you know what I think?"

I knew she would deny it. That wasn't why I was here. I'd brought a warning; that was all. But I breathed in the sweet cherry scent of her pipe and the charred wood smell of her murder and listened. "What?"

"I think you should stay away from fires, Auntie. They're dangerous. And coming too close could get you burned."

Her smile set my stomach to leaping. "Basil. Take Auntie home safely. You know where it is, don't you?"

"I do," Basil said. "Come along, Mrs. Thorpe."

FIFTEEN

Election Day

Election Day dawned cool and bright, and I rose to meet it. I fell into bed nineteen hours later, weary to my bones.

I was at the community hall first thing in the morning, frying up breakfast for volunteers. I left after the last dish was washed, toppling into my bed and sleeping like a log.

I had waited for trains to come, for volunteers loaded with boxes full of votes and their tallies to arrive at the Riverside community hall. We worked around reporters, who acted as our scrutineers, asking questions about every step of our process. We added the results to wheeled chalkboards that listed every electoral riding in Aeland, reading the names of Free Democratic candidates at the top of almost every race.

Millions of ballots showered votes on people who had hastily stood up and volunteered to run for their riding in Parliament. I watched the tallies fill slabs of slate. I watched the sealed boxes of returned ballots pile up. These boxes held the true will of the people.

"Lock them up," I said. "And guard them. We need to bring these boxes to the High Tribunal."

"Mrs. Thorpe, has it been your intention to dispute the election in court all along?" John Runson asked, and I wiped paper dust off my face.

"Bringing the ballots to the High Tribunal has always been an option for further action."

"And are you confident of your victory in South Kingston over your challenger?"

I smiled. "You never know what could happen. I'm pleased and humbled by the support Riverside has shown me in the campaign."

My political career was still in the air. Aeland didn't start counting ballots until all ridings had returned. Rumors said Jarom had under a hundred voters in South Kingston–Riverside, but I had a hundred and fifteen voting collectives who had pooled their money and sent a representative to the ballots.

A hundred and fifteen. Jacob won with only eighty. Agitated butterflies twirled in my stomach. The votes would show the seat was mine, and I'd lead the Solidarity Collective from my place in the Lower House.

It hadn't terrified me before. It hadn't felt real before. To calm my trembling hands, I went out to the hall's loading dock and carried ballot boxes with the rest.

We cheered when the millionth vote arrived. We cheered when the first votes from nearby counties came in by train. We cheered to find that, when given a free vote, the people wanted the Free Democracy Party in charge.

We cheered when the last box, transported by sled from the northern settlement of Agnestown, finally made it into the warmth of the community hall. We double-checked our figures. We audited random ballot boxes. We scrutinized, and inspected, and wrote the final figures on every single riding. Only seven ridings voted for their incumbent, and most of those had been in harmony with Jacob's direction anyway.

We had won Aeland's first free election with a mighty, bellowing roar.

The results on the King's election didn't tell nearly the same tale. Runners came in, reporting the results from distant ridings. They all said the same things, the results starting with Red Hawk. The in-country voters had chosen their incumbents, the results spiraling slowly, inevitably toward Kingston.

West Kingston–Halston Park: Incumbent. West Kingston–Wellston Triangle: Incumbent. West Kingston–Central: Incumbent. The elite of Aeland voted in lockstep, and that was no surprise. I waited until the last messenger came in, breathless from running.

I shook my braids off my shoulders. This was it.

She shook her head at the offer of a glass of water and gasped out, "South Kingston–Riverside: Jarom Bay."

The room went up in surprise. "That can't be!" someone shouted.

"We had more votes! This is impossible!"

The runner waved her hands. "Carlotta was scrutinizing the riding. There's something rotten. Thirty votes were declared spoiled ballots and weren't counted. Twenty-three of them were for Robin. Jarom Bay won by two votes. If they hadn't disqualified those votes, you would have won."

The hall exploded with shouts. I shook, so angry I vibrated. Anyone voting for a collective would know better than to spoil a ballot. They were too careful to make that kind of mistake—to have twenty-three of them unclear or defaced was unbelievable.

"Mrs. Thorpe," a reporter asked. "Will you concede to Mr. Bay's victory?"

"Do you believe this is evidence of election tampering?"

"Have you heard of other spoiled ballots in other ridings?"

"Mrs. Thorpe, after the gigantic effort to hold a mock election which your people dominated, are you disappointed to lose in the legitimate election, or did you expect it?"

He had cheated, and I hadn't anticipated it. I should have. But I had been so busy with the free election I hadn't taken much time to think about the seat I had been sure I would win. But the Bays had bribery in their blood, and I had dropped the ball by not telling my scrutineer to expect chicanery.

It stung, losing to a thief. But it proved something to me: I couldn't do two jobs at once.

I turned away from the reporters. I shuffled ballot boxes on top of one of the folding tables near the front of the crowd and clambered to stand on them.

I had written a speech. I tossed it aside as the crowd quieted to hear me.

"You're expecting me to fight these results," I said. "You're expecting me to question the validity of spoiled ballots, to drag the matter into court, to fight for the seat of South Kingston–Riverside, for the right to speak for the largest electoral riding in Aeland and its one hundred and twenty-nine thousand constituents. But that's not what's important."

Confused silence. My supporters glanced at each other. Some of them looked at me, pleading with their expressions. Don't give up. Don't give in, their faces said. Fight this.

I swept my arms wide, taking in the slate chalkboards. "This is what's important. The will of the people. Not the hundred and some votes for a seat in the Lower House. The six million votes from all over the country. This is the will of the true Aeland. This is what our country wants. And I mean to give it to them."

A few murmurs, but I paid them no mind. "If not for tampering, the King's election would have invited me to sit in the Lower House of Parliament, one protesting voice in a small party. But the people have commanded the Free Democracy Party to lead the country and serve their will. And so I say: I am grateful and humbled by your support, and I accept the position of Prime Minister of Aeland as the leader of the Free Democracy Party."

Gasps. My own people gawped at me in utter shock. The journalists leaned closer. "Does this mean—"

"I care not a bit for the King's election. My place is in your service. My heart and my hands belong to Aeland. And so I call upon every member of my party elected by the people to come and serve the people. Do you want us?"

My volunteers cheered. "Yes!"

"Do you call on us?"

"Yes!"

"Then I send this message across Aeland, from the Elected Member of Agnestown to the Elected Member of the Ayersian Archipelago: Come to Kingston. Show up to Government House. We're going to have our first session witnessed by the people whose mandate we obey. For the sake of the people of Aeland, we're going to get to work."

THE MOB THAT WOULD GOVERN, the *Kingston Herald* proclaimed, with a crowd photo of people raising their fists. I studied it, but the picture was cropped to only show an endless sea of people, yellow ribbons on the sleeves of their coats, most of them surplus Service coats the army had produced in anticipation of the Laneeri War before the standard uniform issue kit changed to suit the conditions of the tropics. I couldn't tell where it had actually been taken.

The *Star of Kingston* had a full-body picture of me standing on a ballot box, my expression captured as I spoke. I looked angry. I pointed toward the headline, a single evocative word: UPSTART!

I picked up a copy of the *Herald* and read the article, but Jedrus slid it out of my hands. "Later."

I reached for the paper again. "They're saying I'm grasping for power, using the threat of a violent mob to prop me up—"

Jedrus hid it behind kher back. "And that's nonsense. Put it out of your mind and eat your breakfast."

I followed kher out of the parlor and across the hall. "I'm not hungry."

"You'll blow away in a stiff wind if you don't have some eggs."

Grumbling, I took a seat at the table and poked at goose sausage. "They're making us look like brutes. That's not what I want for the people's government. We're just making our presence known. We're going to talk about what's important to us."

"And you're going to fight to have the election legitimized in court," Jedrus said. "What if the tribunal says yes?"

"What if the sky turned bright purple?"

Zelind entered the dining room with one last platter of sweet toast and sat beside me. "You don't know they'll deny all your points."

"It's a nice thought," I said, cutting my sausage into tiny bites. "I don't know if they want to be responsible for upending all order and tradition. Not yet."

"You have a storage room filled with millions of votes," Zelind said. "But let's do something nice today. You won't have much time for fun when you're prime minister."

"You won't have much time for fun when you're an energy tycoon."

"So how about we go skating again?" Zelind asked, heaping four slices of toast on kher plate. "It'll be fun."

"Unless we get swarmed by photographers."

"Then it'll be an opportunity. How can they demonize skating?"

"They might find a way," I said.

The loud rap of the door knocker made everyone jump, but Amos was off the bench and out of the dining room in a trice.

"Robin, go and see who it is," Aunt Bernie said, and I followed down the hall to find a court clerk with a sealed scroll. A lawsuit?

Then I saw the ribbon. Not red, for criminal charges. Not blue, for a civil case. Purple, signifying a royal order. This was the official word of King Severin. That document must be an order for me to stop calling myself prime minister. He must have hated the idea, to send a royal order so quickly.

"I guess that's for me," I said. "I'm Robin Thorpe."

The clerk twitched the tube out of my reach. "The order is for Zelind Thorpe."

Zelind? And then I realized what it must be. That bastard. That villain! He couldn't just demand Zelind's invention!

The clerk's shoulders went up. "I just deliver them."

"It's not your fault." I hastily fixed my expression to something more neutral. "I'll get kher."

"I'm here," Zelind said. "It's for me? Is there a reply needed?"

"Not at the moment," the clerk said. "I just deliver them. Good morning."

The clerk handed the scrolled paper to Zelind and left, walking to the bicycle parked on the road.

Zelind stared at the tube in kher hands. "Do you want to wager on what it is?"

There was only one thing it could be. "Just open it."

Zelind broke the seal, untied the ribbon, and read. "His Majesty demands that I relinquish my right of invention to the Thorpe turbine within the next three days." Zelind let the paper curl shut. "There's no mention of cash prizes or medals. I guess revoking them is my punishment."

Severin had the power to do this. He was the King, Parliament was out of session, and the only oversight he could have had was the advice of the Chancellor, if he had bothered to consult her.

"I'm sorry," I said. "It shouldn't have come to this. I'm not sure you can fight it in court."

"I'm not going to fight it," Zelind said.

"You have to do something," I said. "There has to be something you can do."

"There is," Zelind said. "Put on your coat. I'll be right back."

Zelind took the stairs two at a time. Khe didn't seem like someone about to admit defeat. I buttoned up my coat and boots, and Zelind came back, bearing the turbine model and a stack of papers.

I pulled Zelind's double-breasted coat off a hanger. "Are you sure you just want to surrender your rights? It's your invention."

"It is," Zelind said, grinning. "But we can't disobey a king, can we? Hold this."

Khe handed over the turbine. It was lighter than I had supposed. "You're plotting something."

"Me?" Zelind said, kher expression innocent. "I'm shocked that you would suggest such a thing."

I couldn't help the smile blooming over my face. This glimpse of Zelind, the mischievous, clever Zelind from our schooldays who used to mix fun and trouble, was sunshine peeking through the clouds.

"What are you planning?"

"The King wants me to surrender the rights to my invention," Zelind said. "So I'm going to relinquish them to the public wealth. We're going to visit every newspaper office in town with copies of the original plans and building instructions, and then anyone can build a turbine, and anyone can go into business building them for others. That's news, isn't it? How to get the lights back on?"

Oh. It was pure Zelind—clever, defiant, and subversive. I laughed. We were courting trouble, but it was too perfect.

"Where to first?"

"Merchant Printers," Zelind said. "We need to leave behind copies for the papers."

The *Riverside Examiner* took the materials and stopped the presses, but the *Herald* and the *Star* offered tea, wheat cookies, and disinterested questions. When I asked for John Runson at the *Star*, he wasn't available.

"They're not going to print it," Zelind said. "Even after I showed them the light."

"The *Examiner* will, at least. They'll just get the scoop, is all."

"I could make more copies. I could send my last copy to *Mechanics and Devices*. They might publish it."

They'd be fools not to, but Zelind continued on kher glum-shouldered way to the palace, waiting in line at the security booth. I didn't know how to cheer kher up and settled for running my hand along kher arm for comfort.

And then it was our turn. "Do you have an appointment?"

Zelind shook kher head. "I just have this order."

The guard slipped on glasses that magnified his eyes and looked over the document King Severin had sent. "You can leave the materials here."

Zelind backed up a step. "I don't think I should do that."

"You've been ordered to," the guard said. "Are you disobeying a royal order?"

"I am taking great pains to make sure that I do not," Zelind said. "I think I'll feel safer if I take this to the Chancellor."

"Do you have an appointment with the Chancellor?" the guard asked, and his blank expression paired with his intent stare unnerved me.

"We don't need one," I said. "The Chancellor is a friend. Good afternoon!"

Zelind clutched kher materials to kher chest. We hurried out of line, walking fast and squinting into the wind.

"I don't like this," Zelind said. "This device is too important to leave to the mercies of a bureaucratic internal mail system."

"You could have surrendered it and let it get lost," I said.

"If the papers had been more keen I probably would have," Zelind said. "But this will turn on the lights and power the coldboxes, and that's more important than being petty."

"You're right," I said. "This way."

We trotted up the steps of Government House and through the corridors that branched to more junior offices before we came to Grace's. A tidily dressed young white woman, buttoned to the neck and ornamented with a hand-painted scarf, looked up from her typing and smiled.

"You must be Robin Thorpe," she said. "Chancellor Hensley has an appointment, but if you'd care to wait?"

"Thank you," I said. "We just need to drop something off."

"If she can't see you, would you care to leave it with me?" the secretary asked.

"That would be fine. I'm sorry, I don't know your name."

The secretary nodded. "It's Onora. I'm Onora Wright."

Zelind cocked kher head. "Any connection to Clan Wright of the Clever Hands?"

"You know them," she said. "I married in three years ago."

Zelind's smile was sad. "I knew Audric Wright. He was in Clarity House."

Dismay blanketed Onora's face. "I'm sorry. I didn't know him."

Behind us, the door opened, and Miles stepped inside. "Robin! Good! I've come to force my sister to eat. You should come too."

"The Chancellor is with the King," Onora said.

Zelind and I glanced at each other. "I'm sorry," Zelind said. "I didn't know."

"He probably won't be long. He just dropped in."

Miles claimed a seat next to the fireplace. "Then we'll wait. What have you got there, Zelind? It looks like a model box. Is that your invention?"

"It is," Zelind said. "I'm surrendering it to the King."

Miles glanced at the door to Grace's office. "Something happened."

"You could say that," Zelind said.

Miles's face went sour. "That's just wonderful."

The door lever sank with a click, and King Severin walked out, dressed in sporting clothes. Safety goggles hung from a rubber cord around his neck. His tweed jacket was quilted at the suede-covered shoulder. He halted, regarding the three of us.

"Is that my turbine?" King Severin asked. "Good of you to bring it so quickly."

"How could I do otherwise, Your Majesty?"

How Zelind managed to say that without a hint of bitterness, I'll never know.

"Take it out," the King said. "I want to see it work."

Zelind lifted the deep lid from the box, displaying the model turbine and lightbulb. Khe presented it to the King and exerted kher power, making the rotor blades spin so fast they blurred. After a moment, the lightbulb glowed.

Severin watched the rotor spin with a delighted smile. "It works. And you brought your design plans, detailing how you made the device?"

"I brought everything," Zelind said. "Including my notarized surrender of my rights of invention to the public wealth."

Severin's mouth dropped open. He stared, completely speechless, closing his mouth, and opening it again. He pointed at Zelind, at the glowing lightbulb shining in kher hands. "Your surrender—what have you done?"

"I demonstrated my model in the offices of Kingston's biggest newspapers and left behind copies of these documents for them to print," Zelind said. "The fastest way to get aether back into the hands of the people is to freely distribute the means to produce and install turbines. I expect local businesses will start building them as fast as they can, and the country's households will have a source of aether powering their homes before long."

"You defied me," Severin said.

"You asked me to surrender my invention to you, Sire. I'm here surrendering it. You—and every other Aelander—can build as many Thorpe turbines as you wish."

"Some households and businesses will still have need of power from the national network," Grace said. "Mx. Thorpe has acted for the sake of the public good—"

"And broken the monopoly on aether in the simplest, fairest way," Miles said. "I'm certain the Grand Duchess will approve."

"I'm sure she will," King Severin said. His mouth twisted. He stared at Zelind for a long, unspeaking moment. "You've forfeited the prize money, you know."

"I accept that," Zelind said. "Where would you like me to take these plans, Sire?"

"I'll take them." Severin held out his hand. "Give them to me."

"The Chancellor's office will acknowledge receipt," Grace said, and Severin's face went red.

"That would be helpful, thank you." Severin took the plans and marched out of Grace's office.

We watched the door swing closed. We didn't utter a word for one breath, then two, until Grace let out a sigh.

"Well," Zelind said. "Huzzah for me; I've enraged a king."

Tristan nodded. "Grace, does Severin carry grudges?"

"Over something this big? Yes." Grace frowned at Zelind. "Are you sure you want this fight?"

"I'm sure I'm the only one who can fight it," Zelind said. "I can't let him use my turbine the way he used me, or any of my friends."

"All right. I'll try to talk him down, for your sake." Grace turned to her brother. "I imagine you came to chide me into eating lunch, even though it's long past."

"Did you eat lunch?"

Grace smiled. "No."

"Then let's all go back to the suite," Miles said. "Besides, Robin had me looking into something for her. I have some interesting information as a result."

"What? About the—" I went silent. "I'd like to know what you found. Are you hungry, Zelind?"

"I'm always hungry," Zelind said. "And curious."

"I'm curious too," Grace said. "Onora, please take messages from anyone who calls on me. I don't know when I'll be back."

SIXTEEN

Yellow Ribbons

Lunch was simple fare—creamy mushroom soup and sandwiches we had to make ourselves. We each had two before retiring to the sitting room.

Miles sat tucked under Tristan's arm as we shared short glasses of spirits, warmed and mixed with syrup and bitters. "There. I have ensured that my sister won't fall down from exhaustion because she never remembers that there's such a thing as mealtimes."

"Thank you, Miles. Did you ever think I skip lunch just so I can spend an hour in your company?"

"Is that true?"

Grace smiled against the rim of her glass. "I'm going to miss having you at the palace."

Miles smiled back. "I'll have to interrupt you with a basket. But I had to tell Robin about my progress in investigating Jacob's murderer."

"Yes. I've been politely dying for the last hour," I said. "Did you find a woman like the one we were talking about earlier?"

Miles leaned away from Tristan and walked across the sitting room to a desk. "I found five women who held the rank of corporal-specialist currently residing here in Kingston."

"Five? That many?"

"Just in Kingston," Miles said. "There's more who went in-country. Here."

Miles returned with files. Each one had a grainy photograph of a woman clipped to the front.

"How'd you get those?"

"I took photos of their Service portraits." He passed one to me, and I inspected a round-faced woman with a tiny smile as she looked at the camera. Did murderers smile?

"This is Millicent Roebuck. She was an archery champion in school, and volunteered for Service in exchange for paid tuition, where she exhibited her abilities with long-range shooting."

"She served in the war?"

"She was discharged a month before Stanley declared war, and she declined to return to the Service. She's going to have a baby any day now, but it's touch and go. She's been on bedrest for the last month."

"Poor woman. And not our woman."

"I don't think so, no." Miles produced another grainy photograph of a woman who kept up the constant battle to stay blond. "This is Caitrin Scholar. She's a housewife, also pregnant, and she's in a string quintet. She plays cello, violin, and viola."

"Sniper rifle would fit in a cello case," Zelind noted, and passed the photo to Grace.

"It would. I haven't gotten close enough to her to know if she has an alibi for the murder."

I nodded. "Who's this next one?"

"Probably not one of our suspects," Miles said. "Have a look."

I picked up the photograph. I recognized her immediately, though her gaze looked at something above the camera and her mass of thick braids was pulled back from her face. "Isn't that Amelia Summer? From the battle fatigue units at Beauregard?"

"She is, and she's still there," Miles said. "I don't think she's recovering swiftly."

"Easy enough to find out if she took out a pass."

"Indeed. These last two are interesting. This is Evelyn Plemmons. She's a brand-new constable on patrol in Riverside—but she's out of East Hillside, not Central."

Evelyn stared at the camera as if she wanted to fight it. She had a long chin and a thin mouth, and wisps of pale hair slipped free of the style that was supposed to keep her hair back.

"I want to know everything you can find out about her. Who's the last one?"

"Laura Debenham."

"Laura?" Grace sat up. "What about her?"

Miles lifted the photograph. "You know her? I was about to say that she's a royal guard."

"She's one of Severin's bodyguards. He's always preferred women for the job."

Laura Debenham was perfectly composed in her recruit file picture. She didn't smile. She didn't frown. Dark hair, an oval face possessed of that peculiar symmetry that made it pretty.

I tapped the corner of the photo. "Does he usually pick pretty ones?"

Grace nodded. "Usually."

"So she's got a demanding job that keeps her busy," I said. "So. Caitrin Scholar or Evelyn Plemmons, with Laura Debenham as the outside possibility."

"I checked the duty roster at the palace. Miss Debenham was on shift with the King when Jacob was murdered. The report had them in the basement gun range—Severin's an excellent shot himself, you know."

"I had heard that." I spread the photos out, pushing Millicent and Amelia off to the side, and then, after a moment, I pushed Laura's photograph aside too.

Had I ever seen Caitrin or Evelyn? Caitrin didn't live in Riverside, but her address was inside Albert Jessup's electoral riding. Evelyn lived in the neighborhood she policed, however, and her address wasn't that far from Clarence Jones Memorial. Or the stately, luxurious house where the Bays lived.

"Can you connect either of these two to Albert Jessup?" I asked. "He's our most likely enemy. He has the reason to want Jacob dead—personally and professionally—and he certainly has the money to pay an assassin."

"But how would he find one?" Miles asked. "Assassins don't advertise in the paper, do they? What sort of access do you think he has to the criminal underground?"

I huffed. "I don't know who Albert Jessup knows. He could have connections."

"This is as far as I've gotten," Miles said. "Where do you want to take this?"

"I don't know," I said. "I don't want to accuse anyone until I'm certain."

"This is where I come in," Grace said. "I can do background on Albert Jessup. Do you mind if I scare him a little?"

"What are you going to do?"

"Audit his office finances," Grace said. "Looking specifically for peculiarities. I'll send in the accountants especially noted for finding fraud and laundered money. And I won't be quiet about it."

"Grace, you're a brick," Miles said. "That would help tremendously."

Grace's efforts might turn up a payment no one could explain. But what if it found regular contributions, smaller consistent payments? Albert could be funding whoever was sharing Solidarity's secrets.

If Albert had hired an assassin, it wasn't that much of a stretch to believe that he was responsible for the theoretical spy in the committee. We had a meeting in two days. I would find out if Tristan was correct, or if I was right to trust my people.

The Riverside Community Clinic held space in the basement of the community hall. I snuck in the back way, unseen, or else people would think I was there to examine patients and lend a hand. Someone had neglected the dishes in the tiny break room, and I washed cups until Theresa could smuggle me into the conference room for the meeting. But it was Tupper Bell who walked into the little kitchen, and my back crawled as I smiled at him.

"Theresa asked me to come and fetch you," Tupper said. "I was hoping you'd have a minute."

"For you, I have two," I said, every nerve on alert. "What can I do?"

Tupper glanced behind him and then shut the door, leaning against it. "Have you heard anything about leads in Jacob's murder? Anything at all?"

Would he be that bold? Did Albert know I was seeking out suspects, somehow? "I'm the best lead the police have right now."

Tupper scoffed. "You?"

"They seem to think I was jealous of Jacob's prominence in the movement."

"Lazy fools," Tupper muttered. "But there's nothing else?"

"Nothing. The police aren't doing a blessed thing."

"And a murderer is walking around free. Maybe we should conduct our own investigation. Go to the papers."

My tongue went dry. I couldn't tell him not to do that. I had to tell him something. "I have someone making some discreet inquiries."

"Discreet?" Tupper looked puzzled. "Don't you think you should be more vocal about it? They suspect you."

"All right," I sighed. "I have someone doing some research into how one goes about obtaining a long-range sniper rifle as a private citizen, but it hasn't turned up any leads yet."

"You'd better find something fast," Tupper said. "That trail's getting colder every minute."

I kept my shoulders square, and I held back the urge to sigh. I wasn't any good at setting a trap for a spy, but Tupper had accepted my word. It was a plausible lie, and if repeated, wouldn't lead to what we did know.

"We'd better get to the meeting before anyone wonders what's keeping us."

Tupper led the way to the meeting room, and I took a seat in one of the scarred but still sturdy rolling chairs around the battered walnut table.

Judita Linton slipped a ribbon bookmark into a hand-sized volume I assumed was a popular novel. "Good morning, Robin. I haven't seen you since Jacob's funeral. How are you?"

So friendly, but was she fishing for more information? If I took Tristan's word for it, one of these people who had directed the path of the Solidarity movement was a spy.

Which one was it? Tupper Bell? Judita Linton? Dr. Smith? Agnes Gable? Gabrielle Meadows? Preston Grimes? These were my friends. These people were pillars of the movement. The foundation of the community. How could it be? I trusted every one of these people. I liked them. And one of them was supposed to be reporting our decisions to an enemy like Albert Jessup?

"I'm sorry I'm late." I took a seat next to the tiny windows set high on the wall. Heat from the radiator warmed my back, but I kept on a pair of fingerless gloves against the chilly room.

"I'm glad you're here." Preston poured water into a glass made cloudy with scratches from years of scrubbing. "At last."

"She couldn't come in through the front door." Theresa took a seat near the black slate chalkboard and put on her glasses. "But that reminds me. Can you take time in your schedule to do a shift at the clinic? The papers could show you as dedicated to the care of your community."

"That's a fine idea," Preston said. "When do you think you'll be able to do it?"

"I don't know," I said. "But I could probably organize something after the Free Parliament goes into session. And I've been trying to figure out where to have those sessions when we're not on display for the press."

"Are you sure you want to have your meetings in the square in front of Government House?" Judita asked. "Maybe we should book Kingston Arena for the next one."

"We'll need to raise more money for a meeting space." I found my pen and uncapped it, notepad in hand. "I think we could keep doing it where the public are welcome to attend, but the weather could turn bad any day. We need an indoor location."

"We're wasting time with this," Agnes declared. "Didn't you all read the papers?" She unfolded a copy of the *Riverside Examiner*'s special pull-out section detailing Zelind's turbine, including the instructions on how to make one. "This is a breakthrough. An incredible break-through! Though I don't know why you didn't tell the bigger papers."

"We did," I said. "We gave them everything the *Examiner* decided to print."

"Huh," Agnes said. "Didn't they believe you?"

"They seemed to." I shrugged. "But only the *Examiner* ran it."

Both the *Herald* and the *Star* had been properly impressed by Ze-lind's model. It should have been front page news. But the *Herald* ran a story introducing the Elected Members of Severin Mountrose's election, and the *Sun* had concentrated on the King promising to get the network back up and running as soon as possible, with a flatter-ing picture of King Severin posing by a glowing lamp. The Thorpe turbine wasn't mentioned in the article.

"It's serious," Agnes said. "Your Zelind has invented a means of producing aether, and the king is claiming to have a solution at the same time."

"His solution is Zelind's turbine," I said.

"But why didn't Zelind enter to win the contest?" Tupper asked. "Why did khe give the design away for free?"

My tongue turned to lead. I picked up the water pitcher and poured cold water into a glass. What could I tell them? Normally I would have told them everything. I wouldn't have thought twice to tell them the whole story. But if Tristan was right, somebody here couldn't be trusted.

"That's a long story," I said.

"You have time to tell it," Judita said. "I believe that Zelind's design works. But what I can't understand is why khe turned down two hundred and fifty thousand marks."

Anything I said was going to leave this room. Anything I told the committee would go straight to Albert Jessup's ears. I couldn't refuse to tell them. That would lead to questions. If we had a spy, I couldn't let on that I knew.

But they were going to report everything said in the meeting, including my "surprise" day at the clinic. All of our information was compromised. Tupper might be the spy, but he might not. Same with Preston, though I winced at the thought. And while Albert would be looking for something damaging, the only person who looked bad in this story was the King.

"The contest had unacceptable conditions," I said. "They required the inventor to give up their right of invention."

"That's so unfair," Gaby said.

"Zelind surrendered kher rights when khe released it to the public wealth," Judita said. "There has to be more to it than that."

"I can guess the rest," Tupper said. "The King wanted to take whatever generator worked and repower the network. And Aeland Power and Lights, which is not a Crown corporation but a private one, would go right back to shoveling in money. Am I right?"

The committee turned to me. "Is he right?"

"That's what we think too," I said. There. It was out. "The King tried to sweeten the pot by doubling the reward and adding a royalty payment, but when Zelind didn't immediately agree, he sent round an order to surrender the turbine."

How could Albert make hay with that information? How would knowing the truth about the King's desperation and greed help him or damage us? It couldn't.

Preston set down his water glass on a colorful crocheted coaster. "And Zelind, undaunted, gave the invention to the people."

"Zelind wants to design a turbine kit a homeowner can mount on the roof," I said. "That way no one is forced to pay APL for their aether, or they can subsidize their network costs with a turbine of their own."

"You don't have the capital for that," Preston said. "And the movement is squashed flat after financing the election. Where are you going to find that kind of money?"

Now this. This Albert could use. He could even convince his family to start up the same idea himself. He had the capital, the connections. What I said next could only help him.

Never lie when the truth will do. But the truth wouldn't do, not at all.

"We have a plan," I said. "An opportunity for small investors and large. Zelind wants the manufacturing process to make jobs, but khe wants everyone to own a share of the business operations."

"But if that doesn't work, the King wins," Gaby said. "Without the money to start a business, we're stuck paying whatever the monopoly decides to charge."

"I can't say more at this time. It's Zelind's business, not mine— but when khe's ready to share, we will announce everything."

And maybe this wasn't a lie so much as it was anticipating the truth. If we could convince enough people to chip in, or order a turbine in advance, maybe Zelind's dream would get off the ground. But if Tristan was right, someone in this room would pass it on.

It made me sick. But I stayed behind as the committee left the basement clinic. I hid in the break room and washed teacups until the kitchen door opened again, and Preston Grimes entered, bearing a stack of small plates.

"You don't have to do that."

"I don't mind."

"I wanted to talk to you, anyway," Preston said. "I'm not sure we're getting anywhere on Jacob's murderer. There's been nothing about it in the papers, and the incuriosity bothers me."

A bowl slid from my grasp and landed in the water with a splash. Was this a coincidence? It could have been. Did I have more than one spy in my midst, then, both of them fishing for the same information?

My mind buzzed with anxiety. "What would be a good reason for the police not to investigate a high-profile murder like Jacob's?"

"They could be holding back information because they don't want to scare their best suspect into leaving town. The trains are running now."

"Could be the killer already left town."

"Do you know what I think?" Preston asked, but he didn't wait for my response. "The killer was obviously a sharpshooter. There are three tenements directly across from the stage. How hard could it have been to get up on the roof?"

I nodded. "That's probably how it happened. But we're stuck. Albert Jessup wasn't standing on that roof, but he probably hired the assassin. But without access to him, we can't prove it."

"The people who live in those buildings are witnesses. We should ask them if they saw anyone suspicious. Why haven't you done that?" Preston shook his finger at me. "I have a friend in the police. We could find out if anyone with ties to criminal organizations trained as a sniper in the army."

Our own guesses, echoed back to me. "Preston," I said. "That's either a long leap or it's brilliant."

But I relaxed a little. Preston wasn't fishing for information. He was trying to push me into doing the detective work he'd guessed at. "Do you want me to look into it?"

"Yes," Preston said. "It's the only thing that makes sense."

"Thank you," I said. "Where is your friend in the police stationed?"

"Halston Circle," Preston said.

"Please keep me updated."

Preston flashed me one of his rare smiles before he left the stack of plates for me to wash and left.

I cleaned until everyone had been gone ten minutes, and then I quietly let myself out the back way and walked around the hall, headed toward Water Street.

But when I turned the corner, my world narrowed down to the yellow strand of ribbon tied to the handle of the community hall's mailbox. I held my breath as I came closer, trying not to appear overly concerned, and glanced behind me as I walked past that bit of sunny betrayal on the handle.

The clockface chalked on the side called for a meeting at two o'clock.

Somebody in the steering committee had something to tell.

SEVENTEEN

The Tyranny of Paper

I was nearly late meeting Zelind and Miss Minerva for tea. A cat greeted me inside the Princess Mary Hotel, moving to rub herself on my legs and purr. I petted her striped back and spotted a gray cat perched atop a shelf full of canned preserves. A third slinked out from behind a stack of crates, his tail curled like a question mark as he strutted away.

The first cat paid them no mind, meowing every time I tried to stand up straight.

"Oh, fine," I muttered, and bent. The cat leapt into my arms, rubbing her furry jowl against mine.

It was harder to worry with a cat's purring affection lavished on you. My frantic vision of first Tupper, then Judita, then every member of the steering committee tying that ribbon onto the mailbox . . . Why hadn't I taken the risk and gone in the front? I would have seen it. And then—

What good would knowing have done? I was trapped, no matter what. I had to forget about that and figure out who was spying. Which of them had betrayed us all. Which of them had let slip the information that put Jacob in a sniper's crosshairs.

The cat butted her head against my cheek and meowed.

"I know. I'm supposed to pet you. That's my only job in the whole world." But the cat's fur was soft, her skin thrumming with her satisfied purr, and her fishy-smelling breath brought me back to the Princess Mary. Minerva wasn't in her apartment. The kitchen was dark and empty. Voices rose and fell, hollowed out by the vaulted roof in the lobby.

I'd stumbled in on a meeting, and from the mood of the voices floating down the hall, it wasn't a happy one. Someone cried out, "They can't do this to us!" and I hurried my way past another tawny striped cat, this one dining on a mangled little mouse.

Clan Cage gathered around Minerva, who held pink sheets of paper in her hands. Pink paper could be personal correspondence, but the shadow of block letters at the top spoke of something official.

"What's happening?" I asked, and Jean-Marie burst out crying.

Zelind hugged her, patting her shoulder, and said, "The newest move in Nolene's battle, I'm afraid. Listen," khe said, talking to everyone. "We have to do everything we can to improve the place. That means we have to clean the whole building, top to bottom. Not a speck of dust. We have to inspect all the gas fittings, test the plumbing, assess the ceilings and walls and floors. We only have a week before they come, so we can't waste any time."

"A week before who comes?" I asked.

Minerva stretched out her hand to give me the notices.

Health and safety inspectors were going to inspect the Princess Mary for hazards and determine whether the structure was safe for habitation. I pored over the documents, having practice with forms and records from working at Beauregard so long, and looked up.

"Under line 8, reason for inspection, they all list 22a, and according to this, reason 22a is citizen complaint. You're being sandbagged."

"You understand all this stuff," Zelind said. "How can we defend ourselves?"

"The only way is counter-inspections, so you can appeal the decision brought down by the city inspectors," I said. "But if the city inspectors declare the building uninhabitable, you have to vacate while the appeal is happening."

Cora cried, and Emma hurried the infant away, half in tears herself.

"So we have to get the building up to code in a week." Zelind swiped one hand across kher brow, rubbing it as if it ached. "How are we going to do that?"

"We ask for help," I said. "Every one of you come from clans who have someone who can help do repairs."

"Honestly the building's in pretty good shape," Zelind said. "I've been around construction and renovation sites. It doesn't need that much."

All around Zelind, the clan relaxed. But the cat pushed away from me, thumping to the floor and wandering off. The warmth from the cat's furry body faded in the cool air.

I couldn't not tell them my suspicions. I couldn't leave them unprepared. I cleared my throat, and fifty pairs of eyes gazed at me. "It might not be that easy."

Jean-Marie turned her tear-spattered face toward me. "Why? Why can't we just fix it and pass the inspection?"

I gave the pages back to Minerva. "A citizen complaint shouldn't be enough to set this process in motion so quickly, but the form has a line for number of occupants, and it says approximately one hundred. That means the complaint is recent. Which means—"

"Birdie," Zelind said. "She made the complaint—and she bribed someone to push the paperwork through."

I nodded. "That's what I think. And she'll bribe them to declare the building unsafe. You have the right to appeal—but the damage will already be done."

All around me were angry faces, tearful faces. Clenched fists. Arms wrapped around skinny ribs, trying to protect their hearts. But I hadn't told them what I worried about the most, and I took a deep breath before handing out more doom.

"I think they could use the inspection against Miss Minerva in her competency hearing, as proof she can't manage her household independently," I said. "It's all a trap."

"It's so like Birdie," Zelind said. "Never defeat an opponent when crushing them utterly will do."

"How do you know Birdie?" Minerva asked. "You seem to know her quite well."

Zelind sighed. "She's my mother."

"And that's how you know so much about building," Minerva said. "You're a Bay."

"I was," Zelind said. "I married out."

"But you could talk to her," Jean-Marie said.

"We don't speak anymore," Zelind said.

"But I saw her at the train station. She came to claim you. She wanted to take you home. You turned away from her."

"Jean-Marie—"

"No." Jean-Marie lurched out of Zelind's arms. "You can fix this. I know you can. She'll listen to you. Just please make her stop this. Don't let her take our home."

Zelind hugged kher arms around kherself. "But I know what she wants."

"Then give it to her!" Jean-Marie cried. "Give her anything she wants! Don't let her take our home away! You're the only one who can save us!"

Zelind's face crumpled. Khe lowered her head, squeezing tight. "Please don't ask me to. Please. I'll fix everything. I'll stay, and I'll fix everything, and they won't take the Princess Mary away."

"They will!" Jean-Marie cried. "You know they will! And I won't ever forgive you, ever!"

"Jean-Marie!" I shouted. "How can you say such a thing?"

"Because it's the truth," Jean-Marie shouted back. "Zelind can fix this, and khe won't! The whole clan needs this, and khe won't do it!"

"You don't know what you're asking," I said.

"I do! I'm asking for my home! For all of us to have somewhere we're safe and we belong, only kher mother is trying to take it away and khe won't stop her!"

"I can't," Zelind whispered. A tear dripped off kher nose. "Please, I can't."

"Get out of here! Get out!" Jean-Marie shoved Zelind toward the door. "If you won't help us, then leave!"

I pushed her away from Zelind. Jean-Marie stumbled. I grabbed Zelind around the waist and steered kher away, guiding kher around the cats and the crates and out into the street, where the cold air froze kher tears.

Zelind went quiet and miserable all the way home, but khe wouldn't let me go. We huddled together through the streets, faces half-frozen from the wind off the river, silent except for the crush and squeak of our boot soles on the snow. Zelind's misery radiated off kher, and I was caught inside its aura.

Clan Cage had no bigger supporter than Zelind. Khe had helped them revive the hotel, taking it from an empire of cobwebs to a haven. Khe had brought in the colony of cats the clan had bribed with promises of meat and warmth in exchange for mousing and affection. And Jean-Marie spared no thought for any of that when she demanded even more of kher.

That wasn't fair. Jean-Marie was, for all her initiative, still a child. She had been through unimaginable horror. Clan Thorpe had never been her home. I had watched her wincing politeness, the hesitance of a guest who was trying their best not to impose. She never quite lost the fear of living through the hospitality of strangers.

Zelind let go of me once we were inside. Khe ignored Bernice's call to step into the parlor and climbed the stairs, leaving me to the tender curiosities of the clan.

"What's the matter with kher?"

"Bad news," I said. "The Princess Mary Hotel is undergoing a safety inspection, and we're pretty sure Birdie Bay and her bribe money is behind it."

Bernice looked up from her knitted cables. "That woman. Her parents spoiled her, and now she thinks that the world only exists to give her what she wants. Go on up; we won't keep you."

I nodded to Bernice and ran up the stairs, the pleated hem of my skirt caught in one hand, and tiptoed into our rooms.

Zelind wasn't in the chair by the window. A splash of water and the running faucet sounded behind the closed door of my tiny bath chamber, and I scooted into the narrow channel between my bed and the cot Zelind slept in. I sat on the edge of my bed and listened until the water drained and the taps fell silent.

The door lever slid open. The door creaked. Zelind sidled between cot and bed and sat beside me.

"I don't want to talk," khe said. "I don't want to discuss options. There are no options."

I had already thought of one. Between us, we could come up with three more. There was a way to solve this. But I leaned against kher, and khe folded kher arms around me and rolled us up onto the bed.

"Just . . . let me be right here," khe said. "Let me stay here. Let me stay."

Here, in the cedarwood-and-orchid scent of kher perfume,

mingling with the sheep-lanolin smell of kher sweater. I found a bump along one of its mended patches near the elbow, and ran my finger over the seam, again, again. Zelind's arm draped over my waist, elbow crooked so kher arm pressed against my back.

We hadn't moved the throw pillows, and so stiff cotton knotted into lace pressed against my cheek. My braids scattered everywhere, and Zelind laid kher cheek on them to breathe in the smell of moss sap and palm butter, roses and rosemary.

We cuddled closer, pressed our foreheads together, and fell into breathing in the same rhythm. My idea danced impatiently in my head, but I kept my tongue still. Zelind didn't need my ideas. Zelind needed the calm anchor that khe usually was for me, the steadying breath and the consistent hereness of touch. Khe needed comfort. Safety.

So I kept silent and let us be. I ignored my itchy nose. I ignored the urge to shift my legs, to flex my ankles. I was what Zelind needed, until khe finally pulled me closer, wiry strong arms wound tight around my ribs.

"You have an idea," Zelind said. "You thought of a compromise."

"She wants you back in her life," I said. "That's what you have to offer her in exchange for the Princess Mary."

Zelind sighed. "I know."

"So she can have some of what she wants," I said. "Promise her you'll visit her regularly. Once a week, for dinner."

Zelind shook kher head. "She won't—"

"And make her feel like she's needed. Ask her for help. Let her advise you on the turbine business—"

"These things would work if my mother was reasonable," Zelind said. "But she'll never settle for a finger when she wants the whole arm."

"Then turn it around on her," I said. "Tell her if she doesn't leave the Princess Mary alone, you will never see her. Not even if she's dying. Threaten her."

Zelind smiled at me, and a needle pierced my heart.

"I love the hotel," khe said. "She's so grand. Her walls are nine inches thick. Her bones are made of steel. That's why she's so tall for her age—every scrap of the best building skills of the time went into her, and every last detail is as thoughtful as it is beautiful."

The smile faded. "And Mother will bash it to the ground so she can build condominiums. I have to stop her. Not just for the clan, but for the grand dame herself—"

"Wait," I said. "That's it."

"What?"

I propped myself up on one elbow. "The Princess Mary. She's historically unique, isn't she?"

"Yes."

"The last of her kind, even?"

"She was one of a kind when they built her."

I squeezed Zelind's arm. "That's how you save her. She's a heritage property of social and historical significance. If Birdie thinks she can knock down a monument, she's going to have to think again."

"She'll be furious. I can hardly wait to see her face."

"You might have to be more politic than that," I said. "Tell her that you'll have dinner with her once a week—and if she disagrees, then we'll wrap the Princess Mary in so much red tape she'll never get her hands on the property. The carrot and the stick. Zel. This will work."

"It might," Zelind said. "I'll choke on every bite, but I will eat dinner with that woman if it will keep the Princess Mary safe."

"We'll start the petition tomorrow," I said. "And you have to write to your mother."

"That's tomorrow," Zelind said. "For right now, I just want to stay right here. With you. Can we stay like this?"

I curled back into kher arms. "For as long as you like."

EIGHTEEN

The First Day in Session

We slept tangled together on the narrow bed until morning came.

I hadn't laid out my clothes the night before, and so I sorted through a closet of decisions before we ventured downstairs to a hearty breakfast. Not long after, we climbed Main Street and came upon the crowd of people waiting in front of Government House. Yellow ribbons fluttered from sleeves, and the uniform gray of Service coats made the people who had come to see the first meeting of the Free Government look like an army. They clapped mittened hands, jostled and laughed, and kept their assembly in a wide horseshoe around the citizens in velvet-collared coats and shiny shoes.

They watched me climb the wide, shallow steps to join them. I counted thirty-five Elected Members on the steps—everyone from Kingston, and a handful from the ridings closest to town. Beyond them stood a dozen people in scarlet tunics and capes. The royal guard blocked the way inside and watched us, alert to any wrongdoing. Cordoned off to one side were the reporters, shoving their way forward to get pictures and a better chance at hearing the proceedings. Everyone had come to see history done, and it made my palms go damp inside the soft lining of my gray leather gloves.

I smoothed my hands along the front of my borrowed short cloak and turned to the Elected Members. "Thank you all for coming."

I went through the gathering shaking hands with each one. I

repeated their names, spoke briefly with locals I recognized, and then turned back to our spectators.

"Thank you—" My own amplified voice startled me. I looked around for the source, and saw Windweavers in the front row. I nodded my thanks to them and tried again. "Thank you for coming today."

Applause rained down on me. The people curious enough to come to the first meeting had bundled up against cold weather. They brought so much hot tea and cider that the scent of it wafted on the air among the cheers.

"I promised you a government that works for you, the people. Here we are on day one, ready to hear you. More are coming into town on the trains, but they can catch up when they get here."

Some laughter.

"What I'm going to ask you to do is write notes. Jot down the things that matter to you most, and if you see your Elected Member here, give them your notes. If you don't, then give them to me. I'll take care of them."

People had to borrow pens and paper from each other, but the first people bearing notes climbed the stairs and gave them to their members. I tilted my face to the puffball-clouded sky and let out a deep breath. This was going well. We'd meet for an hour, and I already guessed the first order of business.

The Elected Members read through their notes, sorting them like a hand of cards. They spoke to the people who brought them notes, thanking them for their votes. *Do you see this?* I wondered, reaching inside for Jacob. *Can you see what we've done?*

Inside me, something warm stirred.

I caught my breath. *Jacob?*

But no other sensations rose. It might have been nothing.

I turned to my notes and read them. *We need raises,* a great many of them said. *We need aether back fast,* said even more. *Start a turbine factory and put us to work.* I sorted through requests for banks to lessen their account fees. I had a dozen requests that Jessup Family Foods be forced to improve working conditions. A few expressed concerns that landlords were deliberately neglecting their buildings and raising rents too fast, but there was nowhere else to move. All around

me, the people settled into the business of directing the aim of the
Free Government, and we were going to fight for them.

While I read through the notes, spots of red caught my eye. More
guards from the palace ventured outside, ringing the crowd with
their presence. People watched them, murmuring to each other, and
unease rippled through the crowd.

That could lead to trouble. I had to settle them, and the guards.
There would be no trouble today.

"I'd like to welcome the brave members of the Kingsguard to our
meeting," I called, and my amplified voice carried over the crowd.
"This is your government too, citizens. If you have a moment, I'd like
to invite you to write a note about the issues that concern you the
most as Aelanders."

None of them moved to accept the paper and pencils on offer.
They stood still, watching the crowd for trouble, or anything they
could call trouble.

"I'm sorry your duties exclude you from participating," I called. "But
when you're at home, I encourage you to write to your Elected Member,
in privacy, and tell them what they can do to help you and your family."

I clapped my hands, and the leather palms of my knitted gloves
thumped together. The other members took up the flattery, and the
crowd echoed us, politely.

Friendly gesture completed. We were a peaceful crowd, for now.

"This meeting will now begin. I call upon Rodney White-Harris,
Elected Member of East Kingston–Birdland. What have your constituents stated is the most important problem in their lives?"

Rodney, a lanky young white man whose ears stood out from
his soldier-short red hair, stepped forward and consulted his notes.
"They want to know more about the designs for a wind-powered
turbine for aether, ma'am. They want to know when the turbine's
coming, how they can help build them and get them up on the roofs
where they're needed."

A new clump of people joined the crowd, snow goggles shielding
their eyes—Greystars. I watched them spread out among the spectators, chatting with their neighbors.

"Same as mine," another Elected Member said. "They talk about
needing jobs and better pay, but everyone's agog over this wind

contraction. They want it as fast as they can get it. What do we need to do to get this moving?"

Nearly every Elected Member said the same thing—if aether wasn't at the top of their people's concerns, then it was a close second. I listened to them all and nodded. Below, the crowd listened, drawing closer to hear what their leaders would decide. A Greystar lifted one hand, two fingers spread out in a "V." A signal I knew from my days in Beauregard Veterans', it meant "all clear."

Why were they signaling to each other? They were dispersed in the crowd, no two of them standing together, and they were up to something.

"It's clear that the lights are our top priority," I said. "The plans explain how the turbines work, but we haven't the means to manufacture them. That resource would come from the Crown. Do we write a petition to present to the Chancellor on behalf of the people? Yea or nay."

"Yea," the Elected Members declared in one voice, and the audience across from us joined in.

"Then let's start planning our proposal now—"

The doors of Government House burst open, and red-coated guards poured outside bearing truncheons and copper-lined manacles.

"You are trespassing," one guard, in the braid and white wig of an officer, bellowed. "Disperse at once. We insist that you disperse at once."

But guards surrounded us. Anyone who approached first would be taken away and arrested. How could they expect obedience, when obeying was such an obvious trap?

I cleared my throat and pointed at the end of the square. "Clear that exit of guards and we'll go," I called. "We don't want trouble."

"Noncompliance will be met with stronger tactics," the officer called out, and I huffed.

"I just said we'd cooperate. Clear your people from that exit and we will leave in an orderly fashion."

"We order you to disperse and leave immediately."

"You're blocking the way, you wooden-headed gumboot!" one of the spectators shouted, brandishing a pair of clenched fists. "Get out of the way! Get out of the way!"

The others took it up. "Get out of the way!"

Greystars in the crowd raised their fists, but the signal was soon lost as others took up the gesture, still chanting at the guards. This situation was three steps past trouble.

The guards who had surrounded the crowd backed up. Beside me, an Elected Member sighed in relief.

"They're moving back," she said. "They're letting us leave."

But trouble crept up my back on a hundred tiny feet. Only the officer stood his ground in front of the crowd. He lifted a hand, and the guards reached into carrying bags and pulled out brown rubber masks.

My heart stopped. Gas masks. Those were army-issued gas masks. Two guards in red coats and rubber masks that made them look like insects dashed forward, carrying canisters.

They pulled the tabs and threw them into the crowd, the canisters' flight made wobbly by smoke ejecting from one end.

"Tear gas!" someone cried. "Run!"

The smoke billowed up. People shouted, running every which way to escape. A man howled in pain and fell to his knees, gasping for breath in the smoke.

My eyes stung. I covered my face with the silk scarf I had tied around my neck, but it wasn't enough. I shut my eyes, but it didn't help the stinging, the tears trying to wash the gas away. I choked on my own saliva.

We breathed fire. My skin burned where the gas touched it.

Coughing, choking people fumbled their way through the crowd, dragging each other outside the gas clouds to fresh air. People screamed as they tried to soothe their distress with handfuls of snow, warning others against that idea.

My throat was too tight to get words out. I squeezed my eyes tight again, but the pain didn't go away, and the tracks of tears down my cheeks burned as if they were boiling.

Around me, people stumbled around, unable to see, sobbing in pain.

"We need water," I tried again. "Soap and water, to wash it off. We—"

I coughed, and tears streamed from my eyes. They gassed us. Citizens! They used weapons of war on us, like we were the enemy, and I couldn't do anything but cough and weep.

How could they do this to us?

Rodney hustled me down the steps, into the middle of the chaos. He ducked through the crowd, his hand tight on mine as he sought a way through—but where was safety? We were surrounded by guards in gas masks, waiting to round us up.

My face still stung, but I had cried enough tears to see more than just blurry shapes. Red smudges mixed with the gray as the guards waded into the near-helpless crowd trying to recover—what were they doing?

A red coat filled my stinging vision as a guard grabbed a woman, pinning her hands behind her back and marching her away. Another guard grabbed Rodney, who let go of my hand, leaving me alone in the swirling, shouting crowd.

I tried to shout, but coughing seized me. I held up my hands, but no one could see—and then another citizen turned on the guard trying to shove him around and shoved back.

All around me, people shoved and got in each other's way, trying to break free of the ring the guards had closed around us. I stumbled, terror leaping at the vision of falling in the midst of a stampede. Off to my left, another guard burst into the crowd, grabbing a young boy roughly by the arm. He cried out, and a woman in a Service coat and snow goggles pulled a chunk of brick from her pocket.

"You mustn't!" I cried, waving my arms. She smashed it into the guard's face, and blood sprayed.

Those sparks of violence caught, and the blaze leapt into the air.

The crowd was a mob, now, and they were shoving at guards, dragging the people they'd arrested away from them.

"We have to run," I shouted. "Run!"

I tugged at people's coats, trying to guide them. I pushed them to head in one direction, but another group in layers of gray and snow goggles crossed our path, shouting and pulling stones from their pockets.

A rock arced through the air.

"No," I said, and horror turned my hands cold.

I needed to get out, but I was a leaf on the tide, elbowed and shoved along the crowd's furious current. They surged forward, shouting, and met the guard with fists and boots. The guard answered with blows—the end of a stick in someone's middle, knocking the breath from them, overhand blows cracking over skulls. Some of the royal guard fought, while others hauled people from the mass, hobbling them together in a line to be processed.

This was chaos. It was wrong, all wrong, the moment to defuse tensions utterly destroyed.

A woman in goggles and a Service coat kicked at the guard attempting to drag her away, fighting to get free until two Greystars came and hauled her off.

The guards caught a teenage boy, and the crowd dashed in to pull him back, determined to hold the line against our opponents. He faded back into the ranks, yanking stones from his pockets to hurl at his would-be captors.

This assembly—this peaceful, orderly first day of the Free Government—lay trampled under the feet of the mob. They attacked the line of royal guards, managing to seize one of their number and pull him into the swirling mess of the crowd. I saw him stretch out one hand, screaming at his fellow guards to help him.

That could not stand. I fought my way through the crowd, desperately searching for the guard's red coat—there! I threw my own elbow shots to get to his side. I threw myself at him, dragging my arms around him. Blood poured down his face from a scalp wound and a broken nose, and I clung to him, bracing myself for a blow meant for him.

None came. The people ready to beat him to death backed off, and I dragged the guard with me. We fought our way back up the steps, where the guards surged forward. A painful, crushing hand closed around my wrist, and something as cold as the air chilled my skin, and then burned it.

My vision warped. Nausea rolled over me like crashing waves. Rough hands hauled me up the remaining stairs, and I would have fallen if they hadn't had me by the scruff. I was tossed to other guards waiting to gather up the arrested, and a woman in gold braid frog-marched me inside the rotunda, reciting a declaration of arrest.

"You are under arrest for civil upset, destruction of property, and violent assault of a royal guard. You may refuse to answer questions, but silence does not guarantee your exoneration, while anything you say could be used as evidence in a future criminal hearing—"

"I rescued that guard," I said. "They were going to kill him. I risked my life to—"

"You have the right to a meeting with a doctor of laws authorized to advocate on your behalf," the guard went on. "I am required by law to ask you for your advocate's name, so they can be informed of your incarceration."

"Chancellor Grace Hensley," I said.

The guard shook me like a misbehaving terrier. "This is no time for jokes."

"I'm not joking," I said. "Tell her you've arrested me. Fetch her to me right away."

It took two hours to regret my choice. Grace was a busy woman. And I hadn't thought about the appearances. We had trespassed in a symbolic act to assert that we were the legitimate government. They didn't have to use tear gas, and the guard started the violence with the crowd after we escaped, but the magistrates weren't going to see it that way. We had rioted, destroyed property, attacked guards, and I was responsible, as their leader.

The Chancellor couldn't come over to the Tower and advocate for me. *"I will help where I can"* didn't include getting me out of the mess I had made for myself. I should have asked for Orlena. She would have sent someone from the firm, who would be here by now.

The Tower cells were centuries old. They didn't have water commodes, so they stank, and I shivered in a hemp tunic and skirt, watching other arrestees get called out of the cells. Every one of them had seen the magistrate. None of them had come back. I was alone, and cold, and I had to swallow my pride and admit to the guard that Grace wasn't coming.

It was another forty-five minutes before the door opened and a guard stepped in.

"Looks like you do have friends in high places," she said. "You've been released on surety."

That was expensive. "Who signed for it?"

"Sir Christopher Hensley."

"What? He couldn't have."

"Nevertheless, he's waiting for you." The guard unlocked the cell and opened it wide. "Unless you'd rather stay here?"

I wavered. If I stepped out of this cell, I would owe that man my freedom, and he would use my debt against me. I couldn't see how, but he would find a way, and I would pay for it. I didn't want to owe Christopher Hensley the time of day.

"I think perhaps I had better. Thank him for the offer, but it's not one I can accept."

"You're a strange one," the guard said, and she closed the cell door. "If I had a handsome young man like that looking out for me—?"

I looked up. "Did you say young man? About thirty or so? Walks with a cane—"

And then Miles himself moved to the door. "I had to use my legal name for the documents," he said. "She didn't say Christopher Miles, did she?"

I eyed her. "No."

"Well, now you know," Miles said. "It's cold in here. Let's get your clothes and go."

My clothes needed a good laundering, but at least they were mine. I shook them out as best I could. I inspected my belongings and found that my wallet and my pen were scrupulously untouched, but my manacle key was gone. I signed a guarantee to appear for a hearing, and I was free of Kingsgrave Prison.

I stood in the thin, chilly evening air, filling my lungs with the cool, clean smell of late winter. It smelled of snow, tinged with the smoke from the bonfire burning on the palace square.

Miles had his sister's sled waiting outside the prison, and he climbed in it. "So. Rabble-rousing."

"That wasn't my intent," I said. "Things just ran away on their own—No. No excuses. I failed out there today."

"You're being too hard on yourself," Miles said. "Maybe holding your meeting in front of Government House was going a bit far, but they didn't have to tear-gas you. That's a weapon of war."

"But then the riot—"

"If it had been me, I would have rioted too."

"What's going to happen to the others who were arrested?" I asked.

"They're all going before a magistrate for mischief hearings. Most of them will be fined."

"Fines they can't afford to pay." My shoulders sank. I hung my head. I had allowed this to happen. My own pride had gotten us into this mess.

Miles patted my shoulder. "Now get some rest. We're going sleuthing tomorrow."

"Sleuthing?"

"I spoke to Amelia at Beauregard Veterans'. She wanted to tell it with you there, instead of having me repeat it back to you."

"Tell me what?"

"Amelia knew all of the Quiet Ones. That's what the Service called the women sharpshooters during the war. A great many of them write to her care of the hospital," Miles said. "She said she'll tell you anything you want to know, as soon as you come see her."

Beauregard still hadn't caged in a more secure area for the dozens of bicycles chained to the wrought-iron fence, even though they were ripe for theft. The sills around the windows hadn't been painted—and that meant they were probably still drafty. We walked up the wide flagstone walk (the loose stones were repaired, at least) and inside the hospital's front doors.

Music echoed in the main hall, and a crowd of young soldiers I didn't know gathered around one man with a guitar. They shivered in the draft from the front door, but only looked at us with some curiosity. I searched for someone, anyone I recognized.

"Robin!" Nurse Harriet Baker rushed over to me, squeezing my shoulders in a hug. "Or should I say Right Honorable?"

I hugged Harriet. "Always Robin to you, Harry."

"I feel selfish for saying it, but we need you so badly. Jenny keeps threatening to strike over the smallest things—we shouldn't have put her in charge over you. That was a mistake."

"Jenny will learn which battles to fight, and which to negotiate," I said. "Miles and I are here to visit a patient," I said. We're here to see Amelia Summer."

"It's so kind of you to come again. Amelia hasn't seen visitors in a while," Harriet said. "I'll take you over."

Harriet told us all the news the nurses had—who was engaged, who was pregnant, who had left to other hospitals, and she didn't leave us until we had escorted Amelia Summer to a small interview room, granting us privacy we wouldn't have had in an eight-bed ward.

Amelia had a bag full of yarn scraps and a crochet hook, and she looked at the lace square in her hands more than she looked at us. "I'm glad you came," she said.

"I wanted to see you," I replied. "Miles said you didn't want to tell it twice, or risk having Miles mis-repeat something to me."

"You're here because of the Clarke assassination," she said. The hook flashed as she drew yarn around it, creating what would be a piece of a blanket or maybe a scarf. "You think it's one of the Quiet Ones."

"Possibly," I said to her bowed head. "That's the avenue we're currently exploring. Miles found four other women living in Kingston who had training in the Service."

Miles reached into his pocket. "I have their pictures."

"Let's see them." Amelia set her hook down and put her hand out. She paged past the first one immediately. "I don't know her," she said. "Never seen her before. Did she go to Laneer?"

"That's Millicent Roebuck, and no."

Couldn't tell you anything about her." Amelia slipped the photo of Millicent to the back of the stack. "This one, though. That's Evelyn Deadeye."

She held up the portrait of Evelyn Plemmons.

"Deadeye?" Miles asked.

"Best shot I've ever seen," Amelia said. "She could shoot the gasper right out of your mouth. And she did. She liked the distraction missions. The ones where you'd stalk a location, just to scare them."

I glanced at Miles. Assassination was dangerous, wasn't it? "She liked the excitement?"

"She craved it. The riskier, the more dangerous, the better she liked it. She did at least fifty successful missions, and most of those were incredibly dangerous, but she was part cat. She could sneak up on a hare."

Amelia slid Evelyn's portrait to the back. "Caitrin! She played the violin. Took that thing with her everywhere. Not on missions, but she used to play it for the boys. Wireless tunes, singalongs—everyone liked Caitrin. I think most of them never really thought of all the murder she did."

"Do you think she'd be likely for the assassination?"

Amelia shook her head. "Caitrin fell in love with an army captain. She got married and is probably busy making babies right now."

That matched what we knew. "She's pregnant."

"She is?" Amelia's smile stole over her face. "That's lovely. I should make her something."

She turned to the last photo. "Ah. Laura."

I tilted my head. "That's an interesting reaction."

"Laura was far too good for the rest of us," Amelia said. "She didn't waste her time on anyone who wasn't an officer. Did she marry Major Briggs? She really liked him."

"She's still Debenham."

"Oh? Too bad," Amelia said. "Though it's rare to meet an unmarried major, wouldn't you say? What's she doing now?"

"She's in the royal guard," I said. "Personal protection for King Severin."

"Oh. She's flown very high, indeed," Amelia said. "I hope she hasn't broken her heart, trying to charm a king."

"These are all the women trained by the army in long-distance sharpshooting who still live in Kingston," Miles said. "You knew them. In your opinion, who would become a contract assassin? If you read an article in the paper about her capture, which one of these women would surprise you the least?"

Amelia handed the photos back. "You have this image in your mind of the Quiet Ones. We were legends. What the Quiet Ones see, dies. Some of the men feared us on sight."

Miles shifted his weight and shrugged. "I've heard the stories."

"Those stories made it hard to mix with anyone who wasn't our team or each other," Amelia said. "I know a bit about how you men were trained to kill. And it's hard to imagine a woman going through that, isn't it? All that shouting and aggression. But it wasn't like that, for us. They didn't teach us that way."

Miles leaned a little closer. "How?"

"I didn't go from national Under Twenty champion target archer to halfway up a tree hoping intelligence was right, that my scouts were safe, and that my target was really inside the structure because I stood in a line with a rifle and shouted 'destroy them.'" Amelia said. "We penetrated enemy ground and risked our lives without wireless backup to creep up to a location and wait hours for our target, and then we had to escape back to safety. I had to trust my scouts. We had to trust our commander to be there when we made it back. We learned to be quiet, efficient, unseen."

"They trained you differently," Miles said. "They used more sophisticated methods."

"They gave us thought experiments where the right answer, the moral answer, was to sacrifice one for the safety of the rest. We learned that murdering one would save a thousand, that one of our assignments could win a battle without any of the boys ever seeing danger."

Miles nodded. "You were protectors."

"That's what they told us," Amelia said. "And when we came back, when we made it back from shooting whoever was key to the enemy's plans, they would hug us. They would praise us. They would tell us who we saved from the fighting, that we were saving Aeland, and freedom, and everything it stands for."

"They used your love," I said. "They used your love to make you kill for them."

Amelia stared at the empty space between us—not at me, but at something only she could see. "I never felt more worthy than when my commander would gather me up and shower me with praise, ordering a hot bath and a good meal and the best liquor in the camp. My team—they were my brothers. And then they would pack up, and we'd go to the next camp. The next mission. The next murder."

"And you were all protectors. You were all saving the boys from having to fight a battle, or from having to fight tooth and nail to occupy a town. You kept them safe," Miles said.

"That's what we were taught. We were never cynical enough, uncaring enough, cold enough to kill for money. We were trained to kill for Aeland," Amelia said. "Aeland and all it stands for."

I went cold. "And if Jacob Clarke dying meant saving the country?"

Amelia looked at me. "Then you are in grave danger."

I sat back, stomach writhing. "Me."

"If I'm right, and the shooter is a patriot, I'd be very careful if I were you," Amelia said. "But if you're right, and the killer is working on contract, then you're looking for the coldest woman I ever met."

She held up the defiant, belligerent photo of Evelyn Plemmons.

"Check her trail. You remember I said she liked the distraction missions?"

My insides were still shivering. "Yes."

"She would shoot people so they hurt. So they screamed. And she'd drop a few stone-dead on the spot, just to make it worse."

I exchanged a glance with Miles. "She liked it."

"Yes. Deadeye liked risks. She liked people being afraid of her. She loved to see fear." Amelia studied the photograph, and then looked at Miles. "I don't know if I helped."

"I think you have," Miles said. "I'm going to tread lightly while I look into Miss Plemmons."

"Be very careful," Amelia said. "Both of you."

NINETEEN

A Step Ahead of the Rest

FREE WITCHES: WAS IT A MISTAKE? I was more than tired of headlines. I should have been washing dishes, but instead I was standing in the corner with the *Herald*, reading an article placed above the fold about the riot on the steps of Government House, and a story about Zelind's disciplinary reports related to violence while khe was imprisoned at Clarity House. ALLEGED INVENTOR A DANGEROUS PATIENT—OVER 300 INFRACTIONS RECORDED, that headline read.

"What garbage," I muttered, and beside me, Zelind shivered.

"They'd write you up for anything," khe said. "I'm not saying I didn't stir things up sometimes, but they wrote me up for dropping a cup, because it landed on my toe and I swore."

That was more than ridiculous. It was small, petty, and exactly the sort of thing that would break a person's spirit over time. "The papers make it sound like you regularly attempted murder."

"I should have attempted murder," Zelind muttered. "What were they going to do, imprison me again?"

"You can't regret your instinct for survival." I folded the paper and dropped it in the bin.

"Well, if they're smearing me, that means they're not smearing you, at least." Zelind picked up a drying towel and handed it to me. "I was getting tired of riot coverage."

The papers had savaged us, calling the Government House mass

arrest an act of thuggish violence. They had called for the imprisonment of the four hundred people arrested. But when Grace stepped
out to apologize to us for the intemperate actions of an overly anxious guard, and dissolved all pending mischief charges, the papers reacted in confusion, their inflated story popped by a pin.

But it hadn't taken them long to find a new target. Zelind was
handling the smear with a shrug, but I was ready to storm the *Herald*
and demand they take it back.

"It doesn't matter. Your turbines will save Aeland. We'll drag
this country into fairness and justice." I nodded at the mail on the
table, where an opened invitation to gather at Winnie and Duke's sat
among letters to the People's Prime Minister. "The work goes on. But
today, we have a hotel to save."

Zelind's expression soured. "I know I have to give in a little. But
I'm not going to like it."

"I didn't expect you would," I said. "Are you sure you don't want
to write to her and arrange a time to meet?"

"I'd prefer her to have no warning," Zelind said.

This meeting made kher nervous enough to line kher eyes and
powder kher cheeks. Zelind changed clothes three times, finally settling on wide-legged cuffed trousers, shiny wine-colored brogues,
and a burgundy silk blouse with a ribbon bow at the neck. Khe put on
perfume that smelled of woods and herbs, grabbed a surplus Service
coat from the closet, and topped kher springy short hair with a pinch-
fronted gray hat with a wide brim. Khe still carried that elegance
that transformed kher fashion choices into ensembles that gathered
admiring glances as khe pedaled down the streets.

We took Water Street to Main and walked our bicycles up the
steep grade of King Philip Hill, all the way to Bayview, the house that
looked down on all of Riverside.

We rode Bay Crescent in silence. My stomach writhed, remembering my other journeys to this house, this redbrick castle. It was
large enough to house three clans but only held a handful, the servants outnumbering the family five to one. We wound around the
street that housed those servants, and Zelind turned kher head and
stared at a line of beech trees planted on the curving road.

"Right there," khe said, and we pedaled past the place where khe
had been arrested without looking back.

We stopped at the gate, and the guards in the gatehouse ran into the driveway to pull the iron gates open, their faces stunned. Zelind pedaled past with scarcely more than a tight smile, but khe nodded to the stone lions who guarded the driveway leading to the house.

I still couldn't believe the size of it. I hadn't accustomed myself to this kind of wealth belonging to people. I helped the maid. I looked for slippers before I remembered that the Bays just wore their shoes all over the house. I reached for Zelind's hand and khe took it, leading me past parlors and receiving rooms and the empty ballroom I had stared at the first time I had come.

Khe led me to a breakfast room, where Birdie waited for a maid to finish preparing her tea. A cellist played music and it made me think of Ramona; it was just that little bit like home.

Birdie Bay dismissed the maid with a little wave. She gazed at Zelind, and her mouth flattened as she studied our clasped hands.

I didn't let go. Neither did khe. But Birdie inspected us both, not saying a word. She picked up her painted glass teacup and sipped at a brew that smelled malty and strong. I don't think we dared even breathe until she set down the cup and laced her fingers together, displaying a portrait ring on one finger.

"So. My child has come home at last."

"I'm here, Mother," Zelind said. "I thought we could eat breakfast."

"Spare me. You want something," Birdie said, one corner of her mouth curved down. "You're too stubborn to be here otherwise."

"Miss Minerva Brown's hotel is under threat," Zelind said. "I think you arranged it."

"And I think your wife was the one who guessed," Birdie said. "I would have expected you to grab a pipe wrench and try to beat the clock."

Zelind shrugged. "She did."

Her gaze bored through me. "You've always been clever, Miss Robin. Clever and proud. Do you realize," Birdie said, picking up her teacup, "that I never thought you had attached yourself to my child for the money?"

"I hadn't, ma'am," I said. "But you're right. I didn't."

"It wasn't that I disliked you," she went on. "Nor was it because I expected my child to take up with someone wealthy. My sole objection was that you were a null. And I was mistaken."

"I appreciate you telling me this, ma'am."

"But I dislike you now," Mrs. Bay said. "There was a right way and a wrong way to handle the situation when Zelind came back. Humiliating me in public was not the right way."

"Mother."

"She isn't welcome here," Birdie said. "She's only staying because she may as well hear what I have to say. I want you to come home."

"This isn't my home anymore," Zelind said. "I came to tell you that I would pay you a visit once a week. For dinner. Alone, if you wish."

"Ah. And in exchange, I call off my dogs and leave the Princess Mary Hotel to those children playing at clanship?"

Zelind nodded, kher jaw tight. "Yes."

She tilted her head and studied her child, her expression going sharp. "No."

"If you don't agree, then we have no choice but to appeal to Aeland Heritage and Preservation about naming the Princess Mary a site of social and historical significance, and then you will never see me again. I will cut you in the street."

Birdie gazed at Zelind through the ribbon of steam rising from her tea. "You have it all thought out."

Zelind shrugged one shoulder. "I had to think ahead, if I was dealing with you."

"A compliment. I'll take it," Birdie said. "But you didn't think far enough ahead, my dear."

My jaw dropped open. I went cold. She hadn't. She was way ahead of us, miles ahead, but—who would do such a thing?

The woman who'd never learned how to live without getting exactly what she wanted, that's who.

She flicked a glance at me, and her smile widened. "Run to the Heritage and Preservation office and do a little research. Take the day. And take tomorrow. And then come home, and I will withdraw my complaint to the Health and Safety inspectors."

My hand hurt. Zelind squeezed harder. "What did you do?"

"Go, and see."

I knew. I could feel it, as if my bones had turned to cold water. If we went and delved into the files, we'd find the documents there, in triplicate, coated in a fine layer of dust. The money, paid into some clerk's pocket and spent possibly years ago, patiently waiting for the moment when Birdie Bay would get everything she wanted.

Birdie smiled at my expression. "Your wife knows already. Ask her."

Zelind turned to me, kher face going chalky as khe saw the expression I couldn't hide. "What did she do? Robin. You look like you're going to faint."

I licked my lips. Swallowed. "There was already an application processed for the hotel," I said. "She prevented it from being awarded protected status."

"How?" Zelind's voice shook. "How could she have known?"

"Minerva said Birdie wanted the land a long time ago," I said. "It might have been that. Did you bribe them?"

"Oh, Miss Thorpe," Birdie said, the rim of her cup balanced between her fingers. "There's a bylaw on the books. If five different charges of prostitution happen at the same address, that address is considered a locus of criminality and not worthy of consideration for protected status."

"That's a load of garbage," Zelind said. "It's a hotel. Find me a hotel anywhere in Kingston that hasn't had its share of vice arrests—"

"You can't save the hotel," I said. "She's blocked our only play. Zelind."

"No," Zelind said. "There has to be something we can do."

"There is, my child," Birdie said. "But I know you'll just dig your heels in if you don't see the truth for yourself. Go. Take today and tomorrow to find a way out. But after that—I'll have the maid clean a selection of suites for your return. You can choose one."

"You want us to live with you?" Zelind asked, kher tone unbelieving.

"Miss Thorpe is not welcome," Birdie said. "I'll send an advocate around with a divorce agreement."

Zelind backed up a step. Khe squeezed my hand and pulled me close. "No. She's my wife. You can't just wave your hand and make her disappear."

"If you want your friends to keep their playhouse, I can," Birdie said. "Miss Thorpe. I know you're more practical than khe is. What choice does khe have?"

"This won't make kher happy," I said. "It won't make you happy either."

"But we'll be unhappy together," Birdie said. "And I will have what I want."

"I won't do it."

"You will," Birdie said, and in the morning sunlight, Birdie's eyes were dull and tired, ringed with deep shadows.

Zelind was stiff as a board beside me. "I will hate you."

"You will," Birdie said. "You'll hate me, and you'll rebel against me, and you'll spend your every breath defying me—but I will have my child back. Go. Return on the morning of the third day, and I will spare the Princess Mary. I'll have Cook make your favorites."

Birdie rang a bell next to her plate, and a man in a formal black suit came to lead us away.

We coasted down King Philip Hill and pedaled home in silence. Zelind avoided the stairs to our room, stopping instead at the second parlor, where Zola was inconsolable.

"Ahoy," Zelind said, and edged into the room. "Rosabelle. Do you mind if I—"

"She's miserable with teething," Rosabelle said.

"We'll be a pair, then." Zelind stretched out kher arms and took the squalling baby, letting her yell in one ear as khe stroked her back. Khe shushed her, gave her a finger to squeeze, and picked up her teething toy when she threw it to the floor and howled.

"We're going for a walk," Zelind said, and took Zola's yelling to the back of the house.

"Not you, Robin," Bernice said. "Something happened."

The carpet was worn in tracks around settees and chairs. It had been time to get a new one for years and let this one rest—

"Robin."

I looked up.

"Birdie happened," I said. "We went to talk to Birdie this morning."

"No wonder you're upset. Was she horrible to you?"

"She was worse," I said. "She was gloating."

Bernice's head came up. She turned her gaze to the back of the house, where Zola's crying came from, and then to me.

"Are you going to let her win, then?" Bernice asked.

"She's won, Aunt Bernie." I swept my hand across my throbbing brow. "She was already three steps ahead."

"She can't do anything to us," Bernice said. "You didn't back down when she put Jarom up against you. What did she do?"

"Clan Cage," I said. I closed my eyes. "She'll have the Princess Mary torn down if Zelind doesn't come home."

The second parlor was quiet. Zola wailed on, screaming her pain and rage against something she couldn't stop.

Bernice didn't touch her knitting. "So she's won."

My voice broke. I couldn't stop it. "What choice do we have? She'll destroy the clan. Zelind couldn't live with that—I couldn't live with that."

"But you can live without each other."

It put a rock in my chest. "We have to."

The parlor was silent of everything but Zola's cries.

"You never stepped out with anyone," Bernice said. "Never even once in all those years you lived without kher. You were strong. So strong, my girl. And void curse Bellina Lee Bay for forcing you to be strong again."

I couldn't breathe right. I tried to, but I just couldn't fill my lungs. My ribs wouldn't expand. And it hurt— Oh Solace shelter me, it hurt everywhere.

I would have to be strong again.

"I need to—" I tried to swallow, but my mouth was dry. "I need to talk to Zelind."

I turned. I walked, my footsteps barely a thump. Hundreds of Thorpes gazed at me from the walls—from photographs, and silver prints, and miniatures. All my family. All my clan. Centuries of ancestors who walked this hall and slept under this roof and married and had babies who grew up and moved through time to meet me here, where I would soon be alone.

Zola wailed. Maybe she would tire out soon. Maybe she would fall into an exhausted, helpless sleep. She was too small to know how to live with pain.

I opened the door to the back parlor, where the drafts and chill ruled. Zelind was trying to get Zola to bite on a flannel soaked in cold water, but she turned her head and kept screaming.

"My poor lamb," khe said. "It's all right to cry. It's all right to be angry. It hurts, and there's nothing you can do to stop it."

I closed the door again, quietly, and took the back stairs up to my rooms.

I missed tea. I skipped dinner. I curled up in my bed and read *Saria Green and the Secret of Blackstone Hall*, immersing myself in the story of a plucky young science-minded girl investigating a haunted academy. I finished it and picked up the next one, where Saria looked for hidden treasure on the black sand beaches of Stormtide Island. I was just at the part where she found a cave full of glowing skeletons when the door creaked open.

Zelind slipped inside, closing the door behind kher. Khe reached for the dial for the gaslights, kher look asking my permission.

I slipped a bookmark in between the pages and nodded, and khe dialed the little room into darkness. The shape of kher sidled closer, then sat on the edge of my bed, kher features lined in the faint glow of ten thousand twinkling stars, the night of kher eyes a pinpoint shine.

The shadow of kher hand rose, sliding toward my face—gentle and tender as it slid on my cheek, trailing to my temple to slide across my brow and stop just at the point between my eyebrows, so faint I had to close my eyes to feel it.

Khe didn't say a word. Khe let kher finger trace down the bridge of my nose, tickle over the upper curve of my lip—pause there, to trace the full outline of my mouth—and then continued, light as a rose petal, down the tip of my chin.

"Is this all right?" khe whispered, and I let out a breath I'd been holding for twenty years.

"Yes."

Khe bent over me in the dark, and I reached up to pull kher down.

TWENTY

Too Many Alibis

I knew before I opened my eyes that Zelind was gone. Most of kher borrowed clothes sat in neat, folded piles, ready to be returned to the cupboards where they had waited for someone to shoot up tall enough to need them, but khe had taken the clan sweater with kher.

The paper had a raft of opinions in letters to the editor, arguing whether witches were safe, whether open democracy was a threat or a menace, and complaints about how nothing was being done about aether.

"You shouldn't read the news while eating," Jedrus said. "It'll give you indigestion."

"Mm-hmm." I finished a letter that suggested Zelind's invention be manufactured immediately, and recognized the name from my volunteer pool.

"And we just want to say how sorry we are that—"

I held up one hand, palm out. "Don't."

Cousin Jedrus, mercifully, left me alone.

The silence was awkward. I didn't care. I read the paper, ate jam toast with one hand, and barely looked up as Amos scrambled to meet the mail carrier at the door with the morning post.

"This is for Aunt Robin," he said, handing over a gray envelope, my name and address written in eerily perfect, flourished script. The return address was the seal of the Chancellor, with the words "Government House" written under it.

A stiff card slid out, reading,

> You are invited to meet with Dame Grace Hensley at ten o'clock in the morning regarding your concern.

It was stamped with the Chancellor's seal, the paper raised and pierced by the mark.

An engraved invitation. She had probably sent it to get me past security. What did she mean, "your concern"? What did she want, and why couldn't it wait until Winnie's gathering tonight?

It had to be too urgent or too private to wait.

"Grace Hensley wants to see me," I said. "I may not be back in time for lunch."

I walked my bike up the steep slope of Main Street. Joy floated beside me, trying to distract me with all the gossip she'd collected just barging in wherever she pleased. Honestly, she was as knowledgeable as Carlotta Brown. I turned my face away from the sparkling windows of Bayview with an ache in my chest. Was Zelind inside, sharing a bitter breakfast across from kher mother? Ignoring Jarom's attempts at reconciliation? Pacing the limits of kher cage, imprisoned so a clan would be free?

It hurt to think about. It hurt to lose kher. I had only just gotten kher back, and I couldn't let Birdie win. There had to be something I could do. There had to be a way to beat her.

Once at the top of the hill, I put Bayview behind me and pedaled across downtown to the palace complex, parking in front of Government House. A guard started down the stairs, headed right for me, and Grace's under-typist, James, rushed down the stairs to meet me.

"I am here to escort the Chancellor's guest to her office," he announced to the guard.

"She instigated a riot," the guard protested. "One of our own was nearly killed."

"You mean the guard I rescued?" I asked. "I am here by invitation. You may confirm it with the Chancellor, if you wish."

I held out the card, stamped by the Chancellor's seal, and snatched it back when the guard tried to take it from me.

"I'd prefer to keep it, thank you."

The corners of the guard's mouth turned down, his angry gaze hot enough to warm my face. "If this is a forgery, you'll be arrested."

"Fair," I said. "Lead the way."

The guard preferred to walk behind me, however. Probably easier to drag me off to prison that way. James headed our little parade, and swung the door open to announce, "She's here."

"Oh good," Onora said. "Please go in, Mrs. Thorpe. You're sorely needed."

Quick, heavy footsteps paced back and forth on the other side of the door. I pulled it open. Grace was wearing a hole in the expensive silk carpet, pacing from her sitting room hearth to a loop around her desk.

I'd never seen her like this. "What's wrong?"

"Shut the door," Grace said. I was sorely needed, her secretary had said. Music started the moment the bolt clicked shut. "Tea's over there."

I moved over to the cart and poured some, admiring the reddish tint against the sides of the cup. "Do you want one too?"

"I'd just smash the glass," Grace said. "I can't believe it! I'm so stupid. I knew he couldn't be trusted, I knew it, and I didn't do anything—"

"Grace," I said. "Slow down and tell me what's going on."

Grace faced the windows and hurled her hands out in front of her. Outside, a gust of wind sent powdery snow flying into the air, and Grace glared at it until a tiny cyclone swirled in the garden outside her office. She directed it, and blew snow off the ornamental paths, scouring them down to the paving stones.

It wasn't the flailing rage of thrown dishes and smashed valuables. Grace's anger whirled in that funnel of wind, but she contained it, controlled it, set it to a task that had some use. I understood it as the same urge that came over me to wash the dishes or beat the dust out of the rugs—anything that would make my anger useful.

She let the cyclone fall apart. The snow fell back to earth. Grace turned back to me, breathing like she'd just sprinted to the finish line. "Sorry. I'm just so angry."

I exchanged a glance with Joy. "Tell me why."

"He's won," Grace said. "I turned my back. I let him have the run of the palace, and he's got Severin in his grip."

I had a guess, but Grace needed to talk. "Who?"

Grace took the seat at my right elbow with a sigh. "My father.

He's got his hooks in Severin, and I didn't move to counter him—I was so concerned with getting Avia out of his clutches that I left Severin behind. I should have known better."

This was bad news. Worse than I had imagined on the day I had seen the man with my own eyes, walking the palace as he pleased. "No one can do everything or see every possibility. What is it?"

"Severin is a power-hungry Chancellor's dream," Grace said. "He takes on any opinion you offer him. I thought I would be of most use to you at the King's side, guiding him to embrace reforms. I had breakfast with him this morning to speak to him about the Free Government. When I reached the table, Father was there."

And Sir Christopher doesn't care for us. "Oh no."

"He hates you, and all of Solidarity. And Severin—" Grace shook her head, resting the weight of it on her steepled fingertips. "It was like those living doll shows. I could almost see Father's hand moving Severin's mouth."

I shifted in my seat. "Chilling."

"'The rabble will not stop until they have trampled the Crown under their heels,'" Grace said, deepening her voice to imitate Severin's. "It was Severin's voice, but they were Father's words."

"Rabble," I said. "That's pleasant."

"I should have known," Grace said. "Father's been treating Severin like a son since he was a small child. Severin's been going to him for advice all along, and he does everything Father wants."

"And your father wants our movement suppressed."

"Completely," Grace said. "I tried to convince him to meet with you, to hear what concerned the people the most, and he said, 'A king does not bow to the mob.' Just like that." Grace pitched forward, resting her elbows on her knees. "I should have put him back in that cell. I should have pushed for the tribunals to begin."

Grace's stomach must be in knots. Did she want my advice, or my understanding? I wasn't sure what path to choose. What would Miles say? I knew what he would say to a patient, but what would Miles say to a friend? "You're asking much of yourself. For one thing, it's no small act, pushing your father to the gallows."

Grace looked down at her clasped hands. "I know."

"For another, I don't see how you could have out-influenced your father, if he's been working on Severin for so long."

Grace's shoulders bunched up. "There was a way. But I turned my back on it."

"How?"

Grace glanced at the window. "Severin proposed to me."

The floor fell six inches. "And you said no?"

"Of course I did."

I didn't say anything for a moment, as all the words had scattered at her statement. "If you had married him, you would have the run of the country."

"And you wouldn't be sitting here right now," Grace said. "You wouldn't have become someone I can talk to. Miles might have understood why I did it, and he'd still love me. But he, you, Avia— even if I reformed this country top to bottom, I would have done it alone."

Grace Hensley had turned down all the power in Aeland to have a real family, a real sweetheart, the chance to make a real friend. She hadn't called me here to speak of policy. She'd wanted a confidante. Someone to share her burden.

She'd come to me.

I sat up, slapping my palms on my bent knees. "So. If you can't influence the King, what are you going to do?"

"I don't know." Grace bit the corner of her lip. "I'm not doing any good here. I don't have Severin's ear. I don't want to have to silence my own opinions just to keep the office."

I knew that ambivalence. I knew what lay underneath it, and that a friend would help dig it up. "What do you want to do?"

"I want to feel like I'm doing the right thing," Grace said. "I thought I knew what that was, and I was wrong."

Gently, carefully, I brushed away another layer. "What does doing the right thing mean to you?"

"Fighting on your side," Grace said. "Aeland can afford all the things the Solidarity movement is fighting for. We can. We're just too greedy to do it."

"So you want to quit."

"Yes," Grace said. "Or get fired in the most spectacular way possible."

She grinned at that, and I smiled back. "They both have the same outcome," I said. "So which one would be more fun?"

Grace sparkled when she smiled. "I have a meeting with him this afternoon," she said. "Do you want to help me prepare for it?"

"Are you quitting or getting fired?"

"Oh, I think I'll resign. But not before I make it plain I'm deserting his side."

"What are you already planning to do?"

Grace tilted her head, looking up at the ceiling as she gathered her thoughts. "I know your spouse wants to manufacture wind turbines."

The words put a needle in my heart. It was going to be like this whenever someone who didn't know talked to me about Zelind. I rubbed at my chest, soothing it away. "Yes. Khe does. What is your thought?"

"If I gave King Severin a document detailing the decision made by the Free Government about getting aether turbines to the people, he'd be angry enough to fire me."

"He could just refuse," I said. "It's not enough. You need to go bigger than that."

Grace leaned a little closer. "How much bigger?"

"What happened to the witches who were taken from their families and imprisoned in labor camps masquerading as asylums can never be fully compensated," I said, "but I've done some figuring."

"I'm not sure King Severin will fire me over asking for an increase to their pensions."

"Not pensions, Grace. Morally, every cent of profit generated by the scheme to monopolize aether belongs to the witches who suffered profoundly to produce it."

"Morally, you're correct. But no one will ever agree to that," Grace said. "Give me a number I can fight for. A number that people will debate over."

I cocked my head. "Really?"

"Really. Make it hurt, but I want to see it happen."

"All right." I took a deep breath. "Twenty-five percent of all the profits reaped by APL in the four decades of its operation, adjusted by base investment interest."

Grace sat back and sighed between pursed lips. "Lump sum or annual payment?"

"Annual payments for twenty-five years, payable to the witch or the witch's estate."

"And for the witches who are already dead?"

"Closest living relative."

"You thought about this," Grace said.

"Do you think it will work?"

"Oh yes," Grace said. "You're much better at this than I am. Let me write this down. "Twenty-five percent of APL's total profits, plus compounded interest, split equally between every witch imprisoned in an asylum, to be paid to each witch, or their estate, or their closest living relative." Grace gazed at her own handwriting for a moment. "It's fair. It's a painful penalty, but it's payable."

"Do you want to hold another conference to announce your support for Solidarity?"

"Not right away," Grace said. "I'm happy to come work for you, but the official announcement can wait."

This was a plum, and I couldn't wait to tell—I rubbed at my chest again and smiled at Grace. "I think we're going to do great things together," I said.

Grace smiled back. "I know we will, Right Honorable. Will I see you at the sitting tonight?"

When I saw Grace later this evening, we would talk of business. And politics. And maybe I could ask her to listen to my problems with Solidarity. Maybe we could talk like this again.

"I'll be there," I said. "I'll save you a drink."

A sitting wasn't the same as a party, though white Aelanders thought it was. You held sittings a few weeks after a funeral. You wore fine clothing, and if you had given the bereaved food, your dish would be returned to you. There was food and drink, but no music unless someone sang. You brought gifts for the bereaved, and no one played any games.

I had stretched a length of silk scarf and painted it in long, pale stripes of blue and green, Jacob's favorite colors. I wore a hand-hooked lace dress with draping sleeves, the beads in my hair silver and blue, for the sea and mourning. I walked in thick, practical winter boots that didn't match my outfit at all, with a pair of delicate, beaded black slippers tucked into the bag slung over my shoulder.

The street outside Duke and Winnie's was jammed with sleds. Horses stood snug and comfortable in quilted blankets, eating from buckets. Drivers stood in a huddle, smoking as they talked among themselves. I waved to them and they waved back, and one of them jogged out of the gathering to open the door for me.

I was perfectly timed—I had arrived after the gathering had begun, but I wasn't rudely late. Voices hummed through the air, blending into unintelligible, comforting sound, leading me up the stairs and to the open door. I let myself in. I put on my fancy slippers; Althea took my coat.

The pianochord was covered in gifts. I left my modestly wrapped package and ran the gauntlet of guests who wanted to shake my hand and ask questions about the new government and my future plans or give suggestions on what to do next.

"You should have fought that spoiled ballot nonsense," Fanny Harper, one of Duke's bandmates, said to me. "That Jarom Bay stole our votes, and you should have fought for them."

"I could have," I said to the woman who played rhythm guitar. "But then the Free Government would have taken a back seat to my duties in the House."

She nodded, and her drink came precariously close to spilling. "But you could have had a place at the table. Now, after the riot—"

"Robin," Preston Grimes said. "I'm sorry for the interruption, Fanny. I need to talk to Robin. It's important."

He didn't wait for a response before he took my arm and hustled me toward Tupper Bell, towering in a corner like a thundercloud.

"We compared notes," Tupper said, staring me down. "On what you told us about your investigation."

They were angry at me. I looked from one to the other, warmth flooding my hands and up my back. I could have wept with relief. Preston and Tupper were gossips, not spies. I could trust them, and my smile stretched across my face.

"I wouldn't grin like that if I were you," Tupper said, in his best school headmaster voice. "You told us lies. We deserve an explanation."

"Indeed," Preston said. "We should be able to trust you. Why are you happy?"

"I'm just so relieved," I said. "I have a terrible secret, and now I can share it with you."

"What secret?" Tupper asked. "Why did you tell us two different stories?"

I stepped in closer. "I have reason to believe someone on the steering committee is spying on us."

"And so you gave us misinformation to see which story leaked," Preston said.

"I did. I'm sorry I tested you to see what information made it free. But neither of you is the spy."

Tupper glanced over our heads at the gathered crowd. "What do you know so far? We can help."

"I don't know anything," I said. "I have guesses. I think the spy informed about Jacob's plan to hold an election, and our enemy—let's call them A—hired an assassin to murder Jacob. I also think the spy leaked the truth about Jacob's marriage, and A used it to tarnish Jacob's reputation."

"To make people think that the leader of the movement, who talked so much about morality, was himself immoral," Preston said. "That makes sense. And you headed it off as well as anyone could."

"It's like I tell my students," Tupper said. "'Never tell a lie when the truth will do.' But who else knew about Jacob's triangle marriage? I did."

"So did I."

"Right," I said. "And Winnie told me as much. So when you both came to me asking about Jacob's murder, I had to test you. I'm sorry."

"I understand," Tupper said. "And I'm glad you know you can trust us—"

"She's here," Preston said. "The Daughter of the Gates."

We turned toward the door, where the spectacularly tall Grand Duchess of the Solace and her constant companion, the dark and staggeringly handsome Ysonde, walked into the room. Ysonde held a rosewood secretary set, and the crowd parted so the two could stand before Winnie and Duke, who had risen to their feet to receive the Daughter of the Gates.

"Thank you so much for the apple bread," Winnie said. "It was a comfort. I have your bread wrap here—"

Winnie picked up a square of waxed cloth and Aife took it, tucking it inside a silken pouch. "I'm glad you were comforted by it. We have a gift."

Ysonde offered the secretary set. "There are books suitable for meditations inside, if you practice in that way."

Winnie opened the top of the lap desk and drew out a hand-bound diary. "I should start," she said. "I could write about him."

The women next to Winnie admired the set with oohs and ahhs. Aife didn't realize it, but she had just started a fashion. Everyone would buy secretary sets and books for meditation. Penmakers were going to have orders out the door.

Duke took out the second book and compared it to Winnie's. "Thank you," Duke said. "This is a great comfort. Do you want to start writing in the morning, Wins?"

"Yes." Winnie cradled the book in her arms. "Let's do it every morning."

Aife glanced toward a seat, and the person who had been resting there stepped aside. Her secretary perched on the wide, padded arm by her side.

"I liked Jacob very much," Aife said. "But I don't know that much about him."

At that, people clumped up to speak to each other again, letting Winnie and Duke tell stories about Jacob, recalling him with fond memories. Stories about the dead were supposed to draw the spirit back to the gathering, to hear all the gossip and be remembered. If Jacob was listening, I didn't know it.

I turned back to Preston. "I need to know if anyone else on the steering committee knew about Jacob's marriage. I didn't know, though I should have figured it out."

"I'll stick my nose into other people's business," Preston said. "Who do you think this person is spying for?"

"I don't know. I thought maybe Albert Jessup—"

"Wait," Tupper said. "I think I know."

He gestured at us to follow him into the crowded sitting room and paused before a photograph mounted on the wall—there had been a still life painted there before, but now there was a photo of a wedding gathering.

Winnie was in the center of the front row, with Jacob on one side and Duke on the other. They held hands and smiled serenely at the camera. Duke was the only white person in the picture—the others were Brewers and Clarkes, and I scanned over the faces, looking at their expressions.

All of these people knew. Did any of them have reason to tell tales to the papers? Did any of them—

I stopped. I pointed at a little girl near the front of the gathering, her skirt covering her knees. She was a child in that photo, but I knew that face.

"There," I said. "There's our spy."

She had the soft, full face of childhood, but the dimple in her chin was there. The shape of her eyes was the same, and so was her smile.

"That's Gaby Meadows," I said. "Isn't it?"

Tupper leaned in closer and nodded. "That's her."

Preston studied every single face in the photograph, particularly the young women. "She would have been Brewer then."

"Meadows is her professional name," I said. "Brewers of the Fragrant Meadows."

I stared at the picture of Gaby as a young girl. What would have led her to spy on the collective? Why would she betray us—to Albert Jessup, of all people? Gaby headed the committee dedicated to price control on dairy products. She had led brilliant protests against Jessup Family Foods. She was working for Jessup? All this time?

"What do we do?" Preston asked. "She's been on the committee for months."

"Because she pushed the deal to supply schools with subsidized staples, and she got that Wholesome Kitchens education program sponsored by Jessup Family Foods." Tupper looked at the picture of Gaby with a fierce frown pinning his lips shut. "We've been had."

"We talk to her," I said. My middle trembled. How could she do this? She had made so much progress—or, at least, Jessup had made it seem as if she had won victories against him. "Is she coming to the gathering?"

"I don't know," Tupper said. "I haven't seen her."

"Let's look around," I said, and a soft hand on my shoulder made me turn to see Tristan, sighing with relief.

"Robin. There you are," Tristan said. "We've been searching everywhere."

"Ahoy." Preston put out his hand, and Tristan shook it. "You're Miles's sweetheart, aren't you?"

"You know Miles," Tristan said, a lovely smile on his face. "I was just searching for Robin on his behalf. Do you mind terribly if I steal her away?"

Tristan was already steering me toward one of the tall glass doors that led to the dining room. I waved at Preston and turned to Tristan, my voice hushed.

"I found her," I said. "I know who my spy is."

"In a moment," Tristan said. "We have to tell you something."

Miles waited next to the punch bowl, but instead of taking over a corner, he led the way out of the apartment completely, stopping at the end of the hall for privacy.

"What are we doing out here?"

"You have a problem," Miles said. "I investigated Caitrin Scholar and Evelyn Plemmons."

My heart beat a little faster. "Which one is our killer?"

"Neither," Miles said. "Caitrin was at a career day at Queen Agnes Junior Academy. She was talking about being a professional musician to twenty schoolchildren when Jacob was killed."

"And Evelyn Plemmons was in court, testifying in a robbery case," Tristan said. "She was in the docket when the murder happened."

"That means they all have alibis," I said. "None of them did it."

"It might be worse than that," Miles said.

"How? We're nowhere."

"Caitrin and Evelyn are innocent, by the virtue of many witnesses. But Laura Debenham only has the word of one person."

"Yes," I said, "but it's the word of the King—"

A king who disparaged the Solidarity movement. Who likened us to rabble. But I shook my head. "He abolished the Witchcraft Protection Act. Why would he set the witches free, and then kill the man responsible for their freedom? He could have just said no."

"The Amaranthines wanted the witches free," Tristan said. "It was a goodwill gesture."

"But it didn't satisfy Solidarity," I said. "He asked me if we were going to stop protesting now that he had given the witches their freedom. But we didn't."

"And what Jacob wanted next directly threatened Severin's rule," Miles said.

"Severin enjoys being thought of as a generous king," Tristan said. "I have no doubt that he intends to bring changes to Aeland. But he's been waiting for his turn at the throne for decades. Aife thought he would be a better choice than Constantina."

"He is," I said. "Or, at least I thought he was. Do you honestly think he sent his bodyguard to kill Jacob?"

"I checked the duty roster," Miles said. "Laura Debenham was on shift. She reported being in the shooting range with him. Who would question the word of the Crown?"

"We would," I said. "But if you're right—what do I do? How do I expose him? How do I prove that the King is responsible for a murder?"

"That's something I thought Grace might help with. You haven't seen her?"

Tristan shook his head. "Nowhere."

"That doesn't make sense," Miles said. "She's never late. I was the late one. She'd literally push me out of bed and make me get ready early when we were children. She should be here."

I watched a well-dressed couple climb the stairs and enter the Clarkes' apartment. "Maybe cleaning out her office took longer than she thought it would."

Miles cocked his head. "What do you mean?"

"Didn't you see her today for lunch?"

"She sent her regrets, and promised to see us tonight," Miles said. "Did you see her?"

"She wanted my help," I said. "She was angry, toweringly angry. She'd said that she couldn't get through to Severin, that Sir Christopher had all the influence, and that Severin wants to put down the 'mob.' That's what he calls the Solidarity Collective."

"What was she going to do?"

"She wanted to quit," I said. "After she made it utterly clear that she was on Solidarity's side. She didn't tell you?"

"No." Miles held onto Tristan for support. "If we're right about Severin being behind Jacob's murder, if he's listening to Father instead of Grace—if she went in there to deliberately make Severin angry enough that he would—"

"What did Grace do?" Tristan asked. "What specifically did she plan on saying to Severin?"

"She was going to outline Solidarity's request for reparations."

Tristan rubbed Miles's shoulder. "How much?"

"Twenty-five percent of the company's total profit, plus interest."

Miles's head came up. "Twenty-five percent? What does that mean in marks?"

"Millions," I said. "Close to forty million marks."

"He'd never say yes to that," Miles said. "He'd fire her. At the very least."

"And what would your father do," Tristan asked, "if he knew his child had turned on him so completely?"

"He'd punish her," Miles said. "He'd— We have to find her. We have to go to the palace. What if he locked her up in prison?"

"Let's do this calmly. We'll start here and go through this systematically," Tristan said.

"Maybe she's on her way," I said. "One moment."

I closed my eyes and stretched out my senses. I thought of Grace's ostentatious orange sleigh, of the horses who trotted perfectly in step with each other, of white-wigged, liveried George who drove her everywhere.

I asked the dead if they had seen the sled, touching every spirit I could reach. They shrugged. They drifted away. I kept searching, kept asking, stretching my senses farther than I'd ever done.

But then one spirit roused, and I could feel the overwhelming fear, the pain, and under it all, the guilt—it rushed toward me, frantic with the emotions of the freshly dead.

"Oh no," I said.

Miles went still. "What is it? What— Oh Solace, Solace no."

I hardly dared open my eyes, despair pooling in my stomach. No. Please don't be, please don't—

But it wasn't Grace's shade standing before me. It was George, his orange greatcoat stained red with his blood, the fabric torn by bullet holes across his body.

"I am murdered," George said. "They took her away. Please, help her."

TWENTY-ONE

The War Measures Act

Grace's sleigh, overturned in the middle of Bigby Street, blocked traffic and attracted spectators. George's body spilled out over the road, his staring eyes wide, his mouth open as if he had shouted at the danger that gunned him down. The horses were stolen.

Miles gripped Tristan's arm with one hand, covering his mouth with the other. "Ambushed," he said. "Look at the street. There are a hundred shadows to hide in. They could have waited here, shot George, stolen the horses, and dragged Grace away."

"Who, though?" Tristan asked. "And were there any witnesses? Did anyone see this happen?"

He addressed the last to the crowd, speaking at top volume, but they avoided his gaze and shuffled backward.

"Shot. George was shot," Miles muttered. "Criminals carry pistols. Gangs."

"So do royal guards," Tristan said. "Or special tactics police."

Miles stared at Tristan, his face bloodless. "We have to find her."

"We can't just run up and down the streets," Tristan said. "We need to retrace her steps, from when Robin last saw her to the moment she was taken. We have to determine which of her enemies this could benefit. We have to consider ransom—"

"Whatever it is, we'll pay it," Miles said. "I don't care how much. It doesn't matter."

"Sir Christopher?" A brown-clad constable approached Miles. "Sir Christopher, I know you want to get your sister back as fast as possible. If you'll come with us, we're going to coordinate a house-to-house search, and we want to ask you some questions."

"Let's go, Miles," Tristan said. "Let's get help from the police."

I stepped closer. "Is there anyone I should inform?"

"Tell Aife," Tristan said. "When we're done with the police, may we shelter at the clan house?"

"For as long as you wish."

"Ask Aife if she brought a finder. That's our best chance."

Tristan guided Miles up the street. They followed the constable who had invited them to the police station. George's spirit hovered by my side, gasping as if he hadn't realized he didn't breathe anymore.

"George. What happened?"

"Shadows rushed the horses, like stagecoach robbers. They shot me. Dame Grace screamed—they dragged her out the back of the sleigh, I think."

"How many?" I asked.

"I don't know. More than a dozen. Twenty, in snow hoods, I couldn't see their faces. Is she dead? Is she dead?"

"Quiet." I reached out, calling to Grace's spirit, relieved as the seconds ticked past without an answer. "No. Her ghost isn't in Kingston. She's alive. Could you tell anything about the kidnappers?"

"They were quiet," George said. "They knew what they were about. They closed on us and did the job, like they'd done it before, maybe?"

Experienced kidnappers. Who had heard of such a thing? Who had experience hiding in a location, executing an attack with speed and deadly force, and then disappearing?

Former soldiers, for one—Amelia had talked to us about her support team, all experienced operators who snuck into range of their target, and then returned in stealth and speed. We'd asked about sharpshooters, but we hadn't asked about the men who supported them.

I walked fast, headed east. George followed, darting into houses and apartments on a frantic search for Grace, just in case she had been taken to ground nearby. The wind shivered through my thin slip and lace skirt, useless for warmth in the middle of Snowglaze. Who else knew how to snatch somebody off the street?

Criminals, like Miles had said. A standover gang experienced in debt collection and swift reprisals.

"George," I said, and the spirit was right next to me, blood shining on his coat buttons. "Were they wearing gray?"

"I don't know, miss," George said. "They had on hoods, like everyone has for deep freezes. Service coats—everyone wears those. Oh. Ribbons on their left arm, like—"

I lifted my left arm, where a yellow satin ribbon fluttered. "My people wouldn't do this."

"They wore them."

"They sell four-foot lengths for a nickel."

No one in Solidarity would kidnap Grace. But someone wanted it to look like they had. And who would that benefit?

The answer weighed a hundred pounds, all of it pressing on my shoulders. I climbed the stairs to the Clarkes' apartment. I made my way inside and stopped at the settee where Aife and Ysonde shared a seat; they turned to stare at me in the exact same moment.

"Tristan sent me," I said. "Grace has been abducted. He wants to know if you brought a finder."

Aife glanced at Ysonde. "We did, but only one."

I sighed, but the stiffness of their postures halted my relief. "What? What's wrong?"

"Our finder is—was," Ysonde amended, "the criminal and life-taker Aldis Hunter."

I shivered. Miles had told me what Aife did to the Amaranthine responsible for the Laneeri scheme to attack Aeland from within its borders, transforming him into a riding beast and putting him in the royal stable. "So you can't find Grace."

"We cannot." Aife gave me a regretful look. "We Amaranthines will help search for her, but your king is deeply fond of Grace. He'll turn the entire city over searching for her, and those responsible will regret ever laying a hand on her."

Would he? I didn't know. At the very least, King Severin was furious with Grace for turning on him. Would he lift a finger to help her? Or was he connected to her disappearance?

I couldn't let my doubts show. I smiled at Aife, nodded my head in agreement. "Miles and Tristan are spending the night in the clan house. They don't want to leave Riverside until she's been found."

"I wouldn't either," Aife said. "I wish I could help you."

"I can," Ysonde said, rising to his feet. "May I open a window?"

"There's a balcony on the other side of those doors," Winnie said. "What are you going to do?"

"Recruit helpers," Ysonde said, and opened both doors wide.

Chill air filled the room, and the sound of beating wings, soft trilling calls, harsh corvid cries, the hoot of an owl. Summoned from their nighttime hunt and comfortable roosts, bird after bird fluttered and landed near Ysonde, jostling each other for the Amaranthine's attention. A nightjay made a sound like a bicycle bell. Sparrows landed on his outstretched hands, then flew off in a flapping hop to the rails. An owl took a prime spot on the railing, joined by a second, and then a third. Flocks of birds. Flights of birds. Braces and broods and bevies of them, all of them bright-eyed and centered on the Amaranthine, who said not a word as they gathered and crowded around him.

They waited, heads cocked as if they were listening, bobbing their heads as if they nodded agreement. Ysonde regarded them all, silent as he gazed on every one of the citizens of the air, and then nodded.

"Go," he said, and the beating of their wings was like thunder. They rose in a great cloud into the midnight sky, their silhouettes blackening the moon. They circled the sky above the street and scattered in all directions.

The gathering had gone utterly silent. Ysonde closed the balcony doors, and the soft puff of a feather floated in the air.

"They're looking for her," Ysonde said. "If she's outdoors for even a minute, they will find her."

"Thank you." I bent my head and my knee and touched my heart as I stood up. "I hope they find her. I have to go—I don't know when Miles is going to need me."

I put my boots back on and walked out into the street.

In a nearby tree, a wakeful sparrow chirped.

I waited for them in the kitchen. I kept the kettle warm and readied a pot of herbs to infuse and soothe frazzled nerves. There wasn't enough sugar for cookies, so I kept a pan of oil on the stove, ready to make fry dough to serve with butter and jam. Miles loved fry dough. I hoped he'd be able to eat some.

After two hours, I paced from the warmth of the kitchen to the chilly front parlor, peering through the windows for any sign of Miles and Tristan, my own thoughts insisting on circling around the whole evening. King Severin could have had Jacob assassinated—and I had already guessed that Jacob had been killed by a spy exposing the steering committee's secrets. That spy could be Gabrielle Meadows, the youngest member of the steering committee. The most passionately devoted to Solidarity. My biggest supporter.

I was so tired. My thoughts raced in weary circles. I walked to the kitchen, checking on the simmering kettle, then drifted back out to stare at the window. Grace had been kidnapped. Severin was a murderer. Gaby was a spy.

I rubbed my temples, massaging a throbbing ache across my forehead. I tried to fit my puzzle pieces together, but they wouldn't fit with a tidy, satisfying click.

A peloton of bicycles rode up to the house, and I flung open the front door, running outside in my slippers. Miles and Tristan hoisted themselves out of sidecars and came to me, speaking quietly for the neighbors' sake.

"The police want to search Hensley House for clues," Miles said. "We're going with them, to smooth the way with the staff."

"We'll stop at my house for rest and come back here after we've gotten some sleep," Tristan said. "Did Aife bring a finder?"

"Only Aldis."

"Blast," Tristan muttered. "I should have known this wasn't going to be easy."

"Ysonde summoned the birds," I said. "They're all searching for her too."

"That's something," Tristan said. "We'll be back in Riverside soon. I still think she's here."

"Get some sleep," I said. "You're no good to anyone groggy."

"Same to you," Miles said.

"We will find her," Tristan said. "We'll find her, and we'll bring her back."

Soothing words. Something to believe in. I nodded and let them go, them and their squad of policemen, and went inside to take the oil off the stove.

Even with strong midnight herbs, I couldn't sleep. I turned my face into the pillow and tried to breathe, imagining my body falling asleep bit by bit, from my littlest toe to the hair on my head, and instead I just watched the sky turn deep blue, streaked by the salmon pink and rose gold of dawn.

I was out of bed before the sun came up, and I opened the front door to two huge black headlines from the papers. KIDNAPPED! read the *Star*, with its usual terse sensationalism, but it was the *Herald*'s headline, taking up half the folded page that chilled my blood:

"I WILL NOT REST": KING INVOKES WAR MEASURES ACT TO FIND ABDUCTED CHANCELLOR

Chancellor? Not former Chancellor? I backed into the house and unfolded the *Herald*. The article put ice in my stomach—in a passionate midnight declaration, King Severin had vowed to find "my loyal friend and most principled Chancellor" and blamed radicalized extremists for her disappearance.

He meant us, Solidarity. And he had mobilized the army, the police, and the royal guard to find her. To leave no stone unturned.

There wasn't a single word about firing her. Or her resignation. *My friend,* the King had called her. *My most loyal friend.*

Lies. All of it lies. Grace had gone to quit her job. She had gone to tell him she was standing with Solidarity. And now she was missing, and the King was not-so-subtly blaming Solidarity for her disappearance. But when Grace was rescued, she'd shatter those lies in a minute. She'd tell the truth about deserting Severin. She'd tell the truth about who had taken her.

So why make up this story? Why lie to the papers like this?

Why lie, unless you knew the truth would never come out?

Nausea rolled through me. Severin had already killed someone, trying to take Solidarity down. He'd murdered a good man for the sake of holding on to power. Grace had turned on him. And once he found her murdered body, he could tell any story he wanted about it. He could use it to crush Solidarity to dust.

I had to go. Now. I had to get out into Riverside and find Grace before it was too late.

I dressed quickly. I called in Joy, and Mahalia, and George. I hauled my bicycle out of the shed and headed east, calling to Grace's spirit.

I prayed she wouldn't answer me.

TWENTY-TWO

A Nice Brick House
with Beautiful Light

No answer as I pedaled out of the neighborhood. Carlotta Brown stopped me and pointed at her left arm while shaking her head vigorously. I stopped, and she crossed the street to meet me.

"They're arresting everyone in Solidarity colors," Carlotta said. "You're no good to anyone locked up in Central."

I wanted to rebel. My first urge was to refuse to take it off, that it would be cowardice, and I was no coward. But Solidarity wasn't a ribbon. It wasn't a color. And I couldn't find Grace if I was locked up in a cell.

I held out my arm and let Carlotta pull the ribbon free. She slipped her own headwrap off her undressed hair and wound it around my head, hiding my distinctive braids. It wasn't even half a disguise, but it might help.

"Go. Keep your head down. Find your friend," she said, and hurried back to the sidewalk.

I tucked the ribbon into my pocket and pedaled on. Half a block later I had to stop at an intersection for a troop of brown-clad police marching young protesters to the police station. Shops had hastily taken down anything yellow in their display windows. The color had vanished, as if the hope of a better Aeland had fallen, trampled under the heavy-soled boots commanded by the King.

Mahalia and Joy moved through shops and returned, telling me the news—Angelus Merchant, vintage home goods dealer and secret book publisher, had been arrested. The Riverside community center had been raided, and police were arresting street peddlers offering spirit readings and other magical claims. They were arresting witches again. Mama's had been taken over as a base of operations by the royal guard and had demanded she feed the guards with only a letter of promise for payment.

Doors were locked. Curtains closed, twitching open only long enough for a furtive peek. I joined a draft of bicyclists and no one even said good morning, let alone the usual talk and gossip that traveled with the people. And everywhere I looked, I saw the headlines.

But the birds flew overhead, singing in whatever tongue their species understood. None of the spirits I spoke to had seen anyone who looked like Grace. And her spirit never came to my call, no matter where I stopped to summon her.

Still alive. Hope beat fiercely in my chest. Grace was still alive, and I kept riding, climbing up King Philip Hill and heading east, calling to her spirit, hope rising with every unanswered minute, every silent mile.

I had gone so many blocks, stopping for soldiers, my gaze respectfully averted, that I had nearly forgotten why they were there and who they were looking for. I stopped at another intersection, but one of the scarlet-coated guards broke free of his unit and approached.

I took my hands off the handlebars, raising them. "Good morning, sir."

"What's your business out here?"

"My name is Janice Baker," I said. "And I'm going to call on a friend who's feeling poorly."

"What's your friend's name?"

Panic battered frantic wings against my ribs. I blurted the first name that fell off my tongue. "Gabrielle Meadows. She's an art teacher."

"You didn't bring her any soup? Any bread?"

"Supplies are low at home," I said. "I thought I'd help her with the washing up, make a little lunch—"

"It's dangerous out here," the guard said, peering at me. "You came out all this way for a friend?"

"She's important to me," I said. "I want to be sure she's all right."

"And what do you do, Janice Baker? Where do you work?"

"Beauregard Veterans'," I said, and bit back a curse. "I'm a cafeteria worker. I work a split week, evenings."

"So you'll be out again. I'll take you to your friend's house. Where does she live?"

Blast it. Blast it to pieces! "Just outside Five Corners, on Quincy Street."

"Come on," he said. "My patrol's in Five Corners. It's on the way."

I did my best to look grateful. "Thank you."

He didn't talk to me. He walked, so I walked, pushing my bicycle as we moved through the streets, and I kept my mouth shut. This was no time to trip on my own tongue. He stopped to get reports from a group of soldiers, who hadn't seen anything, and from some police, who had more people under arrest. I recognized faces among the arrested. One of them saw me and opened her mouth, only to be elbowed by her neighbor.

"You there." A constable pointed a truncheon into the crowd. "What mischief are you up to?"

The elbower spoke up. "She stepped on my toe. Needs to watch where she's going."

"I said sorry," the other one said, sullenly, and didn't look at me.

"Keep order," the constable barked.

My escort moved away, leaving me to follow.

"About time we cleaned up the streets," the guard said. "They've gone too far, taking the Chancellor. Don't know what they thought that would accomplish. The King's not one to bow to the mob."

I kept my silence.

"Don't you agree?" the guard persisted.

"I'd be lying if I said I didn't want a raise," I said, "but it's too much, what they've done. The ribbon wearers, I mean."

"King Severin knows what the people need. He'll do right by all of you. Look at the workweek reform. I'm on four ten-hour shifts. It's loads better. People are getting hired."

"We just have to be patient," I said. "And find the Chancellor before something awful happens."

It hadn't happened yet. Grace's spirit hadn't come to me. She was still alive. We reached Gaby's block, rounding the corner to the brick building where she lived and worked. Just here, at the corner—

Where a length of yellow ribbon fluttered from a mailbox.

"This nonsense," the guard muttered, pulling a knife from a hip sheath. He cut it away, sawing the heavy satin back and forth, an angry grimace on his face. The ribbon came free, and he threw it in the trash bin parked next to the blue metal box. I watched the ragged ends flutter as it landed in the garbage.

We were right outside Gaby's front door. There was a space for my bicycle. I moved for it, and looked over my shoulder.

The clockface chalked on the side of the box read noon.

"This is the place," I said. "Thank you so much for escorting me."

Overhead, a branch swayed under the weight of a sparrow. It chirped, and I called to Grace's spirit once again.

Nothing but silence. Nothing but hope.

The guard nodded. "Just doing my duty. If you run into more guards, tell them your name, and tell them Corporal Jeremy Blounds interviewed you already. Save you some time."

"I will," I said, and smiled at the man. "I hope you find her."

"Me too," he said, and left me on the corner.

Grace had been kidnapped. Severin was lying about it. Gaby was a spy. The top of my head was so hot with anger I imagined it smoked. I opened the front door and marched straight up those stairs, climbing all six flights as I burned and burned with rage.

Gaby answered the door and stared at me in horrified shock. "What are you doing here?"

"I know what you did," I said. "You told the King about Jacob's plan, and the King had him killed. I want to know everything, starting with why you betrayed Solidarity."

"You can't be here," Gaby said. "He's coming any minute."

"Who?" I said. "Your lover? Or should I say, your handler? Good. Because I was going to smoke him out. Grace has been kidnapped, and I mean to find her before she gets killed."

"You have to go," Gaby said. "If he finds out you know about the King's Service, you're a dead woman."

"What's the King's Service? Is that the name for his spies?"

Gaby sealed her mouth shut. I gave an exasperated sigh and

shoved the door open. She gave a surprised shriek and stumbled backward. I shut the door behind me and folded my arms. "Tell me everything."

"I can't," she said. "He's coming."

"Who is your handler?"

"He's killed before," Gaby said. "He'll kill you too. Go home, wait for this to blow over—"

"Wake up, Gaby! There's no way I'm surviving this," I said. "Grace Hensley resigned last night and told the King she was joining Solidarity. Now she's abducted, and the King declared martial law, and when she turns up dead, he's going after everyone at the top. That includes you, unless you think spying for him will get you free."

Gaby turned terror-stricken eyes on me. "You're going to save her?"

"She's not dead yet," I said. "There's still a chance. Who has her?"

"I don't—"

"Don't give me that," I said. "You know something. Tell me. Who has her?"

"If I tell you, you have to hurry. He's coming."

"Your handler. He has her."

Gabby nodded, tears leaking from her eyes. "Now go. Hurry."

"Who is he? Gaby. Tell me who he is."

She froze. Heavy footsteps echoed up the stairwell, rising on the air. Gaby shook her head. "Hide," she whispered. "Don't make a sound."

She shoved me into her supply closet. It smelled like paint, linseed oil, and old, damp-rotted cotton. I hovered in the darkness, peering through the tiny slit that let in light and a sliver of view. The door swung open to admit a tall, blocky man in a gray Service coat, his golden hair shorn short, his pale skin pink with a perpetual blush.

Basil Brown, right-hand man to the Gray Wolf, stood inside Gabrielle's atelier.

"What are you crying for?" he asked, and Gabrielle shook her head.

"It's awful," she sobbed. "I can see them out there, arresting everyone."

Basil moved out of my sight, his footsteps slow. "Shh, shh shh. It'll be over soon."

"Is she going to die?" Gaby asked. "Does she really have to—"

"Boss's orders," Basil said. "Don't you worry about a thing. I've got you, okay? I'll protect you."

They were going to kill Grace. Oh Solace. I was right. They could be killing her right now, while these traitors clutched at each other and lied.

"I don't want her to die," Gaby said.

"People die in wars, sweet Gabrielle. And this is war, but it'll be over soon. I'll go back to my job in the Service, the Greystars will be no more, and they'll never give you trouble for gambling again. Just a few more days, Gabs. Dry your tears; we're almost free."

"But they're arresting everyone. They're taking Solidarity down, not just the Greystars—"

"We don't need Solidarity, Gabs. They're just getting in the way. King Severin knows what's right—he just needs the freedom to do it. All you have to do is show up to trial and tell the truth. And then we'll go and live in a nice brick house—"

"With beautiful light—"

"—and you won't have to teach painting. You can make art all day long."

"I know, Basil, and I want that," she said. "But can't they just put her in jail?"

"I know she's your friend, Gabs. But you were wrong. Solidarity got more effective with her in charge, not less."

Oh, light of the Solace. Me. They were talking about me—

Danger. It flooded my limbs, prompting me to run. I backed up a step, and my heel connected with something that ponged with a hollow thump.

"What was that?"

"Nothing."

"Something," Basil said.

I froze, holding my breath in the solvent-heavy air, but it was too late. Basil was already headed this way.

I groped around in the dark for something, anything. A can sloshed as my fingertips collided with it. I picked up the can as the door swung open, Basil's shadow falling on me.

I dashed the contents of the can straight into his face. He clapped his hands to his eyes and screamed. I had one chance. I sprang toward him, aiming a kick at the base of his kneecap, hands out to shove him to the ground.

But he was too big. He yowled, but it didn't stop him from grabbing me and pinning my arm behind my back. He frog-marched me out of the closet and stopped before a terrified Gaby, who backed away, her hands up.

"Oh Gabs," he said. "And here I thought I could trust you. I thought you were different."

"She's my friend," Gaby said. "And she figured it out on her own."

"Tell me the rest of your excuses, Gabs," Basil said. "I'm interested."

"I tried to make her leave before you came, but she knew I was a spy. She knew who I was spying for. And then we heard you on the stairs and I panicked and I hid her in the closet and—"

"You were going to burn me to save your own skin."

"No!" Gaby said. "She figured out everything!"

"Which is why we can't let her talk. But I'm in a real spot, Gabs. Do you see it?"

Gaby wept. "I didn't want her to find out, Baz, I never wanted this to happen."

"Oh, I believe you," Basil said. "But it doesn't matter. I can't let her go."

He raised his arm, a pistol nestled in his left hand.

"And I can't let you go, either."

"No," I said. "Gaby. Promise not to tell anyone. Promise right now."

"It won't do any good," Basil said. "My Gabs can't stay out of trouble. She'll just get caught again. I don't have a choice."

"Don't," I said.

His shoulder squared up. The gunshot rattled the windows. Gaby fell on a drop cloth. I couldn't tell if she was breathing before Basil dragged me away.

I kicked him. I tried to yank free of his grip. But he dragged me, kicking and fighting, down the stairs and out the back door into an alley.

"You weren't part of the plan just yet," Basil said. "I guess we'll have to improvise."

One more try. I stomped on his foot and yanked, but he grabbed me in a bear hug as I squirmed and struggled. I opened my mouth to scream, but he covered my mouth and nose with his bare hand.

Everything went black at his touch. I couldn't hear my own panicked breathing. I couldn't taste the bile at the back of my throat. I went numb, and the loss of the sense of my own body was a scream inside my mind. Was this death?

No, I should be a ghost. I shouldn't be in this endless nothing, with only my thoughts in an eternity of blackness. This was wrong. This was worse than death.

I couldn't feel the fear wrench my gut, but I screamed regardless.

Hard floor under my back. Dizzy spinning, roiling nausea, and a headache. I felt. I was alive. Tears leaked out of my eyes, spilling into the curving folds of my ears. Rotten-damp paper and dust in the air—and something high and aldehyde sweet, in the background. My shoulders ached terribly.

I stayed very still and tried to feel if I was hurt anywhere. No pain save the shoulders. I opened my eyes, and pale light seeped through a dirty window. I was in a room—a small square thing with peeling arsenic green wallpaper, the tattered leaves drooping and stained with rusty water—with my hands tied behind my back.

An abandoned house. I fought to sit up. Do I call for help, or do I hide my conscious state? I stayed very still and listened. Nothing. No creaking ping from the radiators. No floorboards groaning under the weight of a pacing guard. But I didn't want to give up my only element of surprise.

"If you come and free me, we can make a deal."

That was Grace's shaky voice. She was close by—the next room, even.

"Is there somebody here? Anybody?" she called, and still I stayed quiet as a mouse. They could be ignoring her. But Grace was here, and that meant we could help each other get free.

I got my knees under me. I shifted and struggled to my feet, and promised my joints a nice long soak once we were safe. I put my back to the door and twisted the knob open, and the door's hinges squawked. I froze, listening—they might ignore Grace, but they wouldn't ignore that.

"Who's there?" Grace called. "I heard you, whoever you are. Ahoy? I need water. Please, I'm so thirsty—"

Nothing else in the house stirred. We were alone.

Grace's room had a stiff doorknob. I turned the knob the wrong way, but I finally got it open and backed into the room.

Grace gasped when she saw me, and then melted in relief. She had a bruise on her left cheek and dried blood on her chin from a cut lip. Her fur coat was chalky with dust, and she wore a dinner gown, pearls and diamonds dangling from her ears and neck. She had kicked off her satin shoes, and her stockings were laddered with runs. Her hands were behind her back, and she struggled to her feet.

"They didn't take your jewelry?"

"Who'd be stupid enough to buy three-fifths of the Hensley parure?" Grace said. "They even added to my regalia. There's a ring on my finger that's not mine—never mind that. Come here."

I stood behind Grace and blinked at her hands. "That's quite the ring."

Grace groped into my pocket, fingers wiggling deeper. "What is it?"

"A big sapphire surrounded by diamonds."

"It's what? Oh no."

"What is it?"

"I need to see the ring. What did the papers say about my disappearance? Did they say anything? Did Severin give a statement?"

"He did. He called you his dear friend—"

"That's not what he said yesterday," Grace muttered. "Shit! We're in trouble."

"Turn around and crouch so I can get at your hands. So you did quit?"

"The papers didn't say that I did, did they?"

"Not a word. You're still the Chancellor, according to them," I said. "Crouch a little more."

Grace hunched down, and I felt around the knot. They'd tied us with twine, pulling the knots tight. A knife would have been better, but I felt the knot and tried to pull it loose.

"What did the King say, then?"

"He called you his most loyal friend. That he would find you. That your kidnappers would pay—"

No good. "Hold still. The knot is tight." The ends of the knot were trimmed short, but I closed my eyes and dug the knot free.

"Ah!" Grace sighed. "My hands are all pins and needles. Hold still."

She knelt to get a close look at my tied hands, and her fingernails were long enough to pick the knot free much faster than I'd managed. I moved to the window to see where we were, and froze.

The windows had been nailed shut.

Joy rushed in through the boards. "Robin! The man is here!"

She had to mean our murderer, Basil. If these windows were nailed shut from the inside, this building had been prepared for us. We had to move. "Go get help, Joy. Spread the word to the spirits. Find Zelind. Check Bayview."

Joy zipped through the wall and disappeared.

"Mahalia," I said, and my aunt came, looking scared. "I need you to get Zelind. Make kher follow you. Get Zelind to come. Check the clan house first."

"She should get Tristan."

"She doesn't know Tristan, and he's all the way up at the palace," I said. "Zelind can get to us faster than Tristan can."

"All right," Grace said. "But we have to do something ourselves too. Look."

She showed me her hand. A double row of tiny diamonds surrounding a hefty sapphire rested on her left ring finger.

"It's the Heart of Aeland," Grace said. "Severin tried to give it to me when he proposed. He means for it to be found on my dead body."

"So we wouldn't have murdered just the Chancellor," I said. "We would have murdered his bride. We have to get out of here."

The house shook. The walls shuddered as someone thumped and hammered, striking the walls over and over. My heart leapt into my throat, and I clutched Grace's arm.

"What is that?"

"Hammers," I said. "He's nailing the doors and windows shut."

"We're trapped?" Grace's voice rose.

"Yes. And when he's cut off every escape, he'll—"

I could smell it then, like a spent match or a blown-out candle or the smell of a hearth-fire on a cold day.

"Fire," I said. "He's setting the house alight."

Grace clutched at my elbows. "We have to get out of here. If we die in here—does the water work?" Grace ran out of the room and opened doors, searching for the bathroom sink. "Give me your handkerchief."

I found mine, and Grace soaked it in running water. "Breathe through this."

I tied it over my mouth and nose. I had to work harder to get a breath. "What about that spell you used to protect us from the wind? Can you use it to surround us in clean air? As much of the air as you can."

"Yes." Grace took my hand. "Stay close."

"And don't let the flames touch it," I said.

The odor of burning wood persisted, but it was fainter. Browntinged white smoke rose up the stairwell, but Grace's bubble cut through it, extending a good three feet from our shoulders.

"Tighter," I said. "You can't let the air meet the flames. This bubble takes a lot of its fuel away, but if it gets into our bubble of air—"

"It'll roast us," Grace said. "I've never tried to make it smaller. One moment."

The smoke crept closer to us, rubbing against the barrier that separated its poison from our safe haven. Grace pulled the bubble in, and my outstretched arm disappeared into the smoke.

"Done. How are we going to get out?" Grace shouted above the crackling roar. "They nailed everything shut."

"We have to break a window," I said. "Hurry. The stairs are—"

It was hot as an oven. More smoke filled the upper floor, and the air radiated through my coat. I stepped back, pushing Grace away from the steps, and the air smelled like burning hair.

I felt my face. Tight and hot. My eyebrows crushed under my fingertips, and tiny flakes of ash landed on my eyelids.

"The stairs are on fire," I said.

"What do we do?" Grace asked. "If we can't take the stairs, what can we—"

Smoke billowed out of the tiny room where I had been imprisoned. Flames leapt out of the smoke, and I drew Grace back.

"It spread so fast," she said. "There's nowhere to go."

"The open doors," I yelled. "They gave the fire air."

She groaned. "My fault."

"No time for that. Come this way."

"This is a dead end," Grace said.

"It's our only chance," I said. "If I'm right, it should be right here."

"What?"

I pounded on the panel, and it rang hollow, the way a door carried the sound through the air. It had to be here. If it wasn't, if we didn't escape, the truth would die with us. Solidarity would die, murdered by a king masked with a man's vengeance of a woman's death.

"What are you doing?" Grace asked. "It's getting closer."

I felt a little higher. "This is a kit house," I said. "They built them by the dozens in Birdland. Miles used to live in one."

"What does that have to do with you feeling the walls?"

"There should be servants' stairs right here," I said. "So this panel is actually a door—ah!"

My fingers found a smooth metal bump and pressed. I nearly sobbed in relief. The panel, still cool to the touch, pushed backward with a rusty click. I shoved the hidden door to the side, revealing steep wooden stairs leading down.

Behind us, the fire roared.

"We're feeding it air!" Grace shouted, and the bubble around us grew heavier, denser.

"Come on," I said. "It's our best chance."

Grace made sure to shut the sliding door before venturing down into total darkness. I had hoped for a window, but fortune wasn't with me today.

It was hot in here. Were we escaping, or just putting ourselves in a corner? It smelled like a fireplace, and heat drifted up my skirt. Was there fire below us? Were we about to fall through the stairs?

"Hurry," I said, and leapt for the landing, realizing that the jump could knock me through the boards. If we wound up in the basement, we were dead.

My stomach lurched as I hit the floor, but the boards held. The air smelled more strongly of smoke, but the door lever was only warm. Warm, but not yet hot. Was the kitchen burning?

"I have all the air," Grace said. "Hurry."

I took a steadying breath and swung the door open. The kitchen billowed with smoke. Flames licked at the doorway to the dining room. Grace shut the service door behind her and put her hands on my shoulders.

"It's so hot. What do we do?"

"Shut the door," I said, and we darted closer to the incredible heat to kick the kitchen door shut.

"How much time did that buy us?" Grace yelled.

"Not even a minute," I shouted back. "There's a window over the sink, and that window in the door. If we're escaping, it has to be from here—"

"Is there someone out there?" Grace pointed.

A shadow stood outside the door, holding a—a club, maybe, or a bat. Grace backpedaled away, and smoke rushed around me—darker now. Browner and kind of oily looking. It stung my eyes and I stopped breathing, my lungs fighting to take a breath. I sealed my hands and nose, covering the now-dry handkerchief over the lower half of my face. I couldn't breathe. Not yet. Not—

Grace touched my shoulder. Air enveloped me again, pushing against the kitchen door, and the shadow outside resolved into a figure with close-cropped hair and a steel-headed sledge.

Zelind had come. Khe was just on the other side of the door, right where I could see kher. Khe gestured at me to get back, raising the hammer.

"No!" I waved my arms, crossing them over my head, the police gesture for stopping traffic. Zelind raised the hammer again, and I shook my head.

"No!"

But the five-pound head arced straight for the window. Khe was going to break it and let all that air inside. All that deadly, fire-fueling air, and it was going to kill us all.

"The door!" I shouted, and dodged to the side as Zelind's hammer swung for the window. The sound of shattering glass was lost in the roar behind me. I cringed as shards flew through the air, spinning as they sailed into the wall of smoke just two feet away from the door. The air chilled. It smelled sweet, with the promise of snowfall.

I braced myself for the explosion, but it didn't come.

Grace stood in front of the kitchen door, her hands raised to

protect her face. Glass sparkled in the singed fur of her coat. Her jaw
bled from a splinter of glass caught in her cheek. But she held the barrier of air away from the boiling brown smoke that enveloped us.

Zelind swung kher hammer and knocked out another pane, bash-
ing at the wooden framework that held the glass. Grace's seal held,
but the smoke turned black.

"I see flames," Grace said, and so did I. They crept up the pantry
door, crawling up the panels. We were so close. So close to freedom.

Zelind swung kher hammer, and wood splintered away. Glass
shattered. Grace flinched as they struck her coat. The cupboards
caught. Fire boiled over the ceiling, so hot I thought my skin would
crack, the fat underneath it sizzling as it dripped.

Zelind's hammer crashed into the glass one last time, and then a
heavy blanket landed on the edge.

"You have to go first," Grace said.

"Boost me."

Grace made a cradle of her interlaced hands and I stepped on it,
rising high enough to push myself through the hole. Zelind caught
me with kher magic and pulled me loose. Grace hoisted herself
through the window, and we both caught and dragged her free.

Grace pointed at the street. "Run."

We scrambled off the back porch. Fire blazed all around us—the
bushes had caught, and they burned with the sweet smoke scent of
fruitwood. Behind us, heat blossomed. It pushed at my back as the
fire, starved for air while Grace deprived it, came back with a roar
once she let it go. I was knocked off my feet, flying on a burning hot
thermal.

I landed in deep, freezing snow, and the sensation of it on my face
stung for an instant. So cold. I got to my feet, watching what should
have been our grave go up in flames. The fire, now fed by the outside
air, consumed the walls. I stared at it and wondered why I didn't feel
afraid, why I didn't feel the cold, why I was nothing but my plan to
escape and survive, my humanity paused while I stared at the confla-
gration.

And then I was caught up in Zelind's arms.

I clung to kher. My cheek stung where it scraped against kher
shoulder. I smelled like burning hair, but my wool clothes were only
singed. I held onto kher and concentrated on the pain in my cheek. I

could feel that. I could feel kher beating heart, fast and strong. Kher breath on my temple, the chill in the air—

Sensation flooded back. Feeling flooded back. I shook in Zelind's arms and shut my eyes against the pain. I could have died. Grace could have died. And if we had died, no one would be there to stop Severin and his determination to crush his own people.

"Mahalia found me." Zelind said into my singed hair. "We all came."

"Who's we?"

"I was at the clan house."

The crowd was made up of neighbors, spilled out into the street, and asylum-born witches, distinctive with their short-cropped hair. Zelind pulled back to look at me. "Who did this to you? Who put you in that house?"

"Basil Brown, under orders from the King," I said.

The crowd around me gasped, and a pair of youths in gray shoved forward. "He never."

"He arranged Jacob Clarke's assassination. He killed Gaby Meadows to preserve his cover. He kidnapped us, and he set that house ablaze—after nailing it up."

They went sulky and quiet. Jamille parted the crowd and stood next to her followers. "He told us to meet him here. We were supposed to ransom the Chancellor. That's what he said he planned to do."

"So it was him. He set the fire at the Battle house. And the asylum fire, too," I said. "You wanted revenge for Jack, and Basil had an idea how to get it. He set you up."

"Basil and Jack were friends," Jamille said. "He was almost family. He'd never betray me—"

"He planned to pin Grace's murder on you. He was going to walk away while you all got rounded up for treason. How many of yours are arrested?"

"Cops are everywhere," Jamille said. "They raided the Rook. Grabbed a week's take as evidence."

"And was I right? Was kidnapping Grace Basil's idea?"

Jamille sniffed, squinting at us both. "He said the King would listen to us if we had her. That we'd give her back when we had what we wanted."

"And what did you want?" Grace asked.

Jamille looked at Grace as if she were a fool. "The Free Government to hold real power."

"Is that all?" I asked.

"Money." Jamille shrugged. "Isn't it enough? But the King put the guard in the streets. He's arresting everyone he can. We weren't getting satisfaction out of him. We thought we could end this madness if we let her go."

"To make it stop," I said. "But Basil had other plans."

"I swear to you, Auntie, Basil Brown is a dead man," Jamille said. "And if Dame Grace died, we were all going to swing for it."

"It's worse than you think." Grace said. "He set up my abduction so he could call the War Measures Act. He told lies to make sure the people were all outraged when the firefighters found my body in the house. And this."

She held up her hand, showing off the sapphire ring. "This is the Heart of Aeland. He was going to lie about me being his bride, so everyone would hunger for vengeance against those responsible."

I spoke up then. "He was going to blame Grace's death on us. He was going to crush us under his guard's boot. Try us for treason. Make you all afraid to make Aeland change."

I reached into my pocket and pulled out my yellow ribbon. I raised my fist in the air, and the wind caught the ends, making them flutter.

"He will not stop me," I shouted. "He will not stop Solidarity. He owes the people an apology. He owes the dead justice. And I'm going to the palace to get it."

The crowd roared. Fists rose in the air, ribbons unfurled and dancing in the breeze. A rush of wings struck the air all around us, and birds took to the sky, darting past us and toward the palace, ready to tell Ysonde that Grace had been found.

I shouted, and my voice rang off the low-bellied clouds. "Deathsingers, call the spirits of Aeland! Bring them with us! They deserve his regret. They deserve his amends. To the palace! Let the redbacks stand aside. Aeland, come with me! Louder than thunder! Stronger than steel!"

TWENTY-THREE

Atone or Surrender

The dead outnumbered us ten to one by the end of the first block. Mahalia and Joy stuck close to me, following behind Zelind and Grace, who walked by my side. A guard patrol saw us coming and shouted at us to disperse, but there were only two of them and ninety of us. We walked on.

And as we walked, marchers took up singing a labor song about the fight for better conditions. The next song asked where the witches went, and sprouted a new verse about their return, gaunt and shaven and haunted. But when the crowd broke into "Aeland Eternal, Aeland Forever," people opened their front doors. They stared at us, marching with our fists in the air, holding up the ribbons we'd been forced to hide.

With every verse, more came out and joined us.

By the time the riot police reached us, thumping riot batons against shields and chanting at us to go home, we had collected thousands of people and ten thousand ghosts. They converged on the police, screaming, passing their spectral bodies through flesh. Constables broke the line, fleeing the wrath of the dead. When our force met theirs, they were already shaken. We passed by them, singing.

Young men in workman's tweed and flat caps joined us. Women threw coats over their housedresses and aprons to join us. We filled the block, spilling over to the next, and kept walking up King Philip Hill to Main Street. A shopkeeper ran out of her corner store with an armful of ribbons to share out, and we walked, holding our Uzadalian banners to the sky.

The dead kept coming, called from their aimless wandering by the Deathsingers from Clan Cage, those witches who had been born to captivity, who had suffered unimaginable violation. The dead marched with us, even the ones who were little more than a handful of memories. Attracted to us like moths to moonlight, they came.

We stopped traffic dead in downtown Kingston, making bicyclists in sack suits wait while we marched in the street, dead and living alike, the long river of thousands turning off Main Street to the King's Way. Police stood in front of shop windows, protecting merchandise. But our purpose wasn't looting. We marched past them, plate glass untouched, and the rumors swirled through the crowd.

The marchers told each newcomer that Severin had lied. They recounted the story of my and Grace's escape from the burning house in East Riverside, saying we made it out shortly before it exploded. They said that we were going to the palace to make Severin apologize and recognize the Free Government. The witches were going to curse Severin if he didn't pay them their reparations. The dead were going to get an apology. Revenge. Justice. When the stories threatened to take on a life of their own, we corrected them, holding hard to the truth.

Others joined us, walking bicycles once they had caught up. Someone told me the march was five blocks long. Another said that asylum-born Deathsingers were uniting ghosts with the people who grieved for them. Newspaper reporters joined the flock, talking to marchers, drawing out their stories.

We walked the two miles to Mountrose Palace and met the protesters who held vigil there, waiting for the sun to rise on a better Aeland. We filled the square to overflowing. We pushed against the gates that kept us from the palace—but on the other side, royal guards waited for us with rifles drawn and trained on us, their message clear—rush the gates, and they would fire.

"Stop," I called. I put my hand up and shouted again. "Hold!" My voice was as loud as it would be through a bellower. I startled, and Grace gave me a wink. "Aeland, stay still! There are armed guards at the gates."

The advice to stay still muttered through the crowd, the word rumbling in the frigid air. I turned to Grace. "Can you do that again?"

"Say what you wish," Grace said, and I turned back to the guards.

"Royal guards! Lay down your arms! You have a hundred bullets. We are thousands! We don't want to fight you. You don't want to shoot us."

"Disperse," the guard in captain's braid bellowed. "By order of the King, vacate the square."

"Surrender," I shouted. "There will be no bloodshed. Stand aside."

Their captain barked an order, and the guards sighted down their rifles. We were only targets. They would fire on us. We would fall, and then surge back once they ran out of bullets, and this day would bleed red in history.

I had to stop it—how? How could I convince them?

This wasn't about me. I spread my senses and called to the dead for help.

A chill passed through me. Ghosts drifted through us, passing the barred gates and filling the steps. They swarmed the guards. They surrounded them, touching and groping at their bodies.

One of them jerked. She raised the rifle, pointing it at the sky. Then another guard lurched away from the line, his steps uncertain. Another dropped the rifle as if it had suddenly become hot, and frost rimed the long barrel.

Grace pointed, and frost-covered rifles hit the ground. Zelind pointed, and rifles yanked themselves into the air. Now unarmed, the guards backed up the stairs. Two cut and ran, ignoring the captain's orders. The other guards watched them, looked at each other for guidance—and raised their empty hands, backing away from the gates.

That was enough. The crowd cheered and rushed the gates, which bowed under the force, sagging back as the people backed up and hurled themselves at the barriers again. Once more, and the posts holding the gates bent. Another heave, and the gates leaned precariously, ready to fall.

"Again!" someone shouted. "One, two, three—"

The hollow support posts snapped on one side. Citizens swarmed over the breach. They dashed up the stairs, rifles snatched up as they ran down the guards and hauled the front doors open.

"Watch the guards," I told a clump of ghosts. "Don't let them get hurt."

Citizens cheered as they filled the great hall. They spread into the hallways. A small unit of armed citizens overpowered red-coated guardsmen, passing their surrendered weapons to increase their numbers, and this was going to be a riot if we didn't find a purpose.

I grabbed Jean-Marie. "Find the kitchens. Tell them to feed the people. That will slow them, calm them down."

I sent her on her task and spied another face I knew from Solidarity. "Get a group together and spread the word that we need the Free Elected Members to get together and start working on a statement for the press."

He nodded and summoned up a group of his own. I grabbed a formidable-looking auntie and had her search the crowd for anyone with medical experience, to set up a clinic in the palace hospital.

With the crowd directed, it was time to move. "Grace."

She was at my side in a moment. "Yes."

"We have to find the King. Where would you suggest looking for him?"

"After the overthrow of the palace?" Grace asked. "Inside the temple."

"Take us there," I said. "Zelind. You're with me."

Zelind huffed a soft laugh. "As if I would let you go on without me."

I took kher hand and nodded to Grace. "Let's go."

Grace led us through the gilded reception hall, looking neither left nor right at the people lifting priceless works of art from the walls. It pricked my conscience until I turned my face up to behold our reflections in the mirrored tiles in the ceiling fixed together by gold moldings. Solid gold, I remembered from the time we trooped into the palace as schoolchildren to stare at all the finery I now understood to be hoarded wealth. The taxes of five hundred clan houses held those mirrors together. The wealth in that ceiling could feed the entire country for a year. This ostentation and greed had to end.

I followed Grace down the parquet to a tall, round chamber where the noise of our footsteps carried, caught, and swirled in the overhead dome painted in the most expensive, vivid pigments—this time a mural of the Hundred Knights kneeling before Queen Agnes, who raised her hand in benevolent approval.

Grace flung open the tall doors to the temple, and the scent of sweetwood smoke and burning beeswax filled the air. Every writing desk bore its own censer and pillar candle, waiting for a devoted scrivener to light the candle of divine vision, to burn the offering, invite the makers to guide their pens, and then fall into a light trance of writing whatever entered their mind while meditating on a problem or a gratitude.

At the far end of the rings of writing desks stood Severin, head bent as his pen juddered across a page of his own book. He raised his head at the sound of our entrance, his lips pressed together so tightly they were white. He put down his pen and drew a pistol, its barrel swinging to point at me.

Grace huffed. "Guns. How cute."

"Now," the King said, and a flurry of movement burst from behind us. Basil Brown held his bare hand against Grace's mouth, and she went limp in his arms. She didn't struggle, didn't make a sound—but her unseeing eyes were white all around the iris, wide with terror.

I moved for Basil, but the King's voice stopped me. "Move and she dies."

I stopped. "You're that good a shot?"

"No. But she is."

I followed Severin's gaze up to the banister rails circling the loft and stared up the barrel of a long black rifle. Zelind touched my wrist and shook kher head.

Khe could yank the gun out of one opponent's hands, but khe couldn't see both at once. Whichever khe disarmed, the other would have time to shoot. And the King wasn't gunning us down just yet. We needed to buy some time if we were going to convince him to step aside.

"All right," I said. "Let's just take it easy. I came to talk."

"You came to demand my crown," Severin said. "All the years I ran charitable foundations, funded the Rose Crown scholarships, headed relief programs, and you couldn't see that I was on your side? You couldn't see that as king, I would steer our course toward reform, that my rule would be good for you?" He looked at me with hurt in his eyes. "I had so many plans. Why didn't you trust me?"

"Because we're asking for so much more," I said. "Because a good king is still a king."

"You could have waited to see what I was like. I understood your dissatisfaction with my mother. I shared it, didn't I? I was prepared to bring the change you wanted. Decree by decree, I would show my Cabinet what mattered to me, lead them to a better Aeland. Only you lot wouldn't let up. You wouldn't take what I offered. You didn't even give me the chance to prove myself."

"You would have proven yourself if you had decreed free democracy," I said. "You never called a meeting with Solidarity to hear us. You never expended even the slightest effort to reach out to us."

"A king doesn't ask for permission from his subjects," Severin said. "You were in the way. I had a plan. With you telling the Chancellor what your people wanted, I could employ the best of those ideas myself. But instead, you defied me. I don't understand you people at all. I offered your spouse a fortune. Look what khe did with it."

This need to be in control as the supreme authority—that was why Jacob died. It all led back to Severin's need to rule. To be right. To be loved by his subjects unquestioningly.

"I understand now," I said. "I see what you intended, and your intentions were good, but your plan wouldn't work if Jacob was still putting Solidarity to work against you."

"Exactly," the King said. "I didn't want to see Jacob dead. He was a good man, as you said. He just didn't know when to quit fighting."

"So you had to kill him," I said.

"Yes."

"Are you sorry you had to kill him?" I asked.

Severin paused. "I regret his death."

"Because a king can't apologize," I said.

"Yes."

"Then there's a problem," I said. "Because the dead are here, and they want your apology. They want your amends. And they won't leave until they have them."

Silently, I called to the dead. I opened my senses to them and beckoned them to me. They came in a great rush, their presence swooping through my senses like the fluttering of many wings, their spirits like soft points of cold in the beeswax-scented room.

Joy was first at my side. Mahalia came next. They floated beside me, the strongest-willed spirits I knew, and floated toward the King, who was white as a sheet.

"No," he said. "No, get away."

The gun barrel swung away from me and pointed at Joy.

"Get back!" the King cried.

"Duck!" Zelind cried, and from behind me came a firecracker pop and a shivering chill.

The sniper. I'd forgotten.

I froze in the sliver of a second before the bullet ripped through me. Zelind flung out kher hand, defending me to the last. Kher mouth opened on a shout, kher nose loosed two thin streams of blood that poured off kher upper lip. Khe coughed, and a fine-mist cloud of blood landed on my face. Khe fell, and while khe was falling I realized, finally, that I was still alive, that I wasn't shot and bleeding.

The bullet that had been hovering in midair succumbed to gravity and fell to the floor.

But Zelind was on the ground, chest heaving, blood smearing over kher cheeks. A bullet lay beside her, shining dully on the golden oak floor. Zelind looked past me as khe lifted kher hand, and Laura's rifle sailed through the air.

It crashed to the floor, and Zelind closed kher eyes.

"No!"

I fell to my knees beside kher. I seized kher soul and held it inside kher body.

"You do not get to die today," I said. "You hear me? Your soul is not going anywhere. Joy!" I shouted. "Get Miles. You get him and you bring him here."

As I held in kher soul, a memory of sunlight glittered on the Densmore Canal. I felt Zelind beside me on a canal barge, asking me to explain germ theory and avoiding infection. Khe listened while butterflies swooped in kher stomach, picking out the next question to keep me talking until the barge stopped behind the clan house and I had to disembark.

"Fight," I said. "Void damn it, fight for me."

We walked across the open field toward school, our shoes crunching on the frosted grass. Zelind asked, "Will you help me with my health science report?" with so much tension quivering inside kher, I held my breath until the younger me shrugged and said, "Sure."

We were fourteen, and Zelind's joy at my acceptance made tears blur my eyes.

"You loved me," I said. "We were knee-deep in puberty, and you loved me and I didn't even notice."

Zelind smiled. Kher teeth were bloody. "There was only ever one girl for me," khe said. "Besides, you—"

Blood sprayed from kher mouth as khe coughed.

"Just stay still," I said. "Miles is coming. He's coming."

Zelind heaved, kher breath tattered. "It hurts."

"I know," I said. "It hurts like the blazes. That's how you know you can still fight."

Beyond me, Severin sobbed like a child, the air around him so thick with the dead that he was hard to see. They passed through his shuddering body, pouring everything they'd felt inside the soul-engines into the King's terror and torment.

"Please," he bawled, and tried fighting them off, but they kept coming.

"Make them stop." Basil pointed the gun at me. "Make them stop hurting the King."

"It's over, Basil."

Basil's response was to lower his aim. "Or I could shoot kher. Call off your spirits, or your sweetheart is dead."

"If I let kher go, khe's dead."

Basil shrugged. "I think you're having a bad day, Auntie. Time to choose."

But the spirits closed in on the King, who held his pistol out before him like a talisman, his face taut with horror.

"I can't stop them," I said.

Basil looked regretful. "That's a shame. Should I do you next?"

Joy burst through the door an instant before it flew open. Tristan cut toward Basil, who swung his pistol around—and blinked as Tristan vanished. Basil gasped as blood flew from his mouth, his head snapping back as if he'd been caught unawares by a powerful blow.

Amaranthines poured into the temple, seizing Basil and putting him on his knees.

Grace fell to her knees and gasped, rolling out of the way. Miles knelt beside me, feeling Zelind's throat.

"I've got kher. It will be all right," Miles said, his palm spread against Zelind's forehead. "Get the King."

"Are you sure you don't need me to—"

"Trust me. Go," Miles said.

I dashed toward Severin, who stared at the ghosts as he sucked in rapid, anxious breaths. I lunged for him, and the ghosts closed in. Severin uttered a thin scream, and I snatched the pistol out of his hands.

He grabbed the front of my singed coat. "Help me."

"No."

I grabbed his wrist and Severin whimpered. The ghosts raked their hands over his face, the whole writhing, haunting mass of them whispering. Some of the most damaged couldn't speak. But they could all scream, and they howled at the King while clawing at him, their hands passing into his body.

"You need to apologize to them," I said. "But a king can't apologize, can he?"

"Stop it," Severin wailed. "Make it stop. Make them stop."

"They will never stop," I said. "Not while you're king. They will come to you every day and every night. They will haunt you forever, until you apologize."

"I didn't do this to them! Tell them! I didn't do it!"

"You carry your grandfather's guilt, and your mother's too. You inherited it along with that crown. This is Cynthia Martin," I said. "She died two years ago. She didn't go to the Solace. She went into a soul-engine. It hurt her for two years. It ate her memories. It ate her soul. And you have to apologize. This is Keltan Green of the Sure Winds. He died—"

"Make it stop," Severin said. "Please."

"Only one thing will stop them from coming to you," I said.

"Anything."

"You must make amends to them."

"How?"

"Give up absolute rule," I said. "Or we will fill your palace with the dead. They will find you no matter where you hide."

"You can't."

"I can," I said. "And so can the Deathsingers you had bred to keep the soul-engines running. We will never stop haunting you."

"I'll do whatever you want," Severin said. "I'll pay the reparations Grace proposed to me."

"Not enough."

"I'll recognize the Free Government," he said. "They'll hold equal weight to the Lower House."

"They already are the Lower House," I said. "And it's not enough."

"Please. I'll make aether free. Please."

"You planned and carried out the murder of Jacob Clarke. You sent your spy to murder Grace Hensley. You used her disappearance as an excuse to loose the armed guards on your own citizens. You should be stripped of your crown and tried for your crimes—for which you would hang."

"No," Severin gasped. "I just wanted the chance to prove myself."

"You failed," I said. "You have a choice. Atone for all the dead by restructuring the government. End the rule of the Crown and abdicate. Or spend years where you personally atone for what your legacy has become. Because they won't stop haunting you until you do one or the other."

"Yes! Yes! I'll abdicate. I'll do what you want, only please—"

I looked up. "He's going to do it," I said to the ghosts. "It isn't enough, but he'll do it. Back up."

The ghosts floated away. Severin wept. His body shook, and he gulped down air.

"Stay near him," I said. "Don't let him forget his promise."

I pulled the plain gold circlet from his head and turned back to Miles and Zelind.

Miles wasn't alone. Aife and Ysonde knelt beside him, shoring up Miles's energy with their own strength. Ysonde was veiled in shadows that fluttered like wings, flashing bright as the afterglow of lightning. Aife was bathed in clear golden light, her glamor little more than gossamer over her strange, half-divine beauty.

Miles blazed with power. The thirteen soulstars crowning him glowed, and green light poured from his hands, filling Zelind's body as the power knitted kher back together. Zelind's face was taut with pain, and khe gasped for breath, kher fists clenched.

"Can you save kher?"

"I'm doing it," Miles said. "Khe's a fighter, but I'm borrowing flesh to pay for organ damage."

"Kher soul will not untether," Aife said. "Khe wants to live."

I landed on my knees next to kher. "Breathe," I said. "I know it hurts."

"That's how I know I can still fight," Zelind said, and groaned as khe laughed.

"Don't talk."

"Zelind's going to need total bedrest," Miles said.

"Oh. That sounds fun," Zelind said.

"I wouldn't move kher out of the palace right now," Miles said. "But kher sarcasm is completely intact, so there's hope."

Grace hugged herself around the middle, and Tristan draped an arm around her as they watched my best friend work to save Zelind.

Miles lifted his hands away. "There."

Zelind tried to lift kher head, but Miles stopped it with his hand on kher forehead. "Don't you move. Not after all the work I did to save you."

I wiped at my forehead. "We did it. We won."

Grace looked up, stepping out of Tristan's comforting arms. "There's something I need to do."

"What's that?"

Grace straightened her dinner gown and took the Heart of Aeland off her finger. "I need to make Father pay for all this."

"Grace," Miles said, but Grace strode off, straight-arming the door open.

Miles sighed. "I'm all right here. Go after her. Don't let her do anything foolish."

TWENTY-FOUR

One Last Blow

Grace was halfway down the corridor by the time I made it out of the temple. I ran, gasping at how the heat-singed skin on my legs and face felt tight and hot as I moved. "Grace!"

"I have to do this," Grace said. "I have to make sure he can't hurt anyone else."

"All right, so we can—"

"I should have stopped him in Bywell. Every setback, every difficulty, every treachery traces back to him. Look what he did to Severin."

"Severin wouldn't have surrendered his power with a smile—"

"We could have worked something out." Grace's strides were so long, and she took the stairs two at a time. "Ceremonial duties, the opportunity to give advice or an opinion—but Father had to have it all, at any cost. He'll never stop trying to control Aeland, not as long as he breathes."

"Grace, stop." I jogged by her side and tugged at her elbow, but she kept walking. "Let's get help. Let's arrest him."

"I am."

We were before a golden oak door, unguarded and unlocked. Grace yanked it open and strode inside, facing the frail figure of Sir Christopher Hensley, who stood before a table filled with tonic bottles.

"I wondered if you would come," he said. "I suppose I knew you would."

He stood with his back to us and looked out the window, preoccupied by the sight of the stars—but then he coughed, great horrible coughs that could crack a rib in a man so old, so weakened by his illness. It was a wonder that he could stand, even with the aid of a cane.

Grace waited until the spasms passed. "It's over, Father."

"So. You've fallen in with the rabble," he said. "I did my best for you. I worked for years to bring you the greatest gift a father could give his most beloved child—the hand of a king, a crown of your own—and you dashed it to the ground to cavort with peasants."

"You taught me that I should make Aeland a better place than it was before," Grace said. "You told me to defend Aeland with everything I had. That's what I'm doing. I'm protecting Aeland from you."

"You little fool," Sir Christopher said. "Can't you see what they will do, if you let the mob run wild? I taught you everything you needed to guide a nation. I gave you a king you could rule!"

He turned, finally, his eyes bright with anger, but that glint was nothing compared to the blaze of hatred that twisted his face when he saw me.

"You," he said. "You twisted my daughter's mind."

And then I couldn't breathe. I choked on nothing, my lungs trying desperately to fill. I groped for Grace, but she ran for her father. She leapt over the sofa, landed before him, and wrapped her hands around his throat.

"No one understands how dangerous you are," Grace said. "But I do. You know what else you taught me? To do what must be done and take responsibility after."

She was going to kill him. I tried running forward, to flee the bubble denying me air, but my lungs ached with the effort of trying to get a breath. I struck Grace on the shoulder, but everything was fading out.

"Grace," I croaked, and thankfully she saw me. Air seeped into my mouth, down my throat—it was only a trickle, but I gasped it in. "Grace, stop."

"I can't. I can't let him live."

"If you don't, it's murder."

"He won't stop," Grace said. "He won't stop until he's dead."

"And he will hang," I said. "But I need you to help me heal Aeland, don't you see that? And if you kill him, he will have succeeded in one last blow against Solidarity, one more thing to sabotage us."

Grace looked at me, and Sir Christopher's thrashing weakened. "He has to pay."

"He will. Let him go, Grace. Don't let him cheat me of the best political strategist in Aeland. Don't let him take my friend away."

Grace's eyes flared wider, and she took her hands away. Sir Christopher gulped in air, once, twice, and backed into a corner.

"Get a pillowcase. We need to blindfold him," Grace said. "We're taking him to Kingsgrave."

"He'll appear before the Free Government," I said. "They will pass judgment. He'll see justice. This will all be over soon."

We left Sir Christopher in a copper-clad cell with nothing but a straw mattress and a woolen blanket. Grace stopped at the guard station to speak to the warden, and I continued past celebrating citizens who had found the wine cellar, graciously refusing a draft on the way up to the infirmary.

Miles was still by Zelind's side, and I gasped to see how wasted, how bony Zelind had become. It was worse than kher underfed frame at the asylum, and Miles held kher hand, still trickling strength into kher.

"Khe's in a medically enhanced sleep. I'll have to heal kher daily to help speed recovery, but khe's better than khe looks."

I gazed down at Zelind's sleeping, bony face. "How long do you need to keep kher?"

"Weeks," Miles said. "I'll see if I can get the Amaranthine healer to assist me. But you're going to be in with those burns, so you can stay with each other."

"Thank you."

"Sit here. I want to look at you."

I reared back. "You have to save your energy for Zelind."

"Tell you what," Miles said, the soulstars glimmering around his head. "You can have a nurse clean and tend the other burns, but let me heal your face."

Now I crept closer. "I haven't looked at it."

"You have blisters. Your eyebrows are gone. But I can take care of all that without scarring."

Miles beckoned me to a chair, and I waited for him to wash his hands to the elbows with red carbolic soap and dry them with a clean hemp towel.

"It's going to hurt," he said. "Swear all you like."

"Go ahead," I said, and then gasped as every nerve on my forehead screeched in pain.

"It'll be about like that the whole time."

"How long?" I asked.

"Ten minutes."

"What did you do with Severin?"

"He's here and sedated," Miles said. "He's going to be drowsy until you're ready to deal with him again."

I sucked in a hissing breath as the pain bloomed over my cheeks, but another sensation like snowflakes landing on my skin didn't hurt at all. I held onto it, gritting my teeth.

"Thank you," I said. "What I did to him was cruel."

"Yes. But he's not allowed to flinch away from his legacy."

"But I terrorized him into abdication," I said. "I have his crown. But—"

"But he's alive," Miles said, drawing back when I flinched at his fingertips on my neck. "You could have killed him instead. And then gone to war with whatever Mountrose sprouted up to win back the crown."

"I know that it was expedient." I sighed and lifted my chin to let him heal me. "I know that killing him would have been worse, and that it was life or death in there. I still feel—"

"Guilty," Miles said. "I understand. And I don't want to tell you that you shouldn't."

"Good," I said. "Because I should feel this guilt. I did something wrong, and it got me what I wanted. I don't want to forget that."

"Let me see." Gentle strokes, more soothing snow than painful flames, followed the path of his touch on my face. "You're going to be a hard leader to follow. I hope you know that."

"I hope whoever follows me has an easier time of it," I said.

"I'm sure they will. Here."

Miles handed me a mirror. My eyebrows were gone, but my face was smooth. My skin was the same dark umber brown I knew in the mirror, the same as I had looked before this mess began.

"I should probably find Grace."

"She was coordinating the prison guards last I saw her. Are you going to heal her face?"

"I want to see if she's all right," Miles promised. "Do you want to stay the night with Zelind?"

"Yes," I said.

Miles helped me slide into bed next to Zelind, who curled around me and sighed. Miles drew the blankets up to our shoulders and raised the guardrails on the sides of the bed before dialing down the gaslight and leaving us to sleep.

TWENTY-FIVE

The Last King of Aeland

Ghosts crowded between the seats of the chambers where the Elected Members of Parliament stood waiting for the meeting to start. Down on the center of the floor, Grace stood in the black robes and starched lace collar of the formal dress of a servant of government, directly between a small lectern and a prisoner's dock. She looked to me, and I settled down in the uncomfortable seat Grace had once occupied. The House soon followed.

"You are called to witness the dissolution of the royal line of Aeland," I called. "Severin Philip Mountrose is king no more, and is welcome to return home to his family's holdings in Red Hawk as a free citizen."

Severin stared at the pen in his hand. He pressed his lips together and stared at the parchment for a long moment before he signed it. His signature was the final act of his rule. Scribes took the writ away to register and copy, to distribute for announcement. We were a kingdom no more.

I touched the hundred ghosts in the chamber, thanking them for their help. "You may go, Mr. Mountrose."

Severin rose from his desk and buttoned the top button of his jacket. He stared up at me, his eyes shadowed by violet, and let the federal guards remove him from the chamber. He took two steps before the first person clapped their hands. Others took it up, applauding as Severin Mountrose, the last King of Aeland, walked out of the House of Members and into his new life.

Without the purpose of haunting Severin the ghosts drifted a little, but few of them actually left. Grace waited for the members to settle down and turn their attention to her and to the old man who sat
in the copper-chased mahogany cage. Once she had them, she spoke,
her magic amplifying her voice to fill the room.

"The first task of the House of Members is unusual, but not difficult," she said. "The man in the dock is Sir Christopher Leland Hensley, and I ask you to consider the documents presented when you
decide his fate.

"On the behalf of the people, I accuse him of treason against
Aeland. I accuse him of murder. I accuse him of conspiracy, of fraud,
of obstruction of justice—but most of all, I accuse him of enacting a
fraudulent law in order to enslave Aelander citizens and force them
to commit the most horrible acts, including destroying the souls of
our ancestors."

Grace turned and addressed her next statement to me.

"I ask you to consider all the evidence before you, and once re-
viewed, I ask that you vote to approve or reject the sentence of execution by hanging."

The assembly shifted in their seats and glanced at one another,
but some of them picked up the documents. The stacks of papers
were intimidatingly large, but the top document was a table of contents and an overview of Sir Christopher's crimes, with the relevant
source material provided to each member.

Grace had worked long into the night to make this happen, and
she spoke into the silence once more. "I will do my best to answer
any questions you have."

"Dame Grace," one of the elected women called.

"Miss Hensley, please," Grace said. "What is your question?"

The woman stood up. I glanced at my seating chart. Delora Smith
pushed spectacles up her nose, and asked, "Miss Hensley, is it true
that you are related to the accused?"

"It is true," Grace said. "He's my father."

"And to be clear, you are denouncing him?"

"I am," Grace said. "Are you worried about my bias?"

"That's a consideration," Member Smith said. "But you say that
he's responsible for the asylums?"

"Yes," Grace said. "He was a member of the Cabinet when my

grandfather, Miles Douglas Hensley, used his position as Chancellor to King Nicholas to pass the Witchcraft Protection Act and the Railway Infrastructure Act. These two acts worked hand in hand to persecute common-born magicians and lock them away in what would soon become the power generators for Aeland's national aether network."

"I have a question about the incorporation of Aeland Power and Lights," another member said, standing up. Leden Wilson of the Endless Horizon, from the south coast. "How much money, in total, did the shareholding members see in profit from its years of operation?"

"That exact figure is the top sheet of the financials report on Aeland Power and Lights, which includes the quarterly financial reports since the company's incorporation," Grace said. "I believe the figure was one hundred and seventy five million, two hundred thirty-six thousand marks."

Papers shushed and shuffled against each other as members sorted through documents to find that top sheet. Silence reigned as they stared at the figure, tried to imagine an unimaginable sum.

"Miss Hensley." Edith Powell stood, holding a document in her hands. "Can you explain the discrepancy in asylum populations? This document says that arrests and convictions fell by two hundred percent after the first five years of arrests, but the articles describing the population of witches released earlier this year don't reflect the arrest numbers—"

"That's the asylum-born," one of the members said.

Edith Powell of Aeland East Norton blanched. "They let the inmates have children?"

"They forced certain inmates to have children," Grace said. "As the aether engines collected souls, those free witches with the ability to speak to and summon ghosts had no way of understanding their magical talent. As such, they ceased to be arrested. But the soulengines depended on witches with those skills. The conspiracy's solution was to breed more witches with the talent."

Edith stared at Grace, her eyes round behind thick spectacles. She raised a trembling hand to her mouth and glared sharp rage at the man in the cage, who gazed up at the fresco of Queen Agnes and her Hundred Knights winning the battle of the Edaran Plains.

"Hang him," Edith said. "I've heard enough. Hang him."

The House rumbled in agreement.

I rose, finally, and Grace used that voice-amplifying trick on me. "I ask the House of Members to decide—will you call Christopher Leland Hensley a traitor?"

"Yes!"

"Do you call him the architect of the greatest abomination Aeland has ever seen?"

"Yes!"

"Do you ask for his death by hanging at the next noon?"

"Yes!"

"It is done," I said. "Christopher Leland Hensley is condemned to hang tomorrow. Take him away."

Guards wheeled the mahogany cage out of the chambers to the angry muttering of the members.

"Thank you for attending this session of the House," I said. "There is only one more item I wanted to put to you today. When we organized the shadow election, it was meant as a protest to prove that the will of Aeland was being ignored by the people who had a choke-hold on the country's power. Not many of you actually expected to be here today, but you are, and I thank you."

Members murmured in response, but I wasn't done. "I acted on impulse when I jumped up on a box and declared myself prime minister. Now I want you all to tell me whether we should elect a new prime minister from our numbers, or if you're willing to follow me for three more years while I lead the country through my plans to heal Aeland."

Pages brought in a ballot box and paper while the members questioned each other, asking if they knew I was going to ask for a confidence vote. Most people filled out their vote and stuffed it inside the box quickly, while others took a minute to gaze up at the fresco-painted ceiling and think. But all ballots were collected, and pages sat down to sort and count the votes.

One pile of votes grew considerably faster than the others, and I stared at Grace, who still stood down on the floor. Could she see which was which? I had coerced Severin's abdication; it would be more democratic for us to elect a prime minister than to keep me. That was the sensible thing to do, the fair thing, even if it would be expeditious to vote confidence in me and continue on course.

A page stood up and cleared her throat, startling as the sound filled the room. Grace smiled, and the page spoke again.

"By eighty-two votes against thirty-nine, the vote of confidence in Right Honorable Robin Thorpe of the Peaceful Waters has passed," the page said.

The house applauded. I tried to speak, but they wouldn't stop. Leden Wilson stood up, and his neighbors followed his lead. I swallowed the lump in my throat, blinking to keep the tears at bay, as the Free Democracy party stood and applauded for me.

"Thank you," I said, when the rain of clapping stopped. "Let's meet again on Firstday. I have some motions I'd like you to consider before then, including my plan to manufacture wind-powered aether turbines as our first priority. It will be a long day, so bring a cushion."

The members laughed and gathered their papers. Grace left the floor to stand by me. "Don't you hate that chair?"

"I want to burn it," I said. "You sat in this thing?"

"And considered it an honor," Grace said.

"I think I'll have it replaced," I said. "I'm going to sit in it for three years."

"I would too," Grace said. "You're going to be a great prime minister. I hope you know that."

"I know that I'm going to do my best," I said, "and I'm going to need good people around me, people who will keep me informed and honest. How would you like to keep your office in Government House? I need a policy advisor."

Grace tilted her head and regarded me with a warm expression. "I think you should take my office in Government House, and I should move into something smaller. But I accept the position, Right Honorable. Thank you."

My first Parliamentary scrum went by in a blur, but I smiled to see Avia Jessup, out of hiding and right in the thick of it, throwing elbows and taking pictures. I let her have the first question, and she skipped right over the subject of Christopher Hensley's conviction to ask about wind turbines.

"We're moving at the speed of government at the moment, but we're committed to getting the lights back on as fast as we can. I have reports that local craftsmasters are building turbines as we speak, and the first homes will have wind-powered aether within the next few days. Please tell the people that Johnson and Garrett and Kingston Wind and Power are hiring staff as fast as they can train them, with wages starting at fifty marks a week. They're looking for everyone from floor sweepers to accountants, so please apply."

I answered questions until the bailey rang the bell. I strode back into the halls of Government House, where James, Grace's former under-typist, waited for me with a clipboard and pen, ready to take notes.

"Plans for the second Free Election have been written," James said, walking beside me as I turned corners and poked my head into various offices. Few people had given up their positions within the bureaucracy, a fact that made me sigh in relief every time I remembered it. "We'll have a Senate in forty-five days."

"Just in time. We should be done putting out fires by the time they're on board." Everything had happened so fast, but it couldn't be helped. "How has the quest for diplomats fared?"

"I've gathered about a hundred people on the list."

"I guess I had better get reading. Did anyone give you fuss about my not taking appointments?"

"Yes," James said, and we turned the last corner before arriving at my office. "Him."

Jarom Bay, dressed in his gleaming, expensive coat and tidy hair-locks, stood beside my office door.

"I need to see Zelind," he said.

"Do you ever stop?" I asked. "Khe's recovering. I don't think upsetting kher is a good idea—"

"I know who betrayed kher to the examiners," Jarom said. "Khe told me I had to find out the truth. I did. Please, khe deserves to know."

"Khe didn't talk to you when khe was back in Bayview?"

"Khe never uttered a word to us," Jarom said. "Khe would speak to the servants, but not to us. I had forgotten how stubborn khe is."

"But you think khe will talk now? What do you expect will happen, Jarom?"

He patted his breast pocket. "Once khe knows the truth, I'll leave if khe wants me to. Khe probably will. We don't deserve forgiveness."

I tilted my head. "Who betrayed Zelind, then?"

"I'll tell Zelind. In person. Zelind can decide if you need to know."
I couldn't make the call to keep this information from Zelind.
"I'll take you to the infirmary. But if khe doesn't want to talk to you,
you leave, and you don't come back until you're invited. Fair?"

"Fair. And—I'm sorry," Jarom said. "Why didn't you fight the
scrutineers at the election?"

I shrugged, and started toward the palace infirmary. "Like I said.
It wasn't the important election."

"You were right." Jarom walked beside me, his heels clicking
on the heart pine. "But I was ready to concede. Albert Jessup bribed
those scrutineers."

I looked at his profile. "What did he want from you?"

"Another puppet in the Lower House," Jarom said. "My vote,
whenever he needed it."

"It's too bad I can't run him into a hearing based on that. It would
be petty to persecute him for a nullified election."

"If you want to nail him for corruption, you probably can," Jarom
said. "He held his seat in Birdland for years. I know he bought and
sold favors as an Elected Member. I've bribed him myself. You just
need a clever accountant."

"And one who hasn't been enjoying supplemental income to
not notice irregularities," I said. "That's useful, Jarom. Thank you.
Wait here."

I left him at the door to the infirmary. Zelind lay in kher bed, listening to Miles reading a popular novel by kher bedside. Khe smiled
as I drew near, and Miles tucked a bookmark between the pages.

"Saria is prowling the parapet looking for the Ghost of Redcliff
Hall," Zelind said. "How are you? Still prime minister?"

"They decided to keep me," I said. "Jarom is here."

Zelind's smile faded. "Why?"

"He knows who betrayed you. He's just outside the door, and he's
agreed to stay away until you're ready to—"

"No," Zelind said. "Bring him in."

Miles set the book on the bedside table. "I'll be just outside if you
need me."

"Me too," I said, but Zelind shook kher head.

"Will you stay with me? And kick him out if he won't listen?"

"I will," I promised, and crossed the room, inspecting the supply station by habit. Tidy, and kept in order, and not my job anymore. I opened the infirmary door. Miles stepped out into the hall, looking stern.

"Zelind is recovering from a grave injury," Miles said. "Don't excite kher. Don't upset kher. If you can't promise that, don't go in."

Jarom squeezed his gloves. "I promise."

I opened the infirmary door wider and beckoned Jarom inside. He looked nervous, his mouth pressed thin and stretched wide.

"Solace," he whispered, when he caught sight of Zelind's gaunt face. "What happened?"

"Khe stopped a bullet meant for me," I said. "It would have caused less damage if khe'd been shot."

"Stop talking about me and come here," Zelind said. "Give me the name."

Jarom felt for his breast pocket again. "I didn't want to believe it. But I cross-referenced the journal with the accounts, and it has to be true—"

"Who?"

"My father, Kalman Bay."

Zelind closed kher eyes and let out a slow breath. "Not Mother."

"No. He didn't do it to stop your marriage," Jarom said. "He chafed at being passed over for your mother, not being in charge of the firm. He poured out his resentment and ire over Birdie's domineering, uncompromising attitude in his journals. He wanted to hurt her just as much as he wanted me to run the firm. By having you arrested, he struck two blows at once."

"Uncle Kalman," Zelind said. "I had no idea he hated me."

Jarom shook his head. "I think you were just in the way. It was a secret he kept to his grave. I'm surprised he didn't have these books burned."

Zelind struggled to sit up, and I helped kher by reflex, cranking up the head of kher bed. "You realize I'm not going back."

"Yes," Jarom said. "And I don't blame you. If you want me to, I'll step aside, and you can take charge—"

"No, I don't want the firm. I want to start a turbine manufacturer."

"You're too late," Jarom said. "Everyone and their uncle is making them."

"I never wanted to do it for the profits. I want to give the witches a stable place to work. Veterans too. I want to form an enterprise co-operative. And you're going to bankroll it. Aren't you?"

"Silent partner," Jarom agreed. "And the Princess Mary Hotel is safe. I won't let Birdie drive Clan Cage out of their home."

"Good," I said, "because I'm declaring it a building of social and historical significance. Birdie can try tangling with the Prime Minister's office if she wants to waste her time."

"You don't ever have to come back, Zelind," Jarom said. "I promise you. Anything she tries to drag you back under her roof, I will stop her. My father stole the firm from you."

Zelind shrugged. "Honestly, I never really wanted it. I planned on building clever devices and letting you figure out how to make money from them."

Hope stole into Jarom's eyes. "We can still do that, if you decide you want to. There's no rush."

Zelind licked kher lips. "Miles says I'll be up and walking soon. We can think about it in three days."

Jarom sniffed and bowed his head. "Thank you."

"I expect you'll have found a factory site by then," Zelind said. "We need to move fast. We have a lot of competitors."

"We do," Jarom agreed, and his shoulders sank in relief. "I'll tell you what I've accomplished in three days."

"Good. I'm tired now, and I hurt. I need to sleep."

"We'll let you rest," Jarom said, leaving us alone together.

I kissed Zelind's forehead and khe took my hand. "Will you come back when you're done prime ministering? I sleep better when you're here."

"Try to keep me away."

Zelind smiled and closed kher eyes, but I waited until kher breathing evened out before I left.

The morning of Christopher Leland Hensley's death dawned on a clear blue sky. Clerks and bureaucrats obliged to attend the execution wore snow goggles to protect against the glare, a strange modern affectation when worn with black robes and stiffened lace. Joy and I wove past them to stand before the gallows, stepping to the side of the witnesses who had a right to the best view.

Grace wore pale gray tweed, a subtle plaid that coordinated with the glowing, wine-red ascot at her throat. Her shoulders were hand-eased and bare of the butterfly brooches that grieving Aelanders wore. She held hands with Avia Jessup, who was dressed in the sharp-shouldered suit and pinch-fronted hat of a reporter and had a camera around her neck stowed inside its protective case.

Miles stood on Grace's right, leaning against tall, handsome Tristan. I slipped in beside the Amaranthine, and he shuffled to give me some more room.

"Pretty day, isn't it?" he asked, and the drummers began to play, sparing us further small talk under the gallows.

They'd dressed Christopher well. Snow scudded over the toes of his shiny black shoes. The suit looked new, and a watch chain draped over the front button of his weskit. He wore no hat, and his white hair gleamed in the sunlight. He went quietly to the top of the stairs, stood on the trapdoor with icy dignity, and gazed down at his children as the rope went around his neck. Miles and Grace stood taller, lifting their chins to gaze back. I didn't want to watch this, but I had to be ready.

More people arrived, heralded by the crunch and squeak of the snow under their steps. Birds circled the gallows, landing on nearby trees, and Christopher watched them gather and settle with a little smile. I glanced behind me.

Aife and Ysonde stood in attendance, with a retinue of Amaranthines bearing arms. They stood behind us, Aife arm in arm with her secretary. She glanced at me, giving me a nod.

I nodded back and the drums stopped.

The executioner pulled the lever. The floor yawned open.

Christopher fell.

I had seen a man die of blood loss on the table, of the rotten necrotic insides a surgeon exposed to the light, of the final strain on an overworked heart—those were deaths I knew, defeats in the battle to heal a man with a knife. This death was not like that, but I watched it regardless, flinching as the fall cut itself short of the ground.

Christopher's ghost landed on the snow, crouching to take the impact out of pure habit. He set his sights on Grace and Miles and stalked toward them.

Miles took Grace's elbow. Grace gasped. Christopher took an-

other step, his face younger, his hair dark and combed back with bril-
liantine, and he looked so much like Miles, only Miles never looked
that menacing, that cruel. He meant to haunt them, to lurk in the
corner of their vision and never let them forget. He stared at Grace,
his mouth pursed up tight, his chin jutted out, and I knew he would
never leave her alone, not for a moment.

That wasn't going to happen.

I coiled my power around his form and made him shrink. Smaller,
smaller, though Christopher shouted and tried to fight the constric-
tion. He would not haunt Grace, nor Miles. Not while I could do
something about it.

His struggle meant nothing to me. I gathered up his soul-stuff
and turned it into a tiny ball of light, drawing it to my hands. Mine
now—I could make him my soulstar, set him to float beside Jacob. I
could bind his power to anyone I pleased. Instead, I turned around
and held up Christopher's soul to Aife and bowed my head.

"Your Highness. Death is not enough justice for what this man
has done to our people. I don't want him retiring to the peace of the
Solace. Will you allow me to deny it to him?"

Aife looked at the soul—a shimmering ball that flared with bright
white light—floating in my cupped hands. "What do you propose?"

"I want to trap it in a tree," I said. "An oak will thrive for a thousand years. That might be penance enough."

Aife considered my request. "When that tree falls, when he
crosses over, then it will be my turn to lay justice on him."

My cheeks warmed. "I should have realized you would have justice for him."

"My plans can wait that long," Aife said. "Do as you will."

I chose a red oak, a species that grew tall and thrived for centuries. Bare of all its brilliant red foliage, its empty branches pointed
to the shining blue sky. I approached the trunk and pushed Christopher's soul against the rough bark, forcing it to meld with the living
wood.

The light of Christopher's soulstar spread through the cracks in
the bark, sinking down into the heartwood. This was his domain
now—a living thing that couldn't see, couldn't move, couldn't cast
magic. He would dwell here as long as the tree lived—and I meant to
ensure that it would persist long after I was dead.

I turned back to the gallows. Christopher's body had already been taken away. I stood in front of Miles and Grace and took their hands.

"It's over," I said. "All he can do now is serve his punishment."

"Thank you," Grace said. "It's fitting."

"He can't hurt anyone now," Miles said. "Let's go inside. I asked the kitchen to put something together for us."

"I'm not mourning him." Grace squeezed her eyes shut, scowling at her tears. "After what he did to you? After what he did to all the witches?"

"We're having a drink." Miles took Grace's hand, making us a triangle. "And we're going to be together."

"You're allowed to be angry at how he used you. We don't have to mourn him. He shaped our lives, and now he's gone, but we're still here, and we should do whatever we need to do."

"I'll drink," Grace said. "To a better Aeland. To our freedom. But not to him."

"Good enough for me," Miles said.

We crossed the trampled snow to Kingsgrave Prison, and trepidation shivered at the back of my neck. I stopped, turning back to look at the oak.

Every bare-fingered branch was filled with birds.

TWENTY-SIX

The Light of the Solace

I drank a thimble of peach cordial and spent an hour in the stiff, sardonic conversation that hung like a veil over Grace's feelings—feelings that Miles prodded at with questions and observations. I knew what he was trying to do, and Grace wasn't going to peel out of the tough hide that shielded the emotions Miles wanted to probe while I was there. I slipped out of the kitchen, traveled the quiet halls of the palace, and went to sleep beside Zelind, who woke me up with kher fingers stroking my cheek.

"Can we get married again?" khe asked. "I don't think I'm finished living the rest of my life with you."

"We can get married again," I said, and khe smiled.

"It's got to be a big wedding this time."

"With music and dancing."

"And three kinds of cake, so I don't have to choose a favorite."

"Where do you want to have it?"

"The Princess Mary. In the ballroom."

"We'll ask Clan Cage."

"They'll say yes," Zelind murmured. "They owe me a favor."

I tucked my head under Zelind's chin and drifted back to sleep.

When I woke up again, Aunt Glory had sent a bag of my best clothes. I unpacked in a suite in the palace to wash and change. I took a pasty with me to the office, chewing on eggs, cheese, and goose sausage as I wandered down the halls to my office.

I blinked in surprise to behold Jamille Wolf, alone and waiting for me. She was dressed in her customary smoke-tattered gray, sat with a cup of malty black tea. Her expression was smooth and impassive, the face of someone with plenty to hide.

She rose when I came in and bobbed her head. "Right Honorable."

"Miss Jamille," I said, and her eyes widened when I put out my hand for her to shake. "James, would you play something fitting for the day?"

James picked a melody that thrummed with melancholy, and that was good enough. I led Jamille into the office, now mine after centuries in the hands of one Royal Knight or another. I let her examine the warm, book-filled room and watched her smile when she saw a full set of Saria Green adventure stories, their colorful spines tucked in beside the law books. While she went from looking around to fidgeting, I sat in my padded horseshoe back chair and left her standing.

"You've come without an appointment."

"Surprised I wasn't arrested," Jamille said.

"May I know why you're here?"

Jamille laced her fingers together. "To ask you to put all the blame on me for the fires, Right Honorable. The others only obeyed me, and they should go free."

"So you're here to be punished," I said. "Sent to Kingsgrave to rot for your crimes."

"It's a sacrifice." Jamille shrugged, and one of her beaded hair-locks fell off her shoulder. "The old man swung for his crimes yesterday. I don't think I merit the gallows, but you and I both know what I did."

"And you came willingly to protect your people."

"I came to ask you to take care of them. I can't outrun you, so I have a bargain to offer—I'll go quietly, if you'll protect Five Corners."

My forehead ridged with surprise. "I don't think that's going to happen."

Jamille's expression went stormy. "I thought you'd play me fair."

"Oh no," I said. "I mean that I planned to do something even worse than leaving you to run your operation from behind bars."

"You're going to send me to the gallows?"

"No," I said. "I'm going to legalize state-controlled gambling."

Jamille sucked in a breath. "Five Corners needs that money. People need the little hope to win—and if you're in trouble, the chance at a loan to make things right."

"Charged at prime and a half."

Jamille shrugged. "It's not like gambling debt. We have to make something off it."

"Not anymore," I said. "Your numbers scheme is now under control of the government."

"But—"

I put my finger up for silence. "The proceeds will be used to fund special projects in vulnerable communities, group therapy for veterans and imprisoned witches, retraining projects, and low-income housing initiatives—and you are going to make sure no one skims off the top."

"Me?" If Jamille looked shocked before, she was pie-eyed now. "You're making me go straight?"

"You're going to be so level we could build a house with you. I mean to attack bureaucratic corruption, and I want your numbers crew to burrow into the accounting of every department in government and take everyone's hands out of the till."

"So you want my whole operation to go straight," Jamille mused. "Do you want to know who's crooked in the police departments?"

"Absolutely," I said.

"I just want to know one thing," Jamille said. "Why let me go?"

"Because Basil Brown is going down for the fires. He was the one who wanted to use fire, and I know it was for Severin's scheme to pin us with Grace's death. You trusted him. You chose to believe in him, and he betrayed you."

Jamille tilted her head and regarded me through narrowed eyes. "And if I muck up your anticorruption plans, you can revoke this mercy at any time."

"You have it exactly. I saw what you did with the Greystars. I know you know fraud like no one else. I know that you can do the job, and that you'll never forget you owe me."

Jamille looked at me, thinking. "Of course I'll do it," she said. "But you knew that already."

"I knew it the moment you came in here to bargain for your community. You're now the gambling and lottery commissioner. I'll have an operating budget for you in a few days. Refer some of your best number benders to me, and we'll see how well we like working with each other."

"You won't regret it," Jamille vowed.

"And you're going to shut down the Greystars. You're going to be running a major bureaucracy," I said. "You're not going to have time to get into trouble."

"And if they spring up independent of me?" Jamille asked.

"Stamp them down or go to jail."

Jamille whistled. "All right. Deal. I'll tell the Stars we're going legitimate. You'll have some accountants tomorrow."

She backed up a step before turning around, and I let myself smile as the door clicked shut behind her.

Ten minutes later, the door clicked open, and James stepped inside. "An Amaranthine brought this for you."

He handed me a note. I flipped it open and read, "Please call on me in the glasshouse." It was signed with an "A," and marked with "yf," denoting who had written the note for the Grand Duchess.

I folded the note and stood up. "I'm going out. I don't know for how long. Make appointments for anyone who comes calling."

The Amaranthines were packing. I watched a young man carrying a spinning wheel out of one of the suites join a group carting trunks and crates outside. I hurried to the end of the wing, where I found Aife and Ysonde, out of their dazzling court clothes and dressed in wide trousers that just covered their calves, with belted tunics layered over full-sleeved shirts. Aife dictated a letter to Ysonde, who wrote with a silver-filigree fountain pen.

She broke off when she saw me. "You came."

"And you're leaving."

"You have started Aeland on an unusual path." Aife smiled and put her mass of golden curls over her shoulder. "I trust that everything I required of Queen Constantina as a punishment will be carried out by you as a balm. You don't need us to hover, to remind you that Amaranthine justice is specific and fitting."

"Are you all going back to the Solace?"

"Tristan is going to stay," Aife said. "Miles was willing to come to the Solace, but Tristan doesn't think he'd be satisfied, leaving Aeland when it needs healing the most. If you need us, Tristan will be able to make the journey to Elondel and ask for aid."

My middle loosened. Miles was staying. I could still try to convince him to chair the Health and Hygiene Committee, we would still eat together, and Tristan—clever, charming Tristan—was going to stay too.

"Thank you for coming," I said. "And thank you for the trust you're demonstrating by leaving. Come back whenever you wish."

"I'm taking the dead with me," Aife said. "I sealed off the Solace to punish Aeland, but I also did it because the territory around the Tiandran Marches is so unstable. We're going to be close by for the next while, putting things right."

I bit my lip. "They deserve rest. But they were helping us with a problem I don't know how to solve—the storms that plague Aeland that have grown too powerful for our Windweavers to fight."

"I know," Aife said. "But please trust me when I tell you that bringing the dead to the Solace will help soothe the troubled winds that blow on your shores. Their absence is what made the storms worse. Their return should ease your trouble."

I nodded. "When are you taking them?"

"Now," Aife said. "Would you like to help?"

I nodded. "Please."

She led me through the corridors to the plain field where the King's Stone stood, and I beheld the gathering of the Amaranthines and their fine horses—which weren't horses at all, I had heard. Aife accepted the bridle of a fine chestnut steed, and the beast bowed its head in deference to her. She mounted, and they moved together toward the stone.

Aife dropped the reins and raised her arms, and the air shimmered like a curtain and twinkled open, revealing blinding, golden light.

The sun rose on the plains of the Solace, its light spilling out to throw long, deep shadows on the stone. I glimpsed long lines carved across its face. They sharpened for an instant, and then wore back down, smoothed by ages of wind and rain, the monolith simply stone once more.

Lights shone in the air, tiny sparks that glowed gold and scarlet, violet and green. They floated into the light of the Solace's sunrise and passed through—a handful, then a scattering, then a flood. Tiny and starlike, they came from every direction, streaming through the air as they flocked to the gateway.

Ghosts drew closer, unable to resist the pull of the land across the Way, and as they stepped from Aeland to the Solace, their substances firmed, became less transparent. They gathered on the other side, watching more souls, more ghosts pass through.

"Joy," I said. "Mahalia."

They hovered beside me, the light of the Solace shining on them.

"You have helped me so much," I said. "But it's time for you to go."

"No," Joy said. "You still need me."

"Aunt Joy. I do. But look at it. Don't you want to feel it? Don't you want to go on to peace?"

"We can rest," Mahalia said, but Joy planted her feet in the snow.

"It will still be there when I'm ready," Joy said. "But Aeland is just getting interesting. My sister's baby is going to run a country, and I want to see what happens."

My heart warmed even as my throat choked up with tears. "If you want to stay."

"I want to," Joy said. "Go on, Mahalia. I know you want to rest."

They held each other for a long moment; then Mahalia touched her ghostly lips to my forehead. "You'll do just fine, Miss Robin. Just fine."

We watched her pass through, joining the people bathed in light.

"There's one more thing," I said.

I raised my hand to hover just at my forehead. I felt carefully, learning the edges of the soulstar as I pulled, gently, and drew Jacob's soul out of the tangle that bound it to mine.

Jacob Clarke stood before me, a younger man than the one I had known, handsome and dapper in the tall collar and tailed jacket of his youth. He smiled as bright as the sunshine and touched his fingers to his lips.

"Well done, Robin. You did everything I dreamed of, and more."

Hearing it made my throat swell, but I smiled and kept back the tears. "What do you want me to tell Winnie and Duke?"

"That we'll meet again. I'll be waiting," Jacob said. "I'll stay right where they can find me."

He covered his heart with his hand, bowed to me, and walked into the Solace, whistling a merry song.

I watched until they all passed through, and the Amaranthines crossed over with their wagons and their mounts. Aife and Ysonde waited until last, closing the portal behind them.

No more crowns. No more Guardians. It was only us now, and we had to make our own choices. We had to bring light and healing to Aeland again. I watched the last sparkling lights of the Way fade from sight, and then Joy and I turned back into the palace to get to work.

ACKNOWLEDGMENTS

Writing the Kingston Cycle would not have been possible without the assistance of many people. I would like to thank my agent, Caitlin McDonald, who helped me every time I had a problem or question with her expertise, support, and encouragement. To Carl Engle-Laird, my editor, who in understanding of what I was trying to do in writing this book helped with countless observations and suggestions as I was putting the book together. My copy editor, Deanna Hoak, for taking the time to make sure that I was clear and accurate in my story and prose. Thank you, Will Staehle, for the amazing cover that captured the feeling of the story.

My production team turned out a fantastic-looking book and made the whole process go so smoothly I never had to worry about anything. Thank you so much to Megan Kiddoo, *Soulstar*'s production editor; Steven Bucsok, production manager; designer Nicola Ferguson; and team members Jim Kapp and Lauren Hougen.

Sometimes you need to turn to an expert. I thank Scott Lynch for taking the time to explain what it was like to be inside a burning building, and about the conditions that cause backdraft, and about the tightrope dance of being able to use magic in a way that could help someone breathe—but could also burn them alive. The mistakes I made were all me and not him.

Similarly I need to thank Arkady Martine, who helped me figure out a major part of this story's plot when I was puzzling over what to do next. Her suggestion was directly responsible for Robin jumping up on that box when the election was decided.

Does a book ever get written without the feedback of a great group of story-savvy people who just get you? I wouldn't dream of trying it solo. Dr. Amanda Townsend is always there for everything—character analysis, plot speculations, wild tangents, all of it. Kate Brauning lent me her time and knowledge to help me write deeper character conflict. John Appel spent an afternoon looking over my second half of the story in a plot-breaking session that was as satisfying as knocking over dominoes. Kimberly Bell talked to me about unconventional romance stories, where the story isn't as simple as one person meeting another. Krista Heath did a lot of reading and gave honest opinions—and she got me back on track more than once.

Finally I need to thank Elizabeth Bear, who patiently, lovingly, and consistently gave advice on how to conclude a trilogy, how to keep writing, and how not to freak out (too much) while trying to write an end to the story that was my life for years.

ABOUT THE AUTHOR

C. L. POLK (she/her/they/them) is the author of the World Fantasy Award–winning novel *Witchmark,* the first novel of the Kingston Cycle. After leaving high school early, she has worked as a film extra, sold vegetables on the street, and identified exotic insect species for a vast collection of lepidoptera before settling down to write silver fork fantasy novels. Ms. Polk lives near the Bow River in Calgary, Alberta, in a tiny apartment with too many books and a yarn stash that could last a decade. She rides a green bicycle with a basket on the front.